THE HUMAN LEGION
FREEDOM CAN BE WON
MARINE CADET

Also by Tim C. Taylor
Marine Cadet (The Human Legion Book 1)
Indigo Squad (The Human Legion Book 2)
Renegade Legion (The Human Legion Book 3)
Human Empire – with Ian Whates (The Human Legion Book 4)
War Against the White Knights – with Ian Whates (The Human Legion Book 5)
The Battle of Earth Part1: Endgame (The Human Legion Book 6)
The Battle of Earth Part2: Restart (The Human Legion Book 7)
Chimera Company: Rho-Torkis (8 issues set in the Legion's future)
Chimera Company: Deep Cover (9 issues set in the Legion's future)
After War (Revenge Squad prequel)
Hurt U Back (Revenge Squad Book 1)
Second Strike (Revenge Squad Book 2)
The Midnight Sun (A Four Horsemen Universe novel)
Endless Night (A Four Horsemen Universe novel)
The Reality War #1: The Slough of Despond
The Reality War #2: The City of Destruction

Writing as Crustias Scattermush (YA science-fantasy)
Treasure of the Last Dragon
The Ultimate Green Energy

Also in the Human Legion Universe by JR Handley
The Demons of Kor-Lir (Sleeping Legion prequel novella)
The Legion Awakes (Sleeping Legion book1)
Fortress Beta City (Sleeping Legion book2)
Operation Breakout (Sleeping Legion book3)
Insurgency: Spartika (Sleeping Legion book4)

Human Legion Annals
—Book 1—

HumanLegion.com

Marine Cadet

Copyright © Tim C. Taylor 2014
Cover art by Vincent Sammy

Published by Human Legion Publications
All Rights Reserved

HumanLegion.com

ISBN: 978-1502519658
Also available in
eBook and audiobook editions.

The author wishes to thank all those who work-shopped, proofread, or otherwise supported the making of this book. In particular, Paul Melhuish for allowing me to raid his vault of filthy Skyfirean vernacular, the Northampton Science Fiction Writers Group, James D. Kelker, Melissa Bryan, Nigel Edwards, Midland Road Costa Coffee, The Bromham Swan, Bedford Central Library, and Ian Watson for persuading me to turn a short story into a book series.

PART I
Alien Lover

Extract from the *NEW ENGLISH DICTIONARY*, Patriot Publishing, Human Autonomous Region, 2671CE

human.

n. **1.** An individual of the species *Homo sapiens*, possibly also of derivative species. **See also:** *augmented-human.*

adj. **2.** Characterizing mankind, as opposed to aliens, animals, and machines (including AIs).

adj. **3.** [*meaning derived from common alien usage*] oppressed, the ultimate underclass, the hopeless ones, unwashed: **as in** *The Human Legion.*

Chapter 01

Arun glanced into the darkness of the side tunnel as he thundered past with the rest of Delta Section. His eyes could see nothing in the branch, and his helmet visor didn't ping up any threats. No one said a thing. Arun was sure he wasn't the only one to feel the deep shadows of the side tunnel burning with threat, but what could they do other than ignore them?

Keep running. That was all they could do.

The rest of Blue Squad was pinned down by a Troggie redoubt. Delta Section had been tasked with pushing ahead and left to outflank the enemy position. Every time they passed a branch in the tunnel, Arun felt even more isolated, but there were only eight Marine cadets in the section. To peel off a pair to check out each fork in the tunnel network would be beyond madness. In this crazy twisting warren, there could be no such thing as a front line, not unless they had an entire regiment down here. The enemy could strike from behind at any moment.

He glanced across at Springer, her mottled gray battlesuit pumping her along at a steady 15mph, her SA-71 carbine just one safety away from spitting railgun death. The sight stirred his pride and buttressed his courage. Together they were strong.

"Halt!" called Cadet Corporal Brandt.

Delta Section braked. What was Brandt thinking of now?

As Brandt pondered his move, Arun's resolve began to drain into the dirt floor.

A moment ago, he'd been buoyed by the momentum of his armored unit. Seeing them stationary had the opposite effect. There was an old Marine saying, drummed into them since the start of novice school: *stay still and die.*

Arun scanned the walls and ceiling for signs of ambush.

Scuttlebutt had it that Trogs could swim through the soil as easily as a human diver through water. He shivered, imagining alien eyes observing him through the dirt walls. If that rumor were true, they were utterly flekked.

No point worrying about what you can't change, he told himself, but only half believed it.

Whether or not the Trogs were watching, Arun was certain that his superiors were. None of the humans had ever met a White Knight. Never would, either, but through their vast network of nano-spies, the White Knights knew everything that happened within their empire, and they had no room for disloyalty or incompetence, even when the source was as irrelevant as a seventeen-year-old human dumbchuck. Like Brandt, for instance.

"I don't like it, because…" Brandt's words died away as he tried to organize the dust motes floating around his brain into a plan.

Brandt was indecisive rather than stupid, but hesitation could get you killed just as readily as dumb orders. Brandt had only been made cadet corporal less than an hour before, a temporary promotion that didn't entitle him to be addressed by the rank, only as 'sir'. Cadet Lance Corporal Majanita, Arun's fire team leader, would've made a much better section commander.

"We've penetrated too far without resistance," spoke Brandt in his best semblance of authority. "You heard the briefing. The Troggie guardians we're facing have regressed mentally to the borders of sentience, but we mustn't mistake that for stupidity."

"Do you think they're creeping up behind us?" asked Del-Marie.

"Err, yes," agreed Brandt. "That's exactly what I mean. Osman, go three hundred meters back the way we've come. Check our rear is still clear."

"Sir!" Osman raced off to obey. He wasn't going to give any cause for complaint now, but give him a cup of grok in a rec-chamber, and Osman would cheerfully tell you exactly what he thought of Brandt's order. For starters, sending a lone cadet to check a position was against their training. They should go in a pair. Buddied up Marines could cover each other. They were more than twice as strong as two Marines on their own.

Everyone knew that.

"McEwan!"

Arun only allowed himself to hesitate for an instant before answering: "Sir!"

"Recce that side tunnel we've just passed."

"Yes, sir."

And so Arun McEwan, a seventeen-year-old Marine cadet, chilled with foreboding, entered the shadows alone.

If the tunnels had been constructed by human engineers they would have been wider, well-lit, and level, but Trogs weren't human. As Arun cautiously penetrated the tunnel, he felt the wrap of alienness tighten around him with every step. He flicked his visor display to survey mode and confirmed one of his suspicions: the tunnel was rising and falling in its depth below the surface of the hill above. The change wasn't obvious as you walked, given the frequent twists and turns. Half-expecting an alien warrior to spring at him from out of the shadows, he quickly switched back to tactical mode, and breathed out when no threats were displayed, though it also told him that he was out of comms contact with his comrades.

Suddenly he was gasping, fighting to control his breath. Why hadn't Brandt sent Springer with him?

He calmed his breathing, but his instincts still told him he was in danger. With his visor tac-display showing no movement, no EM activity, and no inexplicable heat signatures, those instincts were indistinguishable from cowardice. To be afraid was inevitable, even for a Marine. To succumb to fear, though… that was punishable by death.

So Arun pressed on around a tight left bend and immediately came to a halt when he saw the tunnel narrow ahead. He would have to turn sideways to squeeze through the gap. Even if he were dressed in fatigues, it would be tight. The bulky battlesuit he wore meant he would have to force his way through.

Or try to. He could easily get stuck in there, deep inside enemy territory with no one to call for help.

He felt the crushing weight of earth envelop him, driving the breath from his lungs. He bent over, hands on knees, and fought to even out his short, rasping gasps. The walls ahead seemed to tremble, all the more eerie in the blue glow of his enhanced low-light display. That had to be his mind playing tricks.

Didn't it?

The tunnel was constructed from nothing more than trampled soil mixed with alien spit. The incalculable weight of soil overhead was not held up by some product of advanced materials technology, as with the human and Jotun Marine base. Just spit. Perhaps the shock waves from heavy weapons fire was bringing the hill down on top of him.

Arun wanted to go back. The fear was so intense he was on the brink of sobbing. If he triggered an ambush, then he'd die. If the ceiling collapsed he'd die. He'd been a cadet for just two weeks. What dungering use would dying be to anyone?

Flushing these tunnels of Trogs was supposed to be a training exercise, but the enemy didn't know that. The danger was very real. He took a deep breath. And another. To push his fears away was beyond him, but he rose above them enough to find sufficient air and calm for his brain to kick in and think!

Brandt wanted a recce. To advance five hundred meters down the tunnel sounded acceptable. Even though Arun had lost his Battle Net connection, he daren't lie about how far he'd gone down the tunnel. The chance that the Jotun officers were recording everything was too great. He would get to the five-hundred-meter mark, count out ten seconds, and then run back.

Now that he had a plan, a little confidence returned.

Pace by faltering pace, Arun squeezed sideways through the gap, using his power-assisted musculature like hydraulic rams to force his way through.

The earth was darker here. Damper too. Bubbles of foam oozed from the soil and stuck to his battlesuit; loosened soil tumbled to the floor, piling up almost to his knees.

It felt like climbing into the throat of an immense and hungry beast.

After a final series of twists, the constriction opened up again. He began to breathe more normally until the very walls began to tremble in a freakishly organic movement, as if the tunnel itself were breathing. Perhaps that was exactly what the tunnel was doing. He'd seen no obvious sign of ventilation and who knew what these aliens were capable of? His battlesuit AI, Barney, confirmed the motion: whatever was happening to the walls wasn't a figment of his imagination. This was for real.

Great, he thought. Just frakking great.

He checked himself. He was a Marine, and Marines *think*. He might not know much about the Trogs, but the Jotuns did and they had selected this exercise. The older cadets he knew, those in Class G and Class G-1, had all lived through similar exercises, though they were not allowed to discuss the experience. They'd survived. Logic said he should too. Probably.

Class G-1. Of all the cadets in the year ahead of him, Arun saw in his mind's eye the smooth oval face and dark midnight eyes of Xin Lee. She'd come through this alive. What would she think of him if she ever found out he'd gotten the scoojubbers in his first live fire exercise?

Emboldened by his logic — and thoughts of Xin — Arun switched his visor back to survey mode, and placed a target marker at the spot that Barney estimated to be five hundred meters into this tunnel. The target appeared as a glowing green cross slightly to his right, past a sharp bend, and an estimated distance to go of only sixty meters.

Once again, the tunnel shimmered.

Switching his helmet to tactical didn't show up anything to fight.

"C'mon, Barney," Arun whispered to his suit AI. "Help me out."

Barney's response was to flash the green target marker at him again.

"Okay. Okay! I'm going."

The conviction that the walls were alive proved too much. Twenty meters short of his target, Arun lost his nerve. He turned and fled. The movement in the tunnel walls gave him something important to report. That was why he was withdrawing, he told himself, not because he was a coward.

From behind him came the sound of scuffling, the dull sprinkling of falling soil.

Something was digging through the walls!

He ran faster, a risky maneuver in a battlesuit over uneven ground. Nothing would be worse than losing balance and tumbling headfirst into the alien dirt.

The frantic scurrying sound grew in volume until it drowned out the digging.

When he reached the narrow gap, he realized he'd been trapped. He turned to face whatever was coming for him from behind.

He saw a blur of black insectoid bodies scuttling toward him along the floor, ceiling and walls. Each creature was half as big again as a human, with a halo of barbed horns surrounding the head, and vicious fighting claws adorning the front pair of legs.

Troggie guardians.

These barely sentient aliens had no concept of the words 'training exercise'. Only one thing drove the guardians: the burning desire to kill any intruder in their nest.

He didn't need to ask Barney to know that they were coming for him faster than he could push through the narrow passageway.

Reason said that his only chance was to stand and fight.

But reason had fled even faster than the rest of Arun.

Fear drove him to bully his way through the narrow constriction, gouging out more clumps of slimy earth from the walls as he went.

Then he was through to the far side. Still alive.

"This is only an exercise," he blurted to himself, but he knew death was only seconds away.

Fifteen meters ahead was a tight right turn and beyond that, the main corridor. He made it as far as the turning, but then his courage failed again and he had to turn and *see*.

Drawing on countless hours of combat drill, as he turned, he seamlessly readied his SA-71 carbine, bracing the stock tight in against his shoulder in readiness for the ferocious recoil kick he knew was coming.

Then he opened fire.

Every ten milliseconds the twisting railgun inside the barrel charged, launching a spinning kinetic dart out of the muzzle at Mach4. For the first two seconds of full auto fire, the darts whistled out the muzzle so gently it was as if Arun were blowing a stream of deadly butterflies. Then the recoil dampener tripped out. The carbine kicked and writhed with such fury that he couldn't aim with more accuracy than to point in the right general direction. But he didn't want sniper shots. He was after a withering barrage.

The SA-71 delivered.

Ichor and carapace fragments flew from the aliens. Horns shattered. Legs were chipped into fragments, making the insects trip and fall and stumble.

When the ammo carousel reported only 15% of the darts remained, Arun ceased firing. The alien advance was still pouring through the gap, drilling in and out of the solid walls as if swimming through a soil sea. *Would nothing stop them?* They powered around their fallen comrades. Every alien heart pumped hard to accomplish a single goal: to kill Arun.

Particulate matter from alien body fragments churned into a black fog that would have choked Arun if not for his helmet filters.

Oh, drent! His carbine wasn't going to be enough. He needed the tripod-mounted beam weapons and missiles of the Heavy Weapons Section.

Without really thinking about what he was doing, he'd turned away from the enemy guardians. Stumbling into a run, he unsnapped a grenade from his hip and rammed it into the launcher underneath his SA-71's barrel.

He swung around.

The lead Trog was about eight meters away.

He fired.

In that half-instant before the grenade blew, he saw more guardians emerging from the ceiling on his side of the defile, burrowing out from the earth. Their numbers were too great to count, but he saw enough to know that any aliens he slaughtered would be more than replenished.

Then the grenade's blast wave hit him, followed by a shower of alien ichor and gore.

Arun too sailed through the air and landed against a curve in the tunnel wall, his ears clearing enough to hear the hard body fragments clatter to the floor like frozen leaves in the fall.

Roof and walls began to drip with purple slurry in which black and brown rubbery chunks were mixed with clumps of falling soil. Then a half-dozen aliens fell through the top of the roof, bringing more showers of earth with them. Flailing all six limbs as they fell, they landed on the jumble of chitin below, skidding down to join the ungainly heap of living aliens scrabbling to right themselves.

The hordes behind kept coming, slipping and slithering into an ungainly mass that could not win purchase, only impede itself.

The grenade's shaped blast front had left Arun dazed but relatively unscathed. His visor had cracked, its display unavailable, including its low-light enhancers. Smart armor had reduced fatal shrapnel to punishing bruises, but his left knee was numb and unbending.

When his senses came back, Arun hurriedly switched on the lights at the side of his helmet. One of them worked, revealing that the wavefront of alien death had slowed more than he'd hoped. He estimated that his grenade had won him a fifteen second remission before he was sliced to a bloody pulp with those front-limb claws, or impaled on the wicked horns.

Last chance, then.

He activated *combat immunity*, the emergency combat-med that would numb all sensation within three seconds, and allowed him to keep focused on killing, even if he were critically wounded. He used his right leg to push up from the floor, feeling his left knee crunching as he did. By the time he'd gotten to his feet, the pain was gone and he charged at the onrushing insectoids. Grinding noises came from his left knee; he heard his leg tearing and splintering. He smelt the moldy stink on the aliens.

By the time he'd brought up the next grenade, and engaged it in the launch attachment, the pain had gone — *all* feelings had gone. He pressed his railgun's trigger with his numb fingers and was lowering his head — too late — before the soil and chitinous armor blew over his face, almost burying him. Reaching round to the utility attachment patch on his back of his battlesuit, he snapped off another grenade, setting it to a new blast mode while he clicked it into place.

Barracks rumor — allegedly from older cadets — hinted that carrying extra grenades would be a good idea for this exercise, and that blast mode 37H might get you out of a tight spot in a Troggie nest. Whether his senseless fingers had actually punched the right code was another matter. Normally he'd tell Barney to set weapons modes, but his suit AI wasn't in a fit state to listen.

He had been trained since birth to be a Marine, bred for it, in fact. Between the years of drill and the combat meds, his mind was not much more than a spectator as he fired the grenade at the mass of aliens.

Another blast of soil and diced bodies flung itself over his disabled visor, but more subdued this time. The grenade had tunneled through the pile of aliens and buried itself deeply into the tunnel wall behind. This blast had wreaked much less destruction, but had won him time by giving the body pile such a kick that many Trogs lost their footing again.

The combat immunity drugs seemed to be trying to tell him something, to make him remember something from training. He didn't exactly have time to sit down and hum a memory-inducing meditative mantra, so he blanked his mind and followed his instincts… *to burrow!*

Instead of firing at the aliens, he turned his back on them, firing another grenade at the curve in the tunnel wall where he'd been flung by the first grenade.

The blast buried itself into the wall, hurling a cloud of spoil out into the tunnel and coating Arun who'd flung himself to the ground just in time. Even before he'd gotten to his feet and wiped his visor clean of soil and sticky gore, he'd set another grenade to code 37H — *emergency excavation blast mode*, an implanted memory informed him — and fired again into the small alcove carved out of the wall by the previous blast.

But it was all too little too late because he felt the impact of an armored claw slashing him from behind, just before the grenade blast blew him backward off his feet to fall onto hard unyielding carapace and slide down onto the sticky floor. His smart battlesuit armor soaked up enough of these blows to keep him alive for now.

Around him, the nearest aliens stirred feebly. Still half-stunned himself, Arun took a gamble. Instead of racing on into the hole his grenades had scooped out, he got himself up to a kneeling position and put one last 37H into the center of the cloud of alien body debris in front of him. This time he braced while the blast front rolled over him. Then he was staggering to his feet and stumbling on into the spray of soil and aerosol blood, and beyond into the hole the grenades had burrowed out of the soil. Clouds of spilling earth blinded him, but he judged he'd crawled in fifteen meters before the hole stopped and he could go no further. He abandoned his carbine, freeing both hands to burrow into the loosened soil, throwing it behind him like a gauntleted mole.

Euphoria gripped him. He'd abandoned his firearm, a capital offense, and the Trogs would dice him into a hundred bloody chunks any moment now, but he couldn't help but grin at the simple pleasure of using his hands like paddles. For this task, his combat immunity numbness actually seemed to help.

Then he reached soil that was still too compacted to shift. Actually, he'd hit that barrier several moments or minutes ago. The sense of time's passage had numbed with most of his other senses. Even in the depths of confusion, one thing rang clear: Arun had nowhere left to run.

He screamed. High-pitched like a child. His scream cracked, turning into some hybrid of a sob and a gasp.

"McEwan, come in!"

Nowhere to run! Flekked!

"Report!"

Those aliens had done this. Those Trogs. He'd make them pay…

Arun twisted around and charged at the Troggie horde who'd gathered around the entrance to his hole.

He'd rip their legs off their stinking alien bodies.

"Report, cadet! Damn you! That is an order."

The irritation in Brandt's voice reached through the helmet speaker and sent a jolt of challenge into Arun's mind. He slowed as he wondered what the frakk he was doing charging along an alcove to head butt a pack of slavering aliens desperate to reach inside and kill him.

Damn those experimental combat drugs.

"I'm under heavy assault," he whispered into the helmet mike, more interested in putting his brain back into order than following reporting protocol. "I seem to be alive. I feel rather good, actually, thank you for asking."

"I didn't. I asked you to report."

"I did."

"I want a sit-rep. What's happening? We came back when Osman reported movement, but now he's dead and we're pinned down. What are you going to do?"

In front of him, Arun could see his carbine half-buried in the dirt where he'd dropped it. The railgun looked so pretty there. Shiny. He wanted it. But the aliens were reaching into his hole, flicking their claws at him, and the weapon was so close to the bad insects.

Big, *fat* insects. They were too big to follow the human into his hole, and whatever had let them swim through the walls earlier wasn't working here.

Arun shuffled around until his feet were pointing at the aliens and slid his left boot towards the waiting creatures, ever so gently.

Ever since they'd emerged from the walls and ceiling, the Trogs had been slavering, chittering beasts climbing over themselves in desperation to rend him limb from limb.

Now they froze. Arun froze too. His pulse was a dull drumming inside his helmet; there were no other sounds — until Brandt growled: "Well?"

"I think I'm going to kill them," Arun said. "Or maybe the other way around. I'm not sure yet. I'll report back when I know."

There was a way to turn off his comms unit, but he couldn't think what that was right now. He asked Barney to switch it off, but Barney wasn't listening for some reason. He tried out emergency eyeball gestures, but they didn't work either. If he could, he would have taken the frakking helmet off and buried it.

Brandt was very annoying. If he couldn't turn him off, Arun decided he would drown out his voice. So Arun began to sing, a stirring ballad about the beauty of Old Earth, the precious homeworld left so very far behind. The chorus was rousing; just the thing to belt out with your pals at the end of a rec-evening.

His song got the attention of the Trogs. Each guardian shifted its head for the best reception of his singing voice. Perhaps his song was charming them to obedience, or sleep, or an even fiercer rage. Maybe they liked the words.

Inch by inch, he shuffled toward them, trying to slip his toe through the strap of his carbine. Ever so slowly… almost there…

"Are they coming in our direction? Report, McEwan!"

Oh, frakk! Brandt's voice had come out of his external suit speakers, spooking the Trogs so they were jumping around as if he'd rammed a red-hot poker up their butts.

Arun abandoned his attempt to be subtle and slid towards the carbine as fast as he could.

At the same moment, the sea of alien motion flowed at his crude little tunnel and launched something at him, a dark blur of motion with hate in its alien head and coming right at him.

Double dung!

He'd wasted a precious heartbeat watching the thing come for him. The tip of his toe reached the gun strap. By yanking back his leg and contorting his torso so forcibly that this muscles spasmed, he whipped the railgun his way and grabbed. Grabbed the *barrel* end.

He started shuffling back as this new thing came close.

Too late!

As he was spinning the railgun round to point the killing end at the attacker, the beast finally reached him.

Arun looked up from his carbine. At first, he thought his opponent was a Troggie child, but it was difficult to make out because it moved so very fast, all flashing limbs and flailing body and jaws. It was so close that the beam of helmet light didn't spread wide enough to pick out the limbs in detail.

When the creature flicked a claw across his leg, a realization hit him with pointless urgency: guardians are the last stage of the Trog lifecycle. There's no such thing as a guardian child.

What faced him was an adult guardian with four of its limbs ripped out. Only the front two remained, held out in front of its head as combined motive force and assault weapons. This was the hive creatures' answer to the narrowness of his crawlspace.

Spikes of pain flickered up his legs as the mutilated Trog cut into Arun, using the young cadet's flesh to pull itself closer until it could make a killing blow.

Arun wiggled his toes. And laughed.

Without most of its limbs, the Trog couldn't get power behind its attacks. Seeing as he could still move his toes, he probably wasn't going to die from its claw strike. Not just yet.

With a slightly firmer hold on his SA-71, he brought it to bear on this crazy alien. But the beast flicked the carbine out of his hands, which were still too numb from the combat immunity to grip properly.

Helplessly, he watched his weapon sail overhead, out of reach, to land with a dull thud behind him, at the far end of the short tunnel gouged out by Arun's grenades.

Then the crippled guardian flopped its middle segment — its thorax, he supposed it was called — onto Arun's legs, pinning him with its weight. Arun flung his body left then right in a frantic attempt to wriggle free. His legs slid slowly towards freedom but not quickly enough.

The two-limbed Trog raised its legs up and sliced down, aiming in a coordinated attack that convinced Arun that these guardians knew a lot more about human anatomy than he'd given them credit for. It aimed that metal-sheathed claw directly at his heart.

At the moment the claws started to bite into his armor, Arun screamed.

He rampaged through his memories, trying to remember all of it while he still had a chance. He screamed all the way, only stopping when the realization hit him that he'd never properly been in love with a woman. It was so unfair to end it all now, when he was just getting his life started.

Then another unexpected thought struck him: he still wasn't dead.

Looking down at his chest, he saw the claw embedded inside his ACE-2/T training suit, and it hurt like frakk, but… his smart armor had caught and held the blow. The constraints of the narrow tunnel dimensions, the lack of limbs… whatever the reason, the claw was stuck!

The guardian thrashed madly, banging each side of the tunnel in turn, making Arun worry about a cave-in but allowing him to free his legs. All this time, the Trog made no sound at all except for the thudding of its carapace on the dirt walls.

Then it abandoned that tactic and reduced itself to flopping back onto Arun, trying to pin him to the ground.

"Only a matter of time before I get out, my friend," said Arun, beginning the work again of wriggling free.

The alien hissed at him. The sound was like a pressure valve release. Perhaps this meant challenge or hatred. It might be its death rattle, or it might mean "Well done, sir, for besting me". How could he know? It was a drenting, skangat alien for frakk's sake.

With his legs about halfway to freedom, Arun heard an answering hiss from the main tunnel, and a second mutilated alien launched itself at him.

One chance remained… Arun activated the emergency release on his battlesuit, gasping as the shock instantly hit his system. Emergency suit release felt like his body was turning inside out. Endocrine pumps retracted from insertion points. Myriad med-points detached from their hold through his skin. Waste pipes released his penis and slithered out of his anus. Clamps popped. Warm lubricants dripped.

Arun slithered free of his clothing in a short series of slurping wrenches.

The second Trog had reached its companion and tried to squeeze past. With three-quarters of its limbs missing, and the first Trog still stuck to the battlesuit's armored torso, the newcomer never stood a chance.

By the time the second Trog managed to push its head and thorax past its companion, Arun had finally reached his railgun. He fired a controlled burst of darts.

The insect's front limbs exploded into chunks. Wet shrapnel of head and jaws and thorax peppered the area.

Arun released pressure on the trigger and inspected his handiwork. Both beasts were still twitching.

He switched the weapon's ammo supply from kinetic darts to rocket rounds: *bangers*. The main purpose of bangers was to be fully recoilless, something very handy in zero-g combat out in deep space. But even here under a planet's surface, the rounds still made a decent bang.

Arun pumped ten seconds of fiery destruction into the two battered Trogs, imagining the blessed day when he would be issued with micro-nukes. Then the carbine pinged that its ammunition was exhausted, and he remembered the downside of bangers: they were far larger than darts, so you couldn't fit many into an ammunition carousel.

After the black rain of chitin chunks had subsided, he tried cleaning his slick hands by wiping them on the walls, but the walls were soggy too. Maybe it was just as well they hadn't issued him with nukes.

The two mutilated Trogs that had attacked weren't moving, weren't even an obstacle any longer. Outside in the main tunnel it was a different story. An ocean of six-limbed aliens waited for him.

"Should have evolved the opposable thumb," he shouted at the enemy. As taunts went, it didn't have much effect. He reached for fresh ammo to reinforce his message.

Oh, drent!

That was when he remembered he had squirmed from his battle dress in order to escape from the aliens pinning his legs. He was naked, save for his helmet and gauntlets. His ammo was still attached to the battlesuit that he'd discarded underneath the two Trogs, the same Trogs he'd just liquidized with a volley of explosive bullets.

Frakk it!

As he crawled over the slurry he'd created, he struggled to spot his battlesuit under its covering of gore. Something of vaguely the right shape was there, pushed farther up his hole toward the waiting Trogs.

As he advanced, the Trogs outside stilled, and silenced. He preferred them manic; this was more menacing somehow. He ignored the guardians waiting just out of slashing range and wiped at the muck coating his half-buried suit. Arun flipped over the armor, which revealed shapes in the slurry underneath. Feeling with his hands, he found an intact fastening from an equipment pack, and two unused grenades. Underneath a shard from his drink bottle, he found an ammunition carousel. In a smooth and swift motion, he rammed the ammo into an unused socket in his carbine, took a kneeling posture, and fired.

Instead of the soft whine of darts, Arun heard an angry whir as his carbine rejected the ammo carousel, and then a faint plop as it fell to the wet ground.

When Arun crouched down to retrieve the bulb of ammunition, a wave of stench hit him: a Trog pheromone signal. It was an earthy smell; probably it carried layers of meaning to the aliens: taunts and an incitement to victory. To Arun it was remarkably similar to the pungent aroma of unwashed socks.

Zug might know what that scent meant, but his friend wasn't here. At this moment, his best friend was the AG-1 Ammunition Carousel, a dull-gray plastic bulb filled with bullets, darts and shells, a reservoir of sabot resin, and a power pack whose ability to recharge itself was as near as frakk to magical. Arun blew into the carousel's opened feed interface. Dark goop spewed out, gobbing into his eye. He blinked furiously.

Willing his tear-smeared eye to remain open, Arun snapped the slightly-cleaned ammo carousel into his carbine, which clicked and whirred hungrily… and carried on whirring. His railgun was unhappy. A blue light lit up on its stock. He couldn't make it out. So he brought the stock to his head and thumbed for the carbine's AI to give an audio status.

"Ammo feed impaired. Risk of explosion. AG-1 contents only partially utilizable."

Partial, eh? Arun squinted out of his hole. He saw aliens as far as he could see. He shrugged. Once the dumb bugs worked out that all they needed to do was widen the opening to his bolt-hole, he was going to die anyway. *Partial* would do just fine.

Arun overrode the warning and fired into the waiting horde. He screamed incoherent sounds of battle fury as his weapon accelerated sporadic volleys of kinetic darts interleaved with frequent misfires. On and on he pumped death through the aperture of his hastily excavated hole, until he realized the ammo supply feed was clicking through an empty reservoir.

Drop by splatter, the aerosol of ichor and soil succumbed to gravity and cleared, engorging the dark pools already on the floor.

Recognizable fragments of carapaces, jaws, horns and legs poked out from the jumble of undifferentiated alien chitin… and… moved!

Icy fear cooled his battle fury. Dead aliens moving… he'd heard of undead aliens in the morbid rumors that frequently washed over the human community on Tranquility. Arun reckoned that ninety-five percent of this scuttlebutt was drent. That left five percent with at least an undercurrent of truth, such as the tales of alien warriors who could not be killed. Every time you snuffed out their life, they reconstituted, coming back stronger than before.

He shuddered. In front of him, as the spray of destruction cleared a little more, he could make out chitinous bodies jerking into movement, reassembling themselves. *Returning to life.*

Relief flooded his body when he realized what was really happening. He slapped a hand on his bare thigh and laughed so hard that he had to sit down. The dead Troggie guardians weren't coming back to life; it was their living nest-siblings removing their fallen comrades to clear the way for another attack.

As if to reinforce that common sense was returning to his world after that fright, he noticed the Trogs had lost their earlier attack mania and were now using their combat claws to widen the entrance to his hole. They frequently stopped to examine the walls and roof, feeling them with their mid-limbs. These were guardians, he reminded himself: the last stage in the Trog lifecycle. He guessed these vecks weren't normally allowed to do any digging.

Arun backed away the short distance to the rear of his hole and counted down his last moments before evisceration. He'd heard you were supposed to cry for your mother when you faced certain death.

That didn't seem to be working for him, so he closed his eyes and tried to bring up memories of his mother.

She had been kind enough, but she had always known that one day she would be shipped out-system, leaving him behind. That she had kept her emotional distance was obvious to him now.

He couldn't even picture her face, just a name and rank: Sergeant Escandala McEwan.

Inefficient yet remorseless, the Trogs dug him out. Arun kept his eyes shut, but the unceasing scraping noise told him they were almost within range of a claw strike. As he waited to be sliced, his thoughts drifted to Stephen Horden. The older cadet had claimed to be descended from the President Horden of Earth who had signed the Vancouver Accord and condemned the ancestors of the Human Marine Corps to perpetual slavery.

Arun had never cared about lineage. What impressed him was how Horden had built quite a following with his secret teachings on Earth history, and compelling arguments about why Old Earth was something worth fighting for — worth *humans* fighting for — and, one day, returning to as free people.

Horden had graduated the year before, part of a replacement list sent off to some garrison fleet around the mining system of Akinschet. Arun's mother had been posted there. Perhaps the two would meet?

Fighting for humanity… as he waited to die a pointless death on behalf of uncaring alien masters, he wondered what it must be like to fight for a cause you could believe in, a new kind of Human Marine Corps that actually fought for humanity.

Without warning, every Trog simultaneously emitted a screech like poorly lubricated wheel brakes. A few seconds later came another pheromone-laden smell. Like rotten fruit this time.

Guess that meant contemplation time was over.

He opened his eyes. The guardians had withdrawn from his hole, standing motionless in the main tunnel corridor. Great! They must have found some digging-caste Trogs to get at him safely without bringing the roof down.

"Cease fire, humans!"

The voice seemed to be coming from within the tunnel walls, not from a single source but diffusely spread throughout this area of the hive. "This exercise is concluded. Cease fire!"

Within moments, the guardians calmed to a stop, listing woozily. If the notion wasn't so absurd, he'd say they had grown sleepy.

A ripple spread through the insectoid mob. The disturbance came from a new kind of Trog. Smaller and more lightly colored, this one lacked the halo of sharp horns. When the newcomer had pushed through the crowd and stood at the entrance to Arun's little cave, he could see its carapace was as black as the guardians but covered in fine red hairs that looked unexpectedly delicate, when picked out in the beam of his helmet lamp. Instructor Rekka had explained in her briefing that this was a Trog in an earlier stage of the lifecycle: a *scribe*.

"The guardians will not harm you now," spoke the scribe via a box hanging around its neck, which whirred with gears as it generated a mechanical version of a human voice.

Arun wasn't convinced. But, what the hell? It beat cowering. He got down on hands and knees and slithered through the floes of spent sabots floating in a carnage sea. It was like crawling through a midden pit dug for an outdoor field exercise, except now he was so close to the chopped aliens, he smelled a tang of sweetened metal.

This had only been a training exercise.

But when he looked around at corpses of his supposed allies, killed by his own hand, he wondered whether the scribe would see things the same way.

Chapter 02

The alien scribe stood motionless amidst the scene of combat carnage. Two pairs of glassy black bulbs — Arun assumed they were eyes — stared at Arun. If the creature was showing any kind of emotional reaction to the death of its fellows, it wasn't in a form a human could recognize.

Arun's combat drugs were beginning to wear off, enough for him to reason that the best thing for him to do was shut up, keep still, and await orders…

Thinking of orders… why wasn't Brandt shouting at him through the comms link in his helmet? Was Brandt dead?

"I have given them a pheromone order to render them dormant," said the scribe's box after a while. "You too should take on a dormant state, human Marine cadet."

He waited for the scribe's box to say more, but the creature had said all it intended to for now. The hairs on the insect thorax looked so soft, he wanted to reach out and stroke them. Although the alien made no menacing moves, Arun kept his hand to himself, worried that his sudden urge for intimacy might be connected to coming down from the combat drugs.

After the gnarled bulk of the guardians, the scribe seemed as cute as a cooing baby. It was only seven feet long rather than a guardian's nine plus, but still had the same three-segment body arrangement that looked like the head, thorax, and abdomen of Earth insects.

Arun was all too familiar with real insects. When his distant ancestors had been transported from Earth, the little buzzing, biting but pollinating pests had come too. The scribe only looked superficially like an Earth creature, though. It carried itself on three spindly pairs of limbs that ended in flexible suckers. Definitely not like an insect. The pre-mission briefing had mentioned these suckers, describing them as analogous to an Earthly elephant's trunk.

Although he wasn't one of the few who resisted the Earth-centric obsession, sometimes Arun thought it went too far. What kind of dumb veck thought it was a clever idea to compare Trogs to an animal on a far-off planet that none of the human Marines would ever encounter?

"I mean," he told the scribe, "really, it would make far more sense to describe an elephant's trunk as like a scribe's limbs, rather than the other way around."

On the scribe's motionless head, its two pairs of eyes blinked. Then it raised its antenna into a frenzy of wriggling.

Without warning, those feelers telescoped outward, directly at Arun's head.

He jumped back, settling into a loose crouch, ready for unarmed combat. But the feelers stopped their advance and Arun amused himself with the thought that he'd never been taught *unclothed* combat.

The antennae retracted slightly into a fixed pattern, a square shape that it maintained for a few seconds before saying: "I agree. I have read the same human texts. As if anyone on this planet would ever encounter an elephant!"

"That's exactly what I was thinking!"

Arun's squadmate, Zug, studied aliens with a passion. He'd be able to make sense of this conversation later.

"So…" Arun continued, wondering how you were supposed to change subject with an alien species you'd never met before, except to shoot at. (Arun glanced nervously at the carnage around him). "Er… did we win?"

"You failed to meet the success criteria of this exercise. We do not know the detailed assessment that will be forthcoming from the Jotuns and your senior humans. Our own assessment is that too many small-unit commanders proved inadequate, and your company commander lacked imagination. Most disastrous of all, you failed to keep reserves. The concept of a front line is tenuous when contesting a three-dimensional tunnel network. Counter-attacks can come from any direction. Have you not been taught the concept of a mobile reserve?"

"Oh." Arun's shoulders slumped. This was the scenario every human on the planet hated: being made to feel like children by older races that had seen it all before. He tried to put every iota of assertiveness into his voice and asked: "Were there any casualties?"

Speaking those words made him think of his fire team buddies: Osman, Madge and Springer. Were they dead? *Properly* dead?

"There were four minor injuries," the alien told him. Arun relaxed. "And one fatality. Name of Isabella de Grouchy."

Arun pictured bouncy brown hair, a hooked nose set into a serious, freckle-dashed face that was often frowning. De Grouchy had flashed him a momentary half-smile once; they'd never spoken but he'd seen her enough to paint a vivid picture of her in his mind's eye. And now she was gone.

Isabella hadn't exactly been the first to die. Not when Arun considered all those who hadn't survived to graduate from novice school as a cadet.

He glanced at the guardians still crowding the tunnel, apparently in deep sleep.

Arun idly flicked the larger chunks of mess off his body. He felt a throb of pain to his left leg and torso. He squeezed his right eye shut against the fierce pain that stabbed through it. Sensation was returning. And he was injured.

He froze, his wounds forgotten. He realized he'd just flicked a piece of Troggie body onto the scribe. Trogs lived in nests. Nest members, the briefing had said, were almost a gestalt entity, a hive whose members were far closer to each other than any human twin.

"Were…" Arun cleared his throat. "Were there many tropied on your side?" He winced, unable to stop himself glancing around at the combat slurry.

He could have phrased that better.

"A little over a thousand nest-siblings were… *tropied*. Is that the right word? You do mean *killed*, don't you?"

The alien had replayed a recording of Arun's voice when it said *tropied*. Seemed the translation software wasn't up to date with the vernacular used by the 412th Marines.

"Yeah, tropied. You know, *entropied*." Arun shrugged. "I'm sorry."

"Why?" The scribe twitched its feelers. "Because you humans killed so many?"

"Well…" Zug always told him that aliens don't do sarcasm, not that a human would ever understand, anyway. So Arun decided to take the alien's words literally. "Yes," he said, looking at the massed ranks of guardians. One word from the scribe and he'd be chopped meat himself within two seconds.

"I feel regret," Arun decided to add, "that so many nest-siblings were… slain."

Slain? He didn't think he'd ever used the archaic word before, but he couldn't quite bring himself to say *killed* with all those alien warriors standing there in the wreckage of their brothers and sisters — or whatever passed for gender within the nest.

The scribe twisted its antennae into spirals and said, "You humans amuse us with your wild flights of emotion." It paused. "We also feel intense emotion at the appropriate stages in our life-journeys, but there is always a purpose to our emotion. But you, human, why do you grieve for fallen enemies?"

"Trogs aren't my enemies. We're all slaves of the White Knights on Tranquility."

"True. Just as those of my race are also slaves to our biological lifecycle, and to our nest's resource constraints."

The scribe relaxed its feelers and swayed slightly. "Today you killed my nest-siblings who were in the stage of our lifecycle you call guardians. An individual's body changes to the guardian state only because they failed in their previous life-phase. They are the oldest, on average, and so are expendable. In primitive nests, guardians are first to form the defensive wedge when rival nests attack. Without war between nests, our guardian population must be culled. For us, it is a kindness for humans to kill so many, because we remember these individuals from an earlier time in their lives when they were our friends, our children and our parents. Better you do it than we kill them ourselves. However they are culled, their role is not yet complete as we will shortly take their remains to be composted."

Arun pointed at one of the nearby corpses that was still relatively intact. "That one," he said. "Are you telling me you're going to chop him up and use him to help grow your vegetables?"

"Of course."

"Frakk!" Arun raised his hands, palms up. "*Aliens!*"

The Trog matched his gesture of bemusement, using its front limbs to approximate a shrug. "*Aliens!*" it exclaimed, playing the sound of Arun's voice through its box. "My thoughts exactly. See how you referred to that maimed Trog as *he* once you felt sympathy?"

"No. But… you're right. I did."

"You humans fascinate me." It paused. "May I ask you a question?"

"Go on…" said Arun, dearly wishing it wouldn't.

"You exhibit two incongruities that have led me to form a hypothesis. I should like to state my hypothesis for your review."

"O-kay."

"Firstly, I note that you are naked."

"No, I'm not."

"Forgive my imprecision. You are naked other than your helmet and your gloves."

"Right. Well, there's a simple explanation. I had to abandon my battlesuit because your nest-buddies had pinned me down."

"Secondly…" The alien extended both its feathery antennae to touch him in a place Arun really didn't expect an alien to ever make contact. Arun yelped in shock.

"Secondly, you have activated your mating prong."

Arun gasped, and slowly lowered his gaze. *Sweet final homecoming! Damn those frakking combat drugs and their drenting side effects.*

"My hypothesis," continued the alien, showing no sign of noticing Arun blush like a nuclear furnace, "is that you wish to engage with me in a sexual encounter."

Arun slapped one hand down to guard his genitals, and the other up to hide his face.

"It is my privilege to study alien behavior for the benefit of the nest. In the course of my research, I have observed many recordings of human copulation, and I surmise that you wish to penetrate first."

Collapsing to a ball on the tunnel floor, Arun willed the world to go away, or for him to die. Whichever came first; he didn't care, just so long as an end came quickly.

Through a crack in his fingers, Arun watched the alien turn side-on. Patches on its thorax had turned bright red, and a section of its carapace was… *puckering*.

"If my hypothesis is correct," said the alien, "you will find my reproductive opening on my flanks. I regret, though, that I cannot reciprocate."

Arun groaned loudly.

"Oh," said the alien, or rather its mechanical voice in a box, which managed to sound offended. "I hear your disappointment. My reluctance to penetrate you in return is not through lack of interest, rather that I would rip your opening and rupture your bowels."

"Cadet McEwan. Acknowledge ceasefire."

For several moments, the new voice confused Arun. It sounded deep and worn and it wasn't coming from the scribe. Then he remembered the comms link in his helmet.

"McEwan. Acknowledge! This is Sergeant Gupta. Acknowledge."

"Roger that. Sorry, sergeant."

"Relax, son. It's those frakking combat meds they keep tinkering with. There's always a few green cadets enter a combat fugue and never snap out. But you're coming round now. You'll be okay. And next time your body will find them a little easier to take. Hopefully."

"Sergeant… Brandt… why isn't Brandt…?" Arun found words that should come easily swirled and slithered away beyond reach. "Sergeant, is he—?"

"—dead? No, cadet. Well, Acting Cadet Corporal Edward Brandt is dead according to the rules of the exercise, but perfectly okay in real life. Mind you, I expect he will hope it was the other way around when I review his sorry performance with your instructors. Yes, I'm your new veteran squad commander."

Arun knew he should be paying attention to the NCO — a real one who had earned his rank. But he couldn't help but stare at the alien instead. Its antennae were bent at an angle. It looked like a person tilting their head when listening with interest. Maybe this gesture meant the same thing.

"Cadet."

"Yes, sergeant."

Gupta paused. "I did three tours of duty before they had me nursemaiding you kids. I've been around for 180 objective years and that means I've seen a little of the galaxy. I want to share some of that with you now."

"Thank you, sergeant."

"Life has a habit of being unfair. Sometimes you just gotta suck it in. Cry on the inside if you have to, wail in private with your best pals if you must, but keep your head high and wait for your luck to change. Remember, a Marine never buckles under pressure. That's easy to say but now is your time to prove it."

"Yes, sergeant."

"Stay where you are, McEwan. Your injuries don't look too serious, but I've marked you for medical evac just in case. So I don't want you walking out because that would make me look a damned fool."

"Yes, sergeant. Umm… Sergeant?"

"Hurry up!"

"Well, what you said. About life being unfair. I didn't quite follow. I survived. What's unfair about that?"

"Ah, frakk it, son. Everything in those tunnels was recorded. Video, audio, the works. What that bug-ugly just said to you is already flying around the base. *Why have you activated your mating prong?* Like it or not your comrades won't let you forget that, so I want you to roll with it. See the funny side. That's an order."

But Arun wasn't listening. He curled into as tight as ball as he could and willed the lurking guardians to end his existence.

Chapter 03

It was only as Arun approached the battalion chow hall, hobbling with the aid of the walking stick the medic had given him, that he knew for certain he hadn't gotten away with his embarrassing episode in the tunnel. At first, the complete shunters of the 412th Marine Regiment — his future comrades-in-arms, sworn to aid him in his hour of need — had acted as if nothing had happened, though he imagined he saw concealed smirks on their faces.

He began to hope he'd actually gotten away with it.

But now the cadets spilling out from the hall and into the approach corridor were no longer hiding their smirks. He ignored the little vecks as he pushed his way through and into the chow hall. As soon as he was inside, the door sphinctered shut.

Marine cadets of all years thronged the room, overwhelming the ventilation system to suffuse it with a sweaty pong, not unlike the stink of menacing Troggie guardians. Everyone in that room stopped whatever they were doing and twisted around to stare at Arun McEwan.

Digi-sheets had been stuck onto every available surface. All of them looped the moment when the alien scribe grasped Arun's manhood with its feelers. Underneath the moving image, some wit had added the caption: 'Arun McEwan: so desperate he'll prong anything.'

The room erupted in a cacophony of cheers, catcalls, hoots and jeers. Some was good-natured. Most of it wasn't.

Osman slid over from somewhere and slapped Arun on the back, laughing along with everyone else in the room.

"Not you, too," groaned Arun.

Slapping his back all the while, Osman leaned closer and said: "Laugh, Arun. Laugh with them. It's your only chance."

"He's right," said Zug, who was standing a few paces behind Osman. "If they sense your humiliation, they will use this against you forever. Your status will be permanently degraded. What then for your sexual fantasy?"

Arun scowled at Serge Rhenolotte. *Zug* to his friends. He was about to remonstrate that Xin Lee was not a fantasy, but a real woman, when he realized that just then, Xin was a little *too* real for comfort. She was sitting only a few meters away.

"You can do it," said Zug. "Like I've done my whole life."

If the stories were true — and one thing you learned early on Tranquility was never to trust what you were told — then when the first humans had been brought to Tranquility, they had come in a variety of shades and shapes, reflecting the regions of Earth that had originally offered up their children to the White Knights. But that had been many generations ago. United in common service to their unseen masters, and with the distinctions between nationalities reduced to misremembered fables, the Earth races had churned and averaged, to a norm of mid-brown skin and black hair. Except for the occasional individual, such as Zug.

"Say something," Osman insisted.

"Shut up!" Arun hissed. "I'm thinking."

Zug possessed by far the darkest skin color in his year, and that had made him stand out his entire life. He'd grown up being picked on and mocked for looking different, but he had never been cowed. He'd never been in with the popular crowd, but neither had Zug ever been isolated, never been singled out as a loser. Zug had even shaved his head bald to emphasize skin that was the color of the void.

If Zug could survive being different, Arun could too.

And so Arun put his trust in his friend and laughed. A brittle sound at first — obviously fake — he eased into the act and slowly the sound grew more natural. Soon, the crowd's interest waned. It was working!

Just when Arun began to imagine his ordeal was over, Xin Lee limbered her toned body out of her seat and sauntered his way.

Arun stood his ground, but his smile cracked.

Osman whispered: "Whatever she says, keep grinning."

Easy for you to say.

The girl who frequently turned his dreams feverish stopped in front of the little group of friends. She put her hands on her hips and gave Arun an appraising look.

"Well then, McEwan," she said. No, not said: *announced*. The class G-1 cadet — one year older than Arun — was addressing everyone there. Everyone listened. "I hear that you're an alien-faggot. Is that true?"

Arun felt his legs wobble. This was the first time that Xin had ever spoken to him in real life, and she had just invented a new term of derision. Just for his benefit. His heart sank. Speech was beyond him.

"Shame, really," she said. "After seeing your attempt at an erotic vid, it seems like a waste of good equipment."

Xin's gaze met his and taunted, those lovely dark eyes set into her smooth face, with the snubby little nose that he adored.

His heart accelerated up his spinal column and crashed into his brain, preventing him from saying anything beyond a plaintive grunt.

Xin decided his audience was ended, and marched out of the hall, flanked by a pair of girlfriends. Her every step was accompanied by catcalls and wolf whistles. She loved it.

In a way, she had saved him. By taking so much of the room's attention on herself, the excitement dissipated the moment she left the hall.

Arun fled to the nearest table and hunkered down.

"Tough luck, pal," said Zug. "Your reaction to the combat drug was unfortunate, but hardly the most extreme on record. Some cadets die, you know, the first time they take combat-meds under life-threatening conditions. It's rotten luck, I know, but Xin was always a far from realistic proposition for you."

Arun frowned at him. "Eh? Didn't you just hear what she said?"

"Yes," said Zug. "Apparently, you're an alien-faggot."

Osman leaned over. "I think, Zug, that our friend was referring to Xin's second comment. Something about good equipment."

"Your friend is bang on correct," said Arun, feeling cheerful, "I'm well in there."

Osman snorted.

Zug scratched his bald pate, trying to make sense. "It's hardly like she gave you her dorm code and invited you over to make icers with her."

"Oh, I think that it was," said Arun, slapping Zug on the shoulder.

Osman face-palmed.

"Combat drugs are still addling his brain," Zug told Osman. "It's the only possible explanation."

"You're just jealous," said Arun, grinning.

Zug and Osman buried their heads in their hands and groaned.

Arun shrugged off his friends' disbelief. Newly entered into class G-1, Xin had nearly two years to go until she either graduated as a Marine, or was cast out of the Corps.

Today she had spoken to him, and with a dose of optimism, he could stretch those words into a compliment. It wasn't much to go on, but he had almost two years to win something more from her.

Arun relished a challenge.

He wasn't a natural leader like Majanita, as brave as Osman, nor as dependable as Springer.

Didn't need to be. Arun knew his strength: he never gave up.

One day, he'd win Xin Lee. Of that he was certain.

Chapter 04

With evening inspection due in fifteen minutes, the atmosphere in Arun's dorm began to chill with fear.

The cadets in Arun's battalion had laughed at him mercilessly, but the story of the naked cadet had spread far beyond the 8th battalion… beyond even his regiment. The laughter had dried up in Arun's hab-disk and the battalion chow halls. Detroit was the home base for two other tactical Marine regiments and one Marine assault regiment, all of whom were now hooting with derision at the 412th.

Arun had brought shame on his regiment, shame on their regimental instructors.

And one of those instructors would be conducting the evening inspection very soon.

"I know what we need," said Arun, trying to raise the mood, "let's list our top five fantasy rack buddies."

The seven other cadets in the dorm groaned, even Cristina who gave an echo of disapproval from the head.

Arun was sitting at the dorm table with Springer and Majanita. He skidded his chair back to give him space to perform his best rendition of the Gallic shrug that Del-Marie had taught him. Del-Marie Sandure was no more French than Arun, but most people who'd survived this far into Marine training had adopted a personality weirdness or two. Everyone understood the need for a coping mechanism. If Del wanted to pretend he was French, his Delta Section mates were happy to indulge him.

"Oh, c'mon. Top fives are always fun," Arun insisted. His grin faded. "Or were until you all lost your sense of fun. Anyway, it'll give us something else to think about during inspection. I've got a feeling we might need distracting."

Lying on his bunk – or rack as they were learning to call them now they were cadets — Del-Marie sighed. "Arun, you're becoming tiresome."

"Oh, am I?" said Arun cheerfully. "You're only saying that because everyone already knows your list. Your favorite is Bernard. He's your number 2, 3, 4, and 5 too."

"His name is not Bur-nerd. It's Berr-narr." Del-Marie rolled his r's in a way Arun had never managed to imitate.

Madge reached over the dorm table and placed a well-manicured hand over Arun's. "Darling, Arun," she said in her breathy voice that some called flirtatious, and others called dumblitted, "I don't like to generalize but listing one's top vulley-buddies is such a boy thing. And an obsession strongest in the least mature of your gender."

Arun smiled, not minding the ribbing from Madge. Her vampish act had all but disappeared in the last few weeks, smothered under a heavy cloak of seriousness.

Springer snorted derisively, flashing her violet eyes at Arun — literally. Scattered through the Marine cadets were many unintended consequences of the genetic manipulations the Jotun scientists had engineered in their ancestors. The vibrant color of Springer's eyes, and the ability to illuminate them, was one of the more obvious. And attractive.

Madge steamed on. "A more useful topic for discussion is whether we're entering any teams in the Scendence competition this year."

"You're getting boring," Springer told Arun, ignoring Madge. He was shocked to see real anger in her eyes. "All you ever want to do is invent excuses to spout off about that skangat girl. For frakk's sake, why don't you ask Xin if she wants you to prong her? Then she'll shoot you down in a ball of plasma and–" Springer rolled her eyes "– we won't have to listen to you prattle on about her ever again."

An impish grin came to Brandt's face. "Springer's only saying that because she wants you in her rack all to herself."

"Shut up, Brandt!" shouted everyone else in the room. He'd been assigned the section leader role in the tunnels, but his temporary rank vanished the moment the exercise ended.

Brandt seethed.

Cristina emerged from the head. "Did I miss something? What's going on?"

Several pairs of eyes glanced at Brandt and rolled in their sockets.

"The question remains," said Zug, ever the one to steer a conversation back on course, "how many Scendence teams are we entering?" He paused from cleaning the personal locker at the foot of his rack. "Alistair LaSalle will want to team up with Alice Belville. They'll take Gunnery and Deception and pick the best players in Charlie Company for the other positions. That'll probably include Hortez. Del-Marie we can trust to keep our secrets but will be playing Gunnery in a team with Bernard. Am I correct, Del-Marie?"

Del nodded. "If I play this season, it won't be with any of you."

"Forget Alistair," said Madge. "As for Hortez, if our temporary squad leader thinks he's too good for the rest of us then let him play with Alistair. I don't care what they do, I intend to play Gunnery in a Blue Squad team." Madge's tone was serious again now. Cadets from other units often used to underestimate Majanita as either a shallow beauty doll or a salacious siren. They were both acts, to be dropped whenever the matter at hand was serious. And Estella Majanita – not many who knew her dared to call her Madge to her face – took the game of Scendence very seriously indeed.

Madge gave Springer an expectant look.

"Me too," said Springer reluctantly. "I'll take Obedience. I know what you're going to say, Zug, and you're probably right, but what the hell? I enjoy playing, and I enjoy winning. Perhaps we'll win some points for the battalion."

"Please understand," said Zug, "that I speak only for myself when I say that I shall not participate in Scendence this year. We've been in this hab-disk nearly three weeks. Three weeks since we ceased to be novices. Our every action now has the potential to win our battalion merit points–"

"Or demerits," interrupted Del-Marie.

Arun's gut churned. The fallout from the regimental humiliation in the tunnels had yet to settle, and if demerits were forthcoming he had scapegoat written all over him.

"Yes, my friend," said Zug. "Or de-merits. Everything we do has the potential to bring our battalion down closer to the Cull Zone if we fail. And if we do well, we put a larger margin of safety away from the Cull. All I'm saying is that if we don't think the time we put into Scendence training will pay off in merit points, then we should spend that time on something that will. The senior cadet companies seem eager to offer us G-2 noobs extra coaching. If they think that's a good investment of their time it's because we're all part of 8th battalion, and helping us gain merit points keeps them away from the Cull just as much as it does ourselves."

"And they're a year or two ahead of us," added Arun. "We should listen to what they're telling us."

"He's right," added Brandt who was hovering near the table. "I've already taken up every offer of coaching I can handle. I can't do that if I'm also doing serious Scendence training."

There was a moment's tense silence. Arun almost felt sorry for Brandt. He might be a dumb veck, and the way he'd led the section in the tunnels had landed them all in the drent, but Brandt hadn't volunteered to be a cadet corporal. Maybe, back in the days when there were human armies on Earth, he might have made a good officer one day. But there was no such thing as a human officer in the Corps, only NCOs. And Brandt just wasn't right to be an NCO.

"Brandt and Zug share an opinion," snapped Cristina, obviously an opinion she did not share. "That doesn't make them right. I'll be in the team too, if you'll have me."

If Brandt's words had been met with a moment of hostility, Cristina's brought out a silence that was altogether more tense.

Scendence was the hope, the passion, and the closest thing to freedom that would ever be experienced in the Corps. And not just the humans: other races played too on occasion.

While in crèche and then as novices, it had been possible – for some individuals, at least – to compete at Scendence purely for the thrill of doing so. Now that they were cadets, though, Scendence was a game played only to win. Not only were merit points a possibility, but the top 16 teams at the end of the season were granted immunity from the Cull. Cristina was not a good player. In any team she would be a liability. Winning immunity would be inconceivable.

"Of course we'll have you, darling," gushed Madge. "I'm playing Gunnery, of course, and Springer'll take Obedience. What role do you want?"

"Save it for later," said Brandt. "It's 20:58. Inspection in two minutes."

All eight cadets in the dorm scrambled to their positions at the foot of their bunks and stood to attention.

Although cadets had to be ready for inspection once in the morning, and again in the evening, on average each dorm was inspected about twice per week.

But after the company had been shot to pieces in the tunnels, and with images of Cadet Prong plastered all over Detroit, Arun's wrenching gut told him they would be certain to get a visit tonight. And he bet it would be the toughest of them all who would come: Instructor Rekka.

When, earlier that day, Brandt had dispatched him alone into that narrow tunnel, Arun had been terrified. Isolated.

He felt worse now.

Springer caught his eye. Her anger had vanished, replaced by a smile of support.

At least I've one buddy I can always rely upon.

Then the door hissed open and Arun snapped his eyes front.

The inspection had begun.

Chapter 05

The dorm for Blue Squad's Delta Section was a narrow room with eight racks lined up against one wall. At the foot of each, a cadet stood at attention, awaiting the laser-sharp scrutiny of Instructor Rekka.

Arun had the sixth rack down. He kept his eyes front, but with four cadets already dealt with, he could sense Rekka advance to the fifth rack like an approaching storm front, her walking stick thumping aggressively on the deck like the sound of thunder.

Then came the worst part: the silence.

Like many of the instructors, Rekka was a former frontline Marine who had been too broken in combat to fight again, but too experienced to throw away.

The instructors who had trained them through novice school were in the process of handing over to the veterans who would command the cadets in battle after they had graduated as Marines. Although he would rather face an enemy division singlehanded than face an angry Rekka, Arun would miss the instructor's wardrobe of prosthetic legs, her habit of whistling in her rare carefree moments, and those precious few moments when she awarded hard-won praise.

Rekka was a hard person to like, but wasn't a sadistic bully, unlike some of the other instructors he'd endured. She was domineering because that was how instructors needed to be, but there was just one thing that made her boil with rage: when she decided the novices in her charge were abusing their precious gift of youth and health.

This evening, Rekka was beyond angry. The madder she got, the quieter and slower she talked. The instructor's words were barely a whisper.

Rekka had found fault with every cadet in the room. Del-Marie's bed covers had been creased. Madge's were folded at the wrong angle, and as for her long, blonde hair, that was a disgrace that needed to be shaved off. Zug had to do fifty one-armed press ups for not standing straight, and Springer a hundred for being caught glancing Arun's way.

Now it was Osman Koraltan's turn.

As Rekka built up to Osman's humiliation, Arun told himself endlessly not to rise to her bait when her attention turned to him. *Just suck it up, McEwan.*

"What is this… this *rag*?" Rekka didn't need to raise her voice. Everyone heard her disdain ringing loud and clear.

"It's a flag, ma'am," said Osman.

There was a faint swish, and Arun could picture Osman's flag picked up on the end of her walking stick and swirled around.

"A *flag*? Is this the regimental flag, cadet?"

"Ma'am. No, ma'am."

"Are you planning an insurrection, cadet?"

"Ma'am. No, ma'am. I would kill a traitor on sight, ma'am."

"Then what is the point of this article?"

"It's… the country I think I might have come from, ma'am."

"*You think?* The country you come from? On Earth. That is nova-frakking amazing. I'd always put you down as an uninspiring irrelevance, Koraltan. Someone I would forget the instant I'd handed you on to your veteran. Only a few days before I get to shake your hand and say good luck and good riddance, with a tear in my eye – you finally surprise me. I had no idea that you were born on Earth, Cadet Koraltan."

Osman kept silent, but Rekka wasn't going to let him off so easily. "Well, Koraltan? Did I get that wrong? Are you Earth-born?"

"Ma'am. No, ma'am. I meant the country I think my ancestors came from."

Rekka snorted. "You credulous imbecile. The very notion of nationality is a fantasy fit only for veck-heads. Do you really think there is any way you can trace your ancestry back to a region of Earth? Let me tell you what really happened. Your grandfather picked an exotic name and backstory out of a history book and used it to impress your grandmother. You, Osman Koraltan, are one of the disastrous unintended consequences of that unfortunate seduction. What country is this rag meant to represent anyway?"

"Turkey, ma'am."

"Turkey? Tur-key! It's the name of an avian species, you frakk-head, not a country."

Rekka limped over to the waste chute, the red and white flag held aloft on the tip of her walking stick. They all heard the grinding noise when the garbage input sensor recognized it had incoming and began ripping apart the cloth at the start of its recycling journey.

Arun could feel the heat rise in his face. Osman had been given that flag two years ago. Two years during which Rekka had made no comment. But today, suddenly, it was a heresy to be rooted out and destroyed. Same as Madge's hair.

As Rekka returned to Osman, her stick once again thumping out her approach, she asked in a sneering tone that made Arun cringe: "Does anyone else know anything about Earth or that flag?"

"Ma'am, the flag was originally made…" Arun couldn't believe he'd spoken. He felt as if he'd stepped over a cliff and was staring in disbelief at the absence of ground beneath his feet.

All that was left to do now was fall.

"Yes, McEwan?" Rekka was in his face now. She was small and wiry, shorter than Arun. And yet she still managed somehow to loom over him, intimidating him with ease. "Did you forget to finish your sentence?"

"Ma'am. No, ma'am. Cadet Koraltan's flag was originally made by Sergeant Horden, ma'am." There, he'd said it! Projectile launched, brace for impact.

Instructor Rekka glowered at Arun for an eternity before spitting out that name. "Sergeant *Hor-den*. Are you referring to the man who *claimed* to be a descendant of President Horden?"

"Ma'am. Yes, ma'am."

Rekka curled her lip into a slow sneer. "According to the story of the Vancouver Accord, President Horden sold a million Earth children to the White Knights. My ancestors, Koraltan's and yours, all were amongst those children. Today we Marines swear by Horden senior and we swear *at* him just as often. *Horden's Bones! Horden's Children! Horden's Sweet Hairy Fanny.* Everyone on this base swears by Horden. Even *you*, McEwan. Have you sworn by Horden?"

"Ma'am. Yes, ma'am."

"Yes, ma'am. Of course you frakkin' have you stupid drent-for-brains. Horden's like all the devils and gods of every religion wrapped into one convenient package. The story also says that topping the list of slave children selected was his own first-born son. To claim descent from a specific person on Earth is the action of a deluded fantasist. But to claim that mega-veck, President Horden, as your ancestor is the deluded rambling of a truly sick individual, with megalomania only the start of the psychoses infecting their perverted mind."

Rekka leaned in even closer. "Feel free to disagree at any time, McEwan."

These past few weeks, Arun had been losing it. Acting wild in those Troggie tunnels, and speaking out of turn to Rekka: they were only today's disasters. He didn't know what had gotten into him, but he did know that right now he had to keep his mouth firmly shut.

"Now that we've established the nature of Sergeant Horden, this *so-called* authority, who produced a scrap of cloth purporting to be the flag of a hypothetical country, please explain to me, McEwan, why you saw fit to cite him."

"Ma'am, Sergeant Horden explained – I mean, *claimed* – that he had identified genetic markers, clues to our Earth ancestry." Arun stopped there. Horden had used Osman as an early test case. A successful one too. Either Horden was a fraud or Osman really was Turkish.

Rekka stepped back a few paces. "I know all about Horden's lies. Haven't you realized yet that we're all such a thoroughly jumbled-up mongrel mess that any genetic markers present in our distant ancestors have long since been lost in the homogeneous genetic paste that fills the bones of every Marine. And that's a good thing! I understand the human need for a tribe to belong to. You already have yours. Have you learned nothing, McEwan? Your nation is the Human Marine Corps. Your clan is the 412th Marines, or the 412th Tactical Marine Regiment for those who enjoy the long-winded version. I don't hold with all this Earth drent that the Jotuns indulge you in these days. I've been out there in the wars, and I can tell you it's the belief in your unit, and in your comrade standing alongside you that holds Marines together. Not some dumb romantic guff about Earth."

She paused to stare at each cadet in turn, daring them to so much as breathe in a manner that she could construe as backchat. She stretched that moment of tension to her satisfaction before continuing. "Last I heard,

Sergeant Horden was en route to the Akinschet system. I expect when he gets there that he'll change his tune pretty damned sharpish."

Rekka rocked back on the heels of her prosthetic legs. They were her everyday pair, encased in gleaming black plastic and silvered metal, except for the rubbery sole to the built-in feet. She lifted her stick and used it to poke Arun in the chest.

"I've warned you before about speaking out of turn, McEwan. Give me twenty squat jumps."

"Ma'am. Yes, ma'am."

Arun's anger returned in ever-increasing waves. Arun tried to suck it back in but today his self-control was shot to hell.

The instructors claimed that many of the rituals of training and command had been gleaned from practices used centuries before on Earth. The Jotuns reasoned that military training evolved over centuries to match the human psyche would be a better starting point than anything they could devise.

And so punishment for minor infractions often meant press ups, digging and filling in fighting holes, or similar pointless physical activity, even though in comparison with the original humans of Earth, the Marine cadets possessed immense physical strength and endurance. Wetware augmentation and genetic manipulation meant Marines were different mentally too. When not succumbing to a tendency toward ill-disciplined rage, they took an iron will for granted.

All of that meant punishment exercise was easy. Normally. But not today.

The anger in Arun's breast tempted him to glance meaningfully at his rack where he'd placed the walking stick the medics had given him.

He didn't. Rekka knew perfectly well that he'd suffered a leg wound. Drawing attention to his stick would be weak, and achieve nothing but win contempt from everyone in the room. Instead, he drew upon his mental strength and gingerly crouched down into a squat position. His wounded leg felt stiff, but only when he got into the deepest position of the crouch did his left knee grind, as if his joints were made from rusting steel that hadn't seen oil for decades. With a supreme effort, he managed to cap his scream of agony. He looked down at his limb, expecting to see the blood seeping out the wound opened up by the Troggie guardian's claw.

There was no blood, no bone shards poking through the skin over his knee.

"Begin!" Rekka ordered.

Arun jumped as high as he could, flinging his arms up as he leaped. He knew that if she decided he'd made a halfhearted jump, she would make him start again at the beginning.

At the top of his jump, Arun pointed his toes down and lifted his head high, as per the prescribed form. The jump was easy. The descent was not.

When he landed and his legs took his weight, it felt as if hot blades were plunging into his injuries. Arun grunted but did not cry out. At the deepest point, when his legs changed from slowing his fall into beginning his ascent, those blades grew jagged edges and jerked around in his wound. Arun gasped before executing a perfect jump.

Determined not to give Rekka the satisfaction of hearing him scream, Arun willed his jaw to clamp firmly shut and stay closed.

I will not scream. I will NOT scream.

The second landing was even worse. The imaginary blades stabbing into his leg grew red hot.

I will not scream. I… I will not scream.

The blades exuded agonizing venom, which spread to his right leg.

I will not scream!

Arun's world became a foggy battlefield where pain fought against Arun's iron will for control of his body. He could even imagine the crump, crump, crump from a far-off artillery battery.

Then he realized that what he thought was incoming shellfire was actually the sound of Instructor Rekka's walking stick thumping the deck in front of him.

"I said stop!" She was shouting. "You've made 24 jumps. I only wanted 20. Can't you count?"

Arun decided he'd better not answer.

She narrowed her eyes. "I suppose there's something you want to ask me?"

"Yes, ma'am. This cadet requests permission to seek medical attention."

Rekka made a point of chewing over his request before replying. "Yes, I noticed your leg looks sore. You may get it patched after inspection."

Not bothering to inspect Zug or Cristina, Rekka turned and walked away. When she reached the door, she looked back at the cadets. "I'm disappointed in you. You were not fit for inspection and your performance in the tunnels today has made us the laughing stock of Detroit. The handover to your veteran NCOs began this week and already you have let us down. Badly. McEwan with his lewd display worst of all. Do not expect this to be the end of the matter. There will be repercussions. Mark my words."

After fixing them all with her baleful stare, Rekka dismissed them and stalked out.

Arun looked down at his leg. His fatigue pants were glued to his leg with sticky blood, but the blood flow had slowed or stopped.

"Hey, hero," said Osman. "Do you want me to help you get to the infirmary?"

Arun grabbed his stick and took a few test paces. "No, I'm good. Thanks, man."

He wasn't, but he didn't want to get his comrades into trouble. In theory they all had until First Sleep at 25:00 hours to do what they liked – training usually – but Arun knew he was toxic right now. He wanted his buddies to keep a safe distance.

As he limped out of the dorm, he was met by a variety of reactions from his squadmates. Pity he'd expected, and the concern he saw on Springer's face, but he also saw contempt and even anger from Brandt and Madge. He only half-cared, though. As he hobbled away to the med-center he kept thinking about what Rekka had said.

There will be repercussions.

Chapter 06

"Rekka is purest evil," said Arun. "Just because she got her legs blown off, she's jealous of anyone still whole. What kind of instructor makes their cadets jump up and down on a wounded leg? Those squat jumps she made me do earlier – she could have saved us all the bother and just shot me in the leg. End result would've been the same."

"Too right, man," said Osman. "She was just worried about looking bad in front of Shlappo. And the senior instructor's no better. She made Brandt section leader and chose Alistair LaSalle to lead the company against the Trogs. What a pair of dwonks!"

Arun, Osman and Zug were sitting around the dorm room table. Zug was listening but saying nothing, as normal.

Cristina and Madge came over to join them. "Are you badmouthing Senior Instructor Nhlappo again?" asked Cristina.

"Osman's just speaking the truth," replied Arun, "because this is the only place we can say it. They're not supposed to listen in on us in the dorm room. I bet they are, though. In fact, I'm counting on it."

Madge shook her head in exaggerated disdain, flinging her long hair out behind her. "It's no use, Cris, he can't help it. It's because Instructor Rekka and Senior Instructor Nhlappo are both women." She leaned over the table, shoving her face against Arun's. "Admit it, you can't handle being given orders by a woman."

"Yes, I can."

"There's nothing to be ashamed of." She settled back in her chair and grinned at Cristina. "Boys of your age are emotionally immature. It's a proven scientific fact. You can't think too well because you've only one thing on your mind."

"Him more than most," added Springer, joining the group.

"Hey, that's not fair," Arun protested.

"Isn't it?" answered Madge. "How would you feel if I had led Delta Section instead of Brandt? Could you handle that?"

"Well, yes. Why wouldn't I?" It was true. Madge was a natural NCO, at least when she dropped the vampish act.

"You hesitated!"

"Leave him alone," said Osman. "I can't believe you're defending what Rekka did."

"We're not, turkey-man," said Cristina. "Rekka was cruel tonight, but we've all of us had that kind of drent in the past and we don't start crying every time an instructor says something to hurt our little-widdle feelings. At least, we women don't."

Springer joined in. "You know, if there's one thing useful I've learned from ancient Earth history, it's that they used to have all-male combat units. If our masters thought of the Human Marine Corps as a serious military force, rather than breeding stock, I reckon we'd have single-sex units. Anyway, lover boy here is always griping about Rekka or Nhlappo. Aren't you, Arun?"

Arun threw his hands in the air in frustration. "Oh, come on, guys. Rekka's given me a hard time, and Shlappo will tomorrow, or I'm a Hardit. And you," he pointed at Springer, "are supposed to be on my side."

Springer gave a curt laugh. "Rekka's giving you a hard time, eh? You seem to be having a lot of those recently. When you had your hard time with that alien scribe, were you thinking of our instructor? Did you imagine Rekka's sweet face on that Troggie body? Is that why you… oh, how did your alien friend describe it? … *activated your mating prong?*"

Cristina dug an elbow into Springer's side. "Lighten up on him will you? Arun's right. He's our squadmate. We should–"

"I know. Sorry." Springer looked serious. "I apologize for my inexcusable behavior… *Cadet Prong.*" Laughter bubbled out of her. "Sorry, Arun. Frakk it, I couldn't resist."

Arun replayed Sergeant Gupta's words in his mind. He wouldn't crumble. He would get through this. "Guys," he pleaded, "get off my back. Please."

Springer studied him for a while before arriving at a conclusion. "Look, I tell you what, Arun. I won't call you Cadet Prong again if you promise not to call us 'guys'. I can't stand it when people talk to me as if I'm neuter, or a man. I'm a woman."

Cristina snorted. "Speak for yourself, grandma. I'm only in class G-2."

"Okay," admitted Springer, "girl or woman at your discretion, and then only until we're in graduation year. Deal?"

Springer extended her hand. Arun shook it.

"Thank goodness for that," said Madge. "Springer's been spouting drivel about you ever since we saw your mating prong performance. I think she's jealous." She winked at Arun and whispered to him loudly enough for all to hear: "You do realize she dreams about you?"

Arun laughed the same as everyone else.

But, no, he hadn't.

Chapter 07

After all the excitement and pain of the day, Arun decided to turn in early, drifting toward sleep as soon as he closed his eyes. On the cusp of dreams, he imagined a familiar and comforting feminine scent.

"I'm sorry about before," said his dream girl.

He opened his eyes and discovered that, for once, reality was better than his dreams. Springer was crouching on the floor by his rack, with her hand on his shoulder. "I thought you could do with some company," she said. "Will you let me make it up to you?"

Arun grinned. "You're the best, Springer, but please don't put any weight on my left leg. Did I mention? I had a Troggie claw go through earlier today."

Cadet Phaedra Tremayne – named Springer by her friends due to her boundless optimism – grinned back and carefully clambered in beside him.

Springer was a squadmate, which meant they'd grown up together, shared the same school dorm for the past few years before making cadet, and then moving to the Charlie Company's underground hab-disk. That made his feelings toward her somehow both complicated and simple at the same time, but always strong. She was more than the comrade he was often buddied with in combat drills. She was a good friend, and several times recently she had *kept him company in his rack*, as she liked to call it. He tried hard not to think what that meant for their friendship.

Later, when they lay together in comfortable silence with Springer idly running her fingers through his hair, she suddenly blurted out: "I bet you're thinking of her right now."

"Her?"

"Yes, *her*. Xin Lee or is it Lee Xin? She can't seem to make up her mind."

Arun fumbled for a denial. He couldn't find one, though, because Springer was right. He'd been drifting into a heavenly dream existence filled with Xin's essence.

"Shhh, it's okay," she said. "More than okay. I think you having a crush on her is kinda cute." She kissed him tenderly on his forehead. "I was only thinking aloud. Xin is class G-1. At the end of next year, assuming she graduates as a Marine, they'll remove her contraceptive implant. She could have kids. *You* could have kids with her."

"Me? But I don't want to. I mean, I'm only 17. You and I are both only 17."

"Yes, but you *could*. I have to wait another two years and only then if I measure up to someone else's definition of what makes a good Marine."

"What's this all of a sudden about kids? Do you want to get pregnant?" Arun sat bolt upright. "Do you want *my* kids, Phaedra?"

Springer narrowed her eyes. There weren't many people she allowed to use her real name and get away without violence. "No and no. Not right now, and anyway, that's not the point. I don't get a choice. That's what gets me. I have to win someone else's approval to use my own body." She gave her head an angry shake. "You don't have the same implant. I guess you don't understand it. Not being a girl."

"We're all slaves, Springer. We're slave Marines. Bred to fight and die for the White Knights. Our bodies belong to them."

"True. But sometimes I think female cadets are slightly more slaves than you are."

He looked down at his friend who was staring wistfully up at the ceiling. She looked lost. Arun found himself echoing Sergeant Gupta's words. "Life isn't fair, Springer. Sometimes all you can do is suck it up and keep your head proud and high, the sign of a Marine. Wait for your luck to turn and then seize your chances with every fiber of your being."

Springer twisted round and stared at him, astonished. Then she rolled her eyes and shrugged.

The words didn't belong to him, and he felt an idiot to have spoken them. Arun didn't know what else to say – he never did – so he hugged her.

At first Springer relaxed into his embrace, but then she wriggled free and slipped away out of his rack. She was fleeing, unsteady on her feet.

"Don't go," begged Arun. "I'm sorry for talking such stupid drent."

"You didn't," she said. "I just want to be in my own bunk, is all." She paused trying to catch her breath. Arun swung his legs out of bed.

"No!" she shouted, her back to him still. "Get back in your rack and wipe that frown off your silly face. I worked hard to replace it with a smile. Don't you waste my efforts. There. That's better. Goodnight… *Cadet Prong.*"

"I know you too well," he shouted, angry because she was hiding something from him.

The unspoken rule of the dorm – and the entire hab-disk – was that you pretended not to notice when its residents moved between racks during the night. Now he sensed hidden eyes alert, their owners poised to intervene.

Springer finally turned back and looked him square in the face. Tears streamed from those eyes, but those *eye*s! They were blazing beacons of violet. The skin of her eyelids was scorching, her tears vaporizing into emotional steam. He reached for the water canister he kept beside his bed and drenched her eyes with its contents. Her eyes were shut now, the lids still steaming.

"More water!" he barked.

Someone got the hint and threw another water canister to him. Arun tipped the contents over Springer's face, quenching the fire in her eyes.

"Thank you," she said, blinking away the drips.

She sounded abandoned, frightened. He would never forsake her, but she was half-hidden behind a fringe of steam, and he could hardly blame her. He tried to hug her again, but again she pushed him away.

"Tell me, what's wrong."

"Nothing."

"Don't give me that. I know you too well. You had one of your visions, didn't you?"

"It's not a vision, Arun. I don't *see* things. I keep telling you that. I just get a feeling. Just now I felt that you…"

"What, that Rekka would hand me my ass on a plate?"

"No, not her. I don't know who. Really I don't, so just drop it. Get some sleep, instead. Please, for me. You'll need your strength."

"Strength for what?"

"Change. Yes, that's it. You're going through changes. Metamorphosis. You'll become something new. Or die trying. No – it's gone. Whatever I thought I'd sensed… it's gone. Arun, honestly, I probably just imagined it."

Unconvinced, Arun framed her face with his hands. "Be fair, Springer. You can't just dangle me by a thread and then cut the cord as if it doesn't matter. Think! What kind of changes?"

She shook his hands away. "Leave me alone, Arun."

Arun felt a confusing blend of emotions as he watched his friend pad away to her rack.

Then she stopped and turned around, bringing a flash of hope to his heart. "I'll tell you one thing, Arun." Her face creased into a frown. "At least you try to understand me. Have you noticed that since we made cadet everyone's turning into emotionless robots?"

Had they?

"There's not a single person in Detroit who could even attempt to understand me the way you did just now."

"Thank you."

She shook her head sadly. "I didn't mean that as praise. I love you, Arun, but I pity you even more."

Yeah well, I love you too, thought Arun. *But I wish you made sense sometimes.*

Solving the mystery of Springer's words would have to wait for another day. She'd retreated to her rack, wrapped in private thoughts.

Arun lay back down on his bed and closed his eyes, basking in the warm glow that came whenever he marveled in his good fortune at counting Springer as his buddy. Before long, though, his thoughts drifted along the passageway outside and down Helix 6 to hab-disk 7/14 where he pictured Xin asleep in her rack, the gentle ebb and flow of her breathing beckoning him.

Today Xin had acknowledged Arun's existence. Everyone laughed at him for falling in love with a girl so far out of his league, but today she had noticed him.

And Arun had a secret weapon to win her.

The meddling in the human Marine genome threw up a host of surprising side effects. Not all were as pretty as Springer's eyes. She had her visions of the future too, although they might be nothing more than vivid waking dreams.

Arun had his own special talent. Freakish genes might be what powered his ability. Or maybe he only thought he had a talent, and really it was a manifestation of psychosis. Whether true or imagined, if he set his mind a problem to be solved, on rare occasions he could feel his subconscious sifting through all the variables until an answer exploded in his mind, sometimes days later, leaving his brain feeling badly bruised.

He gave a brittle laugh.

So far he'd only used his ability to get into trouble.

He laughed again, softer this time. Getting into trouble was another talent of his. What else was youth for? No wonder Rekka was usually pissed at him.

Settling back into his pillow he immersed his mind in a new problem.

He held a woman's face in his hands, idly caressing the infinitesimally fine down on her cheeks. Just like he'd held Springer's face in real life scant minutes ago. The eyes regarding him from this face were not violet, though, they were as dark and dangerous as a Troggie tunnel. And this girl's skin was as perfectly smooth as ablative armor.

How do I get you to notice me? he asked Xin's face. *Could you ever love me?*

Xin gave the slightest of smiles, daring Arun to find out.

A sense of cogwheel teeth engaging filled his head, of noisy gears dripping with lubricant. It was a peculiarly mechanical sensation as if his mind were an apparatus constructed from brass, iron, hardwoods and oils. The gears turned faster; the smell of hot lubricant grew stronger. The floor of his mind rumbled with a low hum of power. This wasn't imagination. This was *real*. He, Arun McEwan, could do something no one else could.

He felt his problem being analyzed from scores of perspectives. Xin was chopped, sliced, and spun around to be measured from every direction. Whole universes sprang into being, filled with strategies and tactics, and their likely outcomes. Unpromising solutions died away, replaced with more promising lines of attack in a fecund blooming and culling of ideas.

Satisfied that he'd unleashed his talent, Arun left the hard work to his subconscious and drifted off to sleep. As his day finally floated away, he noticed the common thread that connected the galaxy-sized rooms containing the most promising solutions to his question.

For some reason he could not explain, the answers all involved him playing Scendence.

Chapter 08

The following morning, Arun settled for a gentle walk in place of his regular pre-inspection workout. He kept away from the busy spineways and transit corridors, settling for the quiet passageway to the neighboring 6/10 hab-disk and back. *Gentle motion, nothing violent, and make use of your stick.* That's what the medic had said the previous night. She seemed to know what she was talking about. Given that less than a day earlier a claw had gouged a great chunk out of his thigh, and a shrapnel fragment had cracked his knee, he'd told the medic he was amazed he could walk at all.

"Why do you think the White Knights spent all that effort redesigning us?" she'd said. "Blast us and we get up again and carry on fighting. But your leg is now mostly filler and wishful thinking. It will still take weeks for your muscles to fully regrow, and knees are always troublesome healers. You'll have to recalibrate your battlesuit every other day to account for the changes in muscle strength."

As his stroll drew closer to his own hab-disk, his breath quickened. It wasn't the exercise; it was the sense of vulnerability. Rekka had left them with a threat and he felt sure it was aimed at him.

Before graduating to become a cadet, the worst punishment a novice could be given was to be discharged. Outside of the Marines there was a pale life of sorts in the Auxiliary, doing maintenance work and the dirtiest jobs in the mines here and on the moons. The luckiest Aux looked after the cadets and the Marines in the underground base as hab-disk servants. Now that he was 17 and a cadet, the penalty for insubordination or gross misconduct was public execution. And it wasn't an idle threat. Arun shuddered at the memories of what he'd been forced to witness.

Not wanting to be on his own, he slipped into the gym nearest to his dorm. There he found Osman pushing weights along resistance channels, and Springer climbing the endless wall.

Whether by coincidence or an empathetic sense of a squadmate needing support, Osman and Springer finished their exercise at the same time and left with Arun for the nearest shower room.

Usually, after stripping off, there would be a heap of banter between squadmates as they progressed through the various stages of the shower tunnel.

Shower time was normally a simple pleasure shared with friends. Not this morning, though. Today there was a new tension in Springer and Osman, something important but unspoken that poisoned the easy-going mood.

Eyes were averted.

Laughter stilted.

Was everyone else as frightened by Rekka as he was?

He thought that must be the explanation until they reached the spray booth at the end of the shower tunnel. Osman was pirouetting with both arms high while the booth sprayed a film of protective oils over his skin. That's when he blurted out the explanation for the discord.

"Arun, I'm joining the Scendence team."

Arun burst out laughing. "Is that it? All that edginess and it's just because you're joining the team? You bunch of dumbchucks. Have you worked out a team name yet? Here's one: three girls and an avian creature descendant. No, that was frakking awful. Give me a minute and I'll work out a better one."

To the sound of Arun's laughter, Osman walked out the tunnel looking mortified.

This was peak time in the showers. Arun, with his hands on his knees as he laughed himself silly, was holding up the flow of cadets in a hurry to get back in time for morning inspection. Springer pushed past and took her turn in the spray booth.

Tranquility's sun was anything but tranquil. Violent stellar flares flung vast quantities of high energy particles at their planet. The hab-disks were deep enough underground that the danger here was minimal, but at the surface, radiation peaks could be lethal. Detroit wasn't just a training depot, it was responsible for planetary defense too. It would not look good if an invasion force took Tranquility unopposed because the Marines delayed their deployment while they applied their sunblock.

"Moscow Express," said Springer indignantly. "That's our name. Majanita, Osman, Springer, Cristina. M-O-S-C-ow. Get it?" She lifted her arms and slowly turned around.

"Oh, I'm getting it," Arun said cheekily.

Springer narrowed her eyes, daring him to stare at her body.

He dared.

She narrowed her eyes even further, which made him laugh all over again. It was all a game, he thought. Springer loved the attention really.

Springer got her retaliation in by pointing at his crotch. "Your Xin said she admired some impressive equipment. As anyone can plainly see, she wasn't referring to you. She must have meant the Trog."

Arun laughed even harder at that, which won a giggle from Springer.

He caught Osman's attention. "You know," he said raising his voice so that Osman could hear above the chatter. "I don't mean to put a boot into a friend, but honestly? When it comes to Scendence, you're as useless as Rekka in a sexiest legs competition."

Osman winced. "I've no love for Rekka, but that's a combat injury you're mocking, man."

"Yeah, sorry." Arun colored with shame.

"You're right, though," Osman continued. "I stink. But they need a Deception player and it's better than letting them down, don't you think?"

"No, I can't say I do. But that's just me. Good luck to you, pal."

Springer stepped out of the tunnel joining Osman in the dressing area.

Arun took his turn under the spray. He could glimpse Osman. It wasn't easy to tell with his friend putting on his pants, but he looked genuinely unhappy,

"The only role I've any talent for is Deception," said Osman. "And even with Deception, I get a red mist. Can't resist going for the outrageous bluff. Promise me one thing. If the Corps is ever dumb enough to make me squad leader, I give you permission to shoot me first before my red mist gets us all killed."

"Acknowledged, future lance sergeant. I will implement your order without hesitation."

"Yeah, well. There *is* a way…"

"C'mon, man," Arun said as he emerged from the tunnel, washed, dried and coated in protective oils. "It's not like you to vulley around in circles. What's your plan?"

"For me to not be in the team."

Arun thought about that while he limped over to the clothing bins and selected underwear in his size. Just as he was about to step into his shorts, he paused. "No frakking way, man. You want me to take your place, don't you?"

Osman nodded. "The way I see it, if you don't then I will. If you think that's a waste of time, an opportunity cost because we won't be getting so many merit points elsewhere, then either way one of us will be wasting time on Scendence. So the way I figure it, there's nothing to lose if you take my place."

"That's butchered logic," said Arun, underwear on and selecting his pants.

"It's not like you have to," Springer told him. She was now fully clothed other than her shirt. "There are plenty of other good Deception players around."

"But will you?" asked Osman.

Arun frowned, thinking about those hints from his planner brain. "Is this what all that awkwardness was about? Is it really such a big deal to ask me?"

"No," replied Osman.

"Yes," said Springer simultaneously. "Well… yes it is a big deal, but…" Her shoulders slumped as if she'd melted slightly. "We're worried about you. I've never seen Rekka as angry as she was last night. She felt wounded, let down, and took that out on you. I'm not saying that's fair but it's the kind of drent that goes on all the time. Big deal. But what if someone more senior decides that they've been embarrassed? What if someone important goes looking for a scapegoat?"

"What? You mean a Jotun?" asked Arun. He hadn't considered the outcomes of petty training missions would be noticed so high up.

"Maybe," said Springer. "Who knows? It's a crazy world we live in. Let's face it, we're G-2 cadets. To us, this world still doesn't make sense."

"Springer!" Osman shouted. "We agreed not to mention being worried about him."

"Arun's not stupid, Osman. Except when he's vulley-dreaming about his skangat fantasy girl. I can't waste time on a bad lie to a good friend."

Osman didn't argue. He didn't agree with her either. He strode away back to the dorm, but at the shower room door he hesitated.

An instant later they saw why when Instructor Rekka burst into the room.

"Get your clothes on quickly and follow me." Her orders were directed at Arun.

Arun stood there, frozen.

"Hurry up, there's no time to waste," said Rekka, grabbing his walking stick.

He finished dressing as rapidly as he could.

Osman slunk back into the room waiting with Springer. Watching.

The instant Arun's boots were on, Rekka threw his stick at him. "You've been summoned."

He tailed her out of the shower room but took a last look back at Osman and Springer, and their expressions of horror.

Were there tears in Springer's eyes?

"Move it!" barked Rekka from the passageway.

Arun hurried after her as best he could. He wanted a chance to say a proper goodbye, maybe to say some things that had gone unsaid.

Too late. The next time he saw his squadmates, he expected to be on the wrong side of an execution squad.

Chapter 09

In the end, Arun couldn't just stand there as silent and rigid as a statue, having his ass chewed out in silence. It was beyond unfair: he was being set up for a fall. He wasn't the sharpest blade in the set, but he knew nothing he did now would make any difference to his fate.

"Ma'am. Why me, ma'am?" he asked.

For a moment, it almost sounded like a reasonable question.

From the more comfortable side of her desk, Senior Instructor Tirunesh Nhlappo regarded him coolly. The braver cadets called her Shlappo behind her back, though they were always careful to do so very quietly. To look at her in a photo you would think she was nothing special: above average height, average build and with a shaven head that was probably the reason, Arun thought, why her ears looked ridiculously large. But when you meet Nhlappo in person you were struck by an intensity of personality that was so fierce you could practically see an aura crackling around her.

Nhlappo was one of the senior humans in the 412th, and one of her roles was as chief instructor for the 8th battalion. Until the handover to the veteran NCOs had completed, that meant the woman he'd just interrupted had power of life and death over him.

After a long pause – a very long and painful one for Arun – she spoke. "Excuse me?"

"Ma'am. Sorry, ma'am. I spoke out of turn."

All it took was an incremental shift in Nhlappo's expression and Arun knew without doubt that his answer was utterly unacceptable. He wasn't getting out of this so easily.

Dread spread through him like a virulent disease.

The other instructors quietly worshiped their senior, but Shlappo wasn't loved by the school novices or the cadets. In the five years in which she had been Arun's senior instructor he had never known her to say a single word of praise or encouragement. And training had been tough. Thirty percent of novices didn't make cadet grade. Horden only knew what happened to them all. The best thing Arun could say about Nhlappo was that she never took out her frustrations in the kind of petty humiliations some of her junior instructors had developed into an art form.

And yet she had spent the past ten minutes tearing strips off him. He'd never seen her do that before.

This was very bad.

Nhlappo's expression shifted once more, indicating Arun would have to answer now if he knew what was good for him.

"Ma'am. Our mission in the tunnels failed," he said. "But I wasn't even leading a fire team, and I did rack up the biggest kill count. Not saying I'm perfect – and I don't like what the combat drugs did to me – but do I really deserve to be the scapegoat, ma'am?"

After peering at him over steepled fingers, Nhlappo picked up her digi-pad and began writing notes. She handed the pad over to the man at her left, a senior sergeant according to his rank insignia. The sergeant read her notes, nodded, and then passed the pad back. His face was coated in the kind of perfect parade ground glaze that showed no reaction to anything.

"You know I admire your courage in standing up to me," said Nhlappo. "You've got backbone, son. I like that."

Relief gushed over Arun. He felt knots of muscles untie themselves. He'd thought he was in for a mega punishment, and here was Nhlappo offering praise for the first time in recorded history.

"To answer your question," she continued, "the reason I have selected you as – sacrificial victim – is because you're the laughing stock of the entire regiment. And beyond. If the Fates cherish you as their darling, it is just possible you might escape with your life." Her face went as hard as rock. "Don't count on it, though."

Arun held himself as tightly as he could, determined not to show any reaction to Nhlappo's honesty.

"I've served the Jotuns for 150 years," she continued in an infinitesimally softened tone. "All that time and yet I still don't understand them. They're lethally capricious, I can tell you that much. I have to guess what they want, and my guess is that they'll give us such a negative de-merit mark that our battalion is guaranteed to be Culled for years to come. If we humans deal with this first by having our squads disciplined and re-ordered, then that could mitigate any punishment. I have to at least attempt to make an example to prove we are taking this seriously. I have decided that it is your role, Cadet McEwan. You shall be that example. I believe the term your generation has rediscovered is *taking one for the team*."

Arun squared his shoulders another notch. "Ma'am. I understand, ma'am."

"Oh, no," said Nhlappo, suddenly angry. "No, cadet, that just won't do." Nhlappo shook her head in such a way that left Arun feeling the biggest idiot on the planet. "Don't misunderstand me, McEwan. I did not mean: *'You're my favorite really, yet I have no choice but to punish you. I'm sorry and I really hope you'll understand.'.*"

"No, ma'am. Of course not, ma'am."

"Good. Because you thoroughly deserved the punishment I was going to give you."

Relief flooded back. She'd said *was*. Had he gotten off somehow?

"Except you've made this worse," she said. "Standing up to me was brave but it was also exceptionally stupid, even for you, McEwan. You stood your ground because you felt your punishment was undeserved. You felt an injustice. Isn't that right, cadet?"

"Ma'am. No, ma'am."

Nhlappo gave an exaggerated cough. "Excuse me, cadet." She cleared her throat unconvincingly. "Nasty cough. Couldn't quite hear what you were mumbling. You know what, McEwan? An element of the novice training program has just come to mind. *Lying to a superior is punishable by death.* Did we remember to teach you that?"

"Ma'am. Yes, ma'am."

"Thank you. I feel reassured. I'll ask again, and speak clearly this time. Tell me, do you feel an injustice?"

"Ma'am. Yes, ma'am."

"Unacceptable!" Nhlappo slammed her fist against her desk. She rose, coming round the front of her desk to fix Arun with a close-up glare. Arun didn't dare to breathe.

"Marines are not permitted justice," she snapped. "Why not?"

Fumbling through her words for booby traps, Arun stumbled upon an answer that sounded plausible. "We are slaves, ma'am"

"Correct." Nhlappo's expression of disapproval lightened up half a notch, enough for Arun to breathe again. "If you live through today, perhaps you do have some chance of survival after all. Yes, of course, we're slaves. Only a fool would forget that for an instant. From the lowest of humans who fail to graduate school and so join the Aux for the rest of their short lives, to the senior Jotun system commander, and even the insectoids you slaughtered in your tunnel exercise: we are all of us slaves. To the White Knights we are nothing more than a rounding error in a troop strength list reported to the nearest million. As individuals we are less than nothing to them, but as battalions, regiments and Marine fleet contingents, our pain and servitude is just enough to earn a semblance of protection for our homeworld. Earth was free from alien occupation last I heard, though I never trust what I hear on that subject."

Arun took a sharp intake of breath. Nhlappo's words could be considered insurrection.

"My words appear to trouble you, cadet. Do you wish to contradict them?"

"Ma'am. No, ma'am."

"Good. You have a lesson to learn. Learn it well. You are a slave. Slaves must never imagine they deserve justice, because that is one short step away from rebellion. Any slaves who do not grasp this will be rooted out and destroyed. Understand?"

"Ma'am. Yes, ma'am."

"I believe you do. To be sure of that, I intend to extend your punishment. All members of your squad will suffer the same penalty I had intended for you. Furthermore, I will make sure they know that you are the cause of their misery, and why."

Even if he were executed, they would curse his name. Springer too, he realized with a jolt.

"Most people would say I've just wasted the past ten minutes of my life by talking to you. By this time tomorrow, you will probably be dead. But the Jotuns possess an infinite capacity to surprise us, and so there remains a chance that you will live. That is why you and I are discussing this matter. *Attention to detail.* In warfare, administration, even romance, drama, literature – yes, I *am* familiar with those activities – attention to detail is frequently what separates success from failure. And, if you are to die, I want you to know why, and I want you to die well. Can you do that, McEwan? Can you die well?"

"Ma'am. Yes, ma'am."

Nhlappo judged him with a look. "Perhaps," she said grudgingly. She activated a control on the surface of her desk. "Let's find out, shall we?"

The door opened. Rekka entered, accompanied by two cadets: Hortez who had led Blue Squad in the tunnel exercise, and LaSalle who had been put in charge of Charlie Company in its entirety. The cadets looked deathly pale. Even Rekka looked troubled.

Nhlappo addressed Arun. "The reason I told you of punishments you *would have had* is because events are now out of my control. We've all been summoned by Colonel Little Scar to explain why everyone on the planet is laughing at his regiment."

She got out from her desk, leading her little group into the transit corridor outside.

Running was Arun's first instinct. Everything was stacked against him. Where could he run to? The one place he might find sanctuary was in the Troggie nest, but he would never make it that far. The forces of inevitability crushed any resistance from him and rooted his feet to the floor. All he could do was attempt some semblance of dignity.

He felt a shove in his back from the veteran sergeant – Arun still didn't know his name. It was enough to get Arun's legs working.

"Move!" he ordered. "The colonel will not expect to be kept waiting any longer."

Arun marched to his fate.

Chapter 10

Senior Instructor Nhlappo led Arun and the doomed group through Gate Three and out into the eddying breeze on the planet's surface. Arun looked back at the heavily fortified entrance that bristled with gun emplacements manned by Marines.

"Eyes front, McEwan!" barked Instructor Rekka from the rear.

Arun reluctantly obeyed. Wrenching his gaze away from his home filled his gut with an aching sense of loss. The colonel hadn't invited them over for coffee and biscuits, that was for sure. Arun didn't expect to ever see his home again. Never see Springer's warm smile. And his plans for Xin were exposed as nothing more than a joke.

Look on the bright side, he thought, *you always enjoy any chance to come up to the surface.*

In Arun's experience there were four main reasons why cadets were allowed on the surface. A visit to the colonel was definitely not one of them.

A Marine was expected to fight in any environment: in the airless void of space, racing through endless hive tunnels deep underground, defending snowy mountain redoubts, or flushing insurgents from sweltering jungle thick with vegetation. Simulating these combat conditions was not an easy task, but the Human Marine Corps on Tranquility had access to an entire planet to provide as many training environments as required.

His use of the topside training grounds was the first reason why Arun was no stranger to the planet's surface.

Marines had to be in superb physical condition. Arun had climbed the endless Gjende Mountains that shadowed the Detroit base and had run, marched, and slept many times on the adjoining plateau, ignoring roads and crude paths to cut through fields of wheat, maize and more exotic crops, to the consternation of the Agri-Aux and the insistence of the instructors.

That was reason number two.

The third reason was to endure the mutual incomprehension of inter-species encounter sessions, where Jotuns and young humans would meet and attempt to get to know one another. In theory, the result would be human Marines who weren't so terrified of their officers that they were unable to function properly in combat. Arun saw no signs of that working, but the Jotuns had such an extreme phobia about being underground that the only way to move them beneath the surface was to render them unconscious first.

Arun's mind refused to think openly of the fourth reason why he might be summoned to the surface, pushing that cruel knowledge deep into his mind so that it only surfaced in his everyday thoughts as a persistent feeling of dread.

They pressed on in silence through service buildings, storage depots, and vehicle parks, and onward to Jotunville.

There was no official title for the complex of palaces topped with soaring spires and connected by glass walkways at obscene heights. Whatever it was called, to be summoned here was an ordeal few cadets ever experienced, and fewer returned to their underground holes to tell the tale.

As defense against orbital bombardment, Jotunville and the underground Marine complex nestled at the bottom of a narrow valley that meandered beneath towering mountain peaks. The transparent building material favored by the Jotuns would have generated a sense of space and warmth if their city had been situated out on the plateau, but most days inky shadow blanketed the valley floor, shrouding Jotunville with a chill aura of doom. Only once had Arun seen this phalanx of crystal spires at midday, when the illumination from the overhead sun caused it to gleam like a polished jewel.

There was little sun now, in the mid-morning. The lack of light made transparent walkways suddenly materialize overhead, making Arun fight hard against the instinct to duck. Distant palaces became ethereal phantoms that defied his attempts to grasp their shape. Jotunville was ghostly and threatening, as if its existence were only partially in the material plane. As they penetrated deeper into the city of glass spires, and the confrontation with the colonel grew closer, Arun's nerves began to shred.

How were the others coping? He hoped the two instructors were wetting themselves with fear, but they both had hearts of granite: they wouldn't be worried. The unknown sergeant following Nhlappo was no different. Maybe it was only Arun who was so scared that placing every foot forward took a supreme effort of courage. His fellow cadets were showing no signs of nerves. Hortez would be singing in his head to *clear his mind of darkness*, as he put it. As for Alistair LaSalle, he adapted to anything life threw at him, which was presumably why the instructors had tried him in the role of senior company sergeant for the tunnel exercise.

Mastering fear was about deflecting the anticipation of danger. The instructors had drilled that into him all his life. So he tried occupying himself by deploying an imaginary Marine company to defend Jotunville. Two squads up on either end of the overhead walkway would catch an enemy below in flanking fire, pinning them down while another squad, ready to launch flechette grenades, would sneak around and catch the invader from the rear. Then the command squad would fire a quick suppressing frag barrage before the remaining three squads charged the confused survivors.

But he was only replaying standard classroom tactics. The mental trick crumbled almost before he'd begun because they were in such deep shadow that he had to invent the layout of the surrounding buildings.

What made the fear so difficult to deflect was that this whole stupid business was so pointless. Arun didn't believe there was ever any glory in dying, no matter how you had to go, but there were deaths that at least counted for something.

To be executed for an embarrassing accident – that would mean his life had been utterly pointless.

He couldn't prevent his hands clenching into fists, his muscles readying to release explosive power. To fight injustice, to fall in a struggle for freedom. Now *that* would be worth dying for…

"Loosen those hands, McEwan," thundered Rekka. "You *will* march like a Marine, not an ill-disciplined brute."

Arun tried for his best parade ground form as they began to ascend a spiraling loop of transparent stairs, sheathed in a twisting tube. A quarter of the tube was open, exposing them to a blustering wind and a sheer drop that grew rapidly more lethal until he soon realized that he could end it all on his own terms by throwing himself off.

Suicidal thoughts haunted him, teasing fingers plucking at him through the opening in the tube. *A few seconds of falling and then it would all be over. The colonel's revenge would be cheated.*

Arun flung his arms out against the walls of the tube, bracing himself against the seductive thoughts in his head.

Jump…

No!

He wouldn't! Not while there was hope. And there *was* a slender hope. Nhlappo had said so.

Or had she planted false hope, in case of just such a moment as this?

"Keep moving, McEwan! Have you no dignity?"

Arun felt his jaw tighten. *No I haven't, you stupid veck!* For days, Arun had struggled to keep wild mood swings in check, and now Rekka's admonishment was like a flamethrower, coating Arun with incandescent fury.

He fantasized about grabbing the skangat of an instructor and throwing them both off the stairway tube. *But there was still hope.* He *had* to believe that. So instead Arun launched his final mental defense, the one marked: 'Do not use except in case of emergency'. He folded his conscious mind away and relinquished control to the unconscious parts of his brain. He had been engineered to do this during sentry duty, or when deployed for ambushes, waiting for hours or days with his finger on the trigger, waiting for an enemy to appear.

But this wasn't sentry duty. Would he wake up when he needed to?

That sense of unease stretched, infusing his mind for an eternity until–

Rekka slapped him… "That was a coward's escape," she sneered. "But at least it got you here."

Arun found he'd arrived on a transparent walkway, about to follow the rest of the group through a glass door that was sliding open. Of the journey here he had no memory.

He glanced down, but the ground was too far away to see.

Then he passed through the door and into the colonel's domain.

The humans were in the lower of two circular rooms built with the same transparent material as the walkway. They looked like two identical glass bowls stacked one atop the other but offset by a quarter of their diameter.

On the upper level, sitting at a double-banked work station, was the colonel of the 412th Tactical Marine Regiment. His name translated as Little Scar.

Only his head was showing over the back of his chair, but the nick in his left ear was enough for Arun to recognize the colonel from parade ground inspections.

From the tilt of his head, Little Scar was staring up at the clouds gamboling across the gleaming blue sky, his dangling bronze earrings in the shape of hammers brushing the back of his neck.

Sky?

The only view through these windows should have been shadowed mountainside. But that had been replaced by a sunny vista. Arun could even hear imaginary birds calling to each other as they flew through the spiraling walkway that led up through the roof.

Curved sofas covered in emerald green velour ran along the walls of the lower room, the huge size of these sofas making him feel like a small child sent to see the grown-ups, or a mortal approaching the gods. They could have been built for eight-foot tall humans if not for the additional armrests at shoulder level. Of course! Jotuns were hexapeds.

Zug would love this.

The thought of his alien-obsessed friend gave Arun a pang of loss. He tried smothering himself with numbness. Around him, he could sense fear begin to come off Hortez and Alistair, the mental defenses that had kept up their spirits on the journey had been stormed and breached by the presence of their officer. He couldn't blame them because they had everything to lose. Arun didn't.

However much he tried to believe in Nhlappo's slender thread of hope, Arun was certain he'd already lost.

Arun stared at Little Scar. *Whatever you're going to do, get on with it!*

As if the Jotun had heard his thoughts, Little Scar finally acknowledged the humans. Still with his back to them, he growled: "Study the softscreens."

Little Scar spoke with his own voice. Most Jotuns used the same voicebox translator technology as the Trogs, but those most skilled in human language could speak in a voice that sounded as if they had swallowed a box of razor blades.

To use his own voice emphasized that Little Scar had issued a critical command to be obeyed instantly.

But what did he mean? What softscreens?

Hortez saw them first, picking up a stack of transparent rectangles. Softscreen material was tough but years of use meant that the ones the cadets normally handled were scuffed enough to be seen even when inactive. These were pristine. Even when Hortez handed him one, Arun could barely see the device until his touch activated it and an image appeared of the Totalizer. He could see every cadet battalion in Detroit listed in merit point order. Arun's 8-412/TAC was two places and a little over seven thousand points clear of the Cull Zone. The image was real-time, with each score flicking up or down slightly, but the gap between each battalion was much too large for the positions to change while he watched.

After about ten seconds, the image changed. It still showed the Totalizer, but this time listing the live killscores for the past month. There he was, Arun McEwan, top of the leader board by a long margin, the result of blasting the insect horde in the tunnels.

The view switched to live plus simulated killscores. Arun was still ranked top, though by a lower margin.

The colonel must consider my killscore rankings to be important, thought Arun, *or else why is he showing them? If all Little Scar cares about are results, then I'm winning his heart.*

The more Arun considered this, the more it made sense. Zug was always saying it was a mistake to assign human emotions to aliens. It felt as if everyone on the planet had pointed out that Arun had made the regiment the laughing stock of Detroit, but now he thought of it, he'd only heard the jeers from other humans. Maybe Little Scar didn't care. Arun had won top killscore and a bundle of merit points for one of the Jotun's battalions. Perhaps Arun had been summoned to be personally commended by his commanding officer?

Suck on that, Shlappo!

The softscreen display shifted again and all his hope vaporized. Arun felt as if he were falling, plummeting farther even than if he had jumped off the Jotunville heights. If he'd suspected he was doomed before, he *knew* it now.

He peered at the screen. It showed a camera shot of Arun naked with the scribe, an image enhanced to simulate a spotlight focused on the source of his humiliation.

Someone had added the caption: *412th Marines. Always ready for ACTION!*

Arun willed the display to change again. It did, but he wished it hadn't. What it showed was so bad that the breath froze in his throat.

Cadets were lined up with their backs to the parade ground dais. This was the main parade ground, the one cut into the Gjende Mountains above Detroit. The camera took a close-up view of their faces. Most wore blank expressions, some were angry, a few trembled with fear.

Human text at the bottom identified the footage, as if it needed an explanation. This was the final reason for coming to the planet's surface that Arun had hidden from his mind. This was the fate that haunted every cadet.

This was the Cull.

The display looped around the moment of execution, but changed camera views from wide shots to close ups of individual twenty-year old cadet faces at the moment they were put to death.

The humans in his quarters had no choice but to watch. Little Scar had ordered that they should.

The Culled cadets died again and again, and Little Scar said nothing, sitting there up the steps in his upper room, not even deigning to glance in the humans' direction.

Minutes went past.

An hour.

While his subordinates watched endless variations on the same slaughter, Little Scar sat motionless in his chair, looking up into a sky that wasn't even real.

Then, at last, the time had come.

Little Scar turned and faced them.

Chapter 11

Little Scar levered himself out of his deeply reclined seat and advanced a few paces toward the humans. His shaggy white fur, shot through with gray, jounced as he moved.

The size and power of the Jotuns was enough to scare the crap out of Arun at the best of times.

And this was not the best of times.

Arun's gaze was fixed on the digits of the alien's upper limbs. At present they were rubbery extrusions through the flat, horn-ridged pads that terminated his arms. But they could be retracted in an instant and replaced by claws like combat knives. With one blow, those claws could decapitate a human.

There was precedent.

The colonel halted at the top of the steps leading down from the upper part of the room, and delivered a roar that liquefied Arun's spine. Somehow Arun remained at attention, distracting himself with the way the colonel's earrings jangled as he folded his ear trumpets flat against his head.

Little Scar's mouth gaped wide. He did not speak, but the sounds of a male human came from his throat speaker. "You have seen footage from 32 years ago, from the last time my regiment suffered the dishonor of the Cull." He held up one upper limb. A single rubbery finger shot outward stretching as long as a human arm. And it was pointing straight at Arun. "I have had to explain to Supreme Commander Menglod why your image is posted throughout Detroit."

The colonel growled again. "Do I need to draw a connection between the two facts?"

Arun's sight glazed over. He couldn't breathe. He daren't.

The colonel retracted his finger. "The human cadets in the tunnel exercise are less than three years from graduation, from fighting in the war. Losing is a valuable lesson. It is best to lose at some point in your training. A warrior who has never been bested has never tasted the ash and tarnished mouth-feel of defeat. They remain untested and I do not wish for untested warriors in my regiment."

Arun breathed.

But then the Jotun extended his claws. They were serrated and so very sharp. "But to lose badly is unforgivable," he continued. "The stink of incompetence can linger forever. I must correct this now or execute the entire battalion. It wouldn't be the first time we had to discard a unit gone rotten. You humans have created this crisis and you are forever grumbling that you should run more of your own affairs. So you advise me. What should I do?"

Little Scar fixed his glare on Nhlappo. "You first."

She didn't hesitate. "Sir. Cadet McEwan is the source of the embarrassment. He should be executed immediately."

Nhlappo looked as if she had more to say but Little Scar pointed to Rekka. "You!"

"Sir. I agree with the senior instructor, sir."

The Jotun narrowed his eyes, glaring at Rekka. Arun allowed himself a little inward smile when he imagined how Rekka must feel under that attention.

Alistair and Hortez were next. Each took full responsibility upon himself but evaded suggesting what punishment they should suffer.

Then it was Arun's turn. What could he say? He was trapped by his predatory superiors. So he spun the line that Nhlappo had ordered him to back in her office, dragging out the toxic words with as much dignity as he could manage. "Sir, you should remove the source of our shame by executing me."

He tensed his neck, expecting Little Scar to leap down the stairs and slash with those claws.

But the alien appeared satisfied and settled his attention on the sergeant whose name Arun still didn't know. "You are senior human sergeant for 'C' Company, 8th battalion. What would you do?"

If he was the senior veteran then he must be Staff Sergeant Bryant. He answered calmly. "Sir. It is the leader's responsibility to preserve the honor of his or her unit. To have lost a unit's honor is a catastrophic loss of authority after which no leader can function. So if a unit has dishonored itself, then its leader should be punished as an example. Even if the punishment isn't fatal, before the leader can return to the same position he or she must not only wait for a suitable period of atonement, but must also earn that position to the satisfaction of the unit."

"Quite so," said Little Scar. He nodded, a gesture of agreement, although with his pronounced brow ridge and bony skull crest the motion looked very much like an armored headbutt. "Of all of us, Staff Sergeant Bryant has most recently been tested in battle. It shows."

He pointed to Alistair and Hortez. "You are no longer Marine cadets."

A third finger extruded from his hand toward Nhlappo. "You! Ensure these failures are out of my regiment by the end of the day. Then hand over your remaining duties to your junior instructors. From midnight you are demoted to the rank of Marine private. Gold Squad has lost its veteran to resuscitation attrition. You will fill the gap. Pray that you are never presented to me again. I shall not be so lenient next time."

The merest hint of a protest sounded in Nhlappo's throat, but she cut it dead just in time.

"I have…" started Little Scar but stopped suddenly. He growled, flicking his ears wildly. "I have discussed your company's performance with Commander Menglod and we have agreed a unit-wide punishment for the 8th battalion. Examine your screens."

Arun looked down at the image of the Totalizer showing the leaderboard of battalions vying with each other to keep out of the Cull Zone. 8-412/TAC was 7,000 points ahead of the cut off. Arun steeled himself to see that safety margin diminish.

The screen refreshed.

8-412/TAC had disappeared. No, it hadn't. It had shifted position. They were bottom!

"We have deducted 25,000 points from 8-412/TAC. This year's graduates *will* be Culled."

The colonel looked from one human face to another, daring them to protest. They were too stunned to speak.

"There is to be no further punishment of the cadets over this issue. Dismissed."

A mix of horror and relief flooded through Arun as he about-heeled to leave. He'd escaped but his friends had not. It should have been the other way around.

"No, not you, McEwan," said the Jotun. "You shall remain here."

Little Scar waited until the other humans had marched away before switching from his thought-to-voice system to speak in his own gravelly words.

"I want a chat with you."

Chapter 12

With a wave of the rubbery tubes that passed for fingers, the colonel beckoned Arun to stand next to him at his workstation.

As he mounted the steps to approach the Jotun, Arun tried to guess what the alien was about to tell him. He had no idea.

Once Arun was standing next to the alien's chair, and had cast his gaze to the ground, Little Scar asked using his own awkward voice: "Would you like to see your brother?"

Not 'you will be executed at dawn' or 'you will be permanently assigned to the punishment battalion'.

Arun was so stunned that he let his pause drag on until Little Scar drew his ears back in annoyance.

"Sir. Yes, sir," Arun said quickly.

Little Scar smiled. There was little about the six-legged Jotuns that was human-like, but when they wanted to, Jotuns could smile just like the most endearing human child. And at that moment, the commander of the 412th Marines chose to smile.

"He is not here," said the Jotun, back to speaking through his artificial voice.

Inter-species familiarity sessions with the Jotuns often went this way. The exchanges mixed boredom on the part of the Jotuns with the terror of the young humans, blending them into an uncomfortable mutual incomprehension.

The worst part was that if you didn't understand, you were expected to ask.

And find a way to do so without having your face sliced off for insulting a superior.

Arun swallowed hard and then cleared his throat, trying to remember whether doing so meant a polite interruption or an insolent invitation to be decapitated. "Sir, this cadet begs permission to ask a question. Sir."

"Speak."

"Why did you ask whether I wanted to see my brother?"

The Jotun narrowed his eyes and stared at Arun, who flinched under this intense scrutiny. "Your incident in the tunnels. I was concerned it might affect your morale."

What? "Sir, that's… very touching, sir."

Arun cringed at his familiarity, but the alien looked more puzzled than angry.

"Touching?" Little scar digested the word. "Ah. You mean you are overwhelmed by my emotional succor. Is that correct?"

"Sir. Yes, sir."

"Hah hah hah!" The voice simulator was stumped by human laughter. You couldn't tell whether the laughter was hearty, ironic, or uncertain. "You are right to think I care about your wellbeing, Cadet McEwan."

Arun couldn't quite believe what was happening. The commander of the regiment was talking to him like an indulgent uncle. Whenever he had spoken to Jotuns before, they had always assumed an attitude that humans were indistinguishable from each other. Little Scar was talking not only as if Arun were an individual sentient being, but an important one too. One that the regimental commander wanted to know better.

What the frakk was happening?

"I care about you…" said Little Scar, before pausing.

"Sir?"

"I care because the Night Hummers say you will be important."

Arun shivered. Floating in their tanks of churning yellow liquid, deep in the bowels of the base, the Night Hummers were bloated gas-sacs, prized for their pre–cognitive ability. Arun struggled to believe that anyone could actually see into the future – though he tried hard to keep an open mind about Springer's ability. Given the fuss the Jotuns made about them on behalf of their masters, the White Knights surely believed that Night Hummers could.

"I don't know why you are special," said the Jotun. "They won't say. Or can't." Little Scar flicked his ears back and bared his teeth, serrated little gray daggers that gleamed in the light from the artificial sky. "Perhaps you will betray us all."

Arun stood rigidly under the lashes of the Jotun's harsh stare.

"Only one other human has ever aroused the Night Hummers' interest. Strange how after several hundred years in which they never saw fit to even mention your species, here you are, both in my regiment at the same time."

Who was the other? Arun burned with the question, but he didn't dare speak. It took all his courage to even breathe under the Jotun's withering gaze.

"And maybe a third human of interest is due to arrive in the system soon. Or… maybe not."

Little Scar moved his ears in circles, each rotating in a different direction. His training told Arun this indicated indecision, deep thought, or a sign of abdominal discomfort.

"Learn this, human. Night Hummers hint at their predictions. Forever they tell us: 'Act now to avert this disaster that will happen… or maybe it will not.'" He growled. "It is not a question of – what is your expression? – *hedging bets*. It is simply how the Hummers perceive the future – and sometimes the present. They allude, imply, and prattle. A collective of Hummers can be noisy, utterly tiresome. It is only by having a troop of Hummers, and keeping them under constant surveillance and analysis by AIs, that we ever realize when there is a temporary consistency to the Hummers' ramblings. Sometimes the pattern dissipates like mist and wind. Occasionally their minds march in lockstep and they all tell the same story, repeating their words over and over. We know then that they want us to listen."

Arun shivered as his pictured the Hummers in their yellow tanks, screaming Arun's name in unison.

"Human, your posture indicates inquiry. Did you want to ask questions?"

"Sir. Yes, sir. Thank you, sir."

"You may ask only one more."

"Sir. Who are the other humans the Night Hummers spoke of?"

Little Scar thought over the answer. "The one who maybe is to come and maybe is a misinterpretation has only the simplest description. No name, rank, scent, or title. All we know is that she is purple." He laughed, the artificial sound accompanied by a bass rumble from the alien. "Purple!"

Little Scar found the whole idea hilarious, but Arun felt something else flooding him with sparkling warmth: hope.

Instructor Nhlappo had described the entire Marine Corps presence on Tranquility as nothing more than a rounding error on a White Knight fleet strength report. What if humans were important after all? And not in the mega long-term species survival plan some veterans talked of – but right here and now.

And, thought Arun, *Little Scar had referred to the purple human as a she…*

The laughter coming through Little Scar's speaker continued as he spoke. "I have seen pink and brown humans. Hrmph. Seen a few red ones too in battle – your species does bleed so energetically – but never a *purple* one."

Little Scar cut the laughter. "Now we discuss your brother." He brought out a mid-limb from where it had nestled in his deep chest hair and pointed it up to the sky. "He's out there."

"Sir? You mean he's out there in the galaxy?"

"Yes. No." Little Scar thought it over. "He is in orbit. A lucky coincidence. I could let you meet if you would like."

"Sir. I would like that, sir."

Having written off the idea of family long ago, to meet a brother would be a curiosity. But it would also be fascinating to meet someone who had been out there, fighting between the stars.

"You would like," said Little Scar. "I would *not* like. But I may enable this in any case."

O-kay. That didn't exactly make sense. When Little Scar made no sign that he was going to elaborate, Arun asked: "Sir, is there something I must do first?"

"Yes. The insect scribe in your tunnel encounter showed sexual interest in you…"

"Not really, sir," Arun blurted out. When the officer didn't react to his interruption, he added: "Sir. The creature was academically interested in my unfortunate physiological reaction to the combat drugs. That's all, sir."

Little Scar showed his teeth again. He was not happy.

"Sir. Sorry, sir," Arun added quickly.

The Jotun allowed Arun's discomfort to continue for a few more seconds before slowly lowering his lips over his fangs. "Only speak when spoken to, human."

Was Arun supposed to acknowledge that? He decided to keep silent.

Little Scar sniffed at Arun, but then relaxed somewhat. "McEwan, you might dismiss your accomplishment, but such a display of sexual interest is unprecedented. These *Trogs*, as you call the hive creatures, run several mining operations here on Tranquility and on moons around the outer planets. They also service the cryogenic facilities, dig the network of defensive warrens, and form the bulk of the planetary defense force. The hive creatures are vital, yet we know very little about them. We need to aid each other to strengthen our defenses and add new contingency plans."

The first question that instantly struck Arun was why had they felt the need to strengthen their defenses. To ask, though, would be madness. He reckoned he had pushed his freakish familiarity with the colonel as far as it would go.

But Arun wasn't renowned for common sense.

"Sir. Permission to speak, sir?"

"There. Politeness was not so difficult, was it?"

A buried memory surfaced. The Jotun colonel sounded like his mom. He shook the thought away. "No, sir. Why are we needing to–?"

Little Scar hissed a warning. Arun had never heard that sound before. It sounded like human flatulence, but it came through the Jotun's teeth.

"I did not offer permission to speak, human. I merely commended politeness. Yes. We need to work more with the hive people. You have this connection with them. Therefore I want you to be our liaison."

Arun blinked repeatedly so that his emotions wouldn't show. His heart fluttered at the memory of the scribe's red flanks puckering…

"You may speak now," said Little Scar.

"*Liaison*. What does that mean, sir? What must I do?"

"Liaison means you will represent the interests of all humans and Jotuns in our dealings with the insect hives on the planet of Tranquility. Learn from them. Learn about them."

"Sir. But what are you expecting me to do?" *Surely he didn't mean…*

Little Scar hissed through his teeth – more a cross between heavy breathing and sighing than the flatulent growl of real anger. Arun interpreted this as irritation.

"Are you a child?" asked the Jotun.

"Sir. I'm 17," Arun replied. "No, sir, I'm not."

"Then you decide what liaison entails. I care nothing for means, only ends. Your first encounter is set for tomorrow." He paused. "Your honor is tarnished, Cadet McEwan. Combat drugs had taken control of your body. I understand. That is why I permit you to live. But the stink of failure hangs around you, makes me want to retch. How sweet it would be if you could take the cause of your dishonor, and transform it into a sweet-smelling triumph that will be celebrated for centuries."

"Sir. I understand, sir."

"Good. Understand this too. If you fail then I shall execute you personally. Dismissed."

— Urgent Info Message —

MESSAGE SUBJECT: Table of Organization & Equipment. Blue Squad, 'C' Company, 8th battalion, 412th Tactical Marine Regiment.

Additional instructions from Squad Leader, Sgt. Gupta:

Attention, Blue Squad.

Memorize the contents of this TOE. It sets out our initial structure, effective immediately. This includes semi-permanent NCO ranks.

'Semi' means that if you screw up, or if you don't look at me in a way I care for, you get demoted.

'Permanent' means you lower-ranked cadets had better get used to addressing your seniors by their new rank.

To cadets newly assigned non-commissioned ranks: do not let your heads bloat! If any cadet NCO affords even the most junior full Marine with any less respect than that due a god, don't expect sympathy from me when I have to scrape up your pulped remains off the deck. Since graduating from novice school, you have risen in status within the Corps family. To a Marine, that now raises you to about the same level as pond scum.

We have yet to meet. Even the most dimwitted among you will therefore realize that I have set out this TOE mostly on the advice of your instructors. Those of you who impress me sufficiently to still hold NCO positions in six months' time will be sent to NCO training camp. There you will begin to understand that NCOs earn their privileges a hundred times over.

I understand that not all of you want to be a leader.

Tough shit.

Notwithstanding the ranks I am assigning today, you will all take turns to train in every role, including specialist, leadership, and those technical roles where your incompetence isn't likely to blow us all to hell. You are all of you only a few casualties away from being squad leader.

Sgt. S. GUPTA, 412th Marines.

Table of Organization & Equipment
==Blue Squad== [Sergeant Gupta]
Current strength: 1 Marine, 28 cadets

Command Section [Sgt. Gupta]
Sergeant Suresh Gupta
Cadet LSgt. - Edward Brandt [responsibility: ammo logistics]
Cadet LCpl. Puja Narciso [chief medic & casualty evac]
Cadet Christanne Cusato
Cadet Stok Laskosk [specialist: missile launcher]
Cadet Vilok Altstein [specialist: Fermi cannon]

Alpha Section [Cdt. Cpl. Hecht]
~~Fire Team Blue1~~
Cadet Cpl. Menes Hecht
Cadet Laban Caccamo
Cadet Giorgio Yakubov
Cadet Marcus Ballantyne

~~Fire Team Blue2~~
Cadet LCpl. Rozalia Naron
Cadet Kamaria Cimini
Cadet Rahul Bojin
Cadet Fadl Vallario

Beta Section [Cdt. Cpl. Khurana]
~~Fire Team Blue3~~
Cadet Cpl. Uma Khurana
Cadet Cheikh Okoro
Cadet Martin Sandhu
Cadet Johannes Binning

~~Fire Team Blue4~~
Cadet LCpl. Mbizi Sesay
Cadet Norah Lewark
Cadet Bernard Exelmans
Cadet Adeline Feria

Delta Section [Cdt. Cpl. Majanita]
~~Fire Team Blue5~~
Cadet Cpl. Estella Majanita
Cadet Osman Koraltan
Cadet Phaedra Tremayne
Cadet Arun McEwan

~~Fire Team Blue6~~
Cadet LCpl. Del-Marie Sandure
Cadet Cristina Blanco
Cadet Serge Rhenolotte
==1 Replacement Requested==

MESSAGE ENDS

Chapter 13

Arun's leg still felt fragile, as if it were knitted together with spent carbine sabots. But as they jogged past the passageway that led from the hab-disk to Helix 62, that meant he'd now managed a full circuit of Ring 3 without his leg giving way.

"Let's pick up the pace, boys," he said, grinning. He felt indestructible.

"Take it easy, McEwan," said Del-Marie.

"I'm fine," Arun replied.

"Arun wouldn't have suggested it, if he didn't mean it," said Osman, who pulled away.

"I know," said Del-Marie as he accelerated to catch up. "But you're forgetting something crucial about McEwan."

"Go on," said Osman. "Tell me."

"The stupid skangat is afflicted with chronic idiocy."

"C'mon, fellas," protested Arun. "Quit joking around."

"I wasn't joking," said Del-Marie. "And I'm not your 'fella'. You saw the message from the sergeant. As of this morning, I'm a lance corporal. *Lance Corporal Sandure*. Still sounds kinda mutated, but you two had better get it right."

"Sorry, lance corporal," they chorused.

Arun refused to let Del get him down. His leg was healing – good enough to put in a few miles before breakfast. He'd even survived the fallout of Little Scar's displeasure. Nothing was going to spoil his good mood, so he changed the subject. "This rendezvous with the Trog I have to make at 14:00, you'll never guess what he's gone and done."

"He?" queried Osman.

"Yeah. 'He'. Referring to the insect as 'it' all the time is way too tedious. Anyway, he's suddenly changed the rendezvous point. We're to meet up in orbit."

"Why?" asked Osman.

"Search me. I tropied a lot of his friends. He might want to tip me out the airlock without a suit."

"You think too much, Arun," said Osman.

"Wouldn't you in my situation, pal? Allow me my thoughts because I might be dead this time tomorrow. I don't suppose Del would be too bothered if I didn't survive. Would you, lance corporal?"

"Stop your whining, McEwan. I don't like you. You're too soft, too distracted by childish emotions. Since the rest of us became cadets we've moved on and left you behind. I'm beginning to think someone else deserved your berth more."

"Finished yet?" Arun quipped.

"No. I also think you're an idiot, but I've got your back all the same because you're part of Blue Squad. So, no, I don't want you to be killed tomorrow."

Arun turned to Osman. "You see, Lance Corporal Sandure does love me! Bernard will get jealous if he carries on like that."

Osman frowned. "Look, I'm your friend, Arun. But Del's right. You're drifting away. Toughen up, man. Get serious."

Arun glared at his friend. *Get serious?* This from the same Osman Koraltan who two years ago converted his training rifle into a water gun and soaked the neighboring dorms in a water fight that spread throughout the company before the instructors shut it down.

"Oh, look at you!" Osman shook his head sadly. "It's all tantrums and emotions with you. You're supposed to be a Marine, for frakk's sake. You're meant to take your orders and then *act*. Marines don't sit down and debate an order, exploring how it affects their feelings. Sometimes I think the others are right about you."

"Right about what?"

"Frakk!" exclaimed Del. "You and your fat mouth, Osman." To Arun he said: "We're your squadmates. If you stay loyal to us, we'll cover your back, come what may. The rest of the battalion doesn't feel so generous."

Coldness suffused Arun. Del didn't have to spell it out. "I appreciate you two keeping down to my pace," he said, "but I'm slowing you down. Why don't you speed up and I'll meet up with you at inspection?"

A curt nod from Del-Marie and Arun's two jogging partners shot off like a starship engaging zero-point drive.

As he watched his comrades disappear around the curvature of Ring 3, Arun's good mood returned. Even at his slow speed, the rhythmic pumping motion of his run energized his body and cleansed his spirit.

Osman was right. Much of Arun's life felt abnormal. In unguarded moments, the others would agree that life as a cadet was cruel, even pointless. But none of that bothered the others – well, possibly Springer sometimes. Arun had always worried constantly, but he'd been able to keep that well-hidden. Until these last few weeks. Now he couldn't even decide whether the Human Marine Corps was a proud family he was privileged to belong to, or a tyranny that should be smashed in the name of freedom.

But jogging… He loved jogging because it felt so natural. The books from ancient Earth said the human body had evolved adaptations specifically for long-distance running. He believed them.

The sound of pounding feet advanced on him from behind. He pulled over to let the faster runners overtake. To reduce congestion, joggers always pounded the rings in an anti-clockwise direction. He was surprised none had overtaken him earlier.

Two runners drew level with Arun, keeping pace with him. He glanced across and saw two cadets, heavy set, good looking, with cold eyes that hid a hot temper. They could almost be twins. Arun knew them: Chao and Burgamy, senior cadets from Checker Squad.

Whatever they had planned couldn't be good. He weighed his chances of sweeping their legs away and burying his fist in their faces before they realized he wasn't ready to be a victim. But with his bad leg, that was never going to work, and fighting was theoretically forbidden, although incidents were usually reclassified as over-exuberance. So instead he nodded a respectful acknowledgment and maintained his speed.

Chao gave a gesture of command to more runners arriving from behind who raced to take up positions in front. They were all from Checker Squad. Horden's Children! It looked as if the entire squad were here.

Some of the Checker cadets pushed between Arun and the wall, boxing him in entirely. Then they slowed, forcing Arun to slow with them until they halted altogether.

If they were trying to intimidate him, they were doing a grand job. Arun's muscles prickled with the need for action but all he could do was clench his fist and bite his lip.

Cameras would be recording everything, every word spoken, every action taken were constantly assessed by security AIs. It was vital that Arun didn't throw the first punch. He couldn't risk being blamed for starting a brawl.

Arun lowered his gaze, took a deep breath, and asked Chao: "Is there anything I can help you with, lance sergeant?"

The intensity of Chao's scrutiny heated the side of Arun's face, but Arun refused direct eye contact.

"I'm proud that my Checkers get first crack at you, McEwan. And in case you think we're some kind of rogue squad, let me assure you of one thing." Chao leaned in close enough for Arun to feel his breath warm his ear. "Every squad in every company throughout the 8th battalion… we're all lined up waiting for a piece of your ass. What do you think of that, loser?"

"Injuring other cadets is a serious offense, lance sergeant. You can be as much of a bullying veck as you like, but if you beat me up, you'll be executed. That's the one advantage of being a thing, owned by aliens. If you damage me, you damage someone else's property. That someone else is a White Knight. Are you big enough to take on the White Knights, Lance Sergeant Chao?"

"Ohh!" Chao sprang back in mock horror. "I'm a bully. Gosh, the shame." He laughed, the rest of the squad joining in on cue. "I'll spell it out for you, alien-faggot. It's not me. It's every last member of Checker Squad wanting to have a quiet word with you about why we're suddenly in the Cull Zone. Look around. Don't see everyone here? That's because the rest of the squad are up the corridor running interference so our little chat isn't interrupted. We're all equally involved. Who will the senior NCOs value most? An entire squad or one insect-loving loser? And if not Checker Squad then the next squad, and the next one. They'll have to choose who they want most – you or the rest of the battalion. They're odds I'm willing to stake my life on."

The world seemed to fall away from Arun. Chao was right. Actually, no… Not quite. "You forgot one thing, Chao. You aren't all equally to blame. You've acknowledged yourself to be the ringleader."

"Oh, yes." Chao gave a predatory grin. "Thanks for reminding me." The lance sergeant cried out in agony, clutching his ankle, scattering his squadmates in all directions – but not enough to leave an opening for Arun to escape.

Chao rolled around on the ground, pretending without much conviction to be in extreme pain. He sat up, still clutching his ankle. "I seem to have suffered a severe ligament strain. I will have to sit here for a short while to recover. Follow whatever course of action you see fit, Checker Squad. In my incapacitated state, I am unable to guide you."

A sinking feeling came over Arun as he waited for his beating to unfold with grim inevitability. He prepared to curl into a ball and bring up his arms to protect his skull.

It did no good. He felt two cadets behind him grab his arms. His legs were kicked away and Lance Corporal Burgamy lined himself up for the first kick.

"Vulley you, Chao." Arun spat in the direction of Checker Squad's leader.

"Really?" said Chao, still sitting on the floor. "Funny. I thought you only wanted to vulley aliens."

Then Burgamy landed the first kick and the breath was knocked from Arun's body.

He felt a burning need to curl over and reflate his lungs, but with his arms restrained he had to take the pain without the slightest respite.

Burgamy and the two cadets holding Arun's arms waited until the first wave of pain had subsided before running off down the passageway, resuming their jog as if nothing had happened.

Cowards!

Red hot anger exploded through Arun. He wanted to punch, kick, and bite. But being on his knees meant he couldn't throw his weight.

His arms were grabbed again and pinned against his back sharply enough to draw a yelp from Arun. As a tall girl, Schimschak, readied to throw a punch, Arun saw a line queue up behind her and sensed more cadets behind him, waiting to take their turn to restrain him.

Schimschak's punch smashed into his face. Arun twisted at the last moment. It was only a glancing blow to his left eye, but still enough to make him see blinding flashes until he shook them away – just in time to see Hardy land a roundhouse kick into his flank.

After that, the blows came in too fast for Arun to tell them apart. He was alone in a sea of pain that roiled with frustrated anger.

Then, suddenly, it dawned on him that the beating had paused. The sounds of a scuffle broke out around him.

Arun marshaled his strength and peered out through his right eye – his left wasn't cooperating. Around him, facing down the Checker Squad cadets, were Madge, Zug, and Springer. Others too, just out of sight.

Arun felt tears threatening to break to the surface. He hadn't cried for years – didn't want to now – but he'd felt so alone. So unwanted.

He collapsed to the floor and groaned. But the vibration of running feet came loud to his ears as he heard Checker Squad run off, hurling curses at Arun as they withdrew.

Arun didn't care. He gathered his strength as rapidly as he could and put everything he had into his dwindled power of speech. "Thank you." He propped himself up on one elbow and looked up at his rescuers.

He'd expected smiles and concerned expressions. Instead, many of the faces of his rescuers were as cold as Checker Squad's had been.

Madge seemed to be in charge. She stood over him, hands on hips, regarding Arun struggling on the ground as if he were something she'd puked up. "Don't get all dewy-eyed on me, loser." She curled her lip. "If you weren't in my section I'd be the first in line to give you the kicking you deserve for putting us in this drent. Don't ever make the mistake of thinking I like you. And don't give me that crap about it not being your fault that you embarrassed the colonel. I don't give a damn whether it's fair or not, I'm still blaming you. Do you understand?"

Arun nodded.

"Frakk you, cadet. I asked you a question. I expect a respectful answer."

"Sorry, corporal. Yes, I understand, corporal."

Hands reached for Arun, helped him to his feet. But they weren't the corporal's. Cadet Corporal Estella Majanita, the friend he'd called Madge until yesterday, turned her back and walked away.

She did not look back.

Chapter 14

The auto-shuttle docked with the unmanned orbital defense platform. Its two passengers alighted and made their way to the platform's observation room, the young human managing this with far more grace than his insect companion.

Arun tried to keep the hive creature in his peripheral vision. He didn't want to acknowledge the unwanted alien by looking directly at it – *him*, he reminded himself. Nor did he want to look completely away in case doing so was interpreted as a gesture of weakness.

Arun's alien masters had felt accurate timekeeping was important enough that they had augmented all human Marines with a range of time-keeping capabilities. So even though it felt like an age, he knew it took only 412 seconds before the alien broke the impasse by speaking through the voice box hanging around his neck.

"Look out the porthole," said the alien. "Tell me what you see."

Until that episode in the tunnel exercise, Trogs hadn't featured much in the lives of Arun and his comrades. The giant insects were grotesque fairytale monsters whose purpose, as far as the cadets were concerned, was to be an ingredient of the most indecent kind of insults. As to why they were really here, Arun had never heard any more than wild rumor until his interview with Little Scar. And who knew what truth lay behind the words of the Jotuns?

More to the point, Arun had been raised since crèche to know whom to salute and whom he could order around. The Trogs simply did not fit into that neat order. He resented this disruption.

And that made him feel dumber than ever. He couldn't help but feel he was a champion of humanity facing off against alien competition, and here he was second-guessing himself into knots.

It was very simple, he reminded himself. Little Scar had ordered Arun to cooperate with the Trog scribe, and the colonel was very definitely in the list of people to be obeyed.

So, after pausing enough to show he was treating the Trog's words as a request and not an order, Arun shrugged and pushed himself off from his perch. Thousands of hours logged in zero-g training meant the maneuver should have been as natural as walking. Not today, though. Arun's body had taken such a pounding these past few days that he gasped in pain as he pushed off.

"Do I need to apologize for the injuries inflicted by my species?" asked the scribe.

"No, you don't. Most of my injuries were handed out by my supposed comrades. I guess we're a pretty aggressive species."

"Of course," said the insect. "That is the species trait your masters recruited you for. What they have been breeding into you ever since."

"What do you know about what they've done to us?"

"Much. I request of you. Please answer my question: what do you see?"

Unsure how he'd been suckered into talking, Arun shut up and looked out the porthole.

"I can see the Serendine orbital elevator, the twin of the one that took us up from the surface. I can see flashes in a ring above the equator. I guess they're other defense platforms and satellites." He adjusted his sight to look farther out. "There's a disk of gleaming silver out at one of the Lagrange points, between us and… one of the moons, I'm not sure which one."

"Antilles."

"Right, Antilles. I've only got about 4x zoom with my eyes, so I can't resolve the disk, but I reckon it's thousands of ore cans shot there from the asteroid belt and ready for processing on the moons."

"What about the planet? Tell me what you see below us."

"Okay… That's Tranquility. Nine light minutes from the sun. Two main continents: Baylshore where I live and the other one's called Serendine–"

"No. That's not what I mean. If you lived a hundred light years away, you could quote all those facts from a database. But you don't. This is your home. Do not tell me facts. Tell me what you see."

"Why?"

There was a pause before the alien replied: "Were you briefed?"

Insubordination from humans was not tolerated. The punishment would be fatal for him, and the demerits would push his battalion comrades further away from ever escaping the Cull Zone. A cadet called Mowad from the 420th had tried to dodge witnessing last year's Cull. The result was that Mowad found herself on the wrong side of the execution squad and her battalion went from fourth place from the top of the leaderboard down to fourth from the bottom.

"Yes, yes, I was briefed." Arun spoke hastily. "When I said *why*, I meant: what do you want me to describe?"

"Tell me what that view means to you."

Arun shrugged with one shoulder. "Like I said, it's a planet. Our planet. I suppose it's beautiful when you stop to look for a while and really *see* it. I like the way the atmosphere glows as it fades into the black of space. It's like your tongue, I guess. You don't think about your tongue 99.9% of the time, but when you do become conscious of it, it's actually really big, like…" He faded. Tongues were something he'd become aware of recently because he and Springer had kind of been exploring each other's, but anything to do with sex was definitely off topic. This was the insect creature who had humiliated him. Cadet Prong. Drenting stupid name. Drenting stupid alien who'd made him look so bad and now just perched there staring at him, saying nothing, only speaking out of his stupid voice box.

"I do have a tongue," said the alien. "If that is what bothers you. We do not consider it a taboo organ."

"Right."

"But I do not possess ears. I sense vibrations through my antennae."

"Okay."

"Nonetheless, I understand your reference. Antennae are with us from hatching through to death and our final recycling. We do not consider them 99.9% of time, as you say. But when we do they are large and awkward. At those times I do not know where to put them or how to angle them. I feel so self-conscious."

"Yeah. Well, the planet's like that. I've clocked so many hours in space doing boarding exercises, or waiting for atmos drops or TU attack exercises, that I take it all for granted."

"Very good, Cadet McEwan. Please continue."

Arun sniffed. It was a dumb exercise but not as difficult as keeping himself from punching this annoying insect. "Down below us," he continued, "is Beta City. It's the twin of Detroit, where I'm based, but on the other side of the world."

"What do you feel about Beta?"

What was with all this about feelings? "It's a dumb name. I feel contempt. No, that's too strong. They're still Marines down there. Mostly."

Arun looked at the alien, but the voice box was silent, and the insect's twin pairs of eyes seemed to be prodding him to say more.

"I guess I feel a little curious about them too," he said. "I mean, Beta is our twin. It's the depot base for three more Marine tac regiments and one regiment of Marine engineers. Do they train their Marines the same? Probably, though some say the Jotuns forbid the Beta regiments to even mention Earth. The rumor mill also has it that Beta has a space-rat squadron based there."

"I apologize to interrupt, but I do not understand the term, *space-rat*."

"Human spacers. Starship crew. Born out in deep space, most of them. Raised there too, mostly. That's so frakkin' alien. Er, no offense."

"I still don't understand."

I still don't understand. Of course you don't. You never will because you're an alien.

That dry mechanical voice got under Arun's skin and shook him from mild irritation toward rage. It had been that voice that played over and over on those mocking vid recordings plastered all over the base. It was this voice and the alien behind him that had caused so much trouble.

When Arun got angry, all those combat enhancements that turned his body into a killing machine kicked in big time. Right now, he needed to either blast something or run 20 miles. Sitting still wasn't an option. So he pushed away from the porthole set into the dull white plastic wall and shot through the open hatch into the next compartment.

When they'd docked, the alien had asked him to stay and talk in the observation deck. Well, they'd done that. He had never said Arun couldn't explore.

He emerged at speed into a cramped chamber with a central spine that fed cables into four transparent blisters set into the hull. He swung around the central spine and landed on a gunnery couch in one of the blisters. They looked like Fermi cannons, point defense weapons that could alter the laws of physics in a localized area, hopefully within the guidance system of munitions flung at the defense platform.

He stretched back and saw the Trog was still in the obs deck, struggling against the absence of gravity. *Good. It can stay there for a bit.*

Floating back to the cannon, he gripped the firing handles and hovered his thumbs over the firing studs, reveling in the power within his hands.

He pressed the studs.

Nothing happened.

The relief took the edge off his anger. He couldn't sense any power feeding through into the cannons. He hadn't really thought they were active, but he hadn't been sure until he tried them.

Arun perched on top of the gunnery couch and waited. The couch was designed for a hexaped – a Jotun, presumably. He'd done a theoretical course on ship weapons, enough to identify the three banks of controls: firing, targeting, and turret traverse. Humans didn't have enough limbs to operate them without doubling up. In a few weeks Blue Squad was scheduled to learn how to fire these beauties.

Strange, though, that there should be manual controls when the defense platforms were all automated.

The alien was still vulleying around in the other compartment. That was one up for the humans. Arun grinned.

Tired of waiting, he maneuvered over to the spine, surveying the controls there. The platform seemed to be on standby. He guessed that if active, he could control the main armament from here, the x-ray laser. It was a big one. Even the biggest enemy capital ship couldn't survive a direct hit from this beast on full charge, unless they launched an ocean of ablatives to soak up the power. Problem was, any enemy would probably know that too. There were 30 orbital defense platforms such as this around Tranquility. There were also several hundred dummy platforms, but Arun doubted you could hide for long amongst the fakes. The power build up on the real platforms was so intense, an enemy would have to be blind not to spot them.

Suddenly, the Troggie scribe came tumbling through the doorway at surprising velocity. It was flailing all six limbs, absolutely the worst thing you could do to stabilize yourself in zero-g.

Without thinking, Arun pushed off to help. Just before he grabbed the alien's limb he nearly panicked. This wasn't a comrade he was assisting; it was an alien with no reason to love humanity. And Arun was only dressed in fatigues. He didn't even have gloves.

Half expecting the alien limb to be bristling with spines, slime, or burning acid, Arun felt nothing unpleasant as he instinctively added his inertia to the alien's, steering him to a stable perch on one of the gunnery couches.

The alien's limb had felt no different from a human arm except the skin was cold, like a corpse.

"Thank you, my friend."

The artificial voice in the box around the creature's neck managed to sound breathless. Arun was impressed. Even the Jotuns couldn't do that.

"But why did you journey from the observation deck to this gunnery room?" added the voice.

"Why? Why not?"

"Ah, curiosity. At appropriate stages in our life-cycle, we too are consumed with curiosity beyond reason. I myself thirst for an understanding of other species, which is why you and I are here today. You see, we are alike more than you think, young human."

Arun laughed. He clutched at his middle and span forward as he floated, a never-ending forward roll.

"Do you need assistance?" called the alien.

"No." Arun calmed down. "Why?"

"Your barking noise. And that spinning. Are you malfunctioning?"

"It's called laughter. It's a sign of amusement."

The alien froze in silence. He had hesitated like that before, and Arun began to wonder whether the big bug was consulting an implanted data store. "I understand. You have a violent way of showing amusement, which suits the violent nature of your species. When we laugh, we emit a pheromone and tilt our antennae like so."

The Trog angled his antennae about 15 degrees to its right. Arun realized the creature had already made this gesture several times, the cheeky little skangat.

Arun shook his head. This was frakking surreal. "Look at you, Trog," he said. "You say we're alike but you're an insect. You live underground in an immense social group and you can't talk with your own voice because you haven't got one. You make smells instead. And for frakk's sake, you've got those wiggly antennae things. How can you possibly say we're alike?"

The alien tilted its antennae about 15 degrees.

"Are you laughing at me?" Arun smacked his palm to his forehead, not quite believing what he was seeing.

"Yes, Cadet McEwan. We laugh together. It is true that we have gross physiological differences, but many of the problems faced by sentient social creatures are the same. Not only do we share similar challenges but many of their solutions too. This is vital because it leads to the possibility of cooperation between species."

"Isn't that what Tranquility is all about?" asked Arun. "Our Marine Corps officers are all Jotuns. You Trogs do whatever it is you do, and the Hardits do a lot of mining and maintenance work."

"Who says that humans must have Jotun officers? Who says that inter-species cooperation must take that particular form?"

Arun had the feeling he was stumbling into a trap. But he was too unimportant to bother with such elaborate deception, so he answered, though with caution. "The White Knights. They say Jotuns must be our officers and that we humans must obey without question."

Arun expected a response. The Trog said nothing, but it flung its antennae back to run flat along its head. Whatever that meant, it sure wasn't laughing now.

Was the Trog hinting that the slave species on Tranquility should – what? – get together to share expertise? Or was this something far more dangerous? Was the Trog proposing they should join forces and rise up against the White Knights? Arun was scared to even form such words in his mind. To speak them aloud was unthinkable.

The alien watched him and said nothing for a long time. Then asked: "*Why do you obey?*"

Arun's brain replayed a memory. Something the Trog had said just after the auto shuttle had left the orbital elevator. "There are no listening devices on the defense platform," it had said. "We may speak freely."

Arun had been bred, upgraded, and trained to fight in space. Being in a tiny bubble of atmosphere in the vacuum had never bothered him until that moment. He suddenly felt cold, vulnerable, and desperately isolated.

Either he was a melodramatic fool dreaming of conspiracies.

Or… he'd somehow been caught up in a rebellion. A fight to win freedom from the White Knights.

Arun kept his mouth rigidly shut, refusing to answer. Neither human nor Trog spoke again, embarking on their shuttle and descending the orbital elevator in silence.

Thoughts of freedom were not just treasonous.

They were insane.

Chapter 15

"I bet Sergeant Gupta mentions you," said Del-Marie from the seat to Arun's left.

"Unlikely," answered Zug to his right.

"Shut up the pair of you," snapped Madge from behind.

Arun let the banter wash over him, happy that his squadmates still acknowledged his existence. And after being hissed at by Colonel Little Scar, and threatened by Checker Squad, any disapproval by their new leader would be nothing.

The 27 cadets of Blue Squad were sitting behind their desks in one of hab-disk 6/14's briefing rooms, waiting for the first official encounter with their new veteran commander.

After the craziness of the past few days, Arun was looking forward to a simple classroom lesson.

Actually, he reminded himself, although the room layout was identical to the novice school classrooms, he'd finished with classes for good. He was a cadet now. This was a *briefing*.

A buzz of anticipation thrilled the cadets. When instructors had taken classes, in the back of your mind you always knew that you would leave them behind when you graduated. This was different: Sergeant Gupta would command their squad in battle. This was *serious*.

The door at the back of the room opened, launching a wave of standing and saluting.

Sergeant Gupta took his place behind the lectern emblazoned with the regimental flag: a black rectangle with the number 412 in silver set over a gold circle. The circle represented that spherical Tactical Unit warboats that put the *Tactical* into Tactical Marine Regiment.

Arun tried to get a measure of the man and found he felt disappointed at how unremarkable Gupta appeared. The sergeant was shortish, his shaven head not hiding that he was largely bald. His body looked more rugged than the cadets', sculpted by life on the frontier. Only Gupta's eyes revealed him as a force to be reckoned with. He was taking his time to study his squad.

Unlike many of the instructors, he wasn't glaring, wasn't trying to domineer and scare. But there was a quiet intensity to the man's scrutiny. Gupta was not a person you would cross without consequences.

"Sit," Gupta ordered in a voice Arun remembered from the tunnels.

As the cadets took their seats, Arun decided he liked Gupta.

"That was me once," said the sergeant. "I was sitting there watching my first veteran commander give her first lecture. I wasn't listening. Not really. Was too busy wondering what kind of woman this was who would one day give me battlefield orders. It was a long while ago. I had yet to learn that your squad NCO is God as far as you lot are concerned. It's my job to keep you alive and pointing your SA-71 in the right direction long enough to do some damage to the enemy before you get hit. How I do that is my business. It is not my job to be your friend."

Gupta stared at every Blue Squad cadet in turn. His earlier scrutiny had been only a reconnaissance and now the cadets were exposed to the full effect. Many of them flinched under the sergeant's gaze. When he stared at Arun, he seemed to draw out every secret, expose every weakness, leaving Arun a shriveled weakling in awe of this terrifying man.

"Let me give you a flavor of just how long ago I was sitting in your place," said Gupta. "I was born on Tranquility and raised by my mother until I was nine. Then I was frozen for thirty years before they sent me to school. In the years before they froze me, a big change was spreading through what we still called Alpha Base. The Jotuns started allowing us to learn about Earth up till the moment of First Contact. When I was born we'd had to rely on race memories and a helluva lot of make believe.

"That's why so many of my age group were frozen. If the experiment had corrupted the older cadets and Marines – left them unwilling to fight – then the Jotuns would have exterminated them all and woken my cadre of sleeping kids from sleep to start over. I'll leave you to draw your own conclusions about why you are still forbidden to contact cadets from Beta Base."

Arun exchanged glances with Zug. This was news!

"These days squads are commanded by a sergeant, and fire teams are paired up into sections and led by a corporal," said Gupta. "Back then we still used the Jotun NCO ranks of 'old commander' and 'young commander'. I have to tell you I'm mighty glad I'm not called an old commander."

That brought out a smattering of laughter.

"We had *hands* instead of companies, *fingers* rather than squads and sections. As for fire teams of 4 to 6 Marines? Fire teams were the same in my day. But for the rest, they've given you a fresh coat of names and drills borrowed from a hotchpotch of ancient Earth armies. Strip all that away and one key detail is unchanged. Old commander or sergeant – that's as far as a human can ever be promoted. Sure, they invented new ranks: senior sergeant and staff sergeant, but all of them are firmly NCO ranks. Humans can never be officers, can never really be in command.

"That's the theory. That's what you've been taught. The truth is that the Jotuns can't provide officers in sufficient numbers for the Marine Corps. We breed more rapidly than the aliens ever accounted for. That's why so many Marines are kept in ice, and why the Cull gets even more of you than it did in my day.

"So they place us in operational command. If you were to read official regimental reports, a human senior staff sergeant is there in the battalion command squad to make the coffee for the Jotun officers, wipe their backsides, and amuse them with his or her performing monkey antics. Let me tell you, that human staff sergeant is actually the battalion executive officer."

Arun glanced nervously around the room. Was Sergeant Gupta allowed to say that?

A hand went up.

"Go on, Hecht. Spit it out."

"Sergeant. If the Jotun commander were killed in action–"

"Would a human take charge? What you really want to ask is this: can a human give orders to a Jotun? Is that it?"

A hush stifled the briefing room. Arun could taste the danger.

After a pained silence, Hecht replied: "Sergeant. Yes, sergeant."

"No. I don't want that sergeant sandwich crap. You aren't novices and I'm not an instructor. You reply 'yes, sergeant.' Got it?"

"Yes, sergeant," they all responded.

"Good," acknowledged Gupta. "That was well done, Hecht. All of you were thinking the same thing, but only this one cadet spoke that thought aloud. I'm going to have to work on this lack of initiative, but first your answer. The very idea of a human telling a Jotun what to do is preposterous. Worse than that, it is against the natural order of things, and we all know some very dangerous people who like to have everything and everyone in just the right place. Don't we?"

No one spoke.

"Don't we?" barked the sergeant.

Yes, sergeant. The White Knights," said Brandt of all people. Arun would have expected him to keep his head down.

"*The White knights*. Yes, indeed. I've never seen one. Don't expect to either and I can't say I understand them. But the Jotuns know them much better. Say they're obsessed with change, with evolution, and mutation, that sort of drent. They even pollute their world on purpose with a mutating cloud. Flek, people call it. The White Knights change themselves, celebrate their mutants and then – usually – cull them. I told you I don't understand them. The point you need to get inside your frail skulls is that our masters have a fascination with change, a fascination tainted with fear. They are alert to variation and if we upset the natural order then that is change, and they *will* notice. I don't know about you, but I would much prefer to be so insignificant that we're ignored. Frankly, I think the Jotuns are working flat out to shield us from White Knight attention."

What the frakk was Gupta up? They were all so flekked.

Gupta paused for effect. "And so back to you, Hecht. No human can ever give an order to a Jotun. However…" He grinned. "There may be circumstances where a senior human NCO could make helpful *suggestions* to Jotun officers. After all, being attached to battalion or regimental HQ, even a dumb human would know what his Jotun superiors have been planning."

Gupta let the tension build. Arun began to wonder whether the sergeant was insane. Sometimes it happened when being thawed. Resuscitation attrition they called it.

"Yeah, I know," Gupta said. "Treason, eh? I'm going to get you all shot. Well, there's plenty that your instructors never told you. I'll teach you what, but all in good time. Here's your lesson for today. Any talk of dissent, to even raise the question of why you fight, of whether the White Knights are worth fighting for… that is treason. But that rule applies to you cadets. Not to we veterans. We're expected to question our role because – or so the Jotun theory goes – we have a psychological need to do so. Otherwise stress toxins build up and weaken us physically. The Jotuns reckon that when humans are in battle and it's either us or the enemy who are going to wind up dead, that's plenty enough motivation for us to obey orders. So long as you're talking with a vet, that treason immunity extends to you cadets too."

Gupta stopped talking and started sniffing the air. *What the hell was he up to now?*

"Anyone else smell hokum?" asked the sergeant.

When no one replied, he pointed to Osman. "You, Koraltan. Do you?"

Osman looked startled to be singled out by this mad veck. "Sorry, sergeant. I don't know what hokum is."

"Sheesh! It's sixty years since I was sitting in your place. I'll have to get used to your language, and you to mine. If you merge with another unit out there in space, you always get vocabulary issues. Frakking language won't sit still. *Frakking!*" He laughed. "That's a new one you kids have made up since I was last here, we used to say it a little differently. *Hokum*. It means bullshit, bollocks, balls, bullcrap – a lie that doesn't stand up to intensive scrutiny. Some of the petty rules and boundaries that you have lived with up all your lives are hokum."

Gupta suddenly pointed across the room at Uma Khurana without bothering to look in her direction.

"You've a face like you're afflicted with terminal constipation, Khurana. Do you want to ask a question?"

Arun glanced across. It was plain to see that Khurana would rather hide under her desk, but she judged that wasn't an option. "Yes, sergeant. Why? Why would we be told… *hokum*?"

"Good. Maybe there's some hope for you worms yet because that is the right question to ask. For an answer, let me share something I've learned about Jotuns. They are meticulous planners. They want to know every detail, to consider every possibly strategy and counter-strategy. We all notice they have six limbs, but if you shaved off all that shaggy fur, I reckon you would find six buttholes too, because Jotuns are so frakking anal. They don't do *petty*. When I said they set us petty rules and boundaries, *they only seem petty to us*. There will be a solid reason behind them. We just don't know what that is and the Jotuns ain't telling.

"So we fight. We fight for the sake of our buddies. We fight to protect our fleet and our Marine family here on Tranquility. Some of you see a big picture and imagine you fight in the long run for Earth. If that makes you run a little harder, prepare a little more thoroughly, and duck a little quicker, then that's fine by me.

"You're cadets now. The time for philosophy and theory is almost over. You've had 17 years of that useless crap. I'm here so some of my practical experience fighting as a Marine can rub off on you, and when you ship out-system I'll be with you, making sure you fight where, when, and how the officer expects. Well, here's a surprise. Just occasionally, sometimes philosophy can be practical too. I'll leave you with a Marine saying. I'm sure you've heard it before, but it's important and it might be a clue to answering Khurana's question of why you should fight. Here it is: Life as a Marine is awash with injustice, hardship and reverses. The mark of a good Marine is to suck that all up, keep your head held high, and wait for the advantage to swing your way so you can seize it! Seize that advantage and exploit it ruthlessly with every ounce of strength and without a second's hesitation. Shout out if you know who first said that?"

"You?" suggested Springer. Arun agreed, remembering that the sergeant had used almost the same words in the Troggie tunnel, but Gupta shook his head.

"Napoleon," said Brandt.

"I think you need to review your history," answered Gupta. "Napoleon wasn't in the Marines on account of he was too short. They wouldn't let him in. You…" He pointed at Hecht.

"Howlin' Mad Smith, sergeant."

Gupta nodded approvingly. "Better with the history, Hecht. General Smith was in the US Marine Corps, and maybe he did say something like that, but he isn't who I heard it from. I said that when the fight turns your way, a good Marine exploits it with *every ounce of strength*. But when I first heard this saying, the actual words were *exploit your moment with all six limbs*. Yes, cadets, it's originally a Jotun saying. Don't forget that Jotuns are Marines too. Perhaps as our fellow Marines, we should trust them to cover our backs."

Gupta appeared to be satisfied with the confusion he'd sown in his squad. "I want you to be very careful in what you say to each other," he said, "but I also want you to think deeply about what I've just said."

Given the nervous shuffling rippling through the room, Arun wasn't the only one thinking hard but understanding little.

"That is all," said Sergeant Gupta. "I'll see you later for EVA drill."

Arun saluted Gupta as he left but his mind was on the sergeant's words, not his back as he walked away.

What was the sergeant on about? Either he was just insane or… or what? The Jotuns always planned meticulously…there was a reason behind what they did even if they kept it hidden. Even if it was as weird as ordering a cadet to make friends with a Trog. Was Gupta trying to send Arun a message?

He'd only met the sergeant for five minutes, and already Arun had learned that after 17 years of such intensive training that a third of the novices hadn't made it to cadet, he still didn't know a damned thing.

—— Urgent Info Message ——

MESSAGE SUBJECT: Our Cull Zone punishment

To: 8th cadet battalion, 412th Tactical Marine Regiment
From: Staff Sergeant E. Bryant.

Our entire battalion has been punished. For some of you, the hard work of years has been undone in an instant.

This is disappointing.

GET OVER IT!

Life is filled with disappointments, but there are many chances for victory too. Good fortune smiles mostly on those who work the hardest at turning around their luck. Good Marines know this. When bad shit happens, they stick together, outlast the bad times, and go looking for their chance to turn things around.

Inadequate Marines turn in on themselves, pointing the finger of blame anywhere but at themselves.

We are in the Cull Zone.

Deal with it. As a unit.

The subject of how we were awarded the punishment is not to be discussed. Speculation regarding who might be to blame is forbidden.

And if I find any member of this battalion threatening a fellow cadet whom they blame for putting us in the Cull Zone, then I will burn out that canker of disunity with the utmost severity.

For those of you who think they can blackmail their superiors by acting as unified squads, I say this. Our Jotun officers and I are equally convinced that it is far better to have one company of good Marine cadets than eight companies of bad ones.

All of you can easily be replaced.

Don't forget that.

MESSAGE ENDS

Chapter 16

384th Detroit Scendence Championships. Day 1 – Practice Match

A cheer exploded through the crush of cadets near the exit to corridor 610. Arun swiveled his smart-plastic chair around to check out the fuss. It wasn't difficult to work out what was up. A group of cadets from Fox Company were jumping up and down in jubilation, pointing up at one of the sixteen large soft screens mounted on the wall.

Their player had just won a Scendence contest.

The fuss died down soon enough and the parade hall returned to the general low level excitement of a Scendence Day.

"Five minutes!" shouted Del-Marie.

Arun couldn't bring himself to cheer. Moscow Express had lost their first three contests of the day, which meant that however well Springer did in her individual match, the team result would be a loss. The Scendence season consisted of two practice matches before the knockout stage began. As the first practice, the result didn't matter anyway, but the mood from the chairs around Arun was still muted.

Another wave of excitement crashed over the parade hall. Arun looked up but couldn't see any cause. It was just your regular burst of Scendence Day excitement.

Just for a moment, his face fell. They were in one of the battalion's parade decks on Level 4. It was a dramatic space with a dais for NCOs to give speeches or lead large-scale training classes. Part of the wall behind the dais was built from the carcass of a Muryani attack cruiser, still scorched from the plasma fire that had disabled it before human Marines had boarded. The ship was a proud battle honor, but parade halls were used for many purposes, some not so positive. Arun had witnessed an execution in this room.

Executions made him think of the Cull. Across all cadet battalions in Detroit – currently there were sixty – the four with the lowest Totalizer score at the end of each year lost a tenth of their cadets to the Cull. If your battalion was one of the four in the Cull Zone then there were only two ways to escape the Cull. One was to die beforehand, the other was to reach the last sixteen in a Scendence championship and win immunity.

It didn't look like Moscow Express was going to be a means for anyone to escape the Cull.

Arun caught himself from slipping into one of his black moods of doom. Today was a Scendence Day. A day's vacation from such worries. An official day of fun.

He looked up at the screen the Fox cadets were watching, trying to borrow some of their jubilation. The screen replayed the moment of victory. This had been an Obedience-Stoicism contest. The players were each subjected to a random horror. If neither of them flinched, they would face a new horror, and another one until one of them gave way.

The match was running late because of an epic contest that morning between a human player and a Jotun opponent. That contest had gone an incredible twelve rounds before the Jotun had given way when they faced the horror of being buried deep underground in a tunnel collapse.

Not many Jotuns played Scendence and it was rarer too for them to lose to a human. Arun had taken a recording of the frenzied reaction in the room when the human had triumphed. A treasured moment to savor at moments of despair.

At any other time, a display of such disrespect toward the Jotuns would be unthinkable, but the officers expected rowdy behavior on a Scendence Day. It was just one more reason for Arun to think aliens would never make any sense.

The wall-screen now replayed a split view showing both competitors in the Obedience-Stoicism match. Each had their heads clamped and positioned in front of a perforated, black screen. A spike emerged from one of the holes turning slowly but relentlessly, aimed at the left eye of each player.

In real time the advance of the spike had been agonizingly slow. The replay sped up the action until the tip stopped a hand's-breadth from the eye. Then a needle emerged from the tip of the spike, pushing on toward the eye. Closer. Closer. Then it pierced the cornea. Neither player showed any reaction.

The spike had advanced in silence but now a motor purred as it pushed the needle deeper into the eye. Arun couldn't help but blink in sympathy.

A depressurization alert blasted out its twin tones. Depressurization drill was so ingrained in all of them that Arun nearly leaped from his seat. Just in time, he realized the sound was coming from the Scendence replay, a cruel trick to distract the players. They didn't react at all.

Then the clamps holding their heads in place fell away in a burst of compressed air.

Each player now had a needle inside their eyeball with only willpower keeping their head steady enough for it to do no damage.

Arun shook his head in wonder. He'd be blubbing like a baby long before this stage.

The loser lasted another four seconds before screaming and shutting his eyes. The scream turned to a wail of agony as the needle gouged a path of pain through his retina.

The Fox supporters jeered.

"Look at those foxies," said Arun. "I'd like to see them take a needle in the eye without blinking."

"I for one couldn't," said Osman who was standing just behind Arun, there not being enough seats for everyone.

"Cristina did," said Del-Marie.

Slumped in her chair across from Arun, Cristina gave a halfhearted smile.

"Yeah, we're proud of you," added Arun.

There was a grunt of agreement, which made Arun feel relief that his squadmates were beginning to act as if her were one of them again.

Cristina ignored them all.

In the morning session, she had taken the needle without flinching, but so too had her opponent. On the second round, she had screamed in pain when the poisonous scorpion in her mouth stung her. Her opponent had shown no reaction.

Osman's Deception-Planning had involved a card game, never a good scenario for Osman. His opponent hadn't even hesitated before he called Osman's bluff. Arun felt bad about that. Osman still wanted Arun to take his place in the team, but Springer had advised him to wait for now. Madge was still too mad at him after the battalion's Cull Zone punishment.

As for Madge, she was still on her way down from orbit after her Gunnery contest. She had done well but her opponent had done better still, which seemed to sum up Moscow Express's day.

Arun looked back at the wall-screen, which was now showing fluid being pumped back into the competitors' eyes.

The Scendence tortures had been virtual, but they had felt real to the competitors because they had been wearing total immersion suits. The irony was that in order to shoot images directly at the retina while bypassing the lensing effect of the eyes, the liquid inside each eyeball was drained when the suit was put on and reinserted before removal.

Arun felt a kick against his chair leg.

"Springer's in position," said Del-Marie gruffly.

Flicking through the several hundred Scendence feeds offered on his softscreen, Arun quickly found several for Springer's contest. He picked one that showed his friend's viewpoint and offered audio commentary too.

Scendence players wore caps that strapped over the forehead rather like the training caps cadets wore during Second Sleep. You could tap into the player's mind, to see what they saw; hear what they heard. Some of the highest rated ACE-3 battlesuits, allowed you to do this too, tapping into the view from your squadmates. There weren't many of these advanced suits to go around and they were reserved for NCOs. They struck Arun as a very good idea.

"Here she goes," said Del-Marie, rather pointlessly as they were all watching Springer from various feeds as she walked out into a transparent box a dozen meters over the chilly water of Lake Tavistock.

The thin ice crust underneath had been melted for the contest. The commentary said the water temperature was only 4 degrees above freezing.

Each player was dressed in fatigues: boots, camo pants, and a thin shirt. Springer's viewpoint was shaking: she was shivering already.

Arun switched to a view with a wider-angle. The two players were in a see-through box with a dividing wall between them. At the bottom of each compartment was sump filled with water. The objective was to fill the bucket they had been given, climb up a spiral staircase which ended in a hole at the top of the dividing wall. You had to throw the water through the hole to fill your opponent's compartment. The volume of water in each compartment started off the same. Once one player's compartment contained two thirds of the combined water volume, its floor would open up, dumping the loser into the lake below.

From his feed, Arun could see in the distance that a duplicate setup was positioned a short distance farther into the lake. A contest was already underway in the other setup.

Something about one of the figures in the other contest drew him in, making him zoom the view onto the other match as best he could.

It was Xin!

Springer's match wouldn't start for a minute or two, so he quickly found a feed that showed a closer view of Xin.

At the top of each compartment was an opaque box. Xin's match had progressed enough for it to open. It looked like it had deposited biting insects and a slimy goop over the competitors. Xin and her competitor looked like they had been half digested and then vomited up by some hideous monster, but Arun would kiss Xin in an instant.

Despite all the drent that had happened recently, he still felt exactly the same about that girl.

He wasn't watching Xin just to stare at her figure, he told himself. He selected another feed, one that showed a close-up of her face. Arun looked beyond her physical beauty at the determination that blazed from her eyes, the steadiness of her stride as she ascended the slippery steps. Her every movement was calculated, efficient, strong.

Xin put him in mind of a common saying about Scendence: *To take part is but a passing diversion. It is winning that matters.*

Her determination to win was almost machinelike. For all that he admired her, Xin scared Arun a little too.

The commentary feed was showing the score: 58% of the water was in Xin's compartment. She was losing!

"Come on," Arun whispered under his breath.

He delved through the commentary stats for the trends. Xin was losing but she was clawing back. She had been on 62% at one point, just 4% away from a long drop into the lake. Xin poured a bucketful into her opponent's compartment. Now she was on 57%. *Keep going!* Xin leaped down into the sump and began refilling.

Meanwhile her opponent slipped from the stairs, spilling out half the contents of her bucket. She took a moment to catch her breath before dipping her bucket in the sump again.

"Yes!"

With a grin, Arun realized that Xin wasn't losing, she was winning! She had paced herself. Her opponent had started off in a frantic burst of energy but had tired so much that she was visibly exhausted. Xin would carry on like a robot until she won.

Minute by minute, bucket by bucket, Xin came back from the brink to draw level with her opponent. And then claw her way into the lead.

"Thank Horden."

Arun looked up. That had been Zug's voice.

Following Zug's gaze to the wall-screens, Arun saw Springer splash up and down with glee in her compartment. She was grinning so wildly that her dimples were dark pits.

"Yes!" Arun punched the air in triumph.

Instantly, he realized something was wrong. A stony silence had replaced the jubilation around him. The guys were all staring at him.

Del-Marie was out of his seat advancing toward Arun.

It was like a bad dream. Arun couldn't quite believe this was happening.

"Give me that!" snapped Del-Marie.

He snatched the softscreen out from Arun's hands, the screen that showed Xin battling her opponent. Del paraded the screen around the squad, holding it aloft like a trophy.

Arun blushed with shame.

Del-Marie pointed up at the screen where Springer was bouncing up and down in delight. "There," he said. "There! That's Springer. You should be paying her attention. She is ours. You are hers. Frakking imbecile! You look at this cheap vulley-flit instead?"

"She's not a…" Arun stopped. Defending Xin wasn't going to help.

"Arun, it's not all right." Zug spoke calmly. Everyone listened. "This is not a small mistake of rudeness. You have let us down. No bulletin from Staff Sergeant Bryant is going to let you off this hook."

"I'm sorry."

"*Oh, I'm sorry*," echoed Del-Marie sarcastically. "Sorry isn't good enough."

"I swear, lance corporal," insisted Arun. "I promise I'll always put my squadmates first, in front of any… distractions outside of the section."

Del-Marie held Arun's gaze, but then he looked away, probably thinking of Bernard, his boyfriend from Beta Section. Where would Del's loyalties lie if pushed?

Osman joined in. "If you and Xin were an item," he said, "then it would be different. Slightly. But you aren't. She's just a vulley-dream. Come on, man, she's way out of your league. Time to grow up a little. Swear you'll put us before her."

"I already did."

"Then do it again."

"I will put my squad before Xin. I do so swear. On my honor and the honor of the Marine Corps."

The icy tension melted a little.

Zug got out of his chair and came over to Arun. He shook his hand, bent over and kissed him on both cheeks.

Zug sometimes claimed doing this was his cultural imperative because he was French. At other times, he admitted he did this to wind people up.

This time he kissed Arun to whisper a message in his ear. "I am still your friend. Make sure it stays that way."

Chapter 17

At 13:00 hours, after a session at the firing range where he'd scored second best in the squad, Arun grabbed a bike from the Spineway B on Level 4 and cycled on his way to another meeting with the alien scribe.

At Helix 6 a thought struck him as he started coasting down to Detroit's lowest depths. This was their sixth talkie-talkie session and the Troggie scribe was showing no signs of growing bored. The opposite, if anything. And that meant they weren't going to end any time soon.

Referring to the creature as 'The Trog' was getting really old.

It was time Arun named his alien.

Arun laughed. He had no doubt that his Trog already had a name, but it was bound to come in the form of a smell or chemical signal. Asking for the scribe's name would have been met with one of those condescending speeches about how humans were stunted little creatures with no sense of smell, and such a limited concept of the world around them that it was a wonder they could get from one day to the next without accidentally killing themselves.

Arun was so lost in lists of candidate names that he'd picked up more speed than he realized. When the ramp curled round into the top of Level 8, he had to swerve suddenly to avoid hitting an assault tank on its side with the grav sleds off. The team of Hardits repairing the tank hurled abuse at Arun as he sped past, narrowly avoiding hitting one of the stupid monkey-creatures who was too engrossed in an engine diagnostic screen to look up.

Before he disappeared around the bend, Arun lifted up out of the saddle and mimed farting at the Hardits. Like the Trogs, the primary sense of this other alien species was smell, so he reckoned that was the best way to communicate his feelings to the Hardits in their own language.

It was only being polite really.

Judging by the roars of rage, Arun's message was received and understood.

Arun whistled cheerfully as he followed the tunnel round and round getting deeper with every turn. The helixes were the only route down for heavy equipment. If there was a major logistics operation going on in Helix 6, then Arun would be warned by the status map mounted on the walls at regular intervals. But today the helix was almost deserted. Being by himself for a short while was such a luxury that he decided it made up for missing the chow time that his comrades would be tucking into right now. By the time he got back, he'd only have the chance to grab a few scraps. And by then his squad would be going up the orbital elevator for an afternoon session of dropboat training. Another training session missed.

But Arun wasn't going to let that bother him today. This was the first time he'd ever cycled to these depths. Normally he met the Trog via one of the main surface entrances of the nest, in the forest to the southeast of Detroit. Today he was going to meet through the connection between the lowest level of Detroit and the nest.

Until last week he had no idea that the human base joined up with the nest. How many more secrets were waiting to be revealed?

Arun turned his mind back to his naming task. How about *Whistler*? Arun rolled the name around his mind, trying it out. He liked the idea: whistling was something only humans could do. It didn't sound right, though.

How about *Bike*? No. *Peddler*?

People said that bicycles were an entirely human invention, one that annoyed the Hardits in particular, given their specialism in technology and engineering. Mining human creativity was the reason Earth had been nurtured for millennia before being fought over and eventually forced into the Trans-Species Union under the sponsorship of the White Knights. Technologically speaking, humanity was a million years or more behind the most advanced of their neighbors, but that also meant they didn't have a million years of precedent saying what works and what does not, stifling the ability to view old problems from an entirely new angle. Or so people said. But people said a lot of things that might be complete hokum, as Gupta might say. Still, it made for a good story.

But Peddler didn't sound right either. The name sounded like a guy he knew from Dog Company: Pedro.

Peddler. Pedro.

The connection was obscure, and it was dumb. But it was dumb in a human way and that was what Arun was after. Pedro it would be.

"What did you call me?" The scribe spiraled both antennae, thrusting one forward and the other back. Arun recognized this as an expression of bemusement.

"I called you Pedro."

"Why?"

"Because that is your new name."

"But why? Why Pedro? What does it mean?"

Arun shrugged. "Why does it have to mean anything? It's just a name. Your name."

"You mean that Pedro is neither descriptive nor has a functional purpose, such as to denote rank or role? The name is a product of pure whimsy?"

Arun rolled his eyes. Pedro could over-complicate the simplest things. "Yeah, that's what I just said, Pedro. It's a frakking name. Don't any of you overgrown bugs have names?"

Pedro touched one antenna to Arun's shoulder. "No one in our nest has a name. We only have… *designations*, I guess you would call them. Just as you name and number the passageways and chambers of your tunnels. I cannot express how pleased this makes me. To be given a name is a great honor."

"Hold on. If none of you guys have names. How come it's a great honor to be given one?"

Pedro did that annoying gesture where he folded over his antennae in a loose approximation of human shoulders and then shrugged them. "Because I have decided that this is so. *My house. My frakking rules.*"

"You what? Are you quoting me?"

"I often repeat your phrases, though do not seem to recognize this."

"Figures."

Pedro rose on all six legs and skittered around in a circle making sudden little leaps in the air as he did. He'd explained once that this was his way of burning off dangerously high levels of excitement.

Even armed with that explanation, Arun couldn't help but be very conscious of the excitable creature's bulk even if it was bounding around playfully. Pedro must weigh upwards of 300 pounds. If he slipped and fell on top of Arun there would be badly broken bones, and broken Marine cadets were not worth the trouble of fixing.

Arun fiddled with the pheromone emitter dangling around his neck. Pedro had organized delivery of the emitter to Arun's hab-disk, with a note explaining that this made him smell like a nest sibling. Without the device, the Trogs defending their nest entrance would have killed him.

He needn't have worried. Despite the chaotic appearance of Pedro's little dance, the alien never once lost his footing. Arun suspected that the tiniest detail of his over-excitement dance was perfectly choreographed in advance, a pattern stored in its memory ready for use. They were obsessive about the details of life these Trogs.

Pedro halted abruptly and turned to stare at Arun. "With this name, you have assigned a gender to me. Do you believe that has significance?"

"I *know* it has no significance. It's you who are obsessed with sex."

"I see."

"*I see*? What in Horden's name is that supposed to mean?"

"You say more than you know, friend McEwan. Sometimes your subconscious tells me more than you consciously say. That's how I learn so much from you."

"Sure. Well I'm glad to be so transparent. Tell me, Pedro, what do you want me to reveal subconsciously today?"

"Today I want to hear about a day in the life of a human Marine cadet."

"*A day in the life*. You've been reading human books again, haven't you?"

Again with the shrugging antennae.

Arun sighed. "Get me some water, will you? I have long days. Better get my throat lubed up if you want to hear about them."

Pedro scuttled over to the water dispenser.

These sessions with Pedro had so inured Arun to the bizarre that he was only just starting to appreciate how weird this new room was. He recorded images through his eyes while Pedro was busy at the water dispenser – the same kind that was dotted around the human areas of the base. The Troggie tunnels were dark, but this room was brightly illuminated with red-tinged lamps. Arun was sitting in a swiveling sofa chair, deeply padded and covered in red faux leather. It looked brand new. Hung on the walls and ceiling were framed photographs of cadets. Arun was in most of the photos. All of Delta Section were there too. So was Xin. He wasn't going to ask why Xin was there. He'd never mentioned her, had he?

"Do you like this chamber?"

"It's... I don't know. I guess it's a good attempt to make me feel–" he glanced at Xin's photo– "I don't know what exactly, but it makes me feel *something*."

"Ahh. I see you like the photograph of your beloved."

"My be-*what*?"

"Your beloved. The female you love."

"She is not my beloved."

"Correction. Ah, but your language is so messy. It is a minefield. This female is not one you are loving but one you wish fervently that you *shall* love in the future. You are in love but not..."

Pedro paused to regroup. Arun felt his face flush, caught precariously between anger and laughter.

"Let me rephrase," said Pedro. "That Xin is one hot chick." *That last sentence sounded suspiciously like it had been sampled from Arun's voice pattern.* "I guess you'd love a piece of her action." *So did that.*

The problem about Pedro, Arun decided, was that his face was an impassive mask. He couldn't help but feel Pedro was laughing at him from behind that mask. Whenever the conversation touched anything sensitive or awkward, Arun just wanted to punch the alien to wipe the hidden smirk off its face, even though that was a totally dumb thing to wish for, given that Pedro was physically incapable of smirking.

Arun stepped back from confrontation. It wouldn't help. That it wouldn't help just made Arun want to hit Pedro even more and that made him feel... feel that he'd rather Barney was there for a little advice and maybe a sedative too.

"You got those words out of movies and TV shows, didn't you?"

"Correct."

"Do me a favor," he told Pedro, "don't mention anything about girls again. You're just annoying when you do. Anyway, if you know all this stuff, why do you need me? I sometimes think you know more about humans that I do. What's the point of these chit-chats anyway?"

"Because…" Pedro twisted his body into something approximating an S-shape. It probably meant something profound. "Because I have read facts about humans. This is not the same as *understanding* your species. The distinction could become vital one day. Our future may present opportunities for cooperation."

Yup! There we have it, thought Arun. *Those stupid hints that I'm meant to be a messiah or freedom fighter or something.* He bit down on saying the words aloud, remembering that Pedro had gone to the trouble of meeting him in a mothballed orbital platform to escape the surveillance that permeated Detroit. After that first meeting, Pedro had never again hinted that there could be ways to live other than as slaves.

He laughed instead, noticing the manic edge to the sound, but why should he care if a dumb insect heard it? Depending on who you talked to, Arun was too soft, too much of a worrier, or just too much of a loser to be a proper Marine. Well, his emotions might have run wild recently, but he was no coward.

No one had ever accused him of being sensible either.

"Am I special?" Arun asked. *There, he'd said it.* And somewhere an AI would hear and record his words. "Is there something special I'm supposed to do? Is there something unique about me, Arun McEwan?"

Pedro pointed his antennae at Arun and then stood motionless and silent for a good minute. He might be a dumb insect, but he was perfectly capable of making Arun feel dumber.

"We are all unique individuals, Arun McEwan." The insect's artificial voice was so quiet it was barely audible.

"Unique? Horden's Organs, you dumbchuck, you're a *hive creature*. A drone. Uniqueness is an alien concept that you're trying to learn from me."

"I see I have upset you," said the scribe. "I apologize."

The alien wandered around for a while. The movement looked confused and aimless. It probably wasn't, but Arun had no idea what it meant.

When he was done, Pedro clambered onto a shelf carved into one dirt wall. Dim orange lamps were directed at the shelf. Basking in the resulting heat was probably a sensual pleasure. Arun had no way of knowing for sure without asking and he wasn't about to do that. The session had already edged too close to the borders of friendship.

"Tell me about a day in your life," said the scribe.

"You mean like an itinerary?"

"Sure. However you want to do it is fine. Then I'll tell you about my day. Shoot."

"Okay. Well, we wake at midnight. That's the end of First Sleep. We're woken gently. Basically, a switch in our heads is turned on by our internal clocks. We might take a leak, have a slurp of drink, but basically we put on our training cap, check it's attached properly and that we've inserted our suit AI chip. Then we go back to sleep."

"This sleep-training cap – what does it teach you?"

"Well, I don't actually know, seeing as I'm asleep at the time. I seem to know a lot of facts that I never learned in class or read in a book. I mean, we'll be training on a new weapon and I'll know burst radius, recoil strength, ammo variants and all that stuff, and yet I've never seen that kind of gun before. What else the caps do, we can only guess. Probably makes us super-brave and ultra-loyal to the White Knights."

"I expect that is correct."

Arun thought about that. He'd been joking, but he didn't think Pedro was. "So that's Second Sleep," he continued, "where they fill our brains with something. Then at 05:00, there's a buzzer sounds in our dorm. Doesn't give you any option but to be awake. I mean, if there were any corpses interred beneath the floor of our dorm then we'd know about it, because they would rise from the dead to complain about the noise."

"And who do you sleep with?"

"Hey! I thought I told you to keep off that topic."

"I have not gone *on* that topic. You have a dormitory, which I understand to be a separate room inside a habitation disk. Your hab-disk is designated 6/14 and houses Charlie Company and Dog Company from 8th battalion, 412th Marines. Is it always the same individuals who sleep in that dorm?"

"Oh, I see. Yeah. Now that we've graduated from the crèche to be full cadets, we get to live in a hab-disk and the dorm members are fixed, far as I know. Two fire teams make a section and it's one section per dorm. That's eight cadets. Me, Springer, Zug, Brandt, Majanita, Osman, Del-Marie and Cristina."

Pedro seemed satisfied, so Arun carried on: "It's quite relaxed first thing. The hab-disk has its own gym and firing range. So we stretch and work out – enough to get fit but not to tire us out before the day has started. Then we wash dress and clean ourselves ready for inspection between 07:00 and 07:30."

"You clean yourselves with water?"

"Sure we do. Why? What do you use to clean yourselves with?"

"Dirt. We sweat out toxins and scrub away by burying through dirt."

"Lovely. Don't you still smell?"

"We like to smell. We are our smell."

"O-kay. Anyway. Yeah, we have showers dotted around the disk. There's five of them. You can fit about ten people in each shower, twelve if you squeeze together. Sometimes you have to. It can get real busy at peak times."

"And these showers, males and females share the same facilities?"

"What is it with you? You're sex-obsessed."

"Possibly. Remember, my species has no genders. If smell defines my people, I think gender defines yours. This gender distinction is so fundamental to your species and yet completely absent from mine. How can we be so different? I do not understand this yet."

The insect made a good point. But how could Arun explain to someone who has no gender the horseplay that went on at the top and tail of a cadet's day? About how they were given license to let off a little steam? How dorm mates might vacate their dorm to give a couple ten minutes of privacy?

"It's different," Arun said. "In the showers, I mean. At other times, taking clothes off can be a big deal, but everyone has to get clean first thing and have their protective spray. It's mandatory. You get on with it. It's no big deal." That wasn't always strictly true, but it would do for an explanation. "Anyway, your idea of gender and sexual attraction is too simplistic. It isn't just a question of males liking girls and vice versa."

"What? You have more genders? Fascinating. Please elaborate… No, on second thoughts, leave that for another session. Please continue with your typical day."

Arun shrugged. "Like I said, inspection is 07:00 to 07:30. We stand by our racks – which I guess you could call single-occupancy sleep pods. Our kit cabins are open. Everything is stripped clean, assembled, washed. Absolutely perfect. Of course, on most days an instructor doesn't come to inspect us. There aren't enough of them to go around. But we have to be ready just in case. Same goes for evening inspection between 21:00 and 21:30."

"Thank you," said Pedro. "I have two more questions. Firstly, how much time do you have to yourselves in the evening?"

"Well, depends what we got to do. Inspection ends 21:30. We're supposed to in bed by 25:00 hours and sleep all the way through the remaining five hours until midnight at 30:00 hours. That's three and a half hours to ourselves. We don't just goof around, though. Some of us practice for Scendence. Sometimes we meet up with seniors from our battalion who will help teach and train us. Our merit points help determine their Cull status, you see?"

"I do. Thank you. Final question. Who prepares food for you?"

"Well, the Aux of course. They do all the cooking and cleaning. Maintenance too. That sort of stuff."

"And these auxiliaries are lower caste humans, yes?"

Arun was about to deny that humans were so primitive as to have castes or a class system. The words caught in his throat when he thought of how he treated the Aux. He always tried to be polite, he supposed, but there was never any doubt in his attitude that he knew he was better than any Aux.

And from the vast majority of other cadets the best the Aux could hope for was indifference. Petty cruelty was more common because most cadets seemed to have had compassion bred out of them. They felt intense loyalty but struggled with the concept of kindness. And since the Aux were not part of their units, they might as well be aliens. Try as he might, Arun struggled to be so cold hearted. That made him a freak.

Before Arun could form an answer, Pedro announced, "I must go now. I apologize for my abrupt departure. I am called away and cannot ignore the summons. I have a request, though. Please learn the name of one of your auxiliaries before our next meeting."

Pedro leaped from his shelf and raced away as if his life depended on it. Perhaps it did. There could have been a major cave in with thousands dead already, but not the smallest fragment of emotion could ever enter Pedro's artificial voice.

As he headed back up to the human levels, Arun silently cursed Pedro. How had the alien guessed that Arun didn't know the name of a single Aux?

Chapter 18

384th Detroit Scendence Championships.
Day 2 – Practice Match

Arun was no xeno-linguist, which wasn't surprising, given there wasn't much call for that skill. If an alien was on your side then the Jotun officers could communicate with the xeno if necessary. For all other aliens, you didn't talk to them; all you had to do was aim your SA-71 and squeeze the trigger.

The only thing he knew about alien languages was that Jotuns used bifurcated nouns – a way of describing things from two perspectives. Zug said it came from the hexapeds having two pairs of hands.

Arun thought bifurcated nouns were an example of woolly thinking. Most humans agreed. But the Jotuns were in charge so they got to name the Scendence contests using their fussy nouns anyway. Equally naturally, the humans usually ignored this and simplified to a single noun.

So the contest of Deception-Planning was usually described as 'Deception' because most matches involved bluff and trickery. But sometimes – as with Arun's first match for Moscow Express – the planning side came to the fore.

After Madge had let him join, Arun was desperate to make a good showing – maybe that would raise his reputation off the deck in the eyes of his comrades?

He'd been taken to one of the tech labs in the Level 5 novice school where he'd faced a G-1 cadet from the 420th Marines whose shrapnel scars to her face gave her a grim appearance.

Their challenge was to plan blockade-running logistics to resupply a besieged planet until it grew strong enough to free itself from blockade. A range of ships was available to each player, each with varying characteristics such as troop-carrying capacity, build time, cruising speed, fuel consumption, nimbleness to evade the blockade, and firepower to blast a way through. The game AIs handled all the simulation mechanics – combat, random hazards, the success of crash landings other such factors – letting the Scendence players concentrate on planning the logistical operation.

Arun concentrated everything on massive troop carriers loaded with defensive fighter squadrons to protect the carriers and their main cargo: great clouds of single-use dropboats loaded with troops and supplies.

The carriers took such a long time to build that his opponent had already made two blockade-running missions to her beleaguered planet before Arun's carriers even reached his. Once there, his boats suffered a brutal 90% casualty rate as they passed through the blockade. And while his Scendence opponent's ships had degraded her enemy's defenses, Arun's had barely touched his, being all about evading rather than blasting a way through.

The 420th supporters watching the Scendence feeds were jubilant, the 412th's disappointed… except for Blue Squad, Charlie Company, 8th battalion. Some of Arun's squad had lost confidence in him as a Marine, but as a Scendence player they knew him too well to give up hope.

Blue Squad was right. Arun himself soon grew confident that victory would be his.

Although his troopship carriers took a long time to build, they didn't need rebuilding – they simply returned home to load the next cargo of cheap-to-build dropboats and the infinite supply of troops, who had no cost or build time. His opponent's fleets were single use, a replacement having to be built each time from scratch.

The key to victory was to exploit the abundance of his virtual Marines by spending their lives freely. Arun repeatedly flooded the blockade with such swarms of dropboats that enough survivors and their supplies got through to rapidly bolster the planet's defenders. It didn't take many waves before the game AI announced that his besieged forces had counter-attacked against the blockade, wiping it from orbit.

He'd won!

Arun allowed himself a smile when his overwhelming victory was announced.

Normally he would leap up and punch the air. But this time he felt dirty. There was a cruel parallel between the cheapness of his virtual soldiers' lives and those of the flesh and blood slaves bred to fight for the Human Marine Corps.

Still, a victory was a victory. And winning was all that counted.

The moment he entered the battalion mess hall after the game, a ragged cheer went up. Then he was surrounded by cadets wanting to slap him on the back, hug him, ruffle his hair or kiss him. After the mess in the tunnels, being mobbed as a hero felt so damned good.

It only took a few seconds for the mob to thin out and then disappear, revealing the cold truth: Arun had only ever had a handful of well-wishers. Most of 8th battalion was watching him with stony indifference or outright hatred. Gods! He hadn't seen many cadets outside of Blue and Gold Squads since he'd seen Little Scar – since his battalion had been demoted into the Cull Zone.

It didn't take a genius to work out whom most people blamed for that.

"Hey, well done on your game," called a female voice from behind. "I saw it all. An impressive performance."

Arun was grateful for any sign of support. "Thanks, pal. I do my best to…" *That voice!*

He stopped, turned around, and stared into Xin's face.

"Thing is…" Xin cast her eyes to the ground. She looked really uncomfortable. "Thing is, you're a whole lot better than the Deception player in my team."

Arun's reply was simply to gawp, too stunned to speak.

"Yeah, not too good on the vocabulary. I get that sometimes. But I studied your record. You've got good form."

"Well, yes, thank you. I wouldn't say I'm better than your teammate, but thanks. I saw you too. I think you're amazing."

"Oh, man. Don't go all twinkle-eyed on me. This is difficult enough as it is."

Arun chewed over her words, but he still couldn't make sense of them.

"Yeah. Lack of intelligence noted too, buddy. Still, you've got those plus points. And that's why I want you on my team."

"You… but… I can't. I'm already in the Moscow Express team."

"D'uh! I just saw you, remember?"

"Corporal Majanita has only just cooled down enough to let me on the team. I can't leave them."

"Yes, you can. *Can't* is a word only used by losers. Now, *won't* is a word I'd accept, but can't is too pathetic for my ears to process."

Arun tried not to think too hard because he knew he'd hate himself for what he was about to say. "All right, Xin, I *won't*. I won't join you, much as I would dearly love to under any other circumstances, because… Well, you gotta see it my way. I can't let my squadmates down."

Xin gave a curt nod. "Fair enough. But will you at least do me a favor? Let me get you a drink and you give me five minutes of your time, because I've a couple of reasons to change your mind. If you still say no after that, then…" she shrugged sinuously. "No dramas. I won't ask again. Will you do that for me?"

Arun had the feeling he was getting conned here. Xin was dancing rings around him. Zug would know what to say. So would Springer, but Arun's usual way out of this sort of situation was to walk away or punch the person leading him a merry dance.

But with Xin, none of those were options.

"Hey, guys!" Xin was waving at some G-1 cadets sitting by the listening station, a zone of comfy chairs where ancient Earth music was beamed into stripped down battlesuit helmets modified for comfort.

A few minutes ago, Arun had felt like a hero in the making. Now, as he sat waiting for Xin, he felt like a child being bossed around by an adult. Or a bullying older child.

It wasn't long before Xin returned with a couple of drinks in cornboard cups.

Arun took his and drank half in one go. It was a grainer: rich, smooth and cool. He didn't recognize the flavor Xin had dialed up, but it was spicy enough to give a real kick but not enough to overcome the refreshing smoothness of the malt drink.

"It wasn't my idea to call ourselves Team Ultimate Victory. Frakking dumb name if you ask me, but do you think we'll live up to that name, McEwan?"

"Yes." He nodded. "You're superb, Xin. I don't think I've seen anyone play as well as you."

"It's not all about me, McEwan. Let me put it a simpler way. Do you think we'll reach the last sixteen and Cull immunity?"

"No," he said and immediately studied her face for a reaction. He'd given the right answer, he judged. "Too many weak points in the team," he added. "You'll come up against a team with no weak players and then you'll lose."

Xin grimaced. "You're right." Her leg started jerking up and down. Was she nervous?

Arun looked into her face. She looked unsure of herself. Other than that time after the tunnels, he'd only really seen her from a distance or through a camera feed. She'd always looked so perfectly beautiful, so fired up with determination that he thought of her more like an unstoppable force of nature than a flesh-and-blood girl. Seeing her up close like this… he wanted to stroke her straight black hair away from her face, look into those dark eyes, and tell her everything would be all right.

He didn't. Of course, he didn't. How could he when his hands were enormous clumsy lumps resting on his lap, barely capable of holding his drink cup? His tongue wasn't much more nimble, but his mind must have kept some of its sharpness because he found himself finishing off the implications of what he'd just said – *what Xin had led him to say.*

"And I would rate Moscow Express about the same," said Arun. "We won't win immunity either. So what you're proposing is to merge the strongest members of each team. That way we win more merit points for the battalion and start the climb out of the Cull Zone. We might just win immunity for ourselves too. That is what you're proposing, isn't it?"

"Congratulation, McEwan. You're not as dumb as you look. Don't you agree that playing in my team makes the most sense?"

"In terms of cold logic? Yes, I suppose it does. But there are other things beyond logic. Morale, loyalty. They count too."

"That's easy for you to say, McEwan. You're only G-2, this is only just becoming real to you. I'm a year further ahead. The Cull is much closer to reality for me. Much too close."

"Okay, I get that." Arun shuddered. He remembered the softscreen Little Scar had showing the last Cull of the 412th. The looks of resentment on everyone's faces. The dignified silence of the victims made even more poignant by the few who screamed for mercy. But there was no mercy in Arun's world.

"I can see you do," said Xin kindly. She laid her hand on his thigh. "I've witnessed a Cull too, don't forget. We see one at the end of every year." She shuddered, almost retching. "I don't want to be on the sharp end of one, but I don't think my class can escape the Cull Zone. The climb is too high."

"No one does," said Arun. "But I can't see my Moscow teammates going along with your idea. Do you think you can convince your team to bring me in?"

"Team? What team? Olmer quit. And without her, Pardi's thinking about walking too. I reckon I can persuade Lindet to stay, but I need reasons. You are reason number one."

Arun shook his head. The way Del-Marie had reacted after he'd been caught out watching Xin instead of Springer – he didn't even want to even think about how they would react if told them he was joining Xin's team.

"Hey! I'm still here," snapped Xin. "Stop thinking. It's not your strong point."

"Easy!"

Xin sighed. "I'm disappointed. That's all. I thought you'd like to spend more time with me."

"Well, yes of course."

"But you won't even consider my suggestion."

"Well, I–"

"All you need to do is play just one round with us. Then we'll see where we go from there. Just one. It's not much to ask and I'll make it worth your while… you *do* like me, don't you?"

"Like you? I do, I…"

"Oh, for frakk's sake, dunkchunk. When I say, *like*, I'm not talking about modest affection. Let me spell it out. You find me desirable. I find your Scendence talents to be desirable. Let's make a fair exchange."

"No. I can't."

"*Can't*. There's that loser word again. Won't is just as dumb in this case. Listen up, twinkle eyes, if I don't win immunity, I might wind up dead. And, oh, let's think for a moment… A year later, so might you. Bundle up all those soppy love tales you read as a kid, and fire a tac-nuke at them, 'cos this is the adult world you're living in now. I'm not some frakking fairytale princess. I'm not the villain either. I'm just a flesh and guts girl who wants to live long enough to get off this planet and I'll do whatever it takes to survive that long."

"Horden's Children! You're so romantic."

"Romantic? Listen up, McEwan, you'd better sort your drent out fast if you believe in frakking *romance*. Dumb veck. Romance is for... I don't know. People in stories, I suppose. Real people on Earth, even. We're not real people, McEwan. Don't you get that? We're slaves, you dongwit. Some of us are Culled every year. If we survive that, we'll die anyway, fighting out there in the void, warring on behalf of those skangat White Knights who probably don't exist anyway. But that doesn't matter anyway because I'll take my chances in any war. All I'm focused on right now is living long enough to earn my chance to die out there."

In the multitude of conversations with Xin that Arun had dreamed of, there had always been at least an undercurrent of steamy romance, often more like a flood to be honest. All he felt now was pity mixed in with disgust.

He felt mostly pity for Xin.

And mostly disgust at himself because he was actually thinking of joining her.

But then he pictured the disappointment on Springer's face.

"No," he said. He'd had to drag the word out but now he'd turned her down... he felt relief.

Xin cast him a withering look that made him feel two inches tall. She sniffed disdainfully. "There's a chance that if you do exceptionally well, your G-2 class might escape the Cull. For my class that chance is vanishingly small. I will be up for a 1 in 10 chance of being put to death. I have that hanging over me and why? Not from anything I've done. It's not my fault." She leaned in closer. "But it is yours."

Arun shook his head. "That's not fair."

"You're damned right it's not fair. Doesn't mean it isn't true. You put me in this situation, McEwan." She gripped his face, forced him to look her in the eye. "You owe me, man."

Arun's world blurred.

He'd heard that some Marines had been altered to allow messages and mood-altering hormonal packages to be passed through skin contact.

Gifting they called it. Perhaps Xin had gifted him. Maybe the hurt, disappointment and vulnerability she'd beamed through her dark eyes had enchanted him. Or perhaps he was simply weak willed.

Whatever she'd done, or he'd allowed her to do, Arun's mind shifted someplace else for a moment, a place he recognized: a noisy world of whirring brass cogs and hot oil where the planner part of his mind was yelling at him to join her. When he blinked and found himself back in the 8-412th's mess hall he realized he'd done it. He'd agreed to join Xin.

"I'll help out," he added hastily. He paused. Gods, his head hurt. "But only because you're in my battalion. I don't want your… your *bribes*. And I don't buy your guilt trip."

"You're a cold fish," Xin sneered.

"*Me?*"

"Yeah, whatever." She flashed a smile that was undeniably beautiful but so too was the void: cold, airless, and bathed in lethal radiation, but still beautiful.

He shuddered.

"Welcome to the team, Alan," she said.

"Arun. I'm *Arun*."

"If you say so, twinkle eyes. Next team training session is tomorrow 21:55 hours in hall 5B. Don't be late and… hey, good luck telling your friends."

That was it. Xin had finished with him and walked off, quickly disappearing in the crowd, and leaving Arun lost in dark thoughts.

Darkest of all: how *was* he going to tell his friends?

Chapter 19

No training was scheduled for Scendence Days. If you weren't competing yourself, you would be cheering on your buddies from parade halls and lecture theaters given over to Scendence and a dozen other lesser sports and shows. After laughing at your buddy up on one of the stages giving a hopeless attempt at conjuring tricks, she might get her own back by trashing you at a game of petanque. Everyone joined in the fun, because enjoying these Marine holidays was not a privilege, it was an order.

After agreeing to join Xin's team, Arun tried to lose himself in the fun going on all around him. He couldn't. He was like a ghost at his own funeral: desperate to connect with his friends in ways taken for granted in life but now impossible.

Eventually, he slipped away to the shooting range, reasoning that he'd participated enough in the Scendence events not to get into trouble.

As soon as he picked up the SA-71, he knew coming here had been the right thing to do. The feel of the carbine close to his shoulder was a comfort, the railgun his most reliable friend who never judged him. He needed this. As he put round after round into the plastic targets thrown in random arcs by the range AI, every target hit made him feel better. Made him feel like he was good Marine material, despite all the drent going on. When he was inside his battlesuit, Barney did most of the aiming. Here in the range, without his suit AI, Arun was still a crack shot.

Detroit's layout was divided up by the four regiments of Marines based there. There was no rule to say you had to stick with your own regiment, but strolling into another regiment's territory wasn't something to do lightly. Arun was banking on Scendence Day being different. Humor was good, rules relaxed. Arun decided he couldn't spend the rest of the day at his range and so drifted across the border into the 420th's section of Detroit. He kept clear of the Scendence halls and visited immersion training suites, a library and even spent quiet time in one of the temples, trying to figure out what the hell was messing up his head and making him do crazy things.

Night came. The light in the tunnels and rooms changed, losing its UV content and taking on a ruddy glow. With no clear insights into why he kept inviting trouble, just a wasted afternoon, Arun wandered back to his dorm in hab-disk 6/14.

Everyone stopped and stared when he walked in. He wouldn't have felt more of an outsider if he'd walked into a random dorm in another regiment's hab-disk.

"Where have you been, man?" asked Osman.

"And why?" added Del-Marie.

Arun took a deep breath and then told them everything. He tried to explain how he had this premonition that he needed to be close to Xin and close to her Scendence team. It wasn't so much that he was leaving Moscow Express, he explained, more a merger of both teams.

The others greeted this with jeers and heads shaken with disappointment. Even to Arun his words sounded more feeble excuse than explanation.

Frakk them! I'm a Marine cadet. I don't give up.

"Hey!" he protested. "Don't give me that drent. It's not like I've joined a team from another battalion. Is it? Well, is it?" He dared them to deny the truth. But most of his comrades were already turning away.

"Xin's part of our battalion," he said. "Our scores are pooled each year. If her Scendence team scores well, it helps to keep all of us from getting Culled just as much as it does her and the G-1 companies."

"That's not the point," said Zug. "We're squad buddies. You let us down. Again. When we're in the field and get in a tight spot, we must rely on each other. Trust. Teamwork. And you've just taught us that we can't rely on you."

"But, Zug…"

With his voice of perfect calm and reason, Zug delivered his damning verdict. "No, Arun. I've nothing more to say to you." Every pair of eyes in that room was trained on Arun and Zug. Calmly, Zug picked up a softscreen, and opened it to the book he was reading. Arun recognized the title. It was an ancient work of political philosophy called *Two Treatises of Government*. Only last month, he'd discussed with Zug what kind of world its author, John Locke, had inhabited. Now that easy friendship of many years had vaporized.

Not you too, Zug! Arun had come prepared for a shouting match with Madge and Springer, perhaps Del-Marie who took a lot to anger but had a volcanic temper once roused. Arun might not have changed anyone's opinion of him, but he would have given as good as he got.

But Zug was so calm, so reasonable. So *final*. Arun had no defense against that. All the fight went out of him. Since birth he'd had drilled into him that no plan survives contact with the enemy. He hadn't expected such a practical demonstration in his dorm of all places.

Once again he felt like a ghost at his own funeral. Only one person looked at Arun as if he still lived: Springer.

"Get it over with," he said as she walked his way. "Tell me how much you hate me."

"I don't hate you, Arun."

"Really?" Arun brightened. "Sweet homecoming, Springer. For a moment there…" He shut up when saw the sour look on Springer's face.

"You're an idiot, Arun. But you're my idiot. How could I hate you for being yourself? But disappointment? The universe isn't big enough to contain all the disappointment I feel for what you did. That dirty skangat, Xin, saw what a soft dongwit you are and twisted you around her little finger as if you were one of those pretty ribbons the 420th wear. Let's face it, you have as much backbone as a scrap of ribbon. Xin hasn't one iota of respect for you. You do realize that, right?" She paused to emphasize her point and watch Arun squirm. "You were pathetic today, Arun, but I don't hate you. I hate *her*."

Her words stung. Was she right? No, Arun decided, because she didn't understand the whole picture. To be fair, neither did he. "I'm not sure how it happened. I felt…" What had he felt? He'd already tried to explain the planner part of his brain telling him to do as Xin asked. As excuses went, it stank.

"There is a solution of sorts," said Springer.

He raised an eyebrow.

"I've checked. There's nothing to stop you continuing to play for Moscow Express and play for *her* team too. It's very rare but it's been done before. The game AIs will try to schedule the contests to avoid conflicts.

Springer was beyond wonderful. Arun almost kissed her but stopped himself. She was still too frakked off. Then a dark thought cast a shadow over his hope. "If we did well, the two teams would eventually face each other. I can't compete against myself. What then?"

Springer rolled her beautiful eyes. "Life is strewn with choices that can't be bypassed. Haven't you learned that yet? It's through our choices that we are known."

"I get it. If I want us to stick together, I've got to make the right choice. Is that what you're telling me?"

"No." A faraway look took her. Despite the situation, Arun felt a tingle of excitement as he stared at his only remaining friend. Was he seeing a vision as it possessed her?

The violet color didn't come to her eyes. Instead she sighed and glanced up at him through old eyes that looked as if they'd seen a thousand years pass by.

"Depending on your choices," she said, "I might love you, despise you or tolerate you. But our destiny lies together. I'm certain of that. Good or bad, our futures are entwined. I've seen this many times before."

Arun groaned. Since turning cadet, he'd been threatened, manipulated, had the crap kicked out of him, and had made himself the most hated guy in the 8th battalion. All of that he could deal with, but this talk of destiny was freaking him out.

He never wanted to be a hero.

If Springer's violet visions were right, then that choice wasn't his to make.

Chapter 20

Translation of Annotated Nest Archive
Date: 9519-244
Subject: Interrogation of Human McEwan
Key scents: Conditioning~Marines~drugs~betrayal
Filter Applied: High-value information only

CONTEXT: The human, Arun McEwan, was asked to describe small unit organization and tactics. His answers were of little value. More interesting were his attempts to steer the conversation onto the topic of his relationship with his human nest comrades. The nest scribe decided to permit this deviation, realizing it could provide valuable insights to the suspected brain-altering drug regime secretly imposed at that time on humans entering the 'cadet' phase of their lifecycle.

==INTERROGATION FRAGMENT BEGINS==

HUMAN McEWAN: Don't you think it's an overreaction? All I did was switch teams. I mean, I could understand them getting frakked off, but that was three weeks ago now. That's all! Three frakking weeks and they still act as if… Well, it's as if you'd bitten off your queen's legs and danced on her head.

SCRIBE: You mean the Great Leader.

HUMAN McEWAN: That guy, yeah.

SCRIBE: I understand. You feel your offense is minor but your human nest comrades judge you and your acts as repugnant. Are there other examples where the value that you place on things is very different from your comrades?

HUMAN McEWAN: [Pauses to think while consulting wetware memories. He nods his head. *Interpretation: (93% certainty): indicates agreement.*] No one has fun anymore. Goofing around, joking – it's an important part of human bonding but the only time I've seen my buddies loosen up recently was for Scendence Day. [*Shakes head, looking at floor (91% certainty): indicates sadness*] Even that didn't last long. I asked to keep playing for Moscow Express but Madge wouldn't let me. Last match day, they were knocked out of the competition but I won for Xin's bunch: Team Ultimate Victory. *Team Ultimate Disaster*, more like. Other than Springer, my friends hate me more than ever now.

SCRIBE: Has this been a slow and steady change or a sudden one?

HUMAN MCEWAN: It's grown, but real fast. Everything changed about the same time we made cadet. Maybe a little before.

SCRIBE: And you feel unaffected?

HUMAN McEWAN: [Rolls eyes. *Interpretation: meaning unclear*]. No, it's doing my head in too. I get wildly angry sometimes or feel so low that I whimper in my sleep. I think I'm cracking up. Oh, frakk! Frakk, frakk, frakk! I'm so flekked.

SCRIBE: Is something wrong?

HUMAN McEWAN: Wrong? I've just told you I'm cracking up. That's practically an admission that I'm not fit to be a Marine. I'll be working the mines this time tomorrow.

SCRIBE: You need not fear. The internal security systems monitor for signs of insurrection, not individual performance. We have tested this extensively. You may speak freely to me about your medical concerns.

HUMAN McEWAN: Even if you're wrong about the security stuff... [Sighs. *Interpretation: (97% certainty): indicates acceptance of an unwanted situation*]. I guess I can't make things worse.

SCRIBE: Correct. If I am wrong about the drenting security systems, then you are utterly vulleyed whatever you do.

HUMAN McEWAN: [Sets mouth into 'brittle smile'. *Interpretation: (86% certainty): acknowledgement of humor, comradeship, reasserting anxious state.*]. Good one, Pedro. A little more work on the accent and we'll be able to sneak you into the chow hall and no one will realize you aren't one of us.

SCRIBE: [spirals antennae, indicating acknowledgement of humor] Why don't you tell your medical staff or your human leaders about your concerns?

HUMAN McEWAN: [Shakes head. *Interpretation: (96% certainty) disagreement. Possibly (32% certainty) mild contempt too.*] You don't know much about humans, do you?

SCRIBE: Correct.

HUMAN McEWAN: I know. I know. It's why you want us to have these little chats. I'll try to explain. When your squad goes into danger, knowing your buddies around you are strong helps to keep you strong too. A Marine who wobbles under pressure has the opposite effect. The Corps has no use for a Marine who's going to sit down and start crying because someone is shooting at him. I can't admit my weakness. Majanita and Del-Marie already think I don't fit in anymore.

SCRIBE: If you are truly different, can you really keep this deception for three years until graduation? And beyond, as a Marine?

HUMAN McEWAN: [Shrugs. *Interpretation: (96% certainty) showing disdain for challenges faced*.]. That's something I'll have to find out the hard way. I'm not quitting. Never. That's not an option. Not me at all.

SCRIBE: Is that why you originally agreed to join your comrades' Scendence team, Moscow Express? Did you do this to regain the respect of your comrades?

HUMAN McEWAN: [Shakes head and sighs (*resignation*)] Am I that transparent? Even to an overgrown ant? [Shrugs (*resignation*)] Yes, that's why I agreed to join in. I'm pretty good at playing Deception. Gunnery too, though Madge always wants to take that – I mean, Cadet Corporal Majanita. If I did well, then everyone sees me winning for the team. It worked too, for about ten minutes after I won my first Moscow Express match. Then the madness took me, and I joined Xin's team.

SCRIBE: I am concerned for you, friend McEwan. Your wild mood swings are still unexplained. Are you worried that they will affect your Scendence performance?

HUMAN McEWAN: Not enough to stop me playing.

SCRIBE: [Pauses. Scent signal indicates exasperation that human is failing to connect the probable causes of mental state]. When I first met you, you were singing. Was that an example of your strange mental state?

HUMAN McEWAN: No, that was the… the combat drugs. [Words slowed temporarily during previous sentence. *Interpretation: (82% certainty) intense mental activity limiting speech capability. Conclusion: human has linked combat drugs with continuing mood changes.*] Combat drugs! That's it! They've been pumping combat drugs into us continuously. Low dose. They're meant to keep you focused on fighting, a robot killer. Heightens your sense of loyalty. Everything else in your head is put on standby. That would explain everything. Why I've gone wild and everyone else is a robot. And… [Makes stabbing motion with finger at scribe. *Interpretation: (81% certainty) threat display*]. You knew, didn't you? Go on, deny it!

SCRIBE: I cannot answer that.

HUMAN McEWAN: [Shakes head.] That's not good enough. If you want our talks to continue, it's got to be a two-way thing. I share. You share. We both learn from each other. The colonel will skin me alive if I don't learn anything from you.

SCRIBE: What do you wish to learn, Arun?

HUMAN McEWAN: Did you know I was being drugged?

SCRIBE: [Hesitates. Emits *deliberate falsehood* scent.] No.

HUMAN McEWAN: [Tenses jaw muscles. Narrows eyes. Adopts aggressive stance. *Interpretation: (92% certainty): dominance challenge.* Scribe shows no reaction. Human soon abandons challenge.] Answer me this, then: do you think I'm being drugged by the Corps?

SCRIBE: This topic cannot be discussed.

HUMAN McEWAN: Figures. Thanks, pal. Okay, try this. Suppose, hypothetically, the Corps was giving us combat drugs. Speculate why they might do that.

SCRIBE: This topic cannot be discussed.

HUMAN McEWAN: [Growls. *Interpretation: (99% certainty): threat display.*] Forget everything I've just said. Let's play pretend instead. Suppose traitors wanted to disable the human Marines defending the base through a non-lethal drug. As a cadet faithful to my White Knight masters and their officers, I would want to know how to protect against such an attack. How would I protect myself from being drugged without arousing the suspicions of the traitors?

SCRIBE: You humans have extremely weak natural defenses. I cannot see what you could do. A drug or toxin could be administered through the air, drink, skin contact, food, nanobots. You could be hypnotized to self-administer every night and then forget what you had done.

HUMAN McEWAN: How about you take my blood sample and use what you find to develop an antidote?

SCRIBE: [Twists antennae to indicate moral conflict.] Although I cannot discuss this topic, Arun, I make a solemn vow on the sanctity of the nest – may I be cast beyond the boundary if I break my word. I shall do whatever is in my power to aid you. Even though you might not understand nor like what I shall do, yet shall I aid you.

==INTERROGATION FRAGMENT ENDS==

[Archivist note: Subsequent events tell us that the scribe was faithful to its promise, and correct in its prediction that the human would hate the scribe for what it would do.]

Chapter 21

"This afternoon you're going to learn a little history."

Arun groaned inwardly. With his recent frontline experience, Blue Squad had expected their new veteran sergeant to give an insight to their future as Marines, not backward to someone else's past. Gold Squad was at the lecture too – the two squads often trained together – and looked like they felt the same. What was it to be? Famous battles of the Seventh Frontier War? Dropboat development over the centuries? Camo pants stitching patterns of the ancients?

From behind his lectern, Gupta grinned wolfishly. "I know what you're thinking. Why aren't we sweating in our battlesuits, and shooting the crap out of each other in a training environment? There will be plenty of time for that, but to win, a Marine needs more than equipment and tactics." Gupta tapped his head. "The ultimate key to victory is up here. And it's in your mental attitude that you stink the most. Until I'm satisfied with the way you think, I'm going to share examples from our forebears of what it means to be a good Marine. If any of you feels your time would be better spent capturing flags and laying ambushes for your comrades, please feel free to share your opinion with me. I hear the Aux welcomes volunteers to work the fields or clean out the head. Does anyone want to hear my history lesson?"

All the cadets rose from their desks and came to attention. "Yes, sergeant."

Gupta ignored them for several seconds before acknowledging. "Sit down, shut up, and listen good. Location: Earth. Date: Common Era 1917 through 1921. Subject: The Czech Legion."

There was a noise, a disturbance in the rigid order of the lecture. Arun followed Gupta's glare to Springer. She was writhing on her seat and screwing her face as if someone had rammed a stun rod up her backside.

Gupta ignored her. "Earth was in the grip of a major war," he said. "World War One. Total combatants approximately 70 million. Casualties: 29 million killed, wounded, and missing – and that's ignoring the civilians.

Major political groupings – countries and empires – would collapse during this conflict. This was not a clash of ideology, culture or religion, but really a civil war that raged throughout the continent of Europe, although the fighting spread around the planet. Soldiers were sucked into the European battlefields from major nations on other continents, such as India and the United States.

"I've mentioned civil wars in an earlier lecture. You might think me obsessed. Well, you could be right."

Gupta smiled, which brought hesitant laughter from a few brave cadets. They were still learning the sergeant's ways. Compared to the instructors, he seemed just as strict but more informal, even outspoken.

"Brother shoots brother and bombs mother," continued Gupta. "Civil wars are just about the ugliest episodes in the human story. But that isn't what fascinates me. Civil war usually ends in the destruction of the old certainties and the emergence of something new. Even if the incumbent political authority wins on the battlefield, it is forever changed by the war."

Gupta fixed Arun with a stare. "In your orientation speech I told you Marines sometimes have to suck up the pain and survive for as long as it takes to fight back and win. That wait could last for generations. For those seeking change to the old order, civil wars *are* that chance to strike back, the one opportunity that must be seized with all six limbs."

What was this? Gupta's gaze still wouldn't release Arun.

Gupta spoke slowly and clearly. "The White Knights, for example, are an immensely powerful race, but they are no more a single unified entity than the human race. In fact the opposite is the case. Their fascination with change and mutation makes our masters particularly prone to civil wars."

The sergeant's gaze kept Arun prisoner for another few seconds before turning back to the rest of the cadets.

"Back in our Earth example, two great empires were about to disintegrate in this European civil war: the Hapsburg and the Russian Empires. Just as we humans are one of the many subservient species in the White Knight Empire, so the Hapsburg emperor ruled many distinct cultural and ethnic groupings. His empire had 27 official languages. One of these groups was called the Czechs."

Gupta looked up and stared at the cadets sitting before him. "Let's find which of you worms was paying attention in my last briefing. What often happens before a civil war battle, especially at the beginning of the war?"

Arun watched hands shoot up.

"Yes, Skull?" Gupta nodded at one of the cadets.

Skull was taken by surprise to hear the sergeant use his nickname. "Sergeant, soldiers lose the will to fight. Desertion rates are high."

"Correct. Of course, it depends on the background to the war, and how a soldier came to be recruited in the first place. In many civil wars, not only do individual soldiers desert but entire units go over to the enemy, often murdering their officers in the process."

A sense of danger snuck into the briefing hall. "Our Czech soldiers were mostly unwilling conscripts who felt a far closer cultural affinity to the enemy and only resentment to their ruler, the Hapsburg emperor. Egged on by Russian propaganda promising freedom for the Czechs and their own homeland, entire divisions deserted to the Russian side. Czech soldiers captured by the Russians were housed in prisoner of war camps. These were rich recruiting grounds for Czechs who were prepared to fight on the Russian side. These Czechs fought in their own units but under Russian orders. In their minds they fought for freedom. To the Russians, they were plasma fodder.

"Freedom is an intoxicating idea. It can drive people to extreme acts. Even I have to take care with my words. I don't want us all executed for inciting insurrection."

Arun joined in the nervous laughter, relieved that the sergeant appeared to realize the danger in his words. Gupta's near-treason hadn't gotten them killed yet.

"These turncoat units were organized into the Czech Legion. With a peak strength of about 60,000 in comparison with the Russian Army's total wartime strength of 12 million they would have been nothing more than a historical oddity if not for two things. In 1917, the Russian Empire collapsed and turned its attention to its own civil war. A year later, the Hapsburg Empire imploded and the wider war ended.

"It was as if the sea had suddenly gone out, leaving the Czech Legion stranded inside the largest country in the world. They'd suddenly transformed from a historical footnote to the only large force of disciplined troops in Russia. They were now important. By that time, all sides in the Russian Civil War distrusted the Czechs at best, and in many cases wanted them dead. What did the Czech Legion do?"

Gupta acknowledged one of the hands. It was Alice Belville, the cadet lance sergeant from Gold Squad. "The Czechs fought their way back home, sergeant."

"They did that, Belville. But their route home lay to the west, through the bulk of the forces hostile to them."

Gupta hadn't invited input from the cadets, but Arun found he had his hand up.

"McEwan?"

"They forced a passage to the east, sergeant."

Gupta nodded. "The Trans-Siberian Railway was the longest railroad in the world, running nearly 6,000 miles from the west to the east of Russia. Over the next three years, the Czech Legion forced passage along this railroad before being evacuated by sea from Russia's eastern coast."

Another disturbance made Arun glance to his left. It was Springer again. The wisp of steam over her eyes and water dripping from her nose explained what had happened. She'd never had visions so close together before. Her eyelids must be brutally scorched.

Gupta continued as if nothing was happening. "If they had simply sat in a train carriage and waited to reach their destination they would have been ambushed and wiped out before they'd gone a hundred miles. The Czech Legion became almost a nomadic state, controlling all the stations along the railroad for a hundred miles or so either direction of their force concentration, and the countryside around that stretch. They negotiated with the local people and rival factions in the Russian Civil War for supplies, security and passage. That required great skill, discipline and organization.

"Why do I mention the Czech Legion? They weren't members of the Marine Corps, but I think of them as if they were, because that is exactly how I expect Marines to think and act. So you tell me. What can the Legion teach us about some of the drent you cadets have gotten yourself into recently?"

"Sergeant," asked Majanita, "Did you pick that example because of Cadet McEwan?"

"Interesting. What makes you think I did?"

"The Czech Legion stuck together under stresses that would have crushed most units. They showed tenacity, initiative, cunning, ruthlessness, all those good things, but most of all they are a lesson in sticking together."

Gupta thought for a moment. "I would have chosen the Czech Legion's story in any case, but I did have McEwan's situation firmly in mind."

Arun almost felt he should wilt with embarrassment from the unwanted attention. He didn't. Didn't feel anything at all. For his failings to be dissected and analyzed was becoming an everyday burden.

"So tell me, cadets," said Gupta. "McEwan broke his commitment to play Deception for his squad team so he could play with… individuals from elsewhere in the battalion. How does that relate to the Czech Legion?"

Caccamo from Hecht's Alpha Section answered first. "Sergeant. Because McEwan let his team down. The Czechs didn't. By sticking together, the Legion gives us a lesson to counter McEwan's example."

Gupta frowned. "Stand up, Caccamo!" he barked. "Idiot! The White Knights consider us nothing more than cheap plasma fodder. The Jotuns hold us in higher regard. Only a few nanometers higher, but that's better than nothing. I, on the other hand, expect nothing less than for you to be Marines, the very best of the human race. We are not dumb fodder. The difference between surviving combat and being a casualty statistic is half training, half dumb luck, and half using your initiative to make your own luck."

No one dared to speak.

Gupta continued in a slightly softer tone. "Anyone who thinks I can't add up hasn't been listening properly. So, now, Caccamo. Instead of repeating what Majanita just said, use that withered lump between your ears to think. Why did I pick the example of the Czech Legion?"

"I don't know, sergeant." Arun was impressed at Laban Caccamo for keeping as cool as a cryo box under Gupta's glare.

"Don't know?" bellowed the sergeant. "You're no use to me, Caccamo. Sit down."

Caccamo obeyed.

"Anyone?"

Majanita had a reply. "The Czech unit structure was crushed. Rendered obsolete. Their army no longer existed. Even their country no longer existed. They had only themselves. Maybe…" She clammed up.

"Complete what you started, cadet. A Marine never starts anything they don't intend to see through to completion. You should know that."

"Sorry, sergeant. Maybe the parable's lesson is that the legion re-framed their world. They formed a new unit from the wreckage of the old. New buddies. New loyalties. A new team. They set themselves a new goal and set about achieving it by any means available. By teaming up with cadets outside of Blue Squad, has McEwan forged a new unit for the benefit of the battalion?"

"I don't think we know the answer to that, Majanita. Not yet. Maybe Cadet McEwan is a visionary, reacting to circumstances by creating a Marine Legion to get us out of the Cull. Or perhaps he's nothing more than a teenage boy who couldn't refuse an offer from a pretty girl. I don't care about the answer. I do care that instead of thinking through the possibilities, you all picked the lazy choice by blaming McEwan for disloyalty."

Gupta tapped at his head. "Up here! This is where you're failing me. Being able to see the same situation as everyone else, but see new possibilities within it, is what makes the difference between a good Marine and the kind of half-evolved plasma fodder those other races think we are. Do you want to prove them right?"

"No sergeant!" replied both squads, Arun right up there with the rest.

The sergeant studied his cadets for a few moments. Arun wasn't sure whether the sergeant had just stood up for him. He sure felt inadequate, though.

"I can see from your faces that I've confused the hell out of you." Gupta's scowl lightened. "That's a good thing because your brains need shaking up. You're too robotic. If Blue and Gold Squads were stranded in the midst of a civil war, I would expect you to turn the situation to your advantage, same as the Czech Legion did. That's all for today. Dismissed."

As soon as Gupta had left through the door at the back of the stage, Arun made for Springer.

"What happened?" he asked her. "What was in your vision? Did you have two?"

Springer closed her eyes and shook her head. Her eyelids were brutally red, her eyes bloodshot and watering. "It isn't clear, Arun, more a vague feeling, triggered by certain words."

Majanita put a supportive arm around Springer. "Leave her alone, McEwan."

Osman stood beside her, glaring at Arun. The rest of the section waited nearby.

"No, he needs to know," said Springer. She sounded exhausted. "Arun, you and the Czech Legion are connected. I think… I think that one day you will create a–"

Majanita slapped her hand over Springer's mouth. "Shut up! Don't even think about how that sentence ends."

She doesn't need to, thought Arun. *I help to create a Human Legion. That's what she thinks. Gupta was practically spelling it out. It fits with what everyone has been hinting at all along.*

"Go away," Osman told Arun.

"No," said Arun. "Springer, can I please ask you something? I've never wanted to ask until this moment."

"I said, go away." Osman was shoving him now.

"Let him ask," sighed Springer. "What is it?"

"Your visions of the future," said Arun, grimacing uncomfortably because he didn't know how to put this without insulting Springer. "Have any come true?"

"No."

Arun relaxed. He let Osman give him a last shove and then watched his friends move away without him.

Springer paused and turned around. "But that's the thing about the future," she said to Arun. "It hasn't happened yet. But it will."

She wanted to say more but she choked back and kept silent, as if suddenly noticing the verbal minefield all around her.

The passageway crackled with tension like a G-Max cannon before an x-ray burst.

"We both know it will happen," she said, sounding as if the words were being forced out of her at gunpoint.

Arun didn't say a word. He scarcely dared to breathe. Microphones in the walls, nano-spies floating in the air. No one knew what form the surveillance systems took, but everyone agreed that they were everywhere, feeding through any signs of disloyalty to the Jotuns.

Springer spoke the three words she shouldn't, the name that meant Arun's life could never return to normal. "The Human Legion," she said.

Arun froze, expecting hidden beams of death to strike him down at any moment. There was no cover to shield him, nowhere to run. If the Jotuns decided he should die then his existence would end as surely as night extinguishes day.

But death, if it were coming, was not immediate.

By the time he unclenched, the rest of the squad had ushered Springer out of sight, on their way to the orbital elevator and dropboat training.

Arun raced after them, desperate not to be left alone.

Chapter 22

The trips to see Pedro were worse than useless: they consumed valuable time that Arun could never get back. With graduation to qualify for, and his battalion in the Cull Zone – not to mention the Scendence commitments that were causing so much annoyance – every hour spent away from training was painful.

But Instructor Rekka had taught them that so long as your position was secure from immediate assault, if you were given a task then you should put everything else out of your mind and do that task to the best of your ability.

Sometimes that required an iron will, but Rekka was right.

Out in the field, if you were assigned to dig fox holes or latrines, then you let the perimeter guard worry about intruders and you concentrated on your digging.

And if you were tasked with a friendly afternoon chat with a seven-foot insect, then you put away thoughts of culls and graduation, you put on your most companionable smile, and you talked with the alien.

If he could, Arun would cancel his chats in an instant. Since he couldn't, he took pleasure in this excuse to roam the bustling underground labyrinth that was the Detroit base.

Pedro encouraged Arun to explore, because that way he could ask endless questions about the human levels.

Arun's hab-disk was on Level 6, near Corridor 622 that ran between Helix 62 and Helix 6, which was the main spiraling ramp in his regiment's portion of Detroit. Today, on his meandering route to Pedro, he cycled up the Helix 6 ramp to Level 3. This was a level of barracks and defensive positions. The topology of the base was the same on all levels: Corridor 622 always connected Helix 62 with Helix 6, whatever level you were on. But the route Corridor 622 took to get there was different on every level. Here on Level 3, the corridors zigzagged to prevent a single blast of firepower sweeping the entire corridor of defenders. In the hab-disks you talked of walls and ceilings, but here the tunnel structures were hardened and you had bulkheads and overheads instead. If not for the gravity keeping Arun's bike firmly on the deck, Level 3 could easily be mistaken for a warboat interior.

Level 3 was deserted. That's why Arun loved it here. There were plenty of Marines to fill the barracks and man the hardened alcoves peppering the corridor. But they were deep down in Level 10 or below, stored in cryogenic iceboxes.

Arun peddled on around Helix 64, crossed the regimental boundary and on to Helix 72. From there he took Corridor 712, which passed by the southern edge of Detroit.

He'd passed by a huddle of Hardit engineers arguing over something in their growling speech, flicking their long tails at each other aggressively. It was unusual to see them so active. When he passed the monkey-like creatures on his travels, they were more often slumped against the wall, apparently asleep.

He pushed on into a long, south-running corridor where the wall glowed red as he passed. It didn't look welcoming but there wasn't a sign or order to turn back. Up ahead should be hangars for shuttles and ground attack flyers. He doubted he'd get close enough to see them but he carried on, wanting to see how far he could get.

The answer came in the form of four Marines who came out of the distance at the double. They wore full combat armor decorated in the gold-and-black diamond pattern of the 101st Assault Marines, specialists in ground assault. They were supposed to have the thickest skulls and smallest brains, the better to survive the frantic descent from orbit to ground. Some said Neanderthal DNA had been used in their breeding program to toughen them up.

Two of these bone heads from the 101st had SA-71 carbines, one carried a plasma gun, and the other a flame thrower. They held their weapons as if they would open fire at the merest provocation. Debating their ancestry might not be a good plan.

"Beat it, kid!"

Arun hated to take that kind of drent from anyone, especially from Marines who weren't even in his regiment, and boneheads at that. Then one of them raised his carbine, and Arun hurriedly made up his mind that staying alive was the best course of action. He turned and pedaled away.

By the time he'd returned to the main ramp at Helix 6, he'd used up any spare time to go wandering, but there was still plenty to see on the ramp as he descended toward Level 9 and the tunnel that connected with the Troggie nest.

Just past Level 4, an electric truck was towing a heavy weapon strapped onto a trolley. What was that? A Fermi cannon perhaps? It was big enough. Probably something for use in the orbital defense platforms.

Between 5 and 6, Arun passed an Aux – a human manual worker – pushing a wheeled trolley down the ramp. The Aux was struggling a little. If Arun had more time, and if the Aux hadn't stank so much, he would have stopped to help.

Up ahead he could hear the sound of running. He listened closer and made out three pairs of boots thumping along the ramp. Most likely they were novices or cadets on a punishment run. He'd had plenty himself at school. If you merely looked at an instructor in a way they didn't care for then you'd be off on a thirty-klick run. The instructors didn't mind where you went so long as you did your fifty. Woe betide anyone who didn't.

The Aux...!

With a squeal of brakes, Arun came to a sudden halt. He looked back at the Aux he'd just passed.

Surely not?

He shifted gears and pedaled back up the ramp.

The Aux slunk against the wall. He seemed to know that Arun was interested in him, but instead of acknowledging the cadet politely – as Arun would expect any Aux to do – he turned to face the wall. Like many Aux, he wore a woven hat with a stiffened peak that shadowed the eyes. Arun leaned his bike against the wall and took off the Aux's hat.

Despite Arun's attempt to be gentle, the Aux flinched as if pained.

Hortez!

This was the novice Arun had admired and envied throughout school.

And it had been Arun with his escapades in the Troggie tunnels who'd taken that shining success of a cadet squad leader and turned him into … into this!

"Man, you look terrible." It was all Arun could think to say.

Hortez finally looked up, straight into Arun's face. Under his scruffy beard, the outer reaches of his face were a mix of black from deeply ingrained grime, and the angry red of flesh peeling after being burned.

Hortez stank.

The Aux who cleaned, washed, and cooked in the hab-disks were expected to be clean themselves, but Hortez didn't look as if he'd had a proper wash since that moment in Little Scar's office when Hortez's star had plummeted to these depths.

Arun looked again into his old friend's face and saw that under the grime there was another pattern, one painted in deep blues and yellows.

"Do they beat you?" he asked.

Hortez nodded.

Rage bubble up within Arun. He kept it in check, for now. "Look, pal, I know that from where you've ended up, my words are worth as much as an ice cube in the backdraft from a fusion engine, but for what it's worth … I am sorry."

"It wasn't your fault."

"I guess not but… but you're here and I'm not and that's kinda hard. I'm sorry about that."

"You're sorry? How do you think I feel?"

It took a moment before Arun realized that Hortez was trying to be funny. He'd always had a wicked sense of humor and had laid down a constant barrage of practical jokes throughout their years together at novice school. Some of that spark was still there. Not much though. Frakk! It was only a few weeks since Hortez had been his squad leader. What had they done to him?

"What are you doing here, anyway?" asked Hortez. Then he frowned and shook his head. "Forget it! You'll have to keep your mysteries, McEwan. I can't talk. Gotta go. Tell Brandt I wish him luck."

"Don't leave. Your face… This isn't right, we need to do something to fix this."

"You can't, McEwan. Don't make it worse for me."

"Why because they'll beat you? I can't stand for that. I need to let the authorities know."

After a bitter laugh that led into a hacking cough, Hortez replied: "I admire your naivety, pal. As if anyone who can make a difference would care."

The fire returned to Hortez's spirit. Arun could see it in his eyes. His spine uncurved somewhat. "They do more than beat us, McEwan. They kill us. A third of final year novices fail graduation. That's several hundred kids suddenly stuck without a role, all at the same time. There's only so much laundry work needed, man. Do you know we sleep in groups back to back because there's no space to lie down? We have to fight each other for food. It's all clean and civilized for those lucky enough to be your servants in the hab-disks, but not for us. We're excess population and the Hardits, who own and run us, take every pleasure they can in reducing our numbers. They're gonna pick one from my team tonight and kill them. Sometimes they tell us that just to enjoy our fear, but don't follow through with their threat. At other times, they killed two, just to keep the rest of us guessing. And I'm almost beginning to believe them when they say that they're only being kind. Starving to death is a tough way to go."

"What can I do to help, Hortez?"

"Stay out of it, McEwan. Don't draw attention to me and maybe I'll get lucky."

Arun took a deep breath. "Fine. I'll do as you say. Just one thing."

Hortez had already turned around and was bracing against his heavy trolley, ready to push it down the gently sloping ramp. "What?" he called over his shoulder.

"How is Alistair?"

Worse than all the horrors he'd ever seen was the deathly look in Hortez's eye when he glanced back at Arun.

"Last I heard, worse than me," said Hortez. "He's out on the surface without adequate protection against the sun's radiation. He's going to…" He shut up suddenly, his eyes widening in horror.

Arun looked behind and stared into the face of a Hardit.

If you looked past the fur and gripping tail that earned them the nickname of *monkeys*, and the three eyes set in a triangle high above the snout, the Hardits were approximately the size and shape of small humans, much more so than the massive hexaped Jotuns or the insectoid Trogs.

Their attitude was what marked them apart from the other species. When they weren't snarling through their teeth-filled snouts, Hardits could often be found snoring, slumped against a corridor wall for one of their many naps. There wasn't a particular enmity between humans and Hardits, but it was a given that if a Hardit were awake, then it would be angry.

"What occurs here?" The Hardit wore a speaker on the collar of its grimy blue overalls. The synthetic voice was that of a human male, but the alien could be female for all Arun knew. If it possessed gender characteristics analogous to humans, they were completely obscured under its scruffy fur and clothing. It looked scarcely cleaner than Hortez. The difference was that it looked healthy. Arrogant too.

"Do you understand question? What occurs here? Answer!"

"It's my fault," blurted Arun. "I asked this Aux for directions. I am lost."

One of the things Arun hated most about aliens is that their faces either did not move or else their facial expressions were unintelligible. Possibly at some level – scent maybe? – the Hardit was sneering, laughing, or fuming with rage. All that Arun could tell was that three cold, yellow-flecked eyes stared at him down that long snout. It looked about to bite him.

Then the Hardit addressed Hortez. "Verify!"

"Yes, Mistress Tawfiq Woomer-Calix. I answered the request for help as swiftly as possible so that I might return my worthless attention to my duties."

This monkey-frakker, Tawfiq, snapped her attention back to Arun. "You wear a scent identifier for insect nest," she said her artificial male voice. "That makes you even more lost than you realize. You must descend four more levels before come to nest. Insects use you for unknown purposes. You human too stupid to understand. Insects very cunning, very manipulative. They have a purpose for you that will not end well when they realize human is worthless species. Better for all of us if humans wiped from galaxy. Go away!"

Arun bowed. "Yes, ma'am. Please forgive me, Mistress Tallfat Woomer-Cat-Licks."

The Hardit growled. "It is Mistress Tawfiq Woomer-Calix. No, do not attempt to correct your speaking. Do not speak at all. Your voice irritates me. I do not forgive you. I want you go away."

Arun nodded with as much deference as he could muster. With a last glance at the pitiful figure that had been his squad leader so recently, he grabbed his bike and set off for the lower levels.

He hoped he had been sufficiently polite to deflect retribution away from Hortez, but he felt anything but deference for the foul monkey-veck.

You haven't seen the last of me, Tawfiq Woomer-Calix.

Chapter 23

"It is a caste thing," said Pedro, after Arun had recounted his meeting with Hortez on his way over. "It is like our guardians. Our people go through many phases as they progress through their lifecycle from hatching to enriching the soil with their rotting flesh. The phases are more than just different roles, there are profound physiological and mental changes too. At the end of a long and useful life our people become a burden on the nest. We can no longer support them. They must give way so others can replace them. It is no different from your brief human lives giving way to the next generation."

"You're wrong," said Arun. He got to his feet and started pacing the hard-packed dirt floor, clenching his fists. Pedro had learned not to become alarmed by Arun's displays of anger and gave Arun time to collect his thoughts.

"We've all got to go sometime," said Arun. "I get that. But Hortez and the kids who failed school? That isn't right. It's like we toss them into a deep well of despair. Then we turn our backs and pretend to forget all about it, because if we ever peered into that well, we would be so consumed by grief that we would throw ourselves in and drown in that despair."

"You are young," said Pedro. "Mortality and youth do not sit together comfortably."

"That's what I mean. Hortez and the kids who failed school are just teenagers. They aren't spent husks like the guardians of your people. They're only just starting out in life. A caste thing? No, we humans don't have castes."

"Don't you? Tranquility is a complex multi-species planet, and part of an even more complex star system that is itself part of the White Knight empire. You humans are the lowest caste of all. And these Aux the lowest human sub-caste. You do not like this, but it is the truth. You are in a caste system whether you like it or not."

Arun chewed that over. He sat down, embarrassed by his need to pace in front of the alien. "Okay – so we're bottom of the heap. How do the Hardits fit in? Are they the next layer up?"

"It is more complicated. They see themselves as equal or superior to the Jotuns, but the White Knights gave the Jotuns the responsibility to run system defense and the supply of Marines. Your Marine base is a relatively recent addition to our star system. It was a mining system for millennia before that. Hardits dislike all other species, but those who share our planet reserve a special level of hatred for the Jotuns for disturbing *their* star system, as they see it, and for you humans for being the cause of the Marine base's expansion. What makes it worse for the Aux is that there are many levels in Hardit society. The Hardit you spoke to will be one of the lowest of all Hardits, probably a criminal. From their perspective, to be tasked with overseeing human Aux workers is a humiliating punishment."

"I always thought they looked perpetually angry. The Hardits I see are failures who take out their frustration on the one group even lower than them – their human workers. Figures. But if they're such losers, why hasn't Hortez stood up to them more? He was a Marine cadet, if only for a few days. That counts for something."

Intoxicating thoughts of freedom and rebellion swirled around Arun's mind. "Tell me more about the Hardits," he asked his friend.

Pedro answered without hesitation. "The species you call Hardits originate on the planet Iradis 3. First contact with the Tans-Species Union was 0.73 million years ago. Unlike most primitive species, the Hardits initiated that contact. They are a sexual species, the sexes barely tolerating each other except during mating season. Their principal sense is smell, and the average lifespan without longevity treatment is 172 years."

The Trog gave no sign of consulting a softscreen or any other gadget. How did he know all those facts? "That's not what I'm after," Arun told Pedro. "Give me more than dull facts. Something that marks them out as different."

Pedro thought a moment. "Sometimes they are said to be able to see through solid rock. In fact, they have a highly developed sensitivity to changes in gravity. In practice that means they know exactly how far they are below the surface of their planet. If two groups of Hardit miners began tunneling toward each other at opposite ends of a planet, you could be confident that the two teams would meet at precisely the same point without needing any technology more sophisticated than picks and shovels."

Arun frowned. "No, that's still not it. Tell me their weaknesses. Give me something I can exploit."

"Since we became friends, human McEwan, I have studied your planet of origin. Your Earth and the Hardit planet are unremarkable except for one aspect you both share: magnetism. Your planet has an iron-nickel core that operates as a dynamo, producing an extremely powerful planetary magnetic field. The Hardit planet's core has more sulfur than iron, and even more significantly, their planet's mantle is highly metalized. This destabilizes the dynamo effect of their core resulting in a remarkably weak magnetic field."

"So? They never grew up knowing about compasses."

"The significance is rather more than that, human. A planet's magnetic field is like a force field, shielding the surface of the planet from the high energy particle stream emitted from the local star. Stellar flares from Earth's star cause power blackouts and damage to unshielded electronics but this has not been enough to place evolutionary pressure on your species' development. With such a weak magnetic field on the Hardit planet, their star has blasted away most of their planet's atmosphere and left the surface a sterile husk."

"Hold on a minute. If there's no life on their planet, how did the Hardits evolve there?"

"I did not say the planet was lifeless, only that the surface is."

"So they're delvers. They live underground, like you in your nests."

Pedro spiraled his antenna in amusement. "They hardly resemble us, but yes their habitat is below the planet's crust. Vast natural caverns extend for depths of many miles beneath the surface. Which is why they are used as miners. Give them a little gravity, and dirt or rock overhead, and they will be happy, whether on a planet, moon, or asteroid.

"Aliens 101 is all very well, but I asked you to give me the lowdown on their weaknesses. Do they go catatonic when you shine a bright light in their eyes? See that's something I could use. Maybe a common human cooking ingredient is a powerful narcotic? Like garlic. That's it! They go wild for garlic because it gives them such a mega-high and leaves them so blissed out they don't know what they're doing. That would work. C'mon, you gotta give me something."

Pedro flattened his feelers in disdain. "As if a human cooking ingredient would be a narcotic for an alien species. Do you realize how incredibly unlikely that would be?"

"Lay off, Pedro. It's just an example. I need to understand how to beat them, is all."

"If you had listened then you would already understand."

"Do what?"

"I have already been telling you what you asked for."

"About magnetic fields and stuff?"

"Yes."

That brought Arun up short, but he couldn't get his head around what the overgrown insect meant. "This is what our inter-species chats are all about, isn't it? Mutual incomprehension. You tell me something alien that makes no sense. Then you give me an explanation that makes even less sense. You love it. You're conducting an experiment. How much alien drent can you fill my poor human head with until my brain melts? Is that it?"

"Your words do not make sense," said Pedro through his voice box. "But I am learning your tangential ways now. I interpret what you just said as the following. One: I am angry. Two: I fear for my friend, Hortez. Three: I am too ignorant to understand your advice."

Arun shrugged. He was learning too – learning that there was no point in getting angry with aliens. "I figure that about covers it."

"Then allay your concern. It is my calling as a scribe to address the shortcomings of the ignorant. That is why I enjoy our conversations so intensely." Pedro gave a little jump. He did that sometimes when excited. "The significance of their evolution is that Hardits are agoraphobic – they do not like large open spaces in general and planetary surfaces in particular. This is not merely psychological, they are very prone to cancers caused by exposure to Tranquility's sun. Ultraviolet radiation is lethal to them. They are easily dazzled by bright lights. Tranquility's air, even the pumped and filtered air we two are breathing in this lovely chamber, is heavy and oxygen-rich to them. You humans call them lazy. They are actually an industrious species, but they find the dense atmosphere very tiring. If they exert themselves, they hyperventilate easily. You think you see them dozing but they are not asleep. They are slowing heartbeat and breathing in order to regulate blood-oxygen levels. They do not acknowledge you because you are beneath their notice."

"Yeah, I got it," interrupted Arun. "We gotta use flash-bombs." He was about to go but paused. The big insect had helped him. He hated to admit it – after all the trouble his contact with Trogs had caused – but he owed Pedro. Rewarding the big lug was child's play.

"Thanks," said Arun. The insect's antennae circled lazily, indicating his pleasure at Arun's word. "Thanks… *friend*." Pedro's antennae circles grew larger.

Arun reckoned he'd done enough alien chat for one day not to earn Colonel Little Scar's displeasure. "Gotta go now. Hortez needs me. Gonna get myself a posse."

"What does that word mean?"

"Look it up, Pedro."

"But you cannot go yet," said Pedro, his circling feelers flopping to an abrupt halt. "Our inter-species learning has not progressed enough in this session."

"You reckon? I'm gonna raise a posse and I've just explained why. That's enough to keep your feelers wriggling for a bit."

"A poss-ee…?" The voice box raised up the last syllable, indicating Pedro's confusion. Pedro must have been mulling over the word, looking it up probably, because when Arun grabbed his bike, the alien said: "You mean an affectionate term for the species *Felis catus,* especially those kept as a domesticated emotional symbiont?"

"No, I don't mean a frakking cat. P-O-S-S-E. Look it up." As he set off along the nest tunnel on the long journey back to his hab-disk, he called over his shoulder. "You wanted to learn something about humans. We have a saying: *No Marine left behind*. Watch and learn what that means, pal."

Chapter 24

The cadet posse finally cornered Tawfiq, the Hardit bully, in a deserted passageway off Corridor 710 on Level 5, not far from their old novice school.

Only Springer and Majanita had joined Arun. As a posse it was pathetic, but at 3-1 odds they didn't fear the lone Hardit as they closed in, blocking her and forcing her to acknowledge their presence. Arun still felt dangerously exposed and kept glancing back over his shoulder.

When he'd returned from his talk with Pedro, Arun had scoured the habdisk and battalion chow halls, looking for allies he could trust.

Most of his squad had been in gunnery practice, but Springer and Majanita had been studying in their dorm. Cristina had been there too and tried to convince them of the insanity of their plan. But once Madge had heard what they'd done to Hortez, nothing would stand in her way. Not reason, that was for sure.

She'd listened to Arun for about three seconds before going to the dorm armory and helping herself to three flash-bombs. Then she went back and brought out six more, which she divided between Springer and Arun.

And now, here they were in a tense standoff with the murdering alien overseer.

Arun felt the pouch on his hip that bulged with the flash-bomb within.

He undid the pouch flap.

"I saw you earlier," he told the alien. "You're Tawfiq Woomer-Calix, aren't you?"

The Hardit gave no indication that she had heard Arun speak. She was looking up at the ceiling as if inspecting a dirty patch.

"We apologize," said Springer hurriedly.

What? Arun looked wide eyed at his friend.

"We do not have experience of interacting with your people," Springer continued. "Please accept our apologies. May we beg permission to converse with you?"

Arun was all for begging permission with his fists, but maybe Springer's way would yield results faster.

The Hardit slowly lowered her head and looked at Arun. "This one thinks I should recognize him," she growled in Hardit speech, a toneless voice translating at the same time into human words through a collar-mounted speaker. Unlike the clanking gears of Pedro's box, this translator was silent and hidden. It wasn't as convincingly human, though.

"All of you look identical," said the Hardit, "and that stench humans have of rotting cheese – you stink worse than nest insects. I refuse to accept apologies. I speak with you because I want you gone and this best way to make you…" There was a pause as the alien selected the optimum translation. "Frakk off!"

"We have questions," said Arun. "About rumors we have heard concerning the human Aux. We would like to know whether they are true." He paused, but the alien gave no acknowledgment. She didn't give a refusal either, so he pressed on. "Is it true that your Aux team is given insufficient food to stay alive, their quarters so cramped that they cannot lie down to sleep, and that you sometimes kill your workers for reasons other than disobedience or treachery?"

It was hard to tell, but Tawfiq seemed to concentrate, to work through the translation. Then she reacted, bringing itself fully erect and confronting Arun.

The alien was a head shorter than the cadets, but she yielded nothing to her taller accuser as she raised her head so that her snout almost rubbed on his chin. She breathed out through a wall of teeth, blowing a smell his way that was rich and meaty, and beginning to choke the back of Arun's throat.

The cadets hadn't thought this through. Arun was acutely aware of that, but he couldn't back down in front of this arrogant murderer. "Are the rumors true?" he pressed.

"I do not deny them."

Arun was trying to work out whether that meant yes or no when Madge took over. "We want assurances," she insisted. "The humans are to be well treated. Enough space to sleep properly as becomes our species. Enough food for them to be healthy. A shower once a week and an end to the killings."

Tawfiq breathed again into Arun's face. He got the feeling it was meant as the ultimate insult. The Hardit ignored Madge's words.

"We have ample food and shelter," said Springer, "and we can share what we have. Let's work something out. If your workers were healthier and happier they would be more productive. Surely that would be to your benefit."

Tawfiq stepped back. "I have indulged your foolishness." She wrinkled her nose. "And your stench. Now stand aside or face the consequences."

That was it! Arun snapped. He brought his flash-bomb out of his pouch and brandished it in front of the murdering veck. "Do you know what this is, alien?"

"We wish no confrontation," said Springer.

"What my comrade says is still just about true," added Arun. "But the prospect of confrontation is feeling better by the second."

"Our two species are allies," said Springer. "But we humans are trained to kill, Hardit. It is what we have been bred for. I think with these flash-bombs we can fight and hurt you without killing. But we might not be able to control our violent nature."

"Yeah," said Madge. "Shall we find out?" She drew out her flash-bomb. "These devices stun enemy soldiers. They give out such noise, light and radiation that they can fry unhardened enemy targeting systems. Show us your human workers. Show us where they live. Let us talk with them, or we shall find out what these bombs do to you."

"You would not dare, human."

"We give you ten seconds," said Madge.

The Hardit folded her arms and looked at the ceiling.

"Nine," said Madge.

Was this an enormous mistake?

"Eight."

Madge sounded impatient to finish her countdown. But she hadn't experienced the glare of an angry Jotun. Arun was in no hurry to explain to Colonel Little Scar that he'd attacked a Hardit.

"Seven."

Arun glanced at Springer. He could see she wasn't sure either, but she was bringing out her own flash-bomb.

"Six."

He'd like to think they were a band of gallant adventurers, living up to the Marine motto.

"Five."

Never leave a Marine behind.

"Four."

But they'd been flung into this confrontation on the crest of a wave of bluster and indignation.

"Three."

Where would that wave spill them when it broke?

"Two."

Was it too late to back out now?

"One."

Madge's hand twitched but she did nothing. She must have had the same doubts all along. Springer stayed her hand too.

"You are as weak as you are stupid," sneered the Hardit. "It is your cowardice that enables us to exterminate you like the vermin you are."

Arun grabbed the flash-bombs from Springer and Majanita, and dashed all three to the ground.

Chapter 25

The flash-bomb was so loud that the noise reached inside Arun's ears and twisted his poor brain into knots, squeezing out his awareness like sweat wrung from a sodden shirt. Arun had turned his head away from the blast just before it went off. Even so, the flash was bright enough to bore through the rear of his skull and sear a white patch onto the back of his retinas.

Unlike the Hardit veck – hopefully – the cadets had experienced flash-bombs many times before. After a few seconds, Arun's brain untwisted and the after-image of the flash began to flake away. Only a high-pitched wail continued, rising in pitch and volume to unbearable levels.

Every ounce of pain ever experienced by every sentient in the history of the galaxy was distilled into that banshee screech.

Arun opened his eyes and looked in wonder upon Tawfiq. She hadn't collapsed to the ground, hadn't even covered her ears or eyes. The alien just stood there, screeching that wail. Suddenly all three of the Hardit's eyes rolled back far enough to show the optic nerve. Then they began to dance crazily in their sockets.

Tawfiq's scream crescendoed, making Arun flinch. It was not a remotely human noise, more like a percussion drill shattering glass.

"Did we go too far?" asked Springer.

"No," replied Madge.

"Not far enough," added Arun. He spat on the alien.

"But how can we negotiate with it?" hissed Springer, the scream setting her teeth on edge. "That *is* why we're here, isn't it?"

Before Arun could reply, a change came over Tawfiq like a fever breaking. Her eyeballs snapped back into focus – glaring at Arun.

"Frakkk-kk-kkk. Frakkk-kkk-kk. Frakkkkk. Frakk. You. Human. Filth!"

"It speaks," said Arun.

Tawfiq raised her lips, revealing the full length of her fangs. She snarled.

"Do we have your attention, darling?" asked Madge. "We have plenty more bombs…"

Arun glanced across at his cadet corporal. She was giving the pitiful creature a sultry smile. This was more like the girl who had been his friend.

"Human scum. You will learn your place. Veck. Veck."

Madge admonished with a wagging finger. "Naughty girl. And such rude words too. Don't we think that's the kind of bad attitude that got you into trouble in the first place? Hmm?"

"Give it another bomb, corporal," Arun suggested.

"Not so hasty," she said. "I've read up on animal training techniques. I reckon I can tame it." She threw a patronizing smile at the Hardit. "You are bad furry thing. If furry thing do bad things to humans, we make furry thing scream with these."

She brought out another two bombs from her pouch.

Tawfiq ceased her snarling and licked her lips nervously, her gaze never leaving the bombs.

"Not so brave when humans bite back, are you?" sneered Arun. He brought out a pair of bombs himself.

"Easy!" Springer put a hand over his arm. "Let's get our demands met. Don't push it."

Arun took a calming breath, but the heat of his anger would not cool. This skangat of an alien was reducing Hortez to a sniveling wreck, and murdering the Aux in her charge.

No, he would not take it easy.

He flourished both bombs in front of the alien's face. "I wonder what would happen if I set these off right in front of your eyes?"

"Shall we find out?" added Madge.

Arun leered at the alien, loving this. It was more than just sweet revenge. Since making cadet, he'd felt pushed ever further to the edge of the squad. Now he was in the thick of things, and Madge was backing him up for once.

He squeezed the bombs against the alien's eyes.

"No. No. Please," begged Tawfiq. She curled her tail into a circle. Was that a submission gesture? "Please let me speak first."

Arun withdrew the bombs a short distance. The alien touched a stud on her collar and then stared into space for a few moments before explaining: "I have summoned an Aux worker so that I may demonstrate the new way of things."

"I don't like this," said Springer.

"You worry too much," said Madge.

"Really? I don't think you worry *enough*, corporal. Look at her," Springer gestured at Tawfiq. "She's not cowed. She's just buying time."

"Is this one of your *visions*, cadet?" Madge sneered.

Springer seethed, but said nothing.

"You could be right, Springer." Arun tried to speak soothingly. "No matter. If the Hardit tries anything, we'll blast her with four bombs and see whether that encourages her to cooperate."

The tension between the humans was nearly as great as that between the cadets and the Hardit. Before either standoff could break into violence, an Aux worker approached, jogging along the passageway.

He was a sorry sight. Head bowed under a grease-stained cap and face half-covered by a shapeless bush of a beard. His blue overalls were so filthy that they could probably get up and walk on their own without the human inside.

The Aux looked suspiciously at the cadets before reporting in. "I am here, mistress."

"Stay there," Tawfiq ordered the Aux. "You!" She used her tail to point at Madge. "Kiss my boots."

A chill traveled Arun's spine as he watched the youthful playfulness in Madge's face replaced by the chiseled steel of a Marine.

"I'd rather die," snarled the cadet corporal. "And if I did, I'd make sure to take you with me."

"The greater your insolence, the more severe the punishment I shall deliver."

"You can't threaten me," said Madge.

Arun readied to release his bombs.

"I think she's threatening to punish the Aux," said Springer. "Not us. Not yet."

"Correct," said Tawfiq.

"Don't you dare," shouted Arun.

The alien moved – lightning fast. Arun threw his bombs but he knew he'd hesitated too long. Tawfiq dove for the floor, her back to the bombs. As she fell, she drew a grubby black box from her overalls and seemed to activate a control, but Arun couldn't be sure because his world filled with pain and confusion as the flash-bombs drove away every other thought.

When his senses returned, the passageway was filled by the sound of screaming as before. But this time the screams were agonizingly human, coming from the Aux who was thrashing around on the floor in some kind of fit.

Springer and Madge went to aid the Aux, but Arun threw himself at Tawfiq who had risen to a crouch.

He wrestled the alien to the floor. Tawfiq was strong and managed a kick to his gut. Arun bit back the pain and landed two good punches on the alien's face.

Frakk, that hurt his fist! This creature had bones as strong as polyceramalloy, but the fight had gone out of Tawfiq enough for Arun to wrench away her black box.

Desperate to shut off the agonized screams from the Aux, Arun thought he'd simply thumb a control and that would be the end of it. What he saw on the box, though, was scrolling alien script that meant nothing to him. There was no icon, no red button… nothing to say *press me*. He jabbed at the face of the control box anyway.

No effect.

"You will never find it, human." Tawfiq was sitting up now, wiping blood from her snout.

"Then you turn it off, or I'll kill you," shouted Majanita.

"No."

The cadets looked at each other. The instructors had often rammed home the maxim that to win battles, you had to seize the initiative and keep it against all odds.

They'd just surrendered initiative to the alien and they all knew it.

"The pain device is still operating," said Tawfiq as if the cadets couldn't hear the Aux's screams. "It is intended to give a sharp shock. Prolonged use leads to neural pathways frying. Your fellow human will soon go from being a lowly cog in a Hardit machine to being a worn out old part that will need grinding down into components and recycled."

"What do you mean by recycled?" asked Majanita.

Tawfiq was in no hurry to reply. They listened as the Aux breached a threshold of endurance. His screams dulled and his writhing slowed.

"Tell me, humans, have you ever seen an auxiliary who was old, or injured, or otherwise functioning poorly?" Tawfiq looked at all three in turn as that Aux's screams turned to low groans. "You can't tell one Aux from another, can you? See how little you value your own kind. Well, let me inform you that you will never see an auxiliary who is unfit because such an individual has no net worth. You humans breed like vermin, which is why you need regular culling. Your human lives are cheap to spend and expensive to maintain."

Madge pointed an accusing finger at the alien. "You evil vecks. You cull the Aux?"

"Give Tawfiq the box, Arun," screamed Springer.

"And Marines too," Tawfiq told Majanita. "We cull you too, of course."

What? For a moment Arun forgot the Aux.

"No," said Springer. "You're wrong. Marines in the reserve are stored in ice."

"Stupid human. We build the ice boxes. That was my job once, in better days. We know how fast you breed and we know how many ice boxes we make. You breed faster than we can make boxes and the insect filth can build their tunnels. The older humans were even more pathetic than you slightly modified versions. Why use a valuable icebox to store an inferior model when you upgraded humans are so plentiful?"

"Wait till we tell our superiors about this," said Arun.

"No, Arun, we can't wait," shouted Springer. "Give her the box. And, corporal, you need to do as she asks."

By now the Aux worker's struggles had died away to an occasional twitch.

Tawfiq spoke to Madge as if oblivious to the life or death drama unfolding. "Do you really think your superiors don't already know?"

Arun couldn't take it anymore. He gave a last ineffectual jab at the control box before handing it over to the Hardit.

"Turn it off," he begged.

"I have machine lubricant on my footwear," she responded. "Clean it off with your tongue. Then I will consider your request."

Throbbing with humiliation, and fighting off his combat-tuned instincts that urged him to punch this veck, Arun sank to his knees, head bowed.

Tawfiq kicked him in the teeth. Not hard but enough to leave a copper tang in Arun's mouth.

He glanced across at the Aux. Froth was coming from his mouth. He was choking.

"First," said Tawfiq, "you must ask permission in the correct manner."

"Please mistress. May I lick your boots clean?"

"Good enough," said the Hardit. She tapped away at the control box, and the Aux went limp. "The Aux is free from pain."

Arun rose into a threatening crouch.

"Wait!" shouted the Hardit. "I have set the device to inflict a lethal dose of pain in eight minutes. If I am satisfied with your efforts then I shall postpone this worker's death sentence by another eight minutes while the next one of you learns your place. If you kill me, you'll kill your precious Aux. Now get licking."

Arun knelt back down, stuck out his tongue, and set to work.

Chapter 26

Arun stood at attention, flanked by Madge and Springer. In front of them, sitting at a polished desk of real wood, was Staff Sergeant Bryant, the senior NCO for the battalion. Sergeant Gupta stood behind his superior.

Also there, to Arun's mounting horror, was Instructor Rekka. Arun had hardly seen her since that day in the colonel's office when her superior, Nhlappo, had been demoted. Rekka would be loving this chance to plant evil thoughts in the heads of the NCOs.

At least Bryant had the decency to let Arun explain what they had discovered about Hortez, about the despicable way the Hardits treated their human workers.

There was no mulling over Arun's words. No heavy sighs through steepled fingers. Bryant's reply was instant and unadorned.

"The stories of individual Aux are news to me but of no interest. The wider fact of Aux mistreatment by the Hardits is known by Detroit NCOs. I fantasize about throttling those wretched monkey-vecks with my bare hands, but the weak cannot openly threaten the strong. And the hand we humans have to play here is even weaker than you can imagine. Therefore, there will be no more talk of using even non-lethal force against the Hardits."

"But, staff sergeant–" pleaded Springer. She meant to go on, but Gupta silenced her with a curt shake of his head. Bryant chose to ignore her.

"Your actions today have brought a formal complaint from the local Hardit leader," said Bryant. "Instructor Rekka has known you for years. Sergeant Gupta has known you for only a few weeks. Even though the handover from your instructors has formally completed, I requested Instructor Rekka to advise me on suitable punishments."

I bet she did, thought Arun.

"You three are to work as auxiliaries for a week. God help you."

"This cadet begs permission to speak, staff sergeant," asked Springer.

"Granted."

"Hortez is one of our own. What about: *No Marine left behind*?"

"He is an auxiliary. A reject. He is not a Marine."

Bryant sighed and slumped a little. He wasn't enjoying this. "It's a hard galaxy," he said, "and if you survive your punishment I hope it teaches you this lesson. Do not expect justice in this life. Fight for it. Build for it over centuries. But never assume justice as your right, because if you do, you will be sorely disappointed. You, McEwan, should know that more than any here after Chief Instructor Nhlappo tried to teach you that only a few weeks ago."

Rekka started chewing them out for forgetting they were all slaves. Arun wasn't really listening. His mind was on Tawfiq and her brutal monkey friends, who would be waiting for Arun to come into their clutches. He might not survive their welcome. Since Pedro had put the idea into his head that someone was drugging the cadets, if he died, he would take that secret with him. He had to speak out about the drugs now.

"Staff sergeant?"

"Speak."

Arun looked into his superior's eyes. Could he trust the NCO? What about Gupta and Rekka?

"Well?" snapped Bryant.

He daren't trust Bryant. If the staff sergeant were a traitor, Arun would be condemning Springer and Madge to death too. No, it was too risky. "I'm meant to be playing in a Scendence match this week."

Gupta's fists clenched. Bryant's lips clenched into a tight, white line, and he glared with such intensity that Arun felt he was being sliced by a laser cutter. The senior NCO seemed to come to a decision. "You know, I must be crazy, but even though you've not listened to a word I just said, I'm going to cut you slack this one time, and pretend I didn't hear you. Despite demonstrating stupidity at every level, you did show good fighting spirit in confronting that Hardit. One day, you might make an adequate Marine. You're all to report to Auxiliary Camp Delta at 07:00 hours tomorrow for a 7-day reassignment. Short of murder, suicide, or insurrection, your orders are to obey every Hardit instruction to the letter."

"Yes, staff sergeant," they chorused.

"This cadet begs permission to speak, staff sergeant," said Arun.

Bryant frowned. He looked about to rip Arun to shreds but then stopped himself. "Granted, because I'm incredulous. What the hell could you possibly think I need to hear?"

"Thank you, staff sergeant. I am also ordered to attend a Trog liaison meeting next week. Colonel Little Scar ordered me to–"

"Yes, I know what the colonel wants of you. Very well. I shall inform the Hardits. Attend your liaison meeting but do not dally."

"Thank you, staff sergeant."

Bryant stared at the cadets, looking them up and down as if they were something foul he'd scraped off the sole of his boot. There was something wrong about the performance. When Rekka glared at you, her contempt ran solidly from her face down into the core of her soul. But not Bryant. He seemed worried.

For a moment, Arun nearly changed his mind again and confessed his suspicions about the cadet drugging. Then Bryant shook his head and hardened his face. The moment was gone.

"Learn your lesson well," ordered Bryant. "Stay alive. Dismissed!"

As Arun saluted and marched off to his fate, he felt bile rise. He nearly choked with the horror of what he was about to walk into. All his life, the truth of his slavery had been something he could push to the perimeter of his existence. This was different. Beatings, torture, malnutrition, and kissing the boots of your mistress – that's what awaited him. It wasn't the prospect of pain and injury that twisted his gut: it was the shame.

How had humans sunk so low?

Then a far better question hit him, and a lightness came to his step.

How could humans rise up again?

PART II

Operation Clubhouse

Human Legion INFOPEDIA

Military Concepts
– Static defenses/ Defensive Warrens

If you're not familiar with star system defense strategies, then you probably think that defensive warrens, such as the infamous Detroit – constructed for our predecessors and rivals, the Human Marine Corps, on Tranquility – are designed to defend against an invader.

It's an understandable mistake. But you would still be wrong.

In fact, the primary objective of warren designers is to build a structure that will be destroyed.

Sure, the warren will have embrasures and powered hardpoints for heavy weapons, not to mention armor and force shields, and workshops buried deep beneath the surface capable of adding to the stockpiles of vehicles, weapons and ordnance.

And, yes, in addition to the broad spineways and transit corridors, wide enough for grav tanks to charge through, the narrower passageways twist and turn back on themselves so that invading troops will not only become lost, but will constantly be checking their rear for a counter attack that could come from any direction.

Then there is the key to the kind of strongly-garrisoned warren at Detroit: self-contained hab-disks that can seal themselves off for years before drilling their way to the surface and spilling out a company-sized unit of defenders bent on revenge. Hundreds of hab-disks will most likely survive the death rained from the skies by conventional munitions. They would be like weeds forever reappearing on a patch of ground you thought you'd cleared.

Warrens are built so strongly, that a better approach for an invader is to stay in orbit and play a longer game. They could douse the planet with so many dirty nukes that the planet is left a sterile, irradiated husk for millions of years to come – let's see if the hab-disks can wait that one out!

Or, if you have the tech, you could use gamma beams rather than nukes to do the same job.

But simplest by far is to nudge the orbits of comets and asteroids to slam into the besieged planet, a rain of destruction unrelenting for years.

In other words, to destroy a defensive warren, you'll probably have to destroy the planet.

Which is what the warren designers want.

Why?

Because forcing your enemy to destroy your planet denies it to him.

And if he can't use your planet for himself, why bother invading in the first place?

Unfortunately for the defenders, that logic doesn't always work: far too many wars are driven by hatred, not economic calculation.

And the story of how our galaxy's civilizations rise and clash plays out over such an extended timescale that it can scarcely be conceived by humans – at least the original ones derived from *Homo sapiens*.

But the aliens who design the warrens have been around far longer than us, long enough to know one thing with statistical certainty.

If they build their warren well, then the day will surely come when it will be destroyed, along with the planet it has doomed.

Further reading

If you delve deeper into Detroit's history and design, you will soon smack up against security walls. It's no secret that Detroit held a lot of secrets. And if you need to ask what they are, you definitely don't need to know.

But whatever mysteries Detroit might have hidden in its depths, in its upper levels and hab-disks – Detroit was built as a defensive warren.

And when the invasion did finally come, it proved a tough nut to crack.

Chapter 27

The domain of Auxiliary Team Beta lay through a restricted access side tunnel off Corridor 710 on Level 5. During their years at novice school, the cadets had used this corridor countless times, but there had never been a reason to explore the restricted passageways leading into the unknown.

Arun had expected his punishment detail would have to cross a guard post or input a security code into a locked hatch. There was none of that. The only physical barrier to prevent the curious from exploring the area was the stench. Cadets were used to showering two or three times per day. They were now entering the realm of the unwashed.

"Hello!" called Springer. "Is anybody there?"

A minute later, a dreary figure in heavily soiled overalls, that might once have been dark blue, appeared from out of the poorly lit passageway and beckoned them to follow.

"Hi," greeted Madge as they walked to meet the figure. "What's your name?"

The Aux ignored her.

It was a woman, decided Arun, a girl. Like the cadets, she was probably still in her teens, though Arun found it impossible to be sure. The overalls hung very heavily over her shoulders, more like armor than clothing. Her face was gaunt and soiled, her hair crudely cropped.

If the spark of life had dimmed in Hortez's eyes, it was guttering in the girl's, kept alive by the simmering heat of sly resentment.

None of the cadets tried again to strike up a conversation. They followed the auxiliary in silence as she led them along a long corridor, ever deeper into their banishment.

To either side were mostly closed doors, but one door had been removed allowing Arun a glimpse of a vehicle park of sorts. Instead of the hovertanks and strike flitters he's seen in other parks, here were trolleys on casters and sit-on cleaning trucks that actually looked kind of fun.

They hadn't even reported in yet but already Arun was feeling an urgent need to lighten the mood of this death march. The Hardits were humorless bullies whose language translator AIs weren't enough to stop them sounding like bumbling idiots when talking to humans. The next week was not going to be pleasant, but it would at least involve Arun mocking the hell out of the hairy monkey-vecks.

Just as he was thinking of something smart to say – anything to break the doom-filled silence – Springer beat him to it. She sprinted ahead and dodged through a door that had been left ajar.

Arun followed, hot on her heels.

A light flickered on as soon as Springer entered the room, revealing it to be a workshop. There were banks of metal boxes, neatly labeled. Tools and power sockets dangled from the ceiling over scarred workbenches.

"Hey, Arun," said Springer. "Remember the workshops on Level 9?"

He grinned back. Their class had been shown around the workshops where repairs were made for weapons mounted on the orbital defense platforms. This Aux workshop was suited more to fixing shelves, or maybe a leaky tap. But that was all right. Taps and shelves weren't as impressive as a 60 Gigajoule Fermi Cannon, but even such humble equipment had their own part to play in the life of the Corps.

Springer and Arun grinned at each other, a connection that extended for several invigorating seconds. *They were going to get through this okay.*

Wandering off for a few moments hardly counted as a great victory for oppressed humanity, but it put Arun in the mood for ripping the hell out of the Hardits.

Bring 'em on. I'll handle them.

He rejoined Madge and the Aux woman. As they pushed farther along the corridor, the air filled ever thicker with the heavy odors of unsanitized humanity.

Eventually they entered a rectangular room that had the same dimensions as the dorms in the hab-disks, though this room appeared much larger at first because there were no racks, armory cupboards or head.

There was a far more serious difference: dorms in the hab-disks housed eight cadets. In this room were fifty human auxiliaries lined up in two rows. They were hunched, faded skeletons more than people. The men, and boys old enough, wore matted beards.

"You are slightly early." The artificial voice came from the only Hardit in the room, a creature in dark blue overalls like the humans, except the Hardit's was relatively clean and, while still rough material, hung more like clothing than semi-rigid armor. The voice was male, but Arun knew that didn't prove anything.

"I am not impressed, though," said the Hardit. "Your species cowers in filth of its own fear. It is this fear that drove you here double fast, not respect for your better. By the time I have finished with you, I will teach you respect and justify your fear. Now remove clothing." The alien gestured at the Aux who had led them in. "Number 87 will provide you with new uniforms."

The cadets started stripping off their fatigues while the girl who had led them here – Number 87 – went over to a box in the back corner of the room and came back bearing three sets of soiled overalls.

"Those too, you dumb vecks," urged 87, when the cadets hesitated to remove their underwear. "As if anyone cares here."

Arun complied. But when, naked, he reached for his new overalls, his eyes popped wide. Number 87 had lied. *She* cared that they stripped off completely, but in a freak-out way. As soon as the cadets discarded their clothes, she scooped them up. Once she had the full set, she flung most them into a heap of sacking, blankets and clothing piled up in one corner of the room, but kept a few items to one side.

Was this a pile of bedding?

For the briefest of moments, the idea tickled Arun that one of these Aux would enjoy his underwear for a pillow tonight. Then he looked again at the occupants of the room. Were 53 people really going to sleep here in this one dorm? There was scarcely enough room for them all to stand.

"Hurry up or we'll all be in the drent," urged 87.

One of the Aux collapsed in a rasping sequence of coughs, attempting desperately to suppress them.

It was a reminder that Arun had new dorm-mates. He couldn't help but begin to feel responsible for them.

When he stepped into his new clothes, they felt oddly familiar – like a flak jacket, which was a crude form of armor with overlapping scales of toughened ceramo-plastics sandwiched between ablative and reflective layers.

"Which one of you threw the light-bang bomb?" asked the Hardit.

Arun raised an arm.

"Your attack caused me mild discomfort. Very little actually. I almost did not notice."

Liar!

"Nonetheless the idea that a human could attempt to harm superior sickens me to the tip of tail. Step forward!"

This was the moment Arun had dreaded. Worse! It hadn't occurred to him that it would be Tawfiq Woomer-Calix herself who would meet them. This was going to be personal.

The Hardit reached into a pouch slung on her waist.

What was it going to be? A stunner? Slow-acting poison? A whip? Maybe the creature thought humans deserved a particularly primitive form of torture, and was about to bring out a rusty knife.

The prospect of pain was something he could bear, but to stand and meekly take it… he wasn't sure he would be capable of that. The future that frightened him most was to end this punishment week alive but damaged. He would be no use as a cadet if he suffered permanent injury. They wouldn't take him back; he'd be stuck here forever.

All three cadets had made a pact. No goading the Hardits; no rising to their bait. They would suck up every bit of drent they were given and get out of here in one piece… unless he saw an opportunity to make the monkey-like aliens look like buffoons. He bet Springer would do the same.

Madge wouldn't. Even if a hidden traitor really was feeding his buddies with low-dose combat drug, it wouldn't change her. When she needed to be, Madge was as hard as a kinetic torpedo. She would stay professional throughout while Springer and he would need to goof around to cope. That was why Springer was his best buddy and Madge was his section leader.

The Hardit brought out a phial of liquid, which she dipped her thumb into and then smeared over a square fabric patch stitched into the breast of Arun's overalls.

Tawfiq replaced the phial and brought out two more – there were dozens in that pouch – mixed them together and smeared the resulting paste onto the fabric patch.

"You are designated number 106," Tawfiq told Arun. "Return to your place."

While Madge and Springer were given the same treatment, numbered 109 and 114 respectively, Arun looked at his breast. Of the alien's fluid there was no sign, but now he looked closer he could make out his new name, 106, marked in faded human numerals.

"Approach your mistress, 106."

Arun obeyed.

Tawfiq stared at him along her long snout. She appeared disappointed that he held her three-eyed gaze and glared back for all he was worth. Being a head taller than his all-powerful mistress made that a helluva lot easier.

"Keep looking into my eyes," she ordered. As Tawfiq spoke, she lifted her tail and snaked it around behind her. Strips of the rough fabric used in their overalls were wrapped around her tail from its base to a hand's width from its tip, which was left bare. The tip was flattened but curled in on itself like a rolled tongue.

Suddenly the tip whipped through the air and smacked into Arun's left cheek. He was still gasping with shock when the tail whipped back behind the Hardit and slapped him on the right.

This time, Arun was ready for it.

He hadn't broken eye contact with the alien. It was a pathetically small victory, but at this point he'd take what he could get.

After that came a steady rhythm of slaps from the Hardit's tail.

On the spectrum of torture implements he had steeled his nerve against, this slapping barely registered. In fact, he suspected it hurt the creature's tail more than his cheek. It was the surprise that had made him gasp.

But that didn't mean it was easy. To stand and take a beating, however feeble it might be, filled Arun with shame. *What kind of Marine would crawl to these ugly creatures?* He bit his lower lip. His body started to shake with the effort to keep from punching that stupid alien veck between its three ugly eyes.

There was a bulbous projection on the end of the Hardit's snout that he assumed was her nose. Arun pictured grabbing that nose in his hand and pulling with every ounce of strength. Would it come off? His hands clenched with the thought. He hoped it would only come half off. Yes, that was even better.

"Return to your place."

Arun came back to himself, realizing his breathing was fast and shallow. He stepped back, still not breaking eye contact.

He was daring the alien to break eye contact with *him*.

"109, come here for whipping."

Madge stepped up and Tawfiq started to beat her the same way.

Arun was still seething with humiliation, quaking with all the anger that had pumped through his muscles but had nowhere to go.

By contrast, Madge barely seemed to register what Tawfiq was doing, which only made Arun feel more humiliated.

Standing there and taking it was bad, but to watch his friend take her slapping was far harder. They were part of a team. Even though Madge thought him no better than pond scum right now, they still looked out for each other. But Arun could only stand there and shake with impotence.

"109 is female, isn't that so, 106?"

"Right," said Arun.

"She has long and yellow hair does not she?"

"Yes." *Your translator isn't worth drent, Hardit.*

"And human males find that very attractive in human females, don't you... *114?*"

114? That was Springer!

Springer didn't answer. Arun couldn't entirely blame her. Did this monkey creature really think she was a guy? Hadn't Tawfiq just seen Springer naked? Actually, come to think of it, the alien hadn't been paying much attention. Just wait till he got back and told Osman.

"Answer," ordered Tawfiq. The voice coming through her speaker was calm, but the alien was twitching with agitation. "Are you attracted to this female's hairs?"

"Yes," said Springer. "Her yellow hairs fill me with such extreme lust that I often faint with the desire to caress them."

Steady on, Springer. Don't push it.

The alien paused, probably to translate Springer's words, before addressing Arun. "And you, 106?"

"Sure," he replied. "109 has pretty hairs and looks really hot."

"I wonder," said Tawfiq, "whether 109 will still *look really hot* by the time I have finished her whipping." The Hardit sped up her tail swipes. "Shall we see?"

The artificial voice was expressionless, but Arun couldn't help but imagine a sly quality to it. A gloating that Arun longed to smack out of the creature. He looked at the lineup of Aux, searching for support, but they glanced away, pretending not to see, or looked bored as if they'd seen it all before. Only Hortez watched from the back row, anger sketched onto his face.

"Keep watching, 106!" The Hardit's artificial voice did not change its expression, but the alien's anger registered as a louder volume. "This is only a gentle introduction to your program of torture."

Madge began to blink. Then she sneezed. The tail had whipped her cheek unerringly but with the sudden movement of the sneeze, it cut into her nose, bringing out a stream of blood. The Hardit's striking tail smeared the beads of red over Madge's cheeks.

Arun bore it for another half dozen swipes, but the sight of his friend smeared in her own blood was too much.

"Okay," he told the Hardit, "you've made your point."

The alien stopped. "The human speaks. What does it mean?"

"I said you've made your point. You're the boss. We'll do what you say. There's no point in carrying on hitting her."

"Oh, but there is. You are just too stupid to understand yet. But you shall."

Glaring at him all the time, Tawfiq's tail curled around her waist and touched a device at her hip.

Every muscle in Arun's body contracted at once. His diaphragm squeezed the air from his lungs. His knees pressed hard against his chest and he fell to the ground, unable to do anything but silently scream against the pain wracking his body.

Then the pressure released enough for him to draw a breath, and relax the clamp that his jaw had become. No wonder the overalls hung so heavily; they contained an electro-shocker system.

Before he had time to speak, the pain was back and his own muscles had been turned against him again, compressing him into a ball. He rolled over in a feeble attempt to escape the Hardit, who he thought was kicking him, but it was difficult to know what was going on since all that mattered was the need to breathe because the Hardit veck was enjoying this too much to release him from the pain. Steam blew out his mouth. Something was smoldering. It might be his skin or teeth or maybe the hairs over his body, but it didn't matter anymore because…

Then he was breathing the sweet, sweet air. Gulping at it greedily, petrified that each breath would be his last.

It took some time for Arun to fully come back to his senses.

"Stand!" Tawfiq ordered.

Arun struggled to his feet.

"I assure you that I have not hit 109 while you were incapacitated." Tawfiq advanced on Arun and pressed her snout up into his face. Her breath stank of stale cabbage and fresh feces.

She growled in her throat. Then the speaker attached to her collar elaborated: "I did not wish you to miss any of 109's pain."

Tawfiq went back to slapping Madge.

After only half a dozen swipes, the beating was interrupted when another Hardit walked in. Tawfiq switched off her translator unit and the two aliens argued in their own growling speech. Their tails touched and stroked each other. Then, without any change in their conversation, their tails stretched longer and thinner and snaked through gaps in their overalls to caress each other's body.

When they began rubbing with their tails, the tone of their voices softened, taking on a crooning quality.

Arun managed to be both disgusted by the lewd alien display and grateful for the interruption to their torture.

The respite only lasted a minute or so before the two aliens broke off contact.

"I enjoyed your pain," said Tawfiq in her artificial human male voice. "But we must save the rest of the female's beating until later. Humans, you have work to do."

Tawfiq gave out the day's assignments. The newcomers were each paired with an experienced Aux, and Arun thought his luck had changed slightly when he realized he was to be paired with Hortez.

But then Madge thumped him painfully in the ribs as they walked out into the passageway.

"Thanks for nothing, you dongwit."

"What? What did I do?"

"Monkey-bitch was obviously trying to goad you. *Watch me strike this attractive female. How does that make you feel?* Well, didn't take long for us to find out, genius? Did it?"

"I got it worse than you, didn't I?"

Madge grabbed him by the shoulders and span him around, forcing Arun to look into her beautiful, blood-spattered face.

"Tawfiq wants your ass. You've just let her know that beating me is a perfect way to get to you. So guess who's going to get beaten and humiliated every chance that monkey-bitch gets."

"Lay off him," protested Springer.

At least someone doesn't hate me, thought Arun.

"Oh, I'm sorry, cadet. Did I say something horrible to your boyfriend?"

Springer stiffened at that but said nothing.

"What would you know anyway?" Madge snapped. "Monkey-bitch took one look and assumed you were a boy. If you ever wondered about your looks, then wonder no more, sister."

Arun watched in horror as his friends squared up to each other, violence in their eyes.

"Keep your mouth shut, McEwan," whispered Hortez. "Let them sort it out. I might be down and nearly out, but I still understand women better than you do. Besides, once you've finished being Tunnel-Aux scum, Madge will be your cadet NCO again. She needs to remind both of you who's in charge."

Springer and Madge broke contact and stormed off down the corridor so fast that the Aux they were supposed to be following had to run to keep up with their charges.

Hortez slowed, grabbing Arun's sleeve to encourage him to do the same. "Let them go," said Hortez "Try to make things right with them tonight.

And don't be too hard on yourselves. Breaking us is about the only pleasure the Hardits have. They've gotten quite good about it."

Arun slapped his friend on the back. "I'm thinking," he hissed.

It was good to hear his friend talk when he'd pretty much given Hortez up for dead, but Arun wanted quiet to think.

Most people when they got angry just wanted to hit something, their higher order cognitive functions on temporary leave of absence. Software system architecture design, problem solving, strategic planning – these were off the menu until the fight or flight hormones had been purged from their system.

Arun was like that too – most of the time. But maybe Arun was an experimental rewiring, a test subject for the human re-engineering program. Because he could take all that anger and shunt the energy into his mind, making it whirl and dance in ways that were normally beyond him.

And that's what happened now.

The Hardits had humiliated the cadets but had revealed many weaknesses as they did so. Inside his head, Arun pictured a mindscape of possibilities. Opportunities to exploit those Hardit weaknesses were laid out across this mindscape, scores of them. Arun knew better than to box in his thinking with conscious thought, so he unleashed his mind to roam wherever it wanted, testing the strength of those possibilities, rejecting most, promoting some. Extrapolating. Dreaming.

By the time his mind calmed, its task completed, he'd only progressed ten paces along the corridor. He couldn't point to any definite plan. Not yet. Nothing like that conviction that had told him to connect to Xin through Scendence. All the same, he was confident that seeds of revenge had been planted in his head, ready to sprout and bloom when the time was right.

He grinned, even though his mind felt bruised by its effort.

This was going to be a week the Hardits would never forget.

Chapter 28

As far as Arun was concerned, when you pooped indoors, you did your business, flushed, and went on with your day. What happened after you flushed had never occurred to him.

Until now.

Banishment to the Aux underclass had already opened his eyes to some of the least glamorous aspects of life in Detroit.

Opened his eyes and made them water with the stench.

That first morning with Hortez, Arun learned what happened after you flushed.

Aux Team Beta was based near the regimental school on Level 5. At seven years old, the most promising kids were enrolled in the school as its new intake of novices. There the children fought, trained and competed to graduate as cadets at the age of 17.

Until a few weeks earlier, Hortez and the rest of Blue Squad had still been novices, sleeping in a 50-bed dorm not five minutes' walk from Team Beta's base. Now, for his first assignment as an Aux, Arun was back, helping Hortez to transfer novices' rotting excrement from the collection vats into wheeled storage tanks. It had been one of these slurry carts that Hortez had been pushing when Arun had first chanced across him on his bike.

Tawfiq had tasked them with clearing out one latrine block in the morning and another in the afternoon. That hadn't sounded too hard, but then Arun had assumed they would be cleaning out a single day's filth.

They weren't.

Underneath the latrines were collection vats where the output of several hundred novice backsides accumulated for 2-3 weeks before the Aux emptied them. The putrid stench hit Arun the moment he opened the door to the access passageway.

The vats were primed with an automated suffusion of bacteria, engineered to rapidly transform the dung into fertilizer, readily digestible by both the crops grown topside by human Agri-Aux, and the Troggie fungus farms in dark underground caverns.

For the first few trips, Arun and Hortez fitted hoses to drainage taps and allowed the lumpy liquid to drain into the tanks of their dung carts. The foul slurry stank and splashed but they wiped themselves off as best they could, and pushed the carts up the long looping main ramp of Helix 1, and then out past the watching Marines of Gate 5 to a topside facility. There they emptied their contents into wagons with sprayer attachments that would be towed by the Agri-Aux to their fields.

Arun had been grateful for the fresh air once they reached the surface, but Hortez had picked up pace, eager to get under cover. He'd already explained that without the protective spray of the shower block oils, Tranquility's sun burned.

Arun thought his friend was making a drama out of all this sun-worry, especially after they emerged into a topside deeply shadowed by the mountains. Even in half-light, the peeling skin and weeping sore on Hortez's cheek were now more obvious, more than enough to convince Arun to follow his friend's example by pulling his hat low and keeping to the deepest shadows. He prayed they never sent him out beyond the protective shield of the mountains.

After their third trip, the latrine slurry stopped flowing and there was no choice but to open the hatch. They got in and shoveled, the brown goop slapping around their calves and sucking at their every step. The sight of endless gallons of semi-putrefied dung churned Arun's stomach so much that he vomited the contents of his stomach into the vat. The wet slurping noise as they dug out another shovel-full was merely disgusting; far more sickening was the toxic stench. In the end, they took it in turns, one spending five minutes shoveling while the other recovered, breathing the air outside. The same putrid access passageway air that had so horrified Arun at the beginning was now sweet-smelling relief, compared with the miasma inside the vat.

A couple more trips later and Arun's sense of smell had been so violated that it finally shut down in protest.

He might not be able to smell his own stench any longer, but it became clear that other people could. They chanced across two novice boys skulking in the passageway outside at the end of a return trip back to the vats. The lads – Arun put them at about 14 – made a show of wrinkling their noses in disgust.

One of the boys placed himself in the middle of the tunnel, barring their way. "Apologize," he ordered.

His friend joined him. "Yeah, say sorry for offending decent people with your Aux stink."

Arun and Hortez halted their carts a short distance away from the roadblock.

"I'm sorry, sir," said Hortez. "Please let us pass."

Arun looked in horror at his friend. Then he turned his attention to the boys. Could he pick up these novices and shove them into the vat of dung? Probably. He started thinking through the consequences.

"You!" The first boy pointed at Arun. "You have to apologize too."

Arun scowled back.

"C'mon, man," Hortez whispered to him. "We've got more to worry about than your stupid pride."

"Sometimes it is only pride that keeps us fighting through adversity."

"You can cut that Marine Corps drent out right away," hissed Hortez. "That doesn't apply to me anymore, or had you forgotten?"

"We're waiting," said the second boy. "Do we have to report you?"

"Do it for my sake," Hortez insisted.

Arun clenched his jaw in fury. He was going to do it. He really was…

Gazing blankly into the middle distance he said vaguely: "I'm sorry."

"Not good enough," said the first boy.

"Yeah, like that would convince anyone," said his friend. "Kneel down and kiss my boots. No, you stink too much. Kneel down five paces in front of me and… and lick the floor." He laughed. So did his little veck of a friend.

That was too much! The stupid skangat was going headfirst into the collection vat and damn the consequences.

Arun had only taken one step toward the nearest boy when they were interrupted by the sound of laughter. Another two novices emerged from farther up the corridor, a boy and a girl, also about 14. When they saw what was happening, the laughter stopped. The new boy shook his head sadly and put his hands on his hips. "What do you think you're up to, Rammy?"

The two bullies looked crestfallen as they glanced at each other, trying to work out how to play the situation. They withered under the disapproving glare of the other novices.

Arun was convinced he knew what he was seeing now. These kids had arranged to meet up for a little privacy. A double date during a gap between classes.

"Well?" demanded the girl. "Why are you causing trouble, Stephan? You know you're already on a warning."

"We're punishing these Aux," replied Stephan without conviction.

"They deserve it," said the other boy, Rammy. "For olfactory offenses." He couldn't help laughing.

"It's not funny," said the unnamed boy. "Leave them alone. They can't help being Aux."

"Can't they?" said Stephan. "I reckon they can. You're not born an Aux. You become one because you're a loser." He addressed Hortez and Arun. "You are losers, aren't you?"

Hortez answered without hesitation. "Yes, sir."

"Why're you a loser?" Rammy asked him. "What didja do?"

"No, don't answer that," the girl told Hortez.

"Why shouldn't he, Ibri?" asked Rammy.

"Because I don't want to hear any of the ways in which we could end up like them. Besides, you're an utter skangat, Ramdas Tammaro. I expect Stephan put you up to this and you were too pussy to stand up to him. You're better than this."

"I don't plan on being a loser," said Ramdas. There was steel in his voice. Arun reckoned he'd already worked out that his date was a wash out. *Tough luck, you veck.*

"Yeah? Well, I don't expect those two did either," said his date, "but look where they ended up all the same."

"I still say they're frakking losers," said Ramdas.

His date glared back, daring him to retract.

Then the other boy upped the stakes. "Apologize to those poor guys," he demanded.

Arun glanced at Hortez. His friend was wearing a glazed expression as if he weren't entirely there. Arun was beginning to see how that worked. Here was an argument going on right in front of their faces. On the surface, at least, the argument was about the two Aux, but the truth was that they weren't really part of the exchange. As Aux, they were expected to wait there in silence until their betters permitted them to go about their business.

Only yesterday, if he'd come here wearing his cadet's fatigues, the novices would have stepped politely aside out of his way. Well, he decided, he was still the same person as the day before. And so he spoke up.

"There's no harm done," Arun said. "Let us go on our way."

"Stay where you are," ordered the girl. She redirected her glare at Arun, if anything, intensifying it. "You're not going anywhere until these two idiots say sorry."

Eventually, after much sighing and rolling of eyes, Stephan and Ramdas made grunting sounds that their dates decided to interpret as apologies. Hortez and Arun were allowed to get back to the collection vat.

They didn't speak for a long time, the only sound the squeak of the dung cart wheels and the slurp and plop of shoveling slurry.

"At first I didn't know what was worse," said Hortez eventually, "the novices who try to grind our face in the dirt, or the ones who pity us. Now? There's no contest. The ones who pity us sometimes throw us scraps to eat. I gulp down every morsel and thank them with every mouthful."

Arun couldn't think of a reply. He wasn't a hero. He wasn't special. It was only the hope that they would let him back into the hab-disks in a few days that separated Arun from Hortez. If he had to stay here forever, he had no doubt he would soon be begging for scraps himself.

And worst of all, it had been him who had gotten Hortez kicked out of the battalion in the first place.

He wracked his mind, trying to think of a way to help out his old friend, hoping his subconscious had worked its planning magic.

But he couldn't. Hortez's plight was hopeless.

The only question was whether Arun and the girls would be joining him.

Chapter 29

That evening, Arun, Springer and Madge joined the roll call of 52 Aux workers, lined up in the back row. They were short one worker, Number 47 having gone off to the kitchen to fetch the evening meal.

Instead of Tawfiq, another Hardit took the roll call. From the faded blue dye in her mane, Arun identified her as Hen Beddes-Stolarz. Hortez had explained before Hen came in that she was as bored by dealing with the human workers as Tawfiq was thirsty for cruelty.

No words were spoken. The Hardit simply stood in front of the lineup, sniffing the scent markers smeared onto the breasts of the humans, and glancing from time to time at the softscreen she was holding.

All of them, Hen included, waited in silence for Number 47, who eventually returned wheeling a catering trolley bearing two metal buckets. One contained stale bread, the other held scraps left behind by the novices from their evening meal.

It wasn't much for 53 people. It wouldn't even feed 10.

Springer cleared her throat. "Mistress, I beg permission to speak."

Hen flicked her ears. Whether that meant interest or anger was something Arun had yet to learn. But when the Hardit walked over to Springer and gave her a sniff, she said in her artificial voice of a human male: "114. A new one. Yes, human, you may speak."

"Forgive my ignorance," said Springer, "but that food is insufficient nutrition for 50 humans, and by adding our mouths to your team, it is even less adequate. I can see that the workers of Auxiliary Team Beta are malnourished. May we please have more food rations so that we may work harder for you?"

Hen closed her eyes but said nothing.

What was Springer playing at? They'd agreed not to wind up the Hardits, to get out of here in one piece. Arun couldn't help admiring Springer, though, even if she was one stupid shunter.

If Tawfiq had been here, Arun had no doubt that she would have activated the pain function in Springer's suit. But Hen Beddes-Stolarz was different. She opened her eyes and waved her ears from side to side in a motion Hortez had told him indicated pleasure.

"You ask a valid question," Hen replied through her voice box, the artificial voice sounding so reasonable. "You argue that we overseers provide ineffective care for our work team. Your reasoning is not at fault, but your error is to start with the assumption that Work Team Beta consists of 53 individuals."

"Mistress, I do not understand."

"That is obvious, 114. Obvious and to be expected. It is your ignorance and stupidity that makes humans inferior. Team Beta's workforce consists of 22 humans. And yet I see 53 bodies when I include you new ones. What we have here is not an insufficient supply of food but an *over*-supply of workers. No, that is not quite right. *You* are suffering from oversupply. Team Beta has work for 22 individuals. We have accommodation and food for 22. The law of supply and demand is universal. Demand is fixed and so eventually supply must reduce to match demand."

"We don't even have food for 22, mistress," said 47 angrily. "Five thugs from Team Gamma – Cliffie's team – were waiting for me on the way back from the kitchens. They stole four of our food buckets."

"Excellent." Hen wiggled her ears. "Number 47 adds a well-timed additional dimension to this matter. We prefer our work teams to have the strongest individuals. Transferring workers between teams is simple. If you want the food back then prove you are strong enough to deserve it. Steal it back."

Springer didn't hesitate. "Team Beta!" she yelled. "Who's with me?"

To hear such fire in a human belly sent a jolt of surprise shooting through the Aux.

Arun and Madge were by Springer's side in an instant. Hortez hesitated for a moment before joining them.

A flicker of fire lit up the eyes of the other Aux.

"Don't forget, they'll be gone in a week," sneered Number 87 – the worker who'd stolen their clothes.

Her words snuffed out the Aux spirit, making them turn their heads and look away.

Hortez whispered into Springer's ear. "You're insane. And I don't mean that in a good way."

Madge ignored him and led the little team out of the room.

The Hardit made no move to stop them. Instead, she called out: "I do so love the spectacle of you humans fighting over scraps of food like flea-ridden, starving animals. Which, of course, is all you are."

The humans marched proudly away until they were out of sight. Then Madge halted.

"First question," she said. "Who the frakk is Cliffie?"

Chapter 30

Arun took point as they stormed into Team Gamma's room. They identified Cliffie immediately. He was fat and clean shaven, the opposite of the males in Team Beta. Their room had the same discarded human clothing, except here the collection was much larger and had been neatly arranged into a crude staircase leading up to a seat. A throne, Arun realized, of tight rolls of clothing bound together by loose fabric strips.

Sitting on his throne was Cliffie.

The Gamma Aux were enjoying their meal. Arun counted eight buckets of food and 35 Aux. Team Beta outnumbered the bullies. It should be them dominating the smaller group, not the other way around!

Arun charged up the textile steps toward Cliffie. Before he reached the throne, Gamma proved their worth, dropping their meals to crowd the invaders. The four Aux who had been eating at Cliffie's feet now formed a protective wall between Arun's group and their leader.

So Cliffie had guards, and his team had discipline and full bellies. None of that was enough to stop Arun feeling this was ridiculous. The enemy was defending the crest of an artificial ridge constructed from dirty shirts and underwear. Insane! But Arun didn't doubt the look in their eyes that said they would defend this position to the death.

Madge had discussed tactics before they moved in. Success, they'd agreed, depended on speed. It was essential they overpowered Cliffie before his team could react.

This wasn't going well.

From the perspective of a full Marine, or even a cadet, the Aux were all failures for one reason or another. But as Arun felt the gaze of angry eyes pierce his body, he was well aware that everyone here was at least partially combat trained.

"We have guests," Cliffie said. He gestured at the crowd to back away. "Give them a little space to speak their piece."

Arun halted halfway up the steps, just outside of punching range of the guards. It had been Madge's idea for him to take the lead, to brutally pummel Cliffie into submission. She argued that one primal male brute ousting another would make the message clear in this primitive world. But the assumptions of macho brutishness crumbled in the face of reality. Three of Cliffie's guards were women, and Cliffie himself was clean and groomed, his voice soft and playful.

"Please," said Cliffie to Arun. "Speak."

Arun snarled his reply: "You took food that belonged to Team Beta."

"Yes." There was no malice in Cliffie's voice. He spoke as if explaining a simple truth to a child. "Did you come to inform me of this," he added while Arun was still thinking of a reply, "or did you want to ask me something?"

"Give us our food."

Cliffie tutted. "This is a grim place, to be sure, but there is no need to coarsen it with rudeness. Do I hear a please?"

"Are you mad? No, you don't get to *hear a please*. Politeness went out the door when you stole what wasn't yours."

Cliffie scratched his chin, making a play of chewing over Arun's words. "I've heard of you. Here on a forced vacation after making some ill-advised threats. Threats you did not follow up properly. But..." He stretched out his arms in a welcoming gesture. "There is no need for unpleasantness. Let me educate you. You speak of *stealing*. That is a legal term. The rule of law is very strong in the Auxiliary camps, my new friends, and our law is called *Natural Law*. Our law says that the strong must take from the weak. Team Gamma is stronger than Team Beta, and that gives us the right to take your food. There is no crime committed here. Permit me, if you will, a demonstration."

He held up one arm and clicked his fingers.

Cliffie's guards dove at Arun.

Arun picked out the one farthest from the wall and leaped at her, plucking her from the air and diving off the steps to the floor. The fall wasn't far but was enough for him to twist in midair so that when they hit the ground, the guard was beneath him and his knees pulled up into her gut, winding her.

He tried to press home his advantage by punching her in the face but one of the guards had grabbed him as he fell, and was now holding back his shoulders.

Arun's punch still thumped into the downed guard's nose, but there was no strength in his blow.

With a supreme effort he got to his feet despite the guard on his back who was throttling him, and the one on the ground grabbing at his legs.

Just as he was preparing to throw back his head to dislodge the guard on his back, the two he'd left behind on the steps fell upon him, dashing him to the ground. Pinned helplessly beneath their weight he could feel the weight of more Gamma Team Aux jump on him, kicking and punching.

Where was his backup? Then he spotted Springer and Madge, already pinned on the ground. Hortez was out of sight.

All he could do now was bring his arms up to offer a little protection for his head.

Arun was dazed. Under the crush of bodies, he was gasping for air. But even in that confused state he knew Gamma was only disabling him. They could easily have killed him, but the pummeling stopped without serious damage. Instead, they hooded him, lifted him, and threw him onto one of the lower steps of the ramp of clothing. All the while, they kept enough of a crush of bodies on top that he couldn't scramble free.

He realized with a shiver of humiliation that he'd been hooded by a dirty pair of shorts. More clothing was thrown at him. The huge mound of clothing that Cliffie's throne sat atop was huge, far larger than Team Beta's collection and easily enough to suffocate someone.

Panic injected fresh energy into tired limbs. Arun tried to buck and writhe his way out, but the press was too heavy. He tried to dig out an air pocket but it was too late, the crush too strong. His desperate gasping for air had sucked in the dirty fabric of the shorts pressed into his face. But he didn't care because his head started swimming. His mind was slipping away.

He felt a brief flicker of regret for getting Springer and Madge into this mess and then… And then he was *breathing*. Through the filter of discarded underwear, he was breathing air. The weight from his back was lifting. He managed to raise himself to all fours, to throw off the shorts around his head.

While Arun still knelt there with his head hung low, trying to come to terms with still being alive, he heard Cliffie crowing. "There, you see? A practical lesson in Natural Law. But your team are hungry, you say. We aren't heartless, are we Gamma?"

From around the room, all the Aux replied: "No, Cliffie."

"You, 45, give the pretty one an empty bucket. I want all of you to tear off a hunk of bread – a generous one, mind – and throw it onto the floor. If our guests want the food, they can pick it up and take it away."

The next few minutes were a nightmare that made Arun shake with shame. Every time they bent over to pick up some bread, they were kicked in the butt. So they took to scrambling around the floor on their knees, but Gamma took that as an invitation to ride on their backs, smacking their flanks and butts with cries to *giddy up!* That brought fresh waves of jeering from the crowd. The need for revenge burned ever hotter in Arun's gut.

They gave Team Gamma spectacular entertainment that night.

Gamma would pay for that!

Once they had put a safe distance from Cliffie's team, they regrouped, the bucket of hard-won bread safely in Arun's hands. Hortez needed a rest. He was so weak he could barely walk.

Arun was fuming, unable to speak because he was too angry at having his ass kicked in every sense.

"What do we say to the others when we get back?" asked Springer.

"That's your call," replied Madge. "After all, it was your dumb idea to get Beta's food back."

"We tell the truth," Springer said through clenched teeth. "We got Beta more food. How we did it is none of their business."

Chapter 31

"There's gotta be a Hardit weakness we can exploit." Arun scanned the slumped forms of the Beta Aux, but he couldn't detect any signs that his pleas were inspiring them. "C'mon, we've all been to the same school. We've been trained to look at a combat scenario and uncover the enemy's weak points."

"Don't you think we've tried," said a tired voice from a figure crumpled against the back wall.

"What's your name, friend?" Arun tried to pitch his words carefully: encouraging and friendly. It wasn't easy. He looked at these wretched almost-cadets. He felt pity for them, but more than that, anger. Fury that these people who were almost like him had been treated so foully, but even more rage that these pathetic specimens had allowed themselves to sink so low so quickly.

"Miller," replied the voice from the back wall. "Adrienne Miller." She sounded as if she had to search her memory for the name. Arun recognized the voice as the girl who had taken their clothes and sneered at their attempt to win back some food. Number 87.

"Well, Adrienne, I don't want to kick a girl when she's down," said Arun, "but there's one big difference between us and you. I fully intend to get out of this. That's tough on you but we all know it's true. I think my hope can spark inspiration, a fresh look at old problems. There's no harm in trying, eh?"

Adrienne simmered with resentment. Until he saw that look, Arun had recognized her voice from before but not her face. All the Aux had the same clothes, cropped hair, grimy faces and look of hopelessness. It was as if their personality had been abraded away, leaving worn stubs where once there had been people. Hortez had a little of his old flair left, and Adrienne had her resentment. Soon even those would be gone.

"How about rivalry?" suggested Madge. "Some Hardits are senior to others. That's got to mean resentment somewhere in the system."

"Never gonna work," said Hortez. "Sure they don't get along like perfect buddies. Sushantat is the number two. She resents Biljah who's in charge and so does no work. Tawfiq is treated like dirt by the others. We think she might be a lower caste. Hen thinks she's too good to be mucking out the humans. She's so deliberately lazy that she actually works hard at her laziness."

"Hold up," said Springer. "You've just given us a host of grievances. Sound like pretty much all the Hardits hate being here."

"That's right," said a new voice from the crowd. "But it won't help you. However big the divide between Hardit clans and individuals, it is nothing compared to the gulf between Hardits and humans. Most of them are arrogant, lazy, and cruel. But they aren't stupid. You'll never be able to play one off against another."

"But this *is* working," Madge insisted.

"Is it?" asked Adrienne.

"Sure it is." Madge sounded excited. "We're just getting started and already we've got a list. They're lazy. They're cruel–"

"–And we already know they struggle with the heavy air and don't like going topside," said Arun. He looked into the Aux faces. Most had turned away, already given up on the stupid newcomers. They'd taken the extra bread Springer's group had won from Cliffie, but that hadn't won the right to lead the group. Hortez was trying to look encouraging but wasn't doing a good job.

They were losing them.

"What about sex?" Arun said. That got a look of contempt and disgust, so he added quickly: "I mean between the Hardits. Are there any romances between them? A couple who would seize a chance to canoodle, thus giving us a chance to do something while they weren't looking?"

Hortez answered. "Forget it. Put Hardits together and they rub each other constantly. They don't understand privacy. I mean Sushantat will be talking to us, giving us a good yelling, and Hen or Tawfiq–"

"Or both," laughed Adrienne.

"Yeah, maybe both will be sneaking their tails inside Shushantat's overalls for a good fondle. Some of the guys think that's rubbing the team scent over each other, but I'm sure it's more than that."

"They're all females," added another voice from the crowd. "If we live long enough, we'll find out about mating season, but most of the time Hardit females and males avoid each other."

Hortez stood up. "I got something. Well, I think. I dunno…"

"C'mon, man," encouraged Arun. "Spit it out."

"It's like this. Looking after an Aux team is like mucking out the pigs."

"What are pigs?" Springer asked.

"An Earth animal," Hortez replied. "Doesn't matter. Point is, our overseers have sunk to the most demeaning job possible. They hate that. They take every opportunity to humiliate us because we're the only people even lower than them. I guess it's some kind of consolation."

"Brilliant!" Arun packed as much enthusiasm as he could as he slapped Hortez on the back. "Knew you'd come through for the team, man."

"He hasn't said anything useful yet," said Miller. "Besides. It's easy for you. *Oh, I'm so clever because I have all these fancy ideas.* You'll go back to your nice clean bunk in a week, sleeping on sheets laundered by an Aux slave, a belly filled with Aux-cooked food. How does any of this drent you've been talking actually help *me*?"

"I don't know yet, Adrienne. But I'm gonna come up with something. I promise."

Adrienne snorted. "What about you, 114?"

"Believe in him, sister," said Springer.

"I know he's annoying," added Madge. "Horden knows I'd leave him here behind with you if I could. He's unreliable, stupid, lazy…" She gave Arun a baleful stare. *"Disloyal.* Frankly, he's an imbecile whose head is ruled not by his brain but by something a few degrees south of there. But there is one thing I can't take away from him. When it comes to Scendence, he's the best Deception-Planning player I've ever seen. Some say his head is wired up like an organic battle computer. You all know that most scuttlebutt flying round the base is steaming with drent, but I am certain of one thing. If there's one person who can come up with a plan to improve your lives, it's Arun McEwan. You just need to give him a few facts to work on, and time to think."

Arun grimaced. He'd hoped to get some fresh ideas to feed into his planning brain. But he'd heard frakk all of any use and now even Madge was building him up into a messiah.

If he was going to come up with any bright ideas they'd better arrive soon, or he would be stuck in this stinking hole for the rest of his short life.

Chapter 32

Arun leaned over and tapped Madge on the knee. "Hey, Corporal Majanita! Can I ask a question?" When she didn't immediately respond, he whispered: "Have you got a blade? I don't mean a weapon, just something that can cut."

Madge lifted the brim of her hat to give him the benefit of a foul look. "And I was having such a lovely dream."

"No, you weren't. You had one eye open, watching that Adrienne. I don't blame you, either."

"Well, keep it quiet anyway," she whispered. "Springer's snoring away. I can feel her rumble through my back. She's sweet when she's asleep."

Arun tried to lean closer still to Madge without disturbing Hortez whose weight was heavy against Arun's spine. Like most of Team Beta, the newcomers slept back-to-back because with over 50 people in a room 8 meters by 4, there was no space to lie down. Even the strongest only managed to slump against the walls, using discarded clothing as a layer of insulation against the cold plastic skin of the wall and still wearing their dirty hats.

The initiation for newcomers varied depending on the mood of the Hardit overseers, but always included the order to strip naked, and don the heavy overalls through which they could send punishing shocks into their human workers. To wear any other item of clothing was punishable by death; the Hardits were very clear on that point.

At first Arun assumed the no-underclothing order was so the effect of the electric shocks wasn't diluted. That may be the case, but after the experiences of his first day, and talking with the Aux, he saw a new pattern of Hardit behavior.

The aliens had no qualms about inflicting pain, mutilation, and death, when it suited them, but they quickly tired of such things. What drove them was not sadism but the desire to lord it over the humans. The lower the Hardits could grind the humans into the dirt, the more superior they felt.

They could have destroyed the discarded human clothing, forcing them to shiver in the cold during their allotted sleep shift. Instead they were allowed to use the moldering and insect-ridden clothing as nesting material. The garments piled against the back wall during the day were now spread out over the floor and piled on top of the slumbering Aux. Forbidden to wear their own clothing, the humans were expected to be grateful for permission to burrow under these reminders of their shattered lives like feral animals.

The Hardit skangats found that very amusing.

By now, Arun had shuffled closer so he could whisper into Madge's ear, Hortez having slumped away to lean against the shoulder of another Aux.

"I know you, Madge," Arun whispered. "You're sneaky. Have you a blade, shiv, sharpened rock? Anything that would cut?"

"Get a grip of yourself, cadet." There was a hard edge to her whisper. "Out of earshot you will address me properly."

"Sorry, corporal."

She glared.

"It's those Hardit vecks, corporal. I can see how this plays out. Every day they'll make me watch you being beaten and humiliated. I can't take that forever. I'll break. I know I will. I'll punch them in their stupid snouts. And then they'll kill me."

Madge thought over his words. "Only if you let them, McEwan," she whispered back. "I know I gave you a hard time when you stood up for me this morning. That was to make you angry. I mean, sure you were dumb to do what you did, but dumb is what you are. I was trying to give you the gift of anger, though Horden knows you don't deserve any gifts after your serial frakk ups. Give in to your rage. Seethe at the injustice all around. Use that energy to fight your instincts and stay alive."

"But do you have a blade? I promise it isn't to use as a combat weapon against the monkey-vecks."

Madge sighed. "You'd better be telling the truth, McEwan." She lowered her voice to the barest whisper. "Springer and I had flexible las-blades sown into our underwear. We've got needle and thread too."

Arun nearly laughed at that but cut himself off just in time. "Good old, Rekka. She always said a well-prepared Marine always goes into battle with needle and thread. Guess she was right. "Now, don't be coy, corporal, it doesn't suit you. When you said underwear, which piece? It's not as if you're actually wearing any."

"First you tell me your plan."

"It involves you making a great sacrifice." Arun looked shamefaced: he'd not fully thought of what his idea meant for Madge. "I'm sorry. Really, but I want you to help me stay alive."

"Stop vulleying around, McEwan, and tell me what you want me to do."

"It involves taking off your clothes."

The flicker of disgust on Madge's face was swiftly replaced by the shock of understanding when she figured out what Arun was planning. She slid into the sexy pout she'd often worn in happier times when they'd still been novices. "For you, darling, anything," she said. "You clever boy. You'll find what you're looking for in our bras."

Springer had sensed the change of mood and woken. Hortez snored on. None of them offered to help Arun in his task of locating the undergarments in the room packed with sleeping Aux. So he set about his task, trying his best to ignore his two grinning comrades while he whispered apologies to the Aux as he jostled them awake. He rammed his hands underneath them in search of two items amongst the sea of nesting material.

His squadmates would be recording this. Of that he had no doubt. The data flow down their optic nerves would be copied into their auxiliary storage implants. If they ever made it back to hab-disk 6/14 alive, the story of Arun and his nighttime bra hunt would spread wide, and he would be a figure of fun for the rest of his life.

Couldn't the girls see that this was important? Just for once he'd prefer them to be more like robots.

Eventually Springer and Madge tired of their fun and joined the bra hunt. A confused Hortez looked on, slowly coming to his senses.

Perhaps the relative freshness of the newcomers' clothing was a highly prized luxury. Everything else placed next to their skin was greasy and stained. Their pants and shirts were in use as blankets, but the bras were more difficult to locate. They found Madge's stuffed down the front of one Aux's overalls. He said it was just insulation; they said it constituted wearing forbidden clothing. He gave up the bra without a fight.

Springer's bra was the most difficult to find. In the end it was the look on Adrienne's face that gave her away. By now, most of the Aux were awake and resentful, offering mumbled curses and scowls but not resistance. Adrienne's expression was different. Underneath the annoyance was a defensive look. She had something to hide.

When Madge and Springer searched her, they found she was actually wearing Springer's bra, even though it was so tight it must have been uncomfortable. Adrienne didn't fight back as they stripped her of the garment, but they knew they had made an enemy there, and a dangerous one. The other Aux seemed afraid of Number 87.

Once they'd gathered the underwear, the Blue Squad comrades pushed their way to one of the walls, huddled together and set to work.

Adrienne spied on them. Arun began to wonder whether she was a snitch, spying for the Hardits in return for some pathetic scraps of food or favors.

Hortez and Arun shielded the girls by standing up, arms folded and glaring at Adrienne. She pretended to lose interest but kept throwing sly glances their way.

Arun caught a whiff of burning and then Springer swapped places with Hortez who was an expert with needle and thread.

You never quite knew what would happen next with Springer, which was one reason why she was so popular. One thing was for sure: she didn't have the patience of Hortez.

The next time Adrienne spied on them, Springer gave a cry of rage and barged through the crush of people, aiming straight for her. Adrienne looked away. Then she looked back, but Springer was still charging toward her. The Aux woman blanched, getting to her feet just in time for Springer to slam her down onto her butt. Springer sat down, straddling Adrienne's lap.

Springer kissed her. She embraced the Aux girl with the same furious energy that had propelled her across the room like a missile. Springer never did things by half, which is why Arun both adored her and was scared of her in equal measure. Her hands roamed down Adrienne's back, squeezing and kneading.

Arun looked on, astonished. Springer's eyes blazed with violet, a light so intense that the glow lit up Adrienne's face. He caught Springer glancing back at him. Her glowing eyes were like a laser range-finder searching for some reaction from him.

Then she was back in Adrienne's face, drawn back by Adrienne herself who had pushed Springer away at first, but was now clutching at her hungrily.

"That's quite a display," said Hortez who had finished his task. He punched Arun on the arm.

"Please, Hortez. Give our Springer some respect. She's not putting on a display for our benefit, and she's not doing that for pleasure. She's making a diversion to distract that snitch."

"Sure, man. It's that too."

Before Arun could think of an answer, Springer gave one of her own. She broke off, shoving Adrienne against the wall. Number 87 looked on helplessly as Springer hawked up a mouthful of spit. But at the last moment, Springer changed her mind and didn't unleash the gobful at the cowering girl.

From someone who a few moments earlier had shown more spirit than any of the other Aux, Adrienne now looked lost and fearful. Then she started to sob.

Springer left the weeping girl alone and rejoined her group.

Arun had no idea what that was all about but Hortez grabbed Springer's arm as she walked past. "You've still got pity in you," he said. "That's good. Don't let them drive it out of you. Don't hate us, not even Adrienne Miller. It's better that you pity us."

"You always did deep-talk nonsense, Hortez," said Springer. "I don't hate you Aux."

"Give it time," said Hortez. "You have plenty left to see."

Chapter 33

"Step forward, 106," ordered Tawfiq.

A ragged human figure detached itself from the roll-call lineup and stood, head bowed, before Tawfiq and Hen.

"Step forward, 109."

A second figure emerged, equally cowed but distinguishable from the first by a blonde ponytail sneaking out the back of a standard Aux hat.

Tawfiq glanced across at Hen, rubbing tails as she did. "This one with long hair is an attractive female," she explained in the growling Hardit tongue but keeping her translator on automatic to give the humans the full benefit of their humiliation. "The other is male. He understands consequences of defiance. Amusing query. Can he control his protective urge toward her?"

Tawfiq appeared to expect a reply, but Hen stayed silent. "He couldn't help himself yesterday," Tawfiq continued, "so I give him level 3 pain. Today I will use level 4 if he intervenes. Do you understand, human?"

106 gave a nod.

"Stupid though these human animals are, surely even they aren't that stupid," argued Hen.

"Query? Shall we wager?"

"Agreed. Ten credits."

"Done."

The two entwined tails.

"If you understood these creatures as I do," said Tawfiq, "you would realize that the male has marked out this female as one of his harem. This means she has exchanged mating rights in return for his protection. His hormones will drive him to protect his female or die trying."

"I'd like to see one of our males claim mating rights over me!" said Hen.

"Hah! Hah! Hah!"

Both Hardits doubled over and made retching sounds. Laughter, Arun assumed, because Tawfiq's translator system accompanied the sounds with 'hah's. Hen's translator was better than Tawfiq's with normal speech. With laughter, it kept silent.

"Let us see," said Tawfiq when she'd recovered. "Stand closer, 106 and 109."

They obeyed.

"Stop staring at ground. I wish you look into each other's eyes."

They complied. There was the faintest of reactions from the crowd, but the Hardits showed no sign of noticing anything wrong.

Even Adrienne kept quiet, persuaded to keep that way by Springer and Hortez who were flicking threatening glances her way.

Tawfiq began to smack the female with her tail, while watching the male's face, daring him to react.

What the humans all saw was the results of the newcomers' activity the night before, the first part of Arun's plan – not that he'd fully worked out the rest just yet.

Arun and Madge had swapped overalls. They'd used the secreted las-blades to cut off Madge's blonde ponytail. Hortez's expert needlework reattached the hair so that it hung down from Arun's hat.

To the humans the disguise was farcically bad.

But their overseers were the products of a very different chain of evolution. Humans all looked the same to them. They suspected nothing.

Under the gaze of Madge and the Hardits, Arun endured a very mild beating that was more than made up for by knowing he was putting one over on the stupid, skangat monkey-bitch Hardits who thought they were beating Madge.

Best of all, Arun was showing them up in full view of every human there.

Eventually Hen grabbed Tawfiq's tail in hers, bringing the beating to an end. "That's enough," she told Tawfiq. "You lose upon this occasion. Time to get to work."

Tawfiq pressed some tokens into Hen's hand and watched as Hen walked off.

After glaring at the humans for a while, Tawfiq darted into the line-up and brought out Springer and Hortez. "I have a task for new ones and–" she tapped Hortez on his head "–this one who I know is your friend. You will go up top surface. Hen Beddes-Stolarz has a delivery waiting in Bay 32 to make to the fields scum in Alabama." She paused, lips curling high about her teeth. "In fact, that will be your task for rest of the week. You go to Alabama every day whether there is a delivery to make or not."

She grabbed Springer's face, squashing her cheeks together. "You do realize why, don't you?"

"Yes, mistress. We will burn."

"Correct. You will burn."

Tawfiq increased the pressure on Springer's cheeks until she winced. Satisfied, the overseer assigned the tasks to the other workers, and then stormed off.

As soon as she was out of sight, Adrienne was in Madge's face, hands on hips and a sneer across her face. "Give me one good reason why I shouldn't run after Tawfiq and tell her the stunt you just pulled?"

"Because you keep your life." Madge didn't put any aggression in to her voice, but she spoke with absolute conviction as if Adrienne's death would be as certain as night follows day.

Adrienne gave a bitter laugh. "My life isn't worth drent. Have you forgotten last night? Do I have to spell it out?"

"Yes," said Arun.

Springer sighed. "I think what Adrienne means is that she–"

"Stop calling me Adrienne!"

Arun watched in silence as a tear came to Adrienne's eye. She wiped it away.

"For a moment you reminded me of who I once was," the Aux girl snarled, beaming hatred at Springer through slitted eyes. "You veck. Your touch reminded me. Once… once there was someone special. But now he's dead and so is Adrienne. I'm Number 87 now."

"That's only what the Hardits call you," said Springer.

"No, it's what they have made me."

"Well," said Madge, "if your life has no value, how would you like more food instead?"

Adrienne pursed her lips, holding back her initial retort. "All right. How?"

"By taking it from Cliffie," said Madge.

Adrienne snorted. "That didn't work out too well last time, did it?"

"No?" Madge smiled. "Trust me. That was just reconnoitering."

"Consider this," said Hortez. "If we put Cliffie out of the picture permanently, what then?"

"Nothing," spat Adrienne. "One of his gang will take his place."

"Eventually," said Hortez, "if left to their own devices. But they will be off balance. Destabilized. Vulnerable while they fought for succession. If there was a strong man–" he looked Adrienne in the eye "–or strong woman waiting to seize the initiative, to take Cliffie's place, to stand up to them… What then? Don't forget we outnumber Gamma by 3 to 2."

Adrienne shrugged. "Perhaps. But we would need to get rid of Cliffie. I don't see how."

"Leave it to me," said Arun. "I have powerful friends and I'm only just getting started here."

Arun watched the changes come over Adrienne's face. She wasn't convinced, but just for a moment she looked away, her eyes glazing as she thought through possible futures. Better futures.

They'd given her hope.

Bay 32 was on Level 9 in an industrial zone of workshops and production lines where the throb and hum of motors and conveyor belts made the floor shake.

Arun's face lit up when he saw their cargo was waiting for them packed into wooden crates and already loaded onto hover-trolleys.

Hover-trolleys! Carrying their load would be easy.

Once they had swung the trolleys out of the corner of the bay on hover power, Hortez spoiled the mood by explaining that the fuel for the hover motors wouldn't be enough to get them topside, let alone all the way to Alabama, which was 17 klicks away through the Trollstigen mountain pass and out into the western plateau.

So they saved the hover capability for more difficult terrain, and had made their way up two levels of the nearest spine ramp before Madge called a rest halt.

Hortez was already tiring.

Let's crack open the crates," Madge suggested. "We'll take out some of your load, Hortez, and redistribute between the three of us."

"No," said Hortez. "We keep going as we are."

"C'mon, man," said Arun. "We're stronger than you. Don't be a dumbchuck."

"It's not pride making me say no, it's self-preservation. I don't know what's in these crates and don't want to."

"Why?" Arun asked. "What do you think we're carrying?"

"I assumed they were machine parts," said Springer.

Hortez shrugged. "They might be."

"And they might not," Arun finished for him. "Spill!"

"It's just rumors," said Hortez reluctantly. "Talk of black-market smuggling."

"Smuggling? Smuggling what?" Arun said. "We get everything we need. Don't the Hardits?"

"Arun, Arun." Springer slapped him on the back. She was laughing, the sound a balm for Arun's bruised spirits. "It's not that we have everything we need so much as you lack the imagination to want for anything."

When Arun showed no sign of understanding, she added: "How did you think the corporal's hair got to be that shade of blonde? There aren't any hair salons in the hab-disks, you know."

"There's always a favor that can be done," added Madge. "A little surplus to be creamed off, help to be given. A thousand ways to make life a little more bearable. And all of that is tradable."

"The Hardits are at the heart of it all," said Hortez. "It's in their nature. They're natural traders. You gotta see it from their point of view. They were here for a very long time before the Jotuns and we humans showed up. We're like unwelcome guests to them."

"I kinda picked up on the unwelcome part already," said Arun.

"Right," said Hortez. "And guests don't go nosing around in the hidden corners of someone else's home. Not if they know what's good for them."

"All right, we'll do it your way for now," said Madge. "Now get off your butts and start moving. If we're to keep down to Hortez's pace, we can't afford to hang around."

Chapter 34

On the far side of Trollstigen Pass, they came to a crossroads. To right and left the road hugged the foothills of the towering mountains. A simple track ran before them as straight as an energy beam, a gravel and dirt causeway leading to Agri-Facility 21, known by most of the humans as the Alabama Depot.

Although they were still in deep shadow, they could see the landscape opening up before them, the sides of the track sloping down into fields of wheat, maize and barley that waved in the gentle breeze like a golden greeting.

Indeed, it did feel as if the land were welcoming their return, even the fresh outdoor smells were inviting. All of them had been here before in happier times, as novices hiking with heavy packs or running in powered suits or unencumbered, running in nothing more than fatigues and peaked caps.

Arun knew the track carried on far beyond Alabama, as far as the timber plantations. The soil was richer there – or at least different, suitable for growing crops for Detroit's non-human residents. There was Gloigas, long-haired, twisting brown columns crowned with lush purple leaves. And the lurid green, but apparently nutritious, roots of the Tarngrip, which snaked through the undergrowth, trying to ensnare slow-moving limbs, trapping them before slowly crushing the life out of them through hydraulic pressure. The Tarngrips were far too slow to trap a human, at least while you were awake. The carnivorous plants were native to the same homeworld as the Hardits, a planet that had little oxygen in its thin atmosphere, which meant most things moved in slow motion.

Tarngrips were on the Universal Food list. Which meant everyone in the White Knight logistical supply system had their digestions adapted to consume them, human Marines included. The times when he'd seen the contorted faces of other novices forced to eat boiled Tarngrip was all Arun needed to understand why Universal Foods were more usually called *Ugly Foods*.

Arun knew all these crops well because he'd run through them, armored boots trampling great swathes through the crops to the consternation of any Agri-Aux nearby.

Instructor Rekka had once told them: "Get to know every culvert, every bank, ridge and irrigation ditch. One day you might be in them, SA-71 braced on their lip, waiting for the enemy assault to draw nearer before opening fire."

Emerging from the shadows, the bright sun swiftly warmed their spirits, despite following Hortez's advice to pull their stretchy woven hats so far over their faces that the fabric covered their eyes. As they counted down the klicks to Alabama, they peered at the world through gaps in the weave.

"In your hab-disks you go through the shower block every day," Hortez explained. "It's for decontamination and protection as much as hygiene. The spray you're given at the end is more than a dumb protective shield. Embedded into the spray oils are scavenger nanites that suck the ionizing radiation out of the air. Neutralizes it so it doesn't screw with your cells. I had no idea, but the Hardits are eager to explain that to us."

"If it works so well," said Springer, "surely it wouldn't take too much to give you Aux the spray too."

Hortez took a minute to bring himself to reply. "Sushantat told us once. You've yet to meet her. She's effectively in charge of the Aux on Level 5. She explained that the effects of the radiation take around a decade to take a hold of your body. Tumors, organ failure, deformed children. They don't want to send you lot off to war, only to have you riddled with cancer by the time you get to fight. So they give you the scavenger nanites. But the Aux? Why bother? The oldest Aux I ever heard of was 29 Terran standard years. Giving us the protective spray would not be difficult or expensive. But our lives have such little value that they're worth even less than the spray."

"Sorry, man," mumbled Arun, his sentiments echoed by Springer and Madge.

Except the girls don't feel the same as me, thought Arun. *They aren't responsible for putting Hortez here.*

It was time, he decided, to raise the matter that he dreaded most.

"Look, Hortez. I landed you in the drent because I frakked up in that exercise with the Trogs. I'm so sorry. I never knew it would be so bad here."

"Stow it, McEwan," replied Hortez. "You tried apologizing before. Don't try again."

"Fair enough. But I'm going to do more than say sorry. I'm going to ask our new company staff sergeant – Bryant – to have me swap places with you. It should be me festering in this hellhole with those sadistic monkeys."

Hortez glared at Arun who had to look away. Arun could look the Hardits in the eye, but not his friend whom he'd let down so badly.

"Do you really think this Bryant would swap us?"

"Probably not," admitted Arun. "But I don't know that for sure. I can always try."

"Make sure you do," said Hortez. He froze, as if distracted.

"Get off the road," shouted Madge. "Now!"

Arun scrambled down the bank but lost his footing, rolling down and crashing into the waist-high wheat stalks. He turned to see what had spooked Madge. In the distance, back up the way they'd come, they saw a dust cloud and heard a rhythmic pounding. They didn't need image enhancers to know what that was: an approaching squad of Marines, thundering toward them at over 30mph.

He heard a cry of frustration and noticed Springer struggling with her trolley. She'd activated hover mode and was trying to guide the trolley down the bank.

Except the load was too heavy.

Springer was pulling back on the handles, trying to slow its fall, but all she managed was to chase it down the bank.

Arun got to his feet, and rushed into the path of the trolley, hoping to push from the front, but its momentum was too great. The load knocked him flying, forcing Arun to roll away desperately, only inches from being crushed.

The trolley righted itself and came to a stop, hovering cheerfully a meter off the ground as if nothing was the matter. The wooden crate that had been on top snapped its straps and kept going, tumbling over once, twice, three times, screaming as the wood splintered and tore at its fastenings.

"Are you all right?" Arun helped Springer to her feet.

"I'm not hurt, Arun. But my crate…"

The crate had come to rest with one corner buried deeply into the soft soil, and half its sides shattered.

Arun glanced at the onrushing Marines. They looked like a wavefront of a silver sea, about to crash upon them like a tsunami. The pure gold color of their ACE-2 battlesuits was distinctive enough that Arun had no need to see insignia close up. These were veterans of the 420th, led by two Jotun officers. To deviate around the abandoned hover-trolleys would be far beneath their regimental dignity. Any second now the tsunami would break over their abandoned cargo.

The Hardits had given them a simple task, and they had already failed.

The Jotun officers – a captain and a major – showed no signs of noticing the trolleys blocking their way. Cantering like centaurs on four of their six legs, massive crested heads held high, they leaped cleanly over the first obstacle without breaking stride. As their trajectory brought them down onto the second trolley, they threw their front limbs in front of them. Their hands morphed, their armored gauntlets matching every change. What had been human-like five fingers and an opposable thumb, thinned, lengthened and bifurcated repeatedly. They now looked more like waving, long-tendriled fronds held out to either side.

The rubbery fronds hit the cargo crate, pressing down against the wood like organic springs. The tension in their hands sprang back, propelling the aliens cleanly over the second trolley and the third too.

As the major and captain cantered away, a brace of senior human sergeants reached the obstruction. Running at this speed in powered armor was a skill the G-2 cadets of Arun's year had yet to master. When they had been out here as novices in their training armor, the motion had been more of a lope than a run. Not only were these Marines running, but the sergeants followed their officers' example and tried to leap over the abandoned trolleys.

Battlesuit AIs interpreted their wearer's intentions, amplifying human muscle power many-fold. The Marines soared over the first trolley like shells from a howitzer.

Out in the emptiness of space, the battlesuits could speed through a battlefield at crushing velocities. The gravity well of a planet enfeebled the propulsion units in the suits so that their flight capability was reduced to a short hop, such as over a tank.

But the officers hadn't activated their suits' flight capability and so neither could the humans who followed. They used augmented muscle power alone.

As the next rank of Marines jumped into the sky, the sergeants began to fall. The air pushed back against their bulky shapes, and the planet's gravity grabbed at the legs of their heavy armor.

Four hundred pounds of bone, muscle and poly-ceramalloy battlesuit bore down on the middle cargo crate through the armored ball of the sergeant's foot. Arun heard the crack and whine of splintering wood, but the wooden box was strong. It held.

For now.

Arun's brain had been trained and engineered to estimate troop numbers. Around five hundred Marines – three companies of veterans – were yet to clear the abandoned carts, and each one would follow their officers' example and go through rather than around.

They watched as Marines flashed past relentlessly, the smart surfaces of their battlesuits, which could make them invisible when stealthed in space, were now set to shine in regimental gold, with company markings proudly displayed on helmets and squad markings on the knee segments. Streamers tied to knees and elbows flew behind in their slipstream. These were smartfabric ribbons of pulsating color that no cadet or Marine in the 412th would be seen dead in. At least not on a planet's surface where these streamers were no more than a gaudy affectation.

Wearing ribbons in void combat was a different matter entirely; even the 412th trained for that. Inertia would spool out enormous ribbons of reflective and radar hard material behind Marines maneuvering through the vacuum. The possibility of becoming entangled with your squadmates' ribbons was a terror balanced, in theory, by the confusion they sowed in enemy targeting systems.

The Marines might only be from the 420th, but they still looked magnificent.

"Does the sight make you proud?" asked Hortez who had been watching Arun.

His companions looked at each other uneasily.

"I used to dream of being one of them," Hortez continued. "Of earning my own personal device to wear on the thigh of my suit. A bolt of lightning perhaps, or a noble hart. I wanted to belong. I used to think that was my inevitable destiny, an inalienable right. But only the best earn the right to be a Marine. Not everyone makes the grade."

"Stop it!" said Springer. "Don't you ever feel sorry for yourself. I know you're better than that. It's only bad luck that brought you here. You still deserve to be one of them." She pointed at the Marines clearing the abandoned carts.

"Sorry," replied Hortez. "You're right. But the end result is still the same. I didn't make it. There's no way back."

"I never bought into the whole Marine mythos," said Arun, wincing when a boot finally stove in the middle crate. "I'm not saying you're better off as you are, man, but life for a Marine isn't all shiny armor and the comforting heft of an SA-71. The reality is that you get stuffed into a cryo box and stored in a ship's hold. If you're lucky, then you might survive long enough to be awoken just in time to die in battle."

Arun was not a great liar. No one believed him. Even the steady thumping beat of armored feet pounding the ground sounded like the accelerated heartbeat of a super-being. The sight of the Marines, the hammering thump of their boots and faint whine of the armor muscle-amplification, even the sweaty smell vented from the exhaust outlets: everything about them filled his heart with pride.

"There's no shame buying into the dream of becoming one of them," said Hortez gently. "I did. But even if you think pride in your Marine unit is just macho dung, or Jotun brainwashing, it's still better to die young as one of them than live a lifetime as an Aux. Even if it's a short lifetime."

Arun grimaced. What could they say? Fate had dealt Hortez a hand of utter drent and they all knew it. "If I can, man, I'll get you out," he said. "I don't know how but I'll try."

Arun looked at Hortez, trying to let the sincerity show in his face, but his friend stared back with flinty disdain.

"I don't mean asking Bryant to swap us around," Arun added. "Sure, I *will* do that, but I don't hold up hope. I mean something new. Something… something I haven't thought of yet."

Hortez's stare held its scorn for a few more seconds before crumpling into laughter. "Arun McEwan, you sure are something! If anyone else had told me that, I'd have spat in their face. To give a hopeless man a false reason to hope – that's about the cruelest thing possible in an unbearably cruel universe. But you… Things happen around you, McEwan. Like you're blessed or something." Hortez stilled his laughter and regarded Arun seriously.

Arun could see a stiffening of confidence in his friend's face, in the squaring of his stance.

"I'll hook all my remaining hope onto your rising star," said Hortez. "It's like Majanita said last night. If anyone can figure out a way to help me, it's you."

Arun patted him on back. "Yeah, man! We'll do it."

For a moment, Arun thought the group was going to whoop and dance. Inwardly, though, the weight of Hortez's expectation was another burden dragging Arun to his knees. All he wanted to do was be one of the team. The half of the planet who didn't wish him dead seemed to be queuing up to label him as some kind of savior, a hero. Now he'd added Hortez to that list.

He sighed. His one great talent was for vulleying up friendships, and what was heroic about that? Those gleaming warriors, flashing by at precisely regular intervals with streamers flying in their own slipstream – the men and women who were reducing their cargo to a pile of splinters and tortured metal – they were the heroes.

Not him.

Tranquility's tactical Marine regiments had a nominal strength of 12 field and 8 cadet battalions, each organized into 24 companies of 6 squads plus command and heavy weapons sections. Each Marine weighed an average of

250 pounds of human meat packed into a 150 pounds of battlesuit armor, life support, motors, and powered exoskeleton.

In all, three companies stormed by, continuing on their way like a lightning bolt in slow motion, giving Team Beta no more acknowledgment than any other bolt of lightning would. What the friends had seen was probably the entirety of the 420th's veteran force that was stationed on Tranquility and awake, rather than stored in freezer pods deep in the bowels of Detroit.

It was display of strength and discipline strong enough to stir Arun's reluctant heart… and pulverize the middle cargo box and the trolley that had carried it. The other two loads on the path were damaged too: their wooden crates broken and their contents scattered.

The middle trolley was shattered far past the possibility of repair. The flat loading panel now sunken into the path was the only piece of the trolley still recognizable. Washers and bolts of metal and plastic had scattered like shrapnel, adding to the stones used by the engineers to construct the path. Amazingly, some of the boxes carried in the middle trolley were still intact.

Arun joined the rest of Team Beta in trying to salvage something from the mess, throwing cargo box shards, plastic fragments and twisted metal away from the path and onto the fields to either side. As they cleared the debris, they revealed more of the plain black boxes. None of them looked damaged.

Arun picked one up. It had a handle and indentations along its side, just like the kind of ammo case he was used to. It probably was the same design. Durable containers were humble but vital engineering patterns, so it made sense to reuse the same design for many purposes. A lock prevented him from getting inside so he gave it an exploratory shake instead. Even if the box was strong, he expected the shattered remains of its contents to rattle, but he heard nothing. Perhaps the load was okay after all.

The yellow writing stenciled onto the plain black box was written in an alien script. He had no idea what was inside. "Hey, what do you reckon these are?" he asked.

"Something illicit," replied Hortez. "Gemstones, narcotics, the colonel's art collection. Or maybe saucy Hardit lingerie."

Arun laughed. "No. I reckon it's Hardit underwear all right, but it's *clean*. Anything that didn't stink would be deviant fetish clothing to those filthy monkeys."

"Shut up!"

"What's the matter, Springer?" Arun asked.

"I know what's in them."

"What?"

"See for yourself."

Arun followed Springer's pointing finger to where Madge had taken the lid off one of the plain dark boxes. The walls of the box were undamaged but the lock hinges on the lid had shattered, allowing Madge to slide off the lid.

Inside were plasma rifles, SA-71 assault carbines, even a flenser cannon lying on a bed of matte black squares. He'd seen squares like that before: composite armor plates on a hovertank.

Cold fear overcame the warm sun and sent shivers down Arun's spine. Until that moment he had secretly believed against all realistic expectation that he would survive to shrug off the week as his *Aux Adventure*.

But now?

This changed everything.

He was part of a gun-smuggling operation!

Were the Hardits the traitors? With everything else falling to drent, Arun had nearly forgotten about Pedro's hints: that someone was drugging the cadets.

He stared at one of the ammo carousels neatly stacked, ready to be slotted into an SA-71 and fired at – at what? – at Marines?

"This all fits," Arun said to himself. Then he raised his voice and announced: "There's something I need to tell you…"

"Traitors?" Madge's way of getting her head around Arun's tale of drugging and traitors was to storm up and down, looking like she wanted to smack something.

Arun looked to Hortez and Springer for support, but they were too lost in thought. "Corporal, don't you think we've all been acting strangely recently?" he called out to Madge.

She stopped and stared at Arun. He couldn't see her eyes properly through the stretched fabric of her worker's hat. But he imagined contempt there. "What has changed, McEwan, is that we're growing into Marines and you are not, and you never will do. Want to know why? Because you're a coward. You screwed up. You aren't as popular as you were. So you've invented this fantasy to justify why you're being pushed to the edge of the team."

"But it all makes sense," Arun protested.

"Does it? What evidence do you have?"

Arun bit his lip.

"There. See? You've nothing."

"If I'm right, then the drugs will wear off. The Hardits won't be keeping up our supply. We'll start to act differently any day now."

"Enough chitter-chatter!" Madge commanded. "This topic is closed. Permanently. We've a job to do. Get to it!"

In grim silence they set about salvaging what they could of the cargo, stacking it on the three surviving hover-trolleys. They ripped off the damaged lids of the wooden crates but many of the crates still had sides intact enough to layer the additional contents within.

It was heavy work and the sun blazing down punished them for their lack of drink. Hortez took it worse, wilting by the minute, until Madge told him to rest.

"No need, I'm okay," Hortez replied.

"You are not, and you know it," said Madge. "Neither are you, McEwan. I think that beating took more out of you than you knew. Go keep Hortez company, out of our way."

"What? But corporal, I'm—" Arun was about to remonstrate further when Springer stomped on his foot.

He frowned a question at her.

"It's a testosterone thing, dummy," she whispered. "Hortez is weak but he won't want to admit that in front of girls. You're his cover. I told you we would be better off with single-sex units. Prove me wrong."

The situation smelled false. Madge had no formal authority over Hortez, but she could browbeat him into doing whatever she wanted. The girls were up to something, but any thought of protesting was cut short by a kick from Springer.

"Hortez needs rest," she said. "Do this for him."

Arun felt sure that when the time came to go into battle as a Marine, he would charge fearlessly at an enemy defensive position, railgun blazing. But against the combined forces of Springer and Madge, he knew he was beaten.

He shrugged. Hortez allowed Arun to lead him away to sit on the bank with their backs to the sun, facing away from the girls.

They sat in silence but the noises of hard work coming from behind made him feel guilty, so Arun started up the conversation no one had yet dared to broach.

"Do you think we should report the weapons?"

Hortez shook his head. "Negative. Feels like we've caught them red handed, doesn't it? But we haven't. By the time we found someone to listen to us, the Hardits will have covered up any evidence. The only thing we'll be able to prove will be to the Hardits. We'll convince them that we need to be murdered to stop us talking."

"We could take some of the weapons out and hide them."

"Oh, yeah. How's that gonna look?"

"Like we're planning a rebellion," Arun replied grimly.

"Exactly."

"But isn't that what the Hardits are planning? I can understand smuggling luxury items, or the means to produce them, but what use are firearms other than to fight battles?"

"My friend, your thinking is too local," said Hortez. "We don't know what goes on out there in the wider star system, out amongst all those moons and asteroids, and the fuel processing plants in orbit around the gas giants. Tranquility is a small part of the system and the rest of it is dominated by the Hardits. Maybe it's one faction fighting another for the best mining sites. Perhaps it's protection against pirates."

"Pirates!"

"Why not? If something's valuable it means it's worth stealing. Stands to reason. So long as the Hardits sling their ore packets out to their destinations

I doubt the White Knights care too much about how the Hardits manage their own affairs. Whatever the weapons are for, it's nothing to do with us. Don't make it into our problem, Arun."

Arun said nothing. He was a Marine cadet. If anyone was taking weapons then that was something he couldn't ignore.

He decided to say no more about it for now. If he lived through today then he would be seeing Pedro tomorrow. He'd never looked forward to their meetings before, but he couldn't wait to see the insect this time. Arun had a lot of questions.

Chapter 35

Other than the occasional dot in the distance, the party didn't see any Agri workers until the squat block of the main Alabama Depot building hove into view. Three Agri-Aux in a field of barley were sheltering in the shade of a portable canopy only a hundred paces from the path.

The Agri-Aux reminded Arun of a picture he'd seen in an Earth history book in which glamorous ladies posed in voluminous skirts, wide-brimmed hats, and long sleeves with flapping cuffs topped off with leather gloves. The ancient women seemed immensely proud of a stick-like device of unknown function called a parasol. He couldn't recall the name of the historical epoch – Victovian perhaps? – but the ornate nature of their fashion could not hide a functional design imperative: the clothing was designed to cover and shade the skin, protecting against solar radiation.

These Earth Victovians must have lived through a period of intense solar flares or ozone layer depletion.

The bombardment of high energy particles from the sun was a constant on Tranquility, which was why the Agri-Aux dressed like those ancient Earth dwellers. Multiple layers of skirts dragged along the ground, veils hung from their wide-brimmed hats, and their gloves were partially shaded under bell-shaped sleeve cuffs. Unlike the variations of lace and patterned fabrics the ancients had worn, the Agri-Aux clothing was white shot through with a fine tracery of pink. It looked as if their clothes were connected to their blood supply, feeding a network of capillaries through the cloth.

Perhaps it was.

Humans were entrusted to use the military and other technologies provided on Tranquility, but the principles that explained how they worked were forbidden knowledge.

The four Team Beta Aux took it in turns to push the three surviving hover-trolleys in single file along the path. Madge took the lead. She called over her shoulder to Hortez, who was walking behind her, without a trolley. "What are they up to?" Madge asked him.

"How should I know?" he replied.

He looked entirely uninterested but Arun hadn't lost his curiosity. Neither had Springer, who was in front of Arun.

"Carrying out some kind of tests," she said. "Soil samples or gene tests?"

"Maybe they're checking for insects or disease," Arun suggested. Then he added: "Do Tranquility's native pests and diseases attack Earth plant species?"

No one could answer. As far as Arun was concerned, food was something born fully formed on a plate. How it got there was a mystery.

"We're not meant to be here," said Madge, vaguely as if her internal thoughts had accidentally spilled out.

Arun frowned. What had that to do with pests?

"Just look at us," she continued. "Then look at them out there in their protective gear."

"We're oversupply," said Hortez. "Why waste effort on preserving our health when they prefer us dead?"

"No, she's right," said Springer, bursting with sudden enthusiasm. "Shut your sad-mouthing, Hortez, and think a moment. Tawfiq and our Hardits don't give us suits because they're smugglers and we're their expendable mules. They won't want to leave an evidence trail by requisitioning protective gear for non-existent workers to carry out tasks that don't officially exist. I don't suppose the Hardits who manage those field workers are any more big-hearted than ours, but they must treat them better if they provide protective suits."

"Let's see," said Arun. He shouted at the Agri workers. "Hey!"

They ignored him.

Under the canopy and their veils, he couldn't see their faces, but Arun sensed from the way they'd momentarily frozen that they'd heard all right.

"Leave them be," hissed Hortez. "No good will come of this."

Arun ignored his former squad leader. In a hostile new environment, gather information before committing to a strategy. That's what they'd been taught and that's what he was doing now. "I know you heard," he yelled. He parked his trolley. "I just want to know whether the Hardits look after you? Do they treat you well?"

One of the Agri-Aux stopped what she was doing and answered. "We do okay."

"Do they torture you for sport?" pressed Arun.

Hortez shook his head, dismayed.

"Put it like this," replied the Agri-woman, "we'd never trade places with you sad vecks. Not from the position we've reached. Now frakk off."

Arun lifted the handles of his trolley and was about to lean into it when he stopped abruptly. Springer had let go of her handles and was racing down the bank toward the Agri-Aux.

Her legs were short but fleet. By the time Arun and Madge started to follow, Springer was already halfway to the Agri-workers.

With Hortez bringing up the rear, they chased after their comrade.

Springer was under the canopy now, remonstrating with the Agris. After a brief, heated exchange, she punched the Aux who had replied to Arun, felling her.

Arun slowed because Springer had turned around and was cutting a way through the field back to the path.

The Agris looked shocked. They didn't follow that up with action.

Springer did.

She'd only made five steps before she turned back and flew again at the Agris. She punched one, shoved another to the ground, and kicked the Aux who was already down.

Once the Team Beta comrades had regrouped on the path, Springer explained: "I asked them about Alistair LaSalle. They murdered him. The vecks admitted it. He's dead."

When he'd first heard that Alistair LaSalle had been assigned the temporary role of senior cadet commander for Charlie Company, Arun hadn't been surprised in the least. Alistair was smart, strong, and enormously popular. He lacked height and bulk. The untamable waves of his light-brown hair were permanently messy, but he wouldn't shave his head like anyone else. Somehow Alistair had taken his unpromising physique and breathed such charisma into it that he seemed to have whomever he wanted in his bunk: boys and girls. And yet he never attracted envy, never needed to bully or intimidate competitors out of the way. He made success seem so easy. Arun couldn't square the Alistair he remembered with a sorry refugee who – if Springer's info was accurate – had died within weeks of his transfer.

"Murder is too harsh a word," said Hortez. "They had no choice. I often ask myself whether I would do the same in their place."

"You knew!" Arun rushed at Hortez. "You frakking knew he was dead."

Arun's hands reached for Hortez's neck but Springer tripped him as he passed.

His chin thudded into the stones and dirt of the path, filling his mouth and nose with dust. For an instant he was winded, but a Marine cadet isn't easily pushed aside. A moment later he was on his knees, ready to spring at Hortez, when Madge crashed into him, pinning him down onto the ground with her butt on his sternum. "Calm down, McEwan," she ordered.

Arun tried to wriggle free, but couldn't. Madge was lithe but strong. He'd have to attack her to get her off him.

Frakk it! He was too angry to care. Arun threw everything he had into bucking her off. He felt her lose balance, releasing her weight. As he struggled back to his feet, she came crashing down on his shoulders, splaying his legs and making him eat dirt again.

Officially they were all demoted. Madge didn't outrank him anymore. No more playing nice. Fueled by anger, he shifted his weight, trying to prepare an elbow strike at Madge's hamstring.

"Explain yourself, Hortez," said Madge. "I can't keep a leash on this attack drone for long."

Hortez hesitated before responding: "To start with, I volunteered to come up here, risking my skin to make contact with Alistair." The fight went out of Arun when he heard that. Hortez's skin was a flaming mass of burns and sores. "I saw him a few times," Hortez continued. "I waved at him. To begin with he waved back cheerfully, his old self. After a while he didn't notice me when I passed by. Not long after that, I stopped seeing him. I didn't know for sure he was dead."

"But it was a safe bet," growled Springer. "And those vecks out there confirmed it. Explain to the others how Alistair died."

"It comes down to this. To live and work out here you must have a shielded suit. There are only so many to go around. You can even out food rations so everyone gets an equal share. You can take turns at the most dangerous tasks. But you can't share a suit."

"Yes, you can," said Springer. "Take turns wearing it. A rota system, worked out hour by hour."

"Negative. The world doesn't work that way, Springer. Not out here. Alistair and another ex-cadet, a woman, were sent here. Everyone else was already established, already won the right to their suits. None of them would ever give that up. Alastair was fearless, and he was fiercely determined. No one I'd rather have beside me in a fight. But he was a nice guy. Too nice to live."

Madge let Arun wriggle free from underneath her and return to his trolley, his anger drained into the dust. What would he do if he had to choose between dying or living in the knowledge that someone else had to free up his place? Probably, he decided, he'd fight the decision as long as possible before choosing to live.

What a choice!

The others seemed to be infested with the same thoughts because no one spoke until they reached Alabama.

Chapter 36

Alabama Depot consisted of a squat building with smaller extrusions around its base. A semicircle of grain silos ringed the main buildings like teeth in a jaw. On the hardened area outside the back of the main building three trucks waited, their human drivers lazing in their cabs. An ordered swarm of Agri-Aux in their pink-laced costumes loaded plump sacks onto the trucks. These sacks had the same pink tracery as the Aux suits, presumably to afford the same protection from the sun.

Without needing to say a word, Arun's group halted about fifty paces away from the Agri-Aux and assessed their options.

"They don't look riled," said Hortez. He glared at Springer. "Despite your stunt."

"I still care, Hortez," she shot back. "I'd rather die than be like you. *Faded.*"

"C'mon, focus!" barked Madge. "Are they a threat or not?"

"Negative," said Arun. "Even if they know about Springer throwing punches, they don't look like there's any fight to them. Besides, what are we going to do? Ram them with our trolleys?"

"Look in your crate, McEwan," said Madge. "Tell me what you see."

Madge made no sense at all, but Arun was too tired to defy her. Checking the brakes were on, he came around the side of his crudely patched-up crate to peer inside. "There's some plastic boxes. Can't see what's inside." He shifted the top layer of boxes aside. "Frakk! You told me they were hidden at the bottom of the load."

Poking out of the crate was an SA-71 Marine carbine, grip angled upward ready to be taken out and used. "I suppose I'd be wasting my breath to ask if it's loaded."

"You would," said Madge. "Got them ready while you boys were chatting away and we loaded the cargo. Didn't tell you because we didn't want to worry your dear little heads."

Arun was about to protest when Madge raised a hand, shutting him up instantly. Who was he trying to kid? Madge was in charge, formal rank be damned.

Madge organized them into a crude wedge formation, taking point with Arun and Springer on the flanks and Hortez – who no longer had a trolley – taking a position at the rear.

They activated hover mode and the wedge of trolleys advanced.

This is madness, thought Arun. *How have I come to this?*

From far back into his earliest childhood, Arun had taken care not to say or do anything that could be considered treasonous or disloyal. Those who didn't learn that lesson fast enough were no longer around.

Were they now so desperate that they would turn their illicit SA-71s on their fellows?

As the laden hover-trolleys breached the perimeter of the hardened loading area, Arun's fears dissipated. For starters, the idea of an attack wedge of trolleys was too ridiculous to hang on to. And far from crowding around to exact revenge for Springer's attack, the Agri-Aux shied away, as if gripped by a group delusion that if they pretended they couldn't see Arun's little unit, the newcomers would go away.

As the Agri-Aux turned to scurry away, Arun expected to see resentment of their faces. Instead, he saw shame.

Only the truck drivers high up in their cabs watched them. They must be shielded, reasoned Arun, because they wore only white vests, their heads bare.

There were three huge doors in the back of the main building, of which two were open. Madge led their wedge toward one of these open doors, a route that took them close to one of the trucks.

The driver was a fat man but powerfully built. He was in his mid-twenties or even older, which made him one of the oldest Aux Arun had seen. His face was grim set and not fearful in the slightest. He peered at their damaged wooden crates with intense interest.

Arun kept his eyes focused on the driver.

The driver stared back. When Arun drew level with his cab, the man shouted. "Hey!"

Arun let go of his trolley's handles and reached into the opening in his crate. He felt for the loaded carbine.

"I ain't seen nothing," the driver said, his voice coming from a speaker set into the cab door.

Arun's hand wrapped around the carbine's grip. The familiar shape felt comforting.

"But if I had, I might say your crates look a little busted."

Arun glanced back at the driver. He looked amused, a little contemptuous perhaps, but Arun didn't see aggression there. Reluctantly, he loosened his grip on the carbine.

"What do you mean?" Madge asked him. Arun looked her way and had no doubt what her hand was gripping.

"Me?" answered the truck driver. "I don't mean anything. I didn't see you, remember? And that goes for anything you might be carrying, because I definitely didn't see *that*. I'm just saying, in a kind of neighborly thinking out loud kinda way, that if anyone did have a busted crate, there's plenty of spare timber in the fab shop they could use to fix it."

"Thanks, man," said Hortez,

"I didn't see nothing nor hear nothing. If anyone felt thankful, they'd do well to remember that." With that, the driver folded his arms and looked out the other side of his cab.

Madge considered a moment before deciding to take the driver at face value. She picked up her trolley and pushed it the final few paces into the loading bay, the others following close behind.

Inside the main building, they pushed their loads to the far end of the bay, as far away from the main doors as possible. Hortez and Arun guarded the cargo while Madge and Springer scouted the complex.

They soon reported back that they'd encountered two humans repairing split grain sacks, and a fab shop with all the materials needed to repair the crates.

Best of all they brought back a 3-gallon water bottle, the same kind used to refresh water fountains back home.

They debated but rejected the idea of keeping some of the cargo behind. Too risky, they decided. So they set to work making good the damage to the shattered crates. By the time they had crates fit for transport onward –

obviously repaired but sturdy – the grain trucks had departed and most of the Agri-Aux loaders had drifted away. A handful, though, had tasks to carry out in the depot buildings. They kept their distance from the Team Beta group.

Hortez had wheeled a few half-filled grain sacks over to where Team Beta sat with their backs to the wall, passing the water bottle between them. He arranged the sacks into a semblance of a reclining armchair. After explaining that the Hardits didn't care what you did during the day so long as you completed your task and stayed out of trouble, he spread his hands behind his head, leaned back, and relaxed.

The others followed suit, taking an unexpected breather before returning through the burning sun to the hellish dungeon that was Aux Camp Beta.

Arun was of the opinion that a Marine should grab any chance to ease off the pace, and make the most of it while he or she could. The apex of the roof about was 20 meters high which made the interior cool, airy and comfortable. There was soft ambient lighting but neither windows nor any opening in the roof, just the main loading doors. Relaxing on his nest of grain sacks, Arun felt proud of himself for being able to forget about the Hardits, who probably intended that he would not live to return to his battalion.

"You know what this could be?" said Arun suddenly.

"What?" replied Springer, without enthusiasm.

"A clubhouse."

"What's that?"

"It's an Earth concept, a place to relax. A place where you don't get bothered by your betters. You can just chill out, watch a game, chat with your friends…"

"Are you serious?" asked Springer.

"Relax."

"It'll never work," said Madge.

"Why not? The Hardits rarely come here. There's space, shielding, and plenty of seating."

"That's not what I mean," replied Madge acidly. "You can't bring your friends here to chat with them because you don't have any friends."

Arun bit back his tongue.

Madge twisted the knife further. "Oh, and I nearly forgot, we've no game to watch either. Not since our star player abandoned us and we got knocked out last round."

I would have carried on playing for you if you'd let me. As he fumed with the unfairness of his victimization, an Agri-Aux woman, approached them carrying her hat in her hand and a haunted look about her eyes. She looked a force to be reckoned with all the same, perhaps because she was older than the group from Team Beta. This woman had to be at least 25.

She introduced herself as Esther.

None of Team Beta acknowledged her, but that didn't stop Esther from standing so close that she was impossible to ignore.

"They come at night," she said.

"Who?" asked Arun. "Hardit smugglers?"

She nodded. "They use orbital shuttles."

"That's what I keep telling this lot," Hortez said to her. "I've seen the telltale scorch marks on the hardened area outside."

Madge had sat up. "Did you know Alistair LaSalle?" she asked of the Agri-woman.

Esther nodded mournfully.

"Did you try to help him?" she added.

"We sewed grain sacks together, which gave them some protection."

"But you didn't offer your suits," added Springer.

"No."

"Don't expect forgiveness from us," Madge snarled. "Is that what you thought? Come over and say sorry and then your sins would be absolved?"

Esther's face pinched with fury. Arun thought she was going to rip Madge's face off. Or try at any rate. Instead she sniffed. "I shouldn't have said anything," she pronounced, with the air of someone dealing with inferiors beneath her notice.

She started walking away.

"No, please don't go," Arun called after her.

She paused.

"What're you doing, McEwan?" Madge didn't sound pleased.

"It's…" Arun couldn't put it into words. He knew the strategy planning part of his brain was running hard because it was manifesting itself as a sense of prickly heat at the exact center of his head, and a vague sense that the Agri-Aux could prove to be invaluable allies one day.

The feeling might be vague, but he knew to trust any hunches accompanied by the prickly heat.

Springer butted in. "What he's trying to say, is that you Agris will be important allies."

Arun shot a glance at Springer. How did she know that? Behind the cute sprinkle of freckles, her eyes were focused on an ethereal sight not of this plane. They blazed with a violet intensity that made his heart race. He was in awe of Springer. He wanted to kiss her, to kneel down and worship at her feet. And at the same time, he wanted to run away from her, screaming in fear all the way back to Detroit.

What was this? Admiration or mind control?

"Horden's Bones!" Madge sounded like she felt the same. "You're a right pair of psyker mutants. Ol' Violet who can see into the future, and lover boy with a battle planner AI in his head. Not that either of your superpowers have delivered anything of the slightest value. I still can't decide whether all your mystic powers are one big load of utter drent, or whether you really are freaks. I do know that you two should never get it together in case Springer gives birth to a Night Hummer."

"Haven't they told you?" said Hortez. "Each squad has a few members whose DNA has been virally rewritten to add a few choice genes from alien species. Most of it makes no difference but every now and again something useful manifests, and they grab you for use in their eugenics program."

The cadets looked at each other, speechless.

A wicked smile planted itself on Hortez's face. "Relax," he whispered. "It's a joke."

"This is no joke!" thundered Arun as he got to his feet. "This is important! It's what Hortez said earlier – to give false hope to the hopeless is cruel. But what if we could do something for the Aux, something better than giving a gesture of hope and a finger flip at the Hardits? What if we could set an example of what humans can achieve though cooperation, an inspiration that outlasted our gesture. I want to see humans everywhere stronger and prouder. United. A force to be respected. To be granted privileges, Freedom. Isn't that a cause worth fighting for?"

Arun's speech ran out of momentum, leaving a shocked silence that Madge eventually broke. "So, all this inspirational stuff… you're still talking about a clubhouse, right?"

Arun nodded.

"And you're going to make all our lives better, and establish an interstellar human empire with you on the throne. All this by, what? Throwing a party?"

"It's more than that. Imagine if we organize a day of defiance against the Hardits. We'll light a beacon of hope that will shine for years to come into the breast of even the most wretched human slave."

"Have you ever seen him do this before?" asked Hortez rolling his eyes. "I've never heard Arun make a speech. I think the sun's gone to his head."

"No, he's right," said Springer. "Trust him."

"Trust!" Madge shot to her feet, her face reddening with fury. "I trusted him to support Moscow Express. He let us down over a frakking girl. *Twice*! We're all going to be Culled because of him. Hortez is up to his neck in drent and Alistair is dead. *Because of him*. You don't make up for that with a pretty speech, McEwan." She nodded at Esther, who was listening to all of this. "And what about your new girlfriend? How does she fit in to your party plans? Do you need her to bring a frakking salad?"

Arun spoke to Esther: "If your people could stage a diversion – I'm still working on the details – something that forces the Hardits to send us all out to the depot to deal with the crisis. A fire. Explosion. Armed revolt. Make the Hardits think they're sending their expendable Aux Team Beta into danger when actually they're sending us to the shiny new Alabama Clubhouse."

"Oh, great!" spat Madge. "I feel so much better knowing that our plan hinges on the brave Agri-Aux. Have you forgotten that they murdered Alistair LaSalle?"

"I know what I did," said Esther. "It wasn't just your friend. We're all of us alive because we forced someone else to die."

"Why tell us that?" asked Madge. "Do you want us to forgive you?"

"I'm not stupid enough to ask for that, and if I did beg forgiveness, it would be from the dead, not you."

"Let me guess how your next line goes," Madge said. "*The terrible knowledge of our betrayal eats at us every day, like a cancer.* Is that it?"

Esther shook her head and turned away. "I knew this was a mistake," she sneered.

"Wait!" called Arun. "I haven't finished with you yet. You can't ask to be forgiven because you know you don't deserve forgiveness. Not yet. What you should be seeking instead is atonement."

Esther paused. "What do you have in mind?"

"I don't know myself yet. Not exactly. But I'm working on it, and a diversion would be a good start. Think you can manage that?"

"My people will do as I say. Yes, I could arrange a diversion, if I thought the payoff worth the risk."

Arun laughed. "My people, eh? Yeah, that figures. Here," he gestured to a nearby sack, "take a seat."

Esther sat down and waited with the rest of them in an uncomfortable silence while ideas crystallized in Arun's mind.

When enough made sense to him, he explained to each of the others what he required them to do. When he later thought back to that time, it seemed to Arun that he was listening to someone else speak. Another part of him was in control. Afterward he was left behind to carry the thumping great headache that he knew was coming.

He heard himself ask Esther whether her people would help. And he remembered her agreeing that they would. "If you need to get in contact," she said, "leave a note in the cab of the dung truck. I wish you good fortune but now I must return to my duties."

As they watched Esther disappear out of the loading bay, something closer to normality returned.

"What the Aux need is hope," said Arun, feeling in control once more. A charge of excitement built within him, and why not? This could be *big*. "The Hardits expect us humans to fight each other, not cooperate. And the Agri-Aux are bent over double with guilt. Those are our two routes in. So long as we don't threaten the Agri-Aux's right to their protective suits, and don't rub their noses in their guilt, they'll do anything for a chance of atonement."

Madge groaned. "Of all your imbecile ideas, McEwan, this is the dumbest yet. I can't believe you two are humoring him."

That hurt. Just for a moment there, when Arun had been in his planning daze, Madge had listened. Now he was back to himself, she wouldn't give him the time of day.

"Leave him be," said Hortez. "He's onto something. If it sounds insane right now, that's only because the details haven't slotted into place. Just one thing, man." He slapped a hand on Arun's shoulder. "Co-opting the Agri-Aux is a good idea, but don't forget you have other allies too."

"Who?"

But even as the word came to Arun's lips, his mind had already filled with the answer: Trogs. He'd already considered the possibility of sounding out Pedro's thoughts on his plan when they met tomorrow. But what if he could persuade the Trogs to do far more than give advice?

After all, the colonel *had* ordered him to liaise with the Trogs.

Enlisting their help would only be obeying orders.

Chapter 37

Instead of Tawfiq, roll call the following morning was conducted by Hen Beddes-Stolarz.

She paraded Springer, Madge and Arun in front of the line, scratching their faces, drawing blood from skin already red from the furious sun's exposure.

"Your skin is raw and peeling. Look–" she gouged a chunk out of Springer's cheek, making her wince but not cry out. "This one bleeds! This is good. Proof that you humans are useful. You take damage from the cruel sun to preserve the health of your mistresses."

Hen shifted position to growl in Arun's face, her breath hot, fetid and alien.

"This one is useful for other superiors than his Hardit mistresses. 106 is the most disgusting of your entire species. Today he goes to the insect nest where the hive drones keep him as a sex pet."

Hen brought her hand back as if to strike Arun.

He braced for the blow but it did not come.

"Number 106 has been immersed in insect sex fluids. He is too disgusting to touch. Tomorrow, 106, you will go to the surface without your hat. You will burn for my amusement. Perhaps the sun will sear away the stink of your depravity." The Hardit made retching noises. They sounded genuine. "I cannot bear the stink of you. Go now! Go away, human!"

Arun hid his grin as he hurried off to meet his Troggie ally.

—— Chapter 38 ——

"Yes, I can provide the equipment you have asked me for and more besides. We do not have the engineering capability to build spacecraft or nuclear weapons, but simple radio communications equipment will be an amusing diversion. We too know how to have fun, friend. And as for your abilities, human Arun, you have skills exceptional for your species. Your planning capability is similar to the way our minds work in the scribe phase of our lifecycle."

"Steady on, pal," said Arun, although he felt warm to hear his ally speak highly of him. "Nearly as clever as a scribe? I wouldn't go that far."

"No, of course not. I exaggerate."

"Hey! What do you mean, *exaggerate*?"

"I mean your mind is still inferior to a scribe's. For example, you are too fixated on your problem with the Aux. Consequently your mind can only think of solutions to that problem by ignoring your other four critical objectives. A scribe would consider all five simultaneously."

"As usual, Pedro, you're not making a shred of sense. I just want to get through the week alive."

"Yes. That is what I just said. Being a member of the hive grants me the gift of specialization. I can leave such short-term considerations as how to survive this week to others in my nest. That leaves me space to ponder your four other strategic objectives, namely: your desire to graduate as a Marine, to regain the trust of your squad, to mate with the female Lee Xin–"

"Wait! I never said that about Xin."

"Not in so many words. And the objective you have mentioned even more than this female is Scendence. Your match in 48 hours is crucial on many levels. You are the star Deception-Planning player. Yet you are banished to the Aux levels. You cannot play that game."

"You don't have to remind me. I can't be there. Done deal. I won't waste time worrying about something I can't change."

Pedro gave a slight outward tilt to both antennae, the equivalent of pointedly raising eyebrows.

"What're you hinting at? What can I do?"

"You? Nothing."

"Exactly. I need a substitute. But we're only three more wins away from immunity. At this stage, you can't just drag a player out of the spineway and expect them to perform at that standard."

"Agreed. You need a player with excellent planning ability. Preternatural by human standards."

"Right."

"An ability to think in what human opponents would regard as radically new ways. To make plays of such originality that our competitors will not anticipate them."

"I suppose."

Pedro didn't reply. He stood impassively and – to the human's eyes – without expression (or had he moved his antennae out a notch further?). Arun recognized this sudden silence. According to Pedro, this was him allowing Arun's slow human brain to catch up with the implications of their conversation. Which meant… What?

"Horden's spiny growths!"

"Indeed," said Pedro, spiraling his feelers.

"You! *You're* offering to be my substitute. And… Xin. She's already agreed to this, hasn't she?"

"There is still some slight reluctance on her part, but her xenophobia is only natural for you humans. The logic of my offer is unassailable."

Some slight reluctance. I'll bet, thought Arun, but then he remembered how to begin with he'd felt revolted by this strange alien friend. He went through all the reasons why the idea of Pedro taking his place in the Scendence match was madness. But every objection flaked away under closer inspection. He was only left with one question.

"Why? Why are you getting involved, Pedro?"

"Friends help each other in times of difficulty. And we are friends, aren't we?"

"I … yes." He thought for a moment. "Yes, we are!" He knew he'd miss Pedro if he never saw the great lunk of an insect again. He also knew him well enough to suspect that Pedro wasn't telling the whole truth. Pedro persisted with this crazy alien notion that Arun was important. In protecting Arun, Pedro believed he was guarding the interests of his nest.

"And that's not all," said the Trog.

Arun's palm went to his forehead. Pedro's artificial voice lacked emotion, as always, but its volume had increased. Which meant he was excited about something. *What now?*

"I am extolling your virtues to this Lee Xin. I have learned much about you, Arun McEwan. Enough for me to embellish the truth so as to draw attention away from your many shortcomings. I am confident that on your return from your banishment to the auxiliary, this Lee Xin will be so filled with mating hormones that her skin will flush red with the need to–"

"Okay, you can stop right there!" Arun spoke from behind both his hands. Being bigged up by a seven-foot long insect. This had to be a new low. If word ever got out… "And for your information, she's Xin Lee, not Lee Xin."

"Really? Try telling her that."

Arun glared into the shiny black bulbs of the alien's expressionless eyes. Damn! He hated the creature for knowing more about Xin.

"I am serious," said Pedro. "Ask her. You and Lee Xin have a unique connection. You share a destiny. This makes the success of your courtship highly likely."

"That's enough about me and Xin! That topic is out of bonds."

Pedro dropped his antennae disapprovingly.

"I don't care what you think," snarled Arun. "That topic is forbidden."

"Very well, friend McEwan. Let us turn instead to your plan, Operation Clubhouse. I have noticed many ways in which I can improve it. My adaptations will help you to achieve the other four objectives you have temporary forgotten."

"When you say adaptations, are you talking a few slight nudges, or it is more *throw everything away and start again?*"

Pedro hesitated before replying: "The second choice." It was sweet of him to act embarrassed enough to pause.

Arun shook his head. "I don't care who came up with the plan so long as it works. What I don't get is that you keep talking about me as this great being of destiny. But you think my plan's so drent you had to rebuild it. Anyone else would think you regard me as a loser, not this great hero."

"I have never described you as a hero. A person of destiny need not make all the decisions or have exceptional ideas. They might not even be a leader. Even an odious imbecile can be a great being of destiny."

"Okay, I get the picture. Maybe if I survive to have more of these discussions, I'll teach you the concept of being *too* honest."

"I haven't finished, Arun McEwan. With me you have established a friendship across species boundaries. You laugh at this but have no idea how rare that is. Perhaps that is where your destiny lies: to build a great interstellar coalition across species."

Arun sobered. A grand coalition free of the White Knights?

Was that his future? Was that the secret behind the Human Legion to come?

Arun laughed at his ridiculous hubris. "I'll leave the big picture to you," he told his friend. "Remember, my poor human brain can only cope with worrying about whether my buddies and I will still be alive this time next week. Go on, tell me your shiny new version of Operation Clubhouse."

Pedro shook his head. It looked like a negative human gesture, but indicated eagerness.

As Pedro explained his ideas, Arun's spirits lifted so high he was practically floating.

Yes, we can do this!

Arun was so excited that he decided not to puncture the triumphant mood by mentioning the other factor he was trying to ignore for now: the contents of the carts they'd helped to smuggle off planet.

The Hardits were gunrunners.

And the more he thought about that, the more Arun was convinced they were connected with the traitors drugging the cadets.

Arun wouldn't let them get away with that. But first he had to survive the week.

Chapter 39

As Operation Clubhouse rolled out over the days that followed, radio equipment was produced in the Troggie catacombs that stretched for miles to the east and southeast of Detroit. After the comms came specialist explosives designed to give out smoke and heat but not consume oxygen. They were intended to confuse thermal and visual targeting systems in the defense of nest tunnels, where conventional explosive munitions could easily overcome ventilation, choking the defenders to death.

Amongst the Tunnel-Aux, as Arun had started calling the Detroit Aux, favors were accumulated and paid. Supplies were cached in places where the Hardits never bothered to look. Following Arun's example of exchanging his clothes with Madge, scent-marked Aux overalls were swapped freely, allowing the humans to move far out of their assigned areas.

Arun almost began to believe Pedro's fantasy that he was a man of destiny. Whenever he had these delusions of greatness, Arun reminded himself that it wasn't his genius but Hardit laziness that made the whole business possible. Rubbing those long snouts in their own drent gave Arun the greatest satisfaction of all. The Hardits had sneered about the law of supply and demand, but now the human Aux were twisting that law to their advantage. With a new sense of purpose – and a little extra food, that initially came in the form of a gray tasteless paste courtesy of the Trogs – the oversupply of human workers meant some Aux could be spared to work for their own ends.

Humans working for the benefit of other humans – for the first time in their lives. It was really happening!

After Springer managed to pass a message back to Blue Squad about the reality of life in the Aux, the word spread amongst the cadets in their hab-disks. Discrete packages of food and medicine were left in laundry bins. Cadets found reasons to wander far and wide through Detroit, making contact for the first time with their discarded brethren of the auxiliary services. But whenever the Hardits were in sight, even when lolling out of breath against walls as they often did, the Aux acted the part of broken, hungry slaves, losers far beneath the notice of any nearby cadets… until the moment the Hardits passed out of sight.

As far as the Hardits were concerned, they had work for a certain number of human workers. So long as the humans carried out those tasks adequately and didn't cause trouble, that was the limit of Hardit interest in their inferiors. They might make exceptional engineers and miners, but as bureaucrats and overseers, Hardits sucked.

Even accounting for Hardit indolence, Arun's original idea would have been a high-risk gamble that might just have poked the Hardits in the eye, but would probably have paid for that shallow victory with the lives of Arun and his friends.

But Operation Clubhouse had grown far beyond Arun's initial idea, a product of cooperation between scores of individuals. Maybe more, Arun had no idea how many Trogs were involved. Thousands perhaps. Arun might have sparked the idea but it was made possible by Pedro's brains, the engineering and logistical capability of his nest-siblings, the guilt of the Agri-Aux, and the bravery and tactical cunning of Springer and Madge.

And the Tunnel-Aux…

They were the greatest revelation of all.

At first the disgraced Blue Squad cadets had kept the other Aux out of the main picture, not fully trusting the others in Team Beta. Broken women and men could have sold them out for the chance of some more bread. But Adrienne was their ally here, helping to breathe some life back into Beta, enough for them to help out with simpler tasks. Perhaps she sensed that her world was changing, that this was her final chance to improve her lot, if only a little.

And it was still only pathetically little that Arun was offering his fellow Aux.

But for those with nothing, he mused one night as he listened to the ragged snoring in Beta's room, a little was a prize worth dying for.

Each day, Arun, Hortez, Springer and Madge would be sent off on a pointless mission to Alabama, the only purpose being to burn in the sun for the amusement of their alien mistresses. That might have been the Hardits' purpose, but the Blue Squad Aux used the time to plan, prepare and negotiate with the Agri-Aux.

Out in the fields the human workers were better organized than their equivalents servicing the tunnels. Fearful of the lethal effect of the sun's rays, the Hardits did everything they could to avoid emerging onto Tranquility's surface. That meant human taskmasters were in place, who reported daily progress toward quotas and milestones. They were very aware of the painful consequences of any slippage, but they were nonetheless free to run their own affairs.

The Hardits were so averse to the surface that it was a mystery the monkeys had fed themselves in the long millennia before human slaves were brought to the planet, the only clues being a crumbling underground ruin the Agri-Aux had discovered. Buried in the mud were plastic manacles far too big for human or Hardit limbs.

Underneath a veneer of pride and discipline a heart of darkness beat within each Agri-Aux, festering with the guilty knowledge that they were alive because they had denied others their protective suits. The outfits looked like pure white dresses patterned in pink, but they were steeped in blood.

Springer proved adept at exploiting this guilt, which she did mercilessly, although Esther put up little resistance.

Number 24 was the first to report the fruits of the Agri-Aux cooperation. She was one of the youngest in Team Beta, a girl much younger than the cadets. Despite coaxing from Springer and Madge, 24 refused to speak her real name, or anything about her former life. The only time Arun saw her smile was when she shyly came up to him one night to tell him that she had discovered protective outdoor gear, left in the topside building where she had emptied her cargo of novice excrement.

There were eight gifted outfits, crude hats and smocks sown from grain bags. Esther had spoken of them. Alistair had lived and died in one of those eight outfits. They hadn't the protective technology of the Agri workers' suits, but the outfits would ease the burn.

They were a welcome gesture.

When Esther came to see them later that afternoon in the Alabama depot, she had more help to offer. As she explained, her people weren't helping out because they were being nice. This operation was all about atonement, a gesture of contrition made for the dead, not for the benefit of the living. It would be a one off. All debts paid.

The final piece of the puzzle slotted into place when the banished Blue Squad cadets decided to let the rest of Beta in on the plan, co-opting Adrienne as their leader. The moment they saw that sly grin on her face when Springer told her what they had planned for Cliffie, they knew for sure then that Adrienne had thrown in her lot with the plot.

After three grueling days, finally everything was either in place or had to be abandoned because the countdown had hit zero.

Tomorrow was the day of the crucial Scendence matches, with the winners only two more steps away from Cull immunity.

Tomorrow was the final day of Arun's banishment to the Aux ranks. If Tawfiq's revenge was unsatisfied then she would want tomorrow to be the last day of his life.

It was time for Operation Clubhouse.

Chapter 40

Before he faced danger, Arun was used to feeling either grim determination, utterly focused on the task at hand, or wild mania that usually led to unfortunate incidents.

But that was artificial, induced by drugs accessing the parts of his brain engineered to make him a good Marine.

There were no combat drugs in the Aux world, which he assumed was why Madge was starting to lighten up. But that meant to find courage today, Arun had to draw deep within himself. It wasn't working. Prickly heat flared along his spine, making the sweat drip down his back. The fear of letting his buddies down kept paralyzing him so that he couldn't move, could only bend over with hands on knees trying to find the courage to keep moving on his way to Team Gamma's room. The place where Cliffie had nearly suffocated him.

The opening act of Operation Clubhouse was down to Arun acting alone. When he planned this, it hadn't occurred to him that he might not have the guts to see it through.

Strangely the same fear of letting his friends down that made him pause, also drove him on, until with leaden limbs, he stumbled into Gamma's room at breakfast time. The memory of being asphyxiated under a mound of clothing made his heart flutter, and put such a wobble into his legs that he had to halt just beyond the threshold, not trusting his limbs to keep him upright if he took another step.

"Err, excuse me," said Arun, putting a quiver into his voice that didn't require much acting. "May I speak with you?"

He'd expected to find Cliffie seated on his throne, but this time he spotted the Gamma Team leader in one corner, hunched over in a secretive discussion with his lieutenants. Cliffie cast a scornful glance at Arun and then went back to his meeting. That was the extent of Arun's audience with Gamma's leader, but one of the lieutenants separated herself from the group and walked over to him.

"What do you want?" she sneered, arms folded in front of her.

She was heavy set with livid bruising around her left cheek. With a start he realized that her wound probably came from the fight the last time Arun was here.

"Please, I wish to beg for more of our food to be returned."

The lieutenant walked around Arun, inspecting him disdainfully. When she'd made a full circuit, she leaned in to his face and said: "You haven't brought any gifts to bargain with. So why should we give you food?"

"Because every day since I was last here, you've taken seven of our eight buckets. We only have one left. We're dying of starvation."

While this exchange had been going on, about a dozen members of Gamma team had formed a ring around Arun and the lieutenant. Each of them carried a handful of shorts.

"I'll give you one more chance," said the lieutenant, playing to her audience. "And think about your answer very carefully, because it will have consequences. Why should we give you our food?"

"Because Cliffie said you weren't heartless."

The lieutenant lifted her hand up high.

Arun's breath came in short gasps. He started to hunch himself over, anticipating what would come next.

"Wrong answer," said the lieutenant. She clicked her fingers and her team sprang into action.

Arun clenched his hands but didn't fight back when his assailants threw the shorts over his head and bundled him into the pile of clothing, burying him.

Events didn't play out as before. This time, Arun used the moments before the weight above him became crushing to snake his arm down into the mound of clothing and plant a gift from Pedro: a radio transmitter.

Today was a Scendence Day, when the cadets and novices would either be playing the game or watching it. The centerpiece of Operation Clubhouse was a radio show linked to the day's Scendence feeds. After all, what was the point of the clubhouse if they couldn't listen in on the game? The radio signal needed boosting from a location close to the surface. Hosting the transmitter in their room on Level 4 was to be Team Gamma's contribution to a day to remember.

As the crush began to deny him the oxygen his brain craved, and the edges of the world grew fuzzier, Arun held on to the hope that the transmitter meant Gamma would take the blame for what was to follow.

On the limits of consciousness, Arun was yanked out of the clothing pile and thrown onto his knees at Cliffie's feet.

"You have at least learned respect and politeness," said Cliffie. "I appreciate that. To show my appreciation I gift you your life. This generosity will not be repeated. If you enter this room again, my people will kill you on sight."

Arun didn't get off his knees, but did raise his gaze to look upon his master. "I understand, sir."

Cliffie raised an expectant eyebrow.

"Thank you, sir. Thank you for your mercy and generosity."

"There, that wasn't so difficult."

Arun had to keep from smiling. Cliffie was right. Playing the part of a groveling fool *wasn't so difficult.* Especially since all the while, Arun knew who the real dunkchunk was.

Natural Law finds in our favor this time, he thought. *Let's see how you enjoy it, you dirty skangat.*

Chapter 41

"Did you do it?" asked Adrienne.

In reply, Arun could only nod. His lungs still burned. Every gasp of air was too valuable to be expended on speech.

Springer put her arm around him. "You've been a total shunter recently, but you did well today, Arun."

She gave a quick squeeze, and then the moment was gone, though the memory lingered for Arun.

Madge spoke into one of the radios the Trogs had smuggled their way. "You there, Hort?"

"Acknowledged." Now that Gamma's transmitter had boosted the signal strength, Hortez's voice came through the radio as cleanly as if he were there. He wasn't. Operation Clubhouse required someone to stay behind. Someone to take the blame too, most likely. What Pedro called the audience chamber – where he and Arun had their chats – had been transformed into a communications hub, with Hortez at the controls.

"We're ready to roll, sir," said Madge crisply.

"*Sir?*" Hortez laughed. "You're a crazy one, Majanita. I declare Operation Clubhouse is a go. Good luck, everyone. And if you do make it topside, I expect you to enjoy yourselves. That's an order."

"Yes, sir." It wasn't just Madge who'd replied. Over the encrypted channel other voices respectfully acknowledged Hortez's instruction.

Before the arrival of Arun and the disgraced Blue Squad cadets, the morale of the Aux teams had been so pitifully low that none of them had tried fooling the Hardits with such tricks as swapping scent-marked overalls. Now that Arun had shown the way and Adrienne had cajoled and bullied her fellow Aux, Team Beta and their allies in other Aux teams were roaming through Detroit almost at will.

Over a hundred Detroit Aux were involved in today's operation. But the plan extended even beyond Detroit. From his Trog sanctuary, Hortez gave the signal to the Alabama Agri-Aux to initiate their diversion.

Chapter 42

As far as Sushantat Feriek-Khull was concerned, the human animals of Aux Team Beta were lined up as normal in their two cowering rows, waiting obediently for her to complete the morning roll call and issue the day's work assignments.

Which only made her appear an utter dumbchuck to her supposed human inferiors, who couldn't help but set a charge of excitement buzzing throughout the room. Any human would instantly spot that something big was going on.

Not for the first time, the Hardit completed the roll call, satisfied that she had accounted for every human worker. The correct scent-marked clothing might be present, but not the bodies inside. Hortez's overalls were currently swamping a petite girl from Team Alpha called Kalynda. As far as the Hardits were concerned, Kalynda was supposed to be bringing food back from the kitchens for Team Alpha's breakfast, a task actually being carried out by an ally from Team Delta. The Aux had jumped into the game of swapping clothing so enthusiastically that Madge had tried and failed to rein it in. What was supposed to be their secret advantage had transformed into a game played for the simple pleasure of flipping a finger up in the Hardits' snouts.

Sushantat started issuing the assignments, giving no sign that she knew any of this.

A call came over the overseer's wrist comm, instantly clamping the room into silence. The humans had been waiting for this.

The Hardit's natural attitude was one of listlessness, as if encountering the humans was an arduous imposition that deserved a long lie down afterwards. Sushantat was the most active of the lot, officially number two, but effectively running the day-to-day Aux operations in Beta's area. That impression of laziness evaporated when the call came through. Her ears flattened against her head; her lips pulled back to reveal a jaw filled with sharp teeth through which she sucked air into suddenly purposeful muscles.

"The situation changes," she said. "All of you wait here."

Sushantat left. Striding as far as the doorway, she then dropped to all fours and cantered away, her motion making a loud skittering noise surprisingly similar to the Trogs.

"Is that it?" shouted Number 72 in disdain. There were murmurs of anger from the other Aux. She was a gaunt woman who wouldn't share her human name. "We risked our lives for what? To stay here?" She spat at Arun. "Look at him, the magnificent General 106. His plan has won us a day cooped up in this hellhole."

Adrienne confronted 72, toe-to-toe. "Shut up!" she barked.

But 72 was right, thought Arun. What had Hortez told him? To give hope to the hopeless, only to snatch it away… that was the greatest cruelty of all. And for all his big dreams, the only thing Arun had actually achieved so far was to store up a great expectation of hope.

He ran, dashing past Beta's supply store, machine room, parts room, and out in the main corridor where the smell was neutral and the floor regularly cleaned.

Sushantat was still out of sight, but Arun's hearing had been gene-optimized and augmented by amplifiers and wetware filters. Following the skittering sound of the speeding Hardit echoing off the hard corridor surfaces was simple. But the Hardit's sense of smell was acute. Could she smell him following? If she could and stopped him, then he was dead.

Too late to worry about that now, he decided.

He was committed.

He followed her in an arc around the edges of the novice area and out again to a passageway off the main corridor where the ceiling had been lowered. Nice and snug for Hardits; just the way they liked it.

As he passed more junctions, he trusted more to his instinctive sense of direction.

Finally he came to a closed door. It had been two minutes since he'd last heard Sushantat. Either she was behind that door or he'd lost her.

Nothing to lose!

He pushed the door access stud. As soon as the door slid into its housing, he was assailed by a wave of Hardit-stink.

The room had been lowered even more than the passageway outside. It was extensive, though, with banks of computer equipment winking status lights in the shadowy depths. He didn't get much of a look because rubbing together in a tail-swishing huddle were four Hardits.

"See, I told you," said Sushantat through her voice synthesizer when Arun burst into the room. "This animal has followed me all the way back from its hovel."

There were three other Hardits here: Hen Beddes-Stolarz, Tawfiq Woomer-Calix, and the boss that the humans rarely saw: Biljah Hilleskill-Khull.

They looked uninterested in Arun's arrival, as if there were more important matters. But what did he really know about Hardits and their politics? He'd have to start laying his bets or his plan would fall at the first hurdle.

"Mistress," he cried, "I beg you. Let me convey valuable information. In Ala… arghh!"

Arun's breath was squeezed from his body as he crashed to the ground, rolled up into a ball of agony. As he fell, his eyes caught sight of Tawfiq holding out the grubby little box that sent waves of intolerable pain through his overalls.

He tried to wrench his jaw open to explain, to beg… to breathe. But the pain gripped him so tightly that all he could move were his eyeballs.

He pleaded with all he had left, forcing his eyes to look up at Tawfiq. She seemed to understand, was showing him mercy, because she switched off the pain device.

Arun's muscles spasmed back into some semblance of working order. He drew in one breath. Then another. Just as he was about to tell them his lie, Tawfiq turned the pain device back on.

She hadn't shown mercy at all! She was taking care that he didn't asphyxiate too quickly. If she wanted to prolong his pain, she had to let him breathe occasionally.

Tawfiq alternated bouts of agony with the briefest of respites until Arun was too dazed and his brain too oxygen starved to feel the pain.

Amazingly, he discovered he was breathing again.

Did that mean he had died?

"… waste our time. This one is diseased. It is better to kill him quickly."

As his brain reconnected with his hearing, Arun noticed artificial human words drifting into his ears. The Hardits were speaking in their own language simultaneously with the computer translation. Each synthetic voice sounded identical, but the angry alien voices did not. Arun recognized the speaker as Sushantat, the one he had followed… the Hardit he could see bringing out her own pain controller and adjusting its setting…

Arun was engulfed in a new level of agony. Instead of his muscles locking up and feeling as if they were being skewered by a thousand viciously barbed needles, this new torture was like drowning in an ocean of hellfire. His muscles were free for him to spasm, to writhe and groan. This setting was not designed to inflict pain.

This was killing him.

He could feel his insides fry, his spirit consumed in the flames that he could feel but not see, the fire that burned inside him.

He tried again to plead but he still could not speak. His jaw muscles refused to obey because any movement was even more agony.

With a supreme effort of will, he opened a tiny gap in his mouth and tried to speak. All that emerged was a primal grunt and an acrid smell of smoldering.

He tried telling himself that this grunt had been only a start, something he could build upon. But he had expended all his reserves of courage and strength to utter it. He was spent.

The pain lessened.

He managed to glance up at Sushantat.

She was talking with the others, her hand still activating the pain device, but ignoring him now.

Sushantat hadn't reduced his punishment, Arun realized, this was his body shorting out, shutting down in readiness for oblivion. His brain numbed too. Thoughts were difficult to form. Blurring. A last thought came clearly: he was dying. This was where he ended.

No! He would not allow it!

Others had thought he had a destiny. The Aux had placed a great expectation upon him. He. Must. Not. Fail. Them.

"Al-a-bam-a," he cried. His voice heaved like a child talking through uncontrollable sobbing. "Not a… fire! Slave… revolt."

Biljah stopped speaking and looked at this writhing human.

"Guns," Arun cried.

The pain switched off.

Waves of sensation replaced the numbness.

He preferred the numbness because the alternative was worse. He screamed with the pain.

Arun sat there moaning for a long time. How long, he had no idea – his timer implants weren't functioning. Then he noticed two things. He was lying in a pool of his own vomit and Biljah was yelling at him to explain himself.

He gave himself another handful of breaths and then answered. "Mistress Sushantat said there was a fire at Alabama."

"I don't remember saying that," said Sushantat.

"You must have," said Biljah. "How else could the human have known?"

Arun tensed, praying that the Hardits wouldn't answer their own question. The humans knew about the fire because they had organized it, but the idea that humans could do such a thing was still inconceivable to the arrogant monkeys. Sushantat appeared to have conceded.

Arun continued. "I connected the news of the fire with rumors I've heard about Alabama. There are secret caches of guns and explosives. Could this be the start of a slave revolt?"

"Preposterous," said Sushantat. "He lies to save his life."

"But can we be sure what he says is not true?" asked Hen.

"If you give credence to this one's words," said Sushantat, "then we should send the Jotuns and their primitive soldiers in their shiny armor to investigate. That is their role, isn't it? To die in battle?"

Biljah considered. "I do not wish to smell their contempt if we cry panic over an incident that turns out to be innocent."

"Well, if you are so worried about them, organize the agricultural humans based at the depot to report on the situation," said Sushantat.

"I cannot," replied Biljah. "There is a crop fire fifteen miles northwest of the depot. I have already sent the local humans to extinguish it."

"What!" Sushantat looked agitated. "Why did you not inform me? I begin to believe this human's words. One or both events could be diversions. Send in the soldiers."

"No," said Biljah. "Not yet. Not until I'm sure."

"What alternative do you have?" insisted Sushantat. "Do you expect me to fight? I refuse!"

Arun looked from one Hardit to the other, trying to understand the balance of the argument. All along he'd gambled that the Hardits would be unable to ignore a major fire in the food depot, but would be so scared of accidentally revealing their gun-smuggling operation that they would be desperate to avoid bringing in outsiders, such as the Marines.

Arun hadn't considered that some Hardits were unaware of the gun smuggling, but that was the only way to explain Shushantat's attitude. She might have just tried to murder him, but she appeared to be the most honest person in the room.

Then he realized that he was best out of the argument and cast his eyes to the ground.

"There *is* a way," said Tawfiq. "Team Beta suffers from a chronic oversupply of workers. If the situation were dangerous, then a few casualties from Beta would be to everyone's advantage, even any surviving humans."

Thank you. Tawfiq had just spoken the words Arun had been praying for.

"Too risky," said Sushantat. "We need military assistance without delay."

"Need I remind you who is in charge here?" Biljah's artificially voiced words were expressionless, but Arun was sure she was issuing some stern scents to her subordinate.

The leader of the Hardits suddenly remembered Arun was there and switched off her human translation. The argument raged on for a short while. Arun couldn't follow a word, but at the end of it, he was still alive and following Tawfiq back to Team Beta's room.

Arun had barely made it out with his life, but he'd done the necessary.

Operation Clubhouse was back on.

Chapter 43

"Mistress, this slave begs to report our status."

Arun shook his head. Adrienne was enjoying this a little too much. Any human listening in would hear the smirk behind her words.

"Report," came Tawfiq's artificial voice through Adrienne's radio, which was turned up loud enough to fill the truck cab.

"Thank you, mistress. We have caught and interrogated an Agri-Aux."

"And?"

"And they are concealing something."

"Concealing what? Explosives? Weapons?"

"We have not discovered weapons. I meant that the Agri-Aux knows something but would not reveal what she knew."

"You're playing a dangerous game," whispered Arun. He was sitting alongside Adrienne in the truck cab. Madge glowered at her from the driver's seat.

"Do not trust the crop slaves," said Tawfiq. "Stay on your guard."

"Oh, mistress. I never knew you cared."

Madge reached over and switched off the radio.

Arun could practically see the sparks fly between the two women.

"Go check the others are okay," Madge ordered him between clenched teeth.

Arun took the hint. He opened up the hatch in the cab and climbed out, leaving Adrienne and Madge to work out between them who was in charge. Arun would back his squadmate without hesitation, but he understood that Madge wanted to prove she was the commander without Arun there to outnumber Adrienne.

He heaved himself up, closed the hatch and clambered over the spine of the lurching dung truck.

The truck's powerplant was completely silent, but the heavy tread tires made enough racket to nearly drown out the angry squawks of the birds they disturbed as they drove along the same track they always used to get to Alabama.

Arun was sore all over from the Hardit's pain shocks, but his sense of balance was undamaged. He stood up and walked toward the rear, arms thrown out for balance. On the road behind them he could see Springer driving the other truck. They waved to each other.

When Tawfiq had sent Team Beta out to investigate the strange goings-on at Alabama, giving them strict instructions to never speak of what they found to anyone but her, it was Adrienne who had requested transport. The result was the trucks that ferried the broken-down human excrement from Detroit to the farmland depot: the *Alabama Dung Express*.

The poop trucks consisted of a wheeled frame to which four pods were attached by mag clamps, two pairs hanging from either side of a central spine. Instead of raw ingredients for fertilizer, today one of the pods had a different cargo.

Arun opened up the hatch on top of the pod and shouted inside. "Everything all right in there?"

He was greeted with a cheer.

"I guess that's a yes then. You want I should close the hatch?"

"No, it's a lovely day. Keep it open."

"You got it."

Arun and many of the Aux inside the pod were wearing skirts and bonnets – the full high-tech protective kit. Esther's people had donated eight crude suits earlier in the week, but today all of her Agri-Aux had decided to forego their full protective gear as part of their atonement.

Arun hoped she wasn't going to be frakked off when she learned they'd taken the dung express rather than walk.

"Hey, McEwan!" came a call from the hatch.

"What?"

"We can't get radio reception down here. Catch!"

Someone threw a speaker up through the hatch. Arun clamped his radio to the hatch, connected the speaker then settled down, sitting astride the truck's spine, looking out over the fields. Now that he was properly shielded, he could appreciate the beauty of the golden crops as they rippled in a light breeze under delicate flakes of pure white clouds. Arun could happily spend the entire day looking at clouds; they were so beautiful and he didn't often get to see them.

In the distance he could see the last few wisps of smoke dissipating in the sky from one of the fake fires the Agri-Aux had started, using the smoke bombs provided by Pedro. Hopefully they had given off enough heat to look like a genuine fire to any orbiting satellite.

Arun turned his back on the smoke. That was someone else's problem now. Having done his bit, he was looking forward to taking the rest of the day off. He'd never had a vacation before.

He settled down to enjoy the broadcast from Radio Hortez.

Chapter 44

So there you have it, Scendence fans, The Stormers from 4th battalion, 101st Assault Regiment have knocked out Divine Inspiration from 5th battalion, 420th Tac. While we wait for the next game, stick with Radio Hortez as we return once again to Team Ultimate Victory's Deception-Planning match from earlier today, against the Fieldgrays from 1st battalion, 410th Tac.

Each match uses a randomly selected game or challenge, and for this contest the Scendence AI has selected an old favorite, Skat. It's an ancient Earth card game, folks. Skat's a popular game because it rewards bluff, risk taking, and a grasp of probability statistics. Up till this point in the game, our bug-ugly contestant from Team Ultimate Victory has lost every hand. Fieldgrays opponent, Kadian Stadeker, has kept a straight face but now I can see his expression soften, a faint smile on his lips. He's coasting to an easy victory against the surprise Troggie substitution for disgraced idiot, Arun McEwan. Or so he thinks. Let's begin our replay by hearing what our scribe friend has to say after losing yet another hand.

"You do realize, Stadeker, that I have bluffed all along. I have allowed you to win up to this point. I have just been dealt an excellent hand and I shall beat you with it. It is not that I especially wish you to lose, but I wish to win more."

"What do you mean? You want to win more than I do?"

"No. I wish to win more than I don't want you to lose."

"Eh? Your language skills are even worse than your card playing. You're talking utter drent."

"I regret to tell you, Stadeker, that you are incorrect. It is your ability to listen and comprehend that is utter drent."

Kadian shrugs that barb away, but you can see on his face that he's rattled.

"Eight of hearts."

"You what?"

"Ten of bells. Unter of acorns."

"What are you playing at, insect?"

"Unter of bells. Ten of leaves."

"Hey stop that!"

"King of leaves."

"That's frakking cheating."

"No, this is using my natural frakking advantages. I can smell your hormones the way you can see words in a book. Shall we ask the referee to adjudicate?"

Have you ever had the sense that you've snatched defeat from the jaws of victory? No? If you could only see Stadeker's face you would understand exactly what it must feel like. Only moments before he was certain of easy victory. Now he's so confused that he isn't certain of anything. If you told Stadeker that his name was Merry Madge, he'd probably believe you.

Mind you, your host on Radio Hortez can hardly believe what he's seeing either. I've watched this scene five, maybe six, times now and it still makes my eyes pop. The competitors are sitting at a small circular table covered in a black velvet cloth. Well, I say sitting, but our insect – who goes by the name of Pedro – is resting its seven-foot-long bulk on a kind of bench that leaves its back two pairs of legs free to wiggle along with its feelers. Its front pair of limbs holds a hand of cards. Its drab thorax – the middle segment of its body – is coated in fine rust-colored hairs, neatly brushed for the big occasion. Its abdomen – the lower and largest part of the Trog – is mottled in shades of brown and gray and coated in semi-transparent carapace armor that gleams like highly polished lacquer. He looks like the kind of ultimate monster. If you met our Pedro in your dreams you'd wet yourself in fright, but our insect hero is calmly lying there, holding a hand of playing cards. It's simply bizarre, my friends. Unbelievable.

Tell you what, though. Our big ant is built for these bluffing card games. It's staring at Stadeker through twin pairs of eyes like glossy black glass bowls, making absolutely no facial expressions at all. And it's speaking through a thought-to-speech device. No giveaway tells there, folks.

I'll hand you back to Pedro…

"I insist we consult the referee, because I play not only for victory but to uphold the good name of my nest."

"Your nest doesn't have a name, insect. Just a smell. A bad one too, I expect."

"On the contrary, we do have a human name. We are Nest Clubhouse."

Yeah! Let's hear it for Nest Clubhouse. Just remember who's made all this possible today. I can't name names without risking getting our benefactor into trouble. Let's just say this Scendence match had us hanging on a Cliff-edge, eh?

Back to the match. The ref confirms that trash talking to your opponent is all part of the game. As for Stadeker – get this! – now he's shielding his face, hiding it behind his hands.

"Unter of leaves. Nine of bells."

"You can cut that out. I'm not talking to you."

"Well, that's a relief. I don't want you to. I don't need to see your face either. I can smell your reaction as I name each possible card you might hold. Seven of bells. Seven of acorns."

"Damn you, skangat insect."

"You smell upset. If I were you, I'd play my first card ASAP. The longer you delay, the more of your hand I will uncover."

Stadeker makes his play. It's the ten of bells, the trump suit.

"A safe play. Very sensible under the circumstances, Stadeker. After all, I will soon know your entire hand and you have no idea what I've been dealt. That gives me a crushing advantage, don't you think? Only a miracle of good fortune can save you from defeat.

Our bug-ugly friend, Pedro, was right. He won that hand. And the next. And every hand after that until he played the winning card and claimed a stunning victory for Team Ultimate Victory, standing in for Arun McEwan who was too busy with his vacation to make it to the match today.

They say a great Scendence player is crushing in victory and stoic in defeat. Was Kadian Stadeker calm? Was he heck! Let's fast forward to my favorite part of the match. Pedro has just won, and Stadeker is on his feet, thumping the table and hurling abuse at the big insect. Looks to me like there's going to be a fight.

"You're a skangat cheat!"

"The referee disagrees."

"The referee can go vulley herself. I'm talking about all the cadets watching this. In their eyes you're a cheat. Maybe you don't care, but the human players in your team are cheats too by association. A stench of dishonor will hang around them for the rest of their lives."

"If I were you, young human, I would sit down. It is you who risk dishonoring yourself. In your human translation of the Jotun bifurcated-noun, the game we have just played is called Deception-Planning, is it not?"

"It is. Notice the word 'cheat' doesn't appear there."

"Indeed not. To win by cheating would be vile. And since you are a much more experienced skat player than me, I planned to win by deception instead. I convinced you that I could smell your reaction when I named each card. I can't. That was a lie."

Dear, Radio Hortez fans. I'd give anything to swap places with each and every one of you right now, so you can see with your own eyes the expression on Kadian Stadeker's face.

To begin with, his face is bloated with disgust and envy. To get the idea, picture a ripe cabbage in place of his head, a vegetable bursting with greenness. Now imagine filming that cabbage being cooked for an hour in a steam bath, until it is the color of bleached bone. Finally, speed up the cabbage-cooking footage a thousand-fold.

There.

Now you know how Stadeker's expression changed as he realized how he'd been artfully played by the latest Scendence sporting sensation.

Okay, let's move on. Pedro gave an interview after the match. I warn you, do not drive, operate machinery or fire tripod-mounted weapons while listening to this interview. It is so hilarious it will have you in fits of hysteria.

Belay that! We'll come back to that laughter-fest in a moment. There's a live interview with Xin Lee just starting. I'll patch you through to the feed now.

"… whose crazy idea was it to field a Trog substitute?"

"A team effort. Everything about today has been one huge team effort. Sometimes, it seems the whole of Detroit and beyond is backing us."

"I think you're right. Team Ultimate Victory is the comeback team of this year's Scendence season. Your Trog is filling in for your previous super-sub, Arun McEwan. Was it strange to play without McEwan?"

"Not really. Arun was with us more than you realize. If you're listening, Cadet Prong, I have a hug and more waiting for you. Oh, and tell your little girlfriend, Madge, hi from me. She sent me such a sweet message telling me all about your predicament."

"Do I detect a hint of team romance, Xin?"

"I don't think so. Anyway, nice talking with you. We've won two of our four matches today, which means there are still two more to win. I'm heading over to the Gunnery arena now."

Well, what can I say? You heard it first on Radio Hortez. Arun McEwan has a little girlfriend called Madge. She sounds a sweet thing. If anyone can see Arun's girlfriend right now, please radio in a description of her face. C'mon, it's only fair. I described Stadeker for you!

While we wait for that, stick around, sports fans. Let's not forget that there are sixteen teams still in the competition and all are playing today. We've just got time to hear that interview with Pedro before the Endurance-Stoicism game between two teams from the 101st Assault Marines, Nevergation and Bluffmore Stags. Don't go away.

"Don't anyone say a word." Madge spoke with slow menace.

There was silence in the clubhouse for about a second before Arun couldn't help himself.

"That goes for me too," he announced. "If anyone upsets my little girlfriend, I'll be really, really cross."

Madge's punch came quicker than he'd expected, catching him a glancing blow even though he was already rolling off his lounger constructed from half-filled grain sacks. He fell onto the floor of Alabama Depot, surrounded by billows of laughter echoing from the roof high above.

Chapter 45

"We are winning the battle, mistress. We will overcome the fire or… or…" Adrienne had to stop a moment. Otherwise she would burst out laughing and even Tawfiq might grow suspicious "Or we will die in the attempt."

"Make sure you do one or the other," commanded Tawfiq over the handheld communicator. "The food stocks are far more valuable than your lives. Are you sure you cannot simply move the food sacks out of danger? I do not understand why you say this is impossible."

Aware of her human audience, Adrienne made a show of looking around the loading bay of the depot. Most of the food stores were safely stacked on pallets to one side, but smaller sacks had been arranged into crude tables and chairs that held food, water, or lazing Tunnel-Aux gesturing for Adrienne to hurry up so they could turn the radios back on and listen to the game.

In the center of the warehouse was a stepped pyramid with a flat top. One of the two young Agri-Aux who had remained behind to greet the Tunnel-Aux had explained this this pyramid was the dance stage.

"I regret, mistress," said Adrienne with great solemnity, "the sacks are underneath immovable objects, but they are not in immediate danger of burning."

"Talk with you wastes my time," said Tawfiq. Arun tried to imagine her jumping up and down in frustration. "Do not report in again until you have defeated the fire."

"If you insist mistress. I return to my endeavors. Number 87 out." Adrienne switched off her communicator to the cheers of her audience. Within moments, the commentary from Radio Hortez blared out once more from a dozen crude portable radio receivers.

"Is the monkey still buying it?" asked Springer, leaving wet footprints on the floor as she padded over from the shower.

"Yup. She's even more stupid than we thought." Arun glanced up at the roof where the young Agri-Aux had climbed the hanging rope ladders and were leaning out of a hatch to smear Pedro's fire gel onto the roof. "Reckon we've got a few hours of firefighting left."

The military-grade satellites orbiting Tranquility would spot the deception in an instant, but the Jotuns controlled those. Whatever system had told the Hardits of the fire was much cruder, possibly thousands of years older too.

For once, everything was going to plan. Arun felt invincible, or would have done if every muscle in his body wasn't still groaning under the abuse heaped on him by the Hardit torture. Even his knee was playing up again, the one he'd damaged firing grenades point blank into a Troggie horde. Setting his pains aside, he opened his arm, inviting Springer in for a cuddle.

"Oh, no," she teased. "Not with someone who hasn't washed."

Arun laughed. "How was the shower?"

Springer laughed too. "Strangely good. Here…" She threw him the sacking material she'd been using to dry her hair. "Your turn."

"I can take a hint," he said cheerfully, winking at Springer as he walked off to the fab shop.

In theory there were no showers at the depot. Why would any expense be allocated to the comfort of human slaves? But what the fab shop did have was a small degreasing booth intended to prepare metals and other materials before powder coating them with paint and other protective outer layers.

The Agri-Aux had modified the booth for the occasion.

How bad could it be?

Arun stripped off the baggy white undergarments of his borrowed protective suit, punched the on/off button and jumped onto the conveyor belt. As the belt pushed him toward the heavy plastic strips that marked the entrance to the booth, Arun sat down, the hollow diamond pattern of the belt cutting painfully into his butt. He brought his knees up and head down; the entrance didn't look designed for comfort.

As the plastic strips parted and lukewarm water began squirting at him, he relaxed and uncurled. It wasn't as bad as he'd thought. He could almost stand up if he wanted.

Then choking clouds of de-greasing agent filled the booth, rubbed in by flailing fabric fingers. His eyes stung. So did every inch of his skin. He yelped when his brutalized muscles screamed in protest.

He was the last one through. All the Tunnel-Aux had experienced this and come out with gleaming smiles to match their grease-free hair. He'd never seen such a transformation in morale.

He squealed in protest when scalding hot water suddenly jetted up from below.

"Are you okay?" came a voice from outside the booth.

Springer's face poked through the strips on the far side of the booth. "Oh, it's you Arun. I could have sworn I heard a little girl screaming in there."

"Very funny."

"Yes, I thought so." She threw him a cheeky grin. "Don't forget to clean behind your ears, Arun. I'll be waiting for you on the outside." Her head disappeared.

Before Arun could reply, he was drenched in a sudden outpouring of cold water. The groan of a motor started up as hot air began to blast him.

He shouted into the wind: "You'd better make it worth my while, Phaedra Tremayne."

Arun smiled.

She already had.

Springer reached over and caressed Arun's furrowed brow. "Loosen up," she said. "Enjoy. You've earned it."

She snuggled beside him as they relaxed with a few other members of Team Beta in a nest of hay in the loading bay. "Stop worrying," she whispered.

After the stunt they'd played today, there probably wasn't going to be any future. But Arun had spent a lifetime worrying about tomorrow and the habit was too strong to break now.

"I've done something for the first time today," he said. "I've gambled with other people's lives. And…" He took a deep breath. "I think I like it."

"I know. I'm surprised at you, McEwan. You told me once that you would hate to be a leader, because you would be paralyzed by thoughts of what would happen if your plans went wrong."

"Exactly. Look around at all these happy faces. I feel so proud to see them, but then I wonder whether it was worth the risks I took on their behalf just to plant those smiles there? Even if that transmitter I planted on Cliffie puts the blame on him, we could all be executed before nightfall. At least we've a chance. Hortez hasn't. He volunteered for a suicide mission. And all that for such a gamble. It was only a guess that the Hardits would send us here because they would be scared that more official help would reveal their gun running."

"Stop it. You're beginning to sound sorry for yourself. There's nothing more pathetic than sad-mouthing, especially when you start to bend the facts to match your sob story. Coming here to the clubhouse wasn't really essential. Aux have been hiding themselves all over Detroit today, listening in on secret radios. This–" she waved around the room, at the smiling Tunnel-Aux staining their borrowed white clothes in their rush to cram food into hungry mouths – "has been brilliant, but we could still have listened in on Radio Hortez if we'd had to stay in Detroit."

Arun wasn't listening. Springer waited for him as he floundered in his thoughts, trying to turn them into words that would make sense.

"You know me better than I know myself," he told her. "The way I've used other people… have I become so cynical, or was I driven by desperation? Hortez will die, maybe others. I ought to feel guilty, but I only feel stoked because I put one over on Cliffie and on the Hardits. What's happening to me, Springer?"

"Dear Arun. It's your true nature emerging. I don't think you'll like what you're becoming."

"I don't follow."

Springer kissed him. Arun noticed nearby Aux point and smile. Madge looked over from the bowl of stew she was eating and gave Arun a dirty look.

"You're fighting a losing battle against overwhelming odds," Springer told him. "Generations of selective breeding and indoctrination have brought you to this point. You can't fight such powerful forces, Arun. You're growing into a Marine."

———

Soon after, the main body of Agri-Aux returned, their skin hot and raw from the merciless sun.

As they made their way to the water canisters, to slake their thirst and pour cool water over hot bodies, the Tunnel-Aux smiles became guarded. The volume was turned down on Radio Hortez.

Water beaker in her hand, Esther emerged from the milling crowd of Agri-Aux. Arun rose to meet her, his own beaker raised high in salute.

"Here's to being human," he announced in a voice loud enough to carry through the crowd.

"To being human," echoed Springer, Madge and many of the Beta Aux.

Some of the Agri-Aux joined in with the toast too, but Esther waved them into silence.

Tunnel-Aux edged closer together for mutual protection.

Arun had missed something. What?

"My people will join your toast," announced Esther, "but not until we have something proper to toast with."

"Like what?" asked Arun.

Esther snapped her fingers. On the other side of the bay from the food, a cover was pulled away from a table to reveal a row of 5-gallon canisters with taps fixed at their bases.

"Like that!" said Esther.

"What is it?" asked Madge. "More water?"

"We work with the grain. We know how to extract its fruit." Esther's explanation was lost on Arun and the others.

"It's beer, man," called out one of the Aux in a peal of laughter.

"What is *beer*?" asked Arun, but that only provoked more gales of laughter. He looked to Madge and Springer for help, but they looked as puzzled as him.

Esther put an arm over Arun's shoulder. "My friend, this is a party you'll never forget."

"More likely it's a party he won't be able to remember," someone called out.

Esther ignored the heckle and steered her ally toward the beer.

―――

"Remind me again," Arun asked Springer when the light coming through the doors to the hardened area outside was beginning to fade and redden. "What're we supposed to be doing here?"

"Partying!"

"No, I mean, like, what did we tell the Hardits we were doing?"

"Oh. Something about a fire, I think."

Arun took a moment to understand Springer's slurred speech. He remembered now. He looked up at the fake fire in the roof and frowned. He didn't remember anyone applying the smoking gel for a long while.

"Getting dark," said Springer. "D'ya think they're getting worried 'bout us?"

She and Arun looked into each other's eyes, trying to keep a straight face. They erupted into giggles.

Arun retrieved the communicator from where Adrienne had last left it. With a flourish, he activated the device.

There was the briefest of pauses before Tawfiq's voice screamed through the speaker. "Report. Report. Report!"

"Tawfiq. How're you, my fine, furry friend?"

"Who is this?"

"197. 222?" Arun scratched his head. "I don't recall. I never forget a name but with numbers… I'm hopeless."

"What occurs? Report!"

"Keep yer fur on. What're we doing, eh?" He looked around at the buzzing party. The dance floor was heaving to the percussive rhythms struck from upturned metal drums. "Umm, we're busy, I guess."

"What is that noise I hear?"

"People. People doing stuff."

"Stunted imbecile. Where is 87?"

"87? Oh, you mean Adrienne? Let me see…" Arun scanned the warehouse and spied Adrienne on the dance floor, grinding out some raunchy moves in front of an eager young buck with his shirt off.

"87 is engaged in an encounter with an Agri-worker."

Springer stifled a laugh.

"I think," said Arun. "Think she's trying to go undercover to discover his secrets."

Springer exploded into laughter, bringing Arun with her in fits of giggles.

"Give it here. Silly veck-ek-eks." Arun looked up to see Madge standing over him with an open palm thrust in his face. She was bathed in sweat having just returned from an expedition to the dance floor herself, bringing back a gaggle of male admirers with her.

Arun handed over the comm.

"Corporal Majajazazaa here, ma'am." Madge's words were slurred worse than Springer's. "Firefighting party will return to home to you–"

"Do so, immediately."

"–as soon as conditions permit. Mazazeeta out."

Madge cut off the sound of Hardit protest, took aim, and threw the device 10 meters into a pan of warm stew.

Madge was so drunk she could barely stand or talk. But she could dance and – it seemed – she could throw. The communicator landed dead center in the pan and disappeared to contribute its favors to the stew.

Springer whistled in admiration. "Your targeting skills are impressive, corporal."

Arun was impressed too, but was relieved to see Madge return to the dance floor. Her hostility to him had reduced, but only by a hair's breadth.

He pulled Springer closer to him. She fitted so perfectly, snuggled under his shoulder, as if they had been engineered to complement each other.

Basking in the warmth of her embrace, he took a gulp of beer and recorded onto his implants the sights and sounds of the party, from the clumps of strangers in conversation to the pounding beat from the ever-changing lineup of drummers. He tried to memorize the scents too, though he had no means of digitally recording them: the smell of fresh perspiration, freshly-baked bread, and sticky beer spills. He nuzzled Springer's neck, drawing in her scent, the most precious of them all.

Then he settled into the simple pleasure of watching everyone else have fun.

Other than a few of the male Agri-Aux who had stripped to the waist to show off muscled torsos, everyone there was dressed alike in loose white underclothes. Arun looked from one happy human face to another, and whether they worked the tunnels and passageways of Detroit or the fields of Alabama he could not tell.

They were all of them human.
And just for a little while longer. Being human was all that mattered.

Chapter 46

It was Adrienne who eventually rounded up Team Beta and herded them back into the dung trucks for the trip back to Detroit. She even managed to bully them back into the Aux overalls they'd left behind in the cargo pod.

After a few hours of blissful cleanliness, persuading the drunken Aux to don their stinking rags took such impressive leadership that even Arun noticed.

She's the one with the keenest eye on the future, he thought, but he kept his assessment to himself. Thoughts of what awaited them on their return pressed everyone into a somber silence as the trucks drove through the night.

Madge had driven them here but she was in no fit state now, so Adrienne took the wheel of one truck, with Springer driving the other. Arun kept Springer company in the cab while Madge slept with their passengers in their dung pod.

The drive back was bumpy, and the track somehow seemed narrower because the drivers continually slipped down the bank, raising groans from their passengers.

Eventually they gave up and drove through the fields, paralleling the track.

At the topside vehicle park back at Detroit, they found a detachment of Marines waiting for them, accompanied by Sergeant Gupta, their railguns leveled at the cabs of the dung trucks.

No one said a thing. There was no need. The Marines grabbed Arun, Springer and Madge and propelled them down the main ramp of Gate Three and down into the tunnels of Detroit.

"Take these," said Gupta, handing them each a capsule.

Arun swallowed his and immediately felt a blinding flash of agony followed by terrifying clarity. All the comforting fuzziness brought on by the Agri-Aux beer vanished, to be replaced by a crystal-clear understanding of just how utterly flekked they all were.

As they were marched down to the battalion administrative section on Level 4, they encountered cadets, novices, Marines, Aux and Hardits. The

Hardits paid them no attention, the military humans gave them wary acknowledgment, but some of the Aux recognized them. There were tears in the eyes of some Aux onlookers, despair in their hearts.

That was the hardest thing for Arun to bear, that the hope he'd encouraged in the slave workers had unraveled so rapidly. Before the day was out, the whole of Detroit would know his fate.

To give false hope to the hopeless is the cruelest deed of all.
What have I done?

Gupta deposited them back where their Aux escapade had begun: at attention in front of Staff Sergeant Bryant's desk.

He glowered, making them sweat for a long while before he spoke.

"I have a request from your Hardit hosts. No, not a request. It is a *demand*, barbed with the most hideous threats. Do you worms realize how dirty it makes me feel to be ordered about by those flea-bitten monkey-vecks? They demand your termination. I thought it advisable to have you escorted here directly upon your return. At least that way I'm spared the further indignity of our monkey colleagues implementing the termination of human cadets themselves."

Arun fought against the temptation to slump. He succeeded in keeping himself absolutely still, not even breathing until the shock eased. Not that he'd expected anything different, but to hear the death sentence passed… it wasn't easy.

Bryant watched with interest as Arun's dismay played out over his face.

"Staff sergeant," said Arun. "This cadet begs permission to speak."

"Go ahead." Bryant's words were filled with subtle poison, as if inviting Arun into a trap.

"I found something out there I need to report."

Madge gave a warning growl, deep in her throat, but that only steeled Arun to his purpose. He would tell about the drugs and the firearms. It was a hell of a risk for everyone, but sometimes you had to take a chance. Arun didn't expect to get another one.

Then Springer gave an identical growl, and Arun's resolve melted away.

"Stop that at once," boomed Bryant. He slammed the table and then shot to his feet, his muscular bulk towering over the cadets. "It's bad enough that you stink like Hardits. To growl like them too is an insult to the Corps. Six days you've been away. Six fucking days, and you've already lost every shred of dignity." He took his seat, his face still livid with contempt. "I pity you, Gupta, to have such sniveling cowards in your squad."

Arun didn't dare to glance over at Madge, but he knew dismay would be etched into her face. Being called a coward would have hurt her more than any Hardit shock torture. To have growled like that, she must be utterly convinced that they shouldn't be talking about gun running.

Bryant turned his stare onto Arun. "Continue."

This was Arun's big moment.

He took a deep breath… and then danced away from the truth. "I reckon my time has been up for a little while now, staff sergeant. Been dodging incoming drent so much it feels like I've cheated death a dozen times. What I mean is that it's all my fault, not the other two."

Bryant's eyebrows shot up. Arun's did too. The staff sergeant had sent them off to the Aux with a lesson about justice ringing in their ears. Arun added quickly: "I don't mean it isn't fair, staff sergeant. Justice and fairness are irrelevant. Please let me take all the blame and spare the others. That's not justice, it's efficiency because these other two have shown through their initiative that they could make good Marines one day. It would be a waste to throw them away now."

"You're wrong," said Bryant. Arun had given the most impassioned speech of his life, and Bryant had instantly crushed it with two crisp words.

But then Arun noticed a twinkle in Bryant's eye… the staff sergeant was laughing at him! "You're wrong," repeated Bryant, "because there *is* a place in the Corps for justice, even compassion. Though they are luxuries that are not often possible, we should never forget them or we will cease to be human."

Arun's heart beat faster.

"Nonetheless, request denied."

Arun couldn't keep it up any longer. He slumped, physically and mentally. This was the end.

"Unlike the Hardit request," continued Bryant. "That we cannot refuse, whether we like it or not." Why was he grinning? "They request termination and I agree. You three were sentenced to serve one week as Aux because your overactive sense of justice caused you to make grave errors of judgment. I believe you have learned your lesson. I am therefore terminating your Aux sabbatical with immediate effect. Report to the medical facility ASAP for anti-radiation treatment. You restart cadet training tomorrow."

Arun couldn't keep the smile from his face.

"We all turned a blind eye to your little adventures," said Bryant, "but no more escapades that might draw the attention of our betters. On the other hand, if I were to fish through the communal laundry shelf one morning and my fingers happened upon a packet of biscuits hidden amongst the shirts, I might put that down to one of life's little mysteries. *I might*. But don't push it too far. Understood?"

"Yes, staff sergeant," answered the cadets.

"This cadet begs permission to speak, staff sergeant," requested Madge.

"Hell no. Of all your sorry little band you are the one who should keep your mouth most firmly shut, cadet corporal. As senior cadet, your task was to keep the other two out of mischief. You failed."

It was Arun's turn to ask. He wanted to ask permission to contact the Aux, to let them know they hadn't been executed, to prevent their morale from shattering. Madge had probably been trying to ask the same thing. But as Arun's mouth moved to speak, Bryant stopped him dead with a flinty glare.

Bryant's face colored red. "You cadets have far too much to say for yourselves." He pointed an accusing finger at Arun. "You most of all."

Arun kept his eyes front as the staff sergeant's scrutiny played over him. He hated that having lifted Aux morale it would be crushed by rumors of his death. But he was too scared of Bryant to even think of crossing him.

"You're trouble, hero," said Bryant. "And you other two are only one step behind him. If you study your military history, you will learn that sometimes the awkward few win finely balanced battles with their different ways of seeing things. But this is a Marine Corps unit. I do not tolerate dissent. I can maybe afford to give a few nanometers of leeway to a handful of exceptional Marines, to pander to their unconventional thinking, because one day they might make the difference between victory and death. However…" Bryant's face went as hard as poly-ceramalloy armor. "You are *not* exceptional! All I can see in front of me are three silly little teenagers. Nothing more. Do I make myself clear?"

"Yes, staff sergeant," they all replied.

"I hope so because you'd better pray to whatever gods you hold dear that you are never brought before me again. Now get the hell out of my sight!"

The cadets gave a crisp salute, turned and marched away.

Fifty paces down the passageway they stopped, looked each other in the eye and whooped with delight.

Level 4 echoed with the sounds of gleeful high fives.

PART III
The Prophecy

Human Legion INFOPEDIA

Military Concepts
–Introduction to ships, boats & platforms

Marines will encounter a wide range of ship and boat types while on active service, as well as orbital platforms and other void-based facilities. The term 'ship' is widely use in a generic sense in the Human Legion Infopedia, but a stricter nomenclature differentiates between *ships* as vessels that have interstellar range, *boats* as vessels designed for maneuver but are not capable of interstellar travel, and *platforms* to mean space stations and other essentially static facilities.

Ship design has changed little since the development of the bacterium bomb about six thousand years ago. The ease with which this bomb — small enough to be carried by a Marine — could penetrate outer hulls made capital ships more vulnerable. This led to an emphasis on smaller vessels and on much greater numbers of Marines skirmishing in an attempt to disable enemy ships and to shield friendly vessels from the enemy's Marines. Indeed, it is probable that the very existence of the Human Marine Corps, and consequently the Human Legion, owes its existence to the bacterium bomb.

Battles between warships typically occur when an invading fleet contests a defending force for control of a star system. Ships will tow warboats to strike range in the outer system, and then leave the boats to take the fight to the enemy who will defend with a mix of boats, orbital defense platforms and many hidden defenses. Some ships have high maneuver and offensive capabilities and may accompany the warboats in an attack.

Although to a Marine the distinction between ship and boat may seem arbitrary and of little interest, this is not true of navy personnel. It is vital that you learn and employ the correct terminology for any vessel to which you have been assigned. Entire Marine complements have been executed for insulting their warboat captain by suggesting she or he commanded a ship. To warboat crew, ships are flown by plodders and cowards who wait in safety while the boats do the real fighting. To ship crew, boats are minor craft, mere passengers whose crew spend most their lives in cryogenic sleep while the ship navigates the deep void between the stars.

By whatever name they are known, the vessels to which human Marines are assigned tend to be less powerful models and toward the end of their active life, many craft already having seen millennia of service.

The ship type a Marine will be assigned to depends to some degree on the regimental specialism, although Marines train for all potential roles.

Assault Marine regiments are trained for assault against a defended planet. Assault regiments can be assigned to almost any ship type. In fact, the ship or boat is unimportant, being merely to tow self-contained Marine pods, which contain habitation, cryogenic, supplies, and dropboats for an approximately company-sized unit of marines to deploy in orbit and launch an assault. The Marine pods have limited maneuver and defensive capability and will detach from the parent vessel before attack.

Void Marine regiments are specialists in vacuum and zero-g warfare. A ship's Marine complement will form a defensive screen and add offensive options against enemy ships.

Tactical Marine regiments are also trained in void combat, but are allied to a small tactical warboat to make a single combined operations unit. The most common warboat type is called a Tactical Unit (often shorted to 'TU'), a roughly spherical craft that is agile and well-armed. A TU will typically have a Marine complement of two squads and be ferried into combat by a *sleeve* ship. The sleeve consists of a command and propulsion sections attached to a hollow tube. The TU boats — and other modules such as engineering and supply pods — are stacked within the tube during interstellar travel.

Another distinction between void and tactical Marines is that the former will egress their ship through an airlock, or through a hanger opening inside a small boat. A tactical Marine will typically egress through an EVA chute which uses amniotic gel to shield the marine from physical trauma while the TU jinks at high gees to avoid enemy fire.

— Some information on this topic has been excluded as you have insufficient access privileges —

Chapter 47

Nestled within the pattern of brilliant jewels embedded in absolute black, the precious gleam from Earth's star pulled at Arun across nearly 50 light years.

Sol was not far away, easily reached by transport ship, but no ship would ever take Arun there. Not even to one of Sol's neighbors.

Throughout novice school, the instructors had rammed home that the Human Marine Corps was a joke in the eyes of other species: plasma fodder equipped with third-rate cast-offs and so stupid that they were sent off to die actually believing they were genuine warriors.

"Look up Earth history," Instructor Rekka had once told them, "for the contempt felt by Earth peoples for Roma, Jews, lepers and dalits. That's how the others see us: unwashed, untouchable, unwanted. The word 'human' has been absorbed by alien languages, a byword throughout this region of the galaxy for the lowest of the low."

Arun wasn't so convinced. Maybe all this humans-are-useless drent was a psych trick to produce Marines who were hungry to prove their worth.

What made Sol so impossibly distant was the White Knight policy of keeping human Marine units well away from Earth. But why would they bother if humans were such a joke?

Arun would go there if he could, but he suspected that was a dream that would sour if it ever came true. He'd heard tales of Earth soldiers marching through captured cities and welcomed as liberators by beautiful girls throwing flowers at their feet. As an armed representative of Earth's oppressors, Arun guessed a more likely welcome would be a knife in the back in some dark alley.

Sol hazed and then vanished behind Tranquility's bulk as the planet swung across his field of view, but Sol was only one of myriad stars, and the circling heavens held endless fascination for those who really took the time to look.

As an underground dweller, Arun equated the starscape with clouds: both provided spectacular sights, made all the more precious because he rarely had the chance to relax and enjoy them.

"Listen up, squads. We head out in two minutes."

With a sigh, Arun reeled in the focus of his attention. Blue and Gold Squads were floating in the vacuum, like a snapshot of swarming insects. Close by was their target, a hulk of functional metal officially labeled *Assault Training Vessel 2*. The Spirit class warship was once a proudly gleaming wedge of metal, just under a klick long from bow to stern, and 300 meters from the viewing blister sprouting from the upper deck down to the main railgun slung under its belly. Now its off-white hull was scorched by beam weapon attacks and its skin riddled with holes drilled through for boarding exercises. As with most things in Detroit, the ship had been unofficially re-designated using an Earth name, *Fort Douaumont,* because — in reference to some obscure battle on Earth — the ship had been fought over countless times but never truly won.

"Ninety seconds."

A grafted-on switch in Arun's head told him that these words came over the command channel. There was no need, because Arun recognized the voice as belonging to Cadet Lance Sergeant Alice Belville, Gold Squad's leader and designated commander for both squads in this exercise.

Alice was okay. Sometimes Arun worried that she was a little too quick to press ahead without consulting with her section leaders.

"Frame-reference on my position," said Alice. "North to *Douaumont's* bow. Center on her dorsal command blister. Green layer through ship axis. Layer height 200 meters."

Zero-g combat had no natural reference for up and down, left and right, so tactical commanders defined a frame-reference for their Marines, sometimes redefining it over the course of a fast-changing battle. With *Fort Douaumont*, the framing was often the same: north corresponded to forward, right to starboard, and so on.

Arun glanced over to the two veterans observing the cadets. Their battlesuits were capable of stealthing their wearers against any means Arun had of detecting them. Today sergeants Gupta and Searl had set their suits to high visibility mode, flickering yellow and orange. They looked as if they were on fire.

Alice issued each section their orders, and reminded the cadets that the vets had given them a ten-second start before activating *Douaumont's* defensive lasers. That's when the fun would begin.

Madge would lead Arun's Blue-5 fire team in an arc over the ship at a distance of around half a klick above the ship's upper hull. Once in place, Blue-5 would watch for counter-attack, covering the backs of Alice and Brandt's teams who would lead the main assault. Del-Marie and Blue-6 would take a similar position but slightly lower and facing aft.

"All units to fire smoke at two klicks to target," finished Alice. *Frakk! That meant he would be exposed to laser fire for a klick before shielding his advance under cover of smoke. It also meant the smoke would be far denser supposing enough Marines made it that far.* "Stealth at one klick. Any questions?"

Alice had left about one minute for any debate. None of the other 54 cadets had any questions to ask, but Arun wondered whether the vets in their fiery suits were questioning why she was leaving her teams exposed for so long.

Arun concentrated his thoughts on an area of space about one half klick closer to *Fort Douaumont* until Barney acknowledged, adding a cream waypoint marker to Arun's tac-display.

"On my mark… 3… 2… 1… Mark!"

A blur of frantic motion erupted into the void from all directions, every cadet performing a crazy dance of perfect unpredictability. Arun whooped with delight in the privacy of his own suit as he corkscrewed, reversed, accelerated and stopped in a complete jinkout maneuver. All he had to do was set the waypoint and enjoy the ride as Barney plotted a constantly changing evasive course.

After about ten seconds, *Fort Douaumont's* point defense systems were activated, immediately acquiring targeting solutions. Lasers opened up, fingers of instant death reaching out to pluck the cadets from their dance.

Arun was under heavy fire, but it felt oddly unreal. It always did in space. With a ground assault you felt the crump of shellfire through your feet and heard the whiplash crack of field railguns. Atmospheric dust would bloom beam weapons into brilliant light-shows, leaving a tang of ozone in the singed air, and an afterimage on survivors' retinas.

Not so in the serene vacuum of space. Here there were no shockwaves, the only sounds that of Arun's own breathing and the commands coming through his internal helmet speaker. With no atmosphere to scatter their light, lasers were invisible unless you looked directly down the beam.

Death was something that happened to someone else, until it happened to you. And even then, any weapon capable of slicing through battlesuit armor would kill the person inside before they knew they'd been hit.

There were no wounded in void combat.

Barney gave him a jolt whenever one of the cadets was hit. In the disorientating rush of the assault, that was the only way he could tell the lasers were finding targets. Arun hadn't time to worry about them. He set Barney a second waypoint, closer to the ship.

After another two seconds of exposing himself to point defense, Barney told him he was now two klicks from *Fort Douaumont*.

Arun fired smoke. *Yeah!* He'd made it through the most nerve-shredding part of the mission.

The defensive munitions canister flew from the launcher beneath the barrel of his SA-71. Moments later, the canister split in two, each section blasting off on different vectors. Those children split again, and then again into a total of 64 final capsules. The assault force launched around three thousand capsules, which exploded over the course of the next twenty seconds, lighting up the vacuum. Marines talked of firing *smoke*, but what really emerged was a mixed shower of decoys and material strips that unwound into streamers. The strips had a range of properties: highly reflective, thermally hot, radioactive, energy absorbent. All were designed to confuse enemy targeting systems and degrade beam strength.

It worked: Arun sensed the rate of casualties slow to a near stop.

Space seemed to have acquired a thousand new stars, a sequined shroud added to by the enemy lasers, which flashed in green or red bursts from myriad reflections.

Arun told Barney to filter out these distractions from his visor, leaving him with the target ship and his waypoints. He was about to add a third waypoint when a gut-wrenchingly abrupt change of velocity grayed and narrowed Arun's vision, robbing him of breath.

It took a few seconds for Barney to ease his acceleration enough for the blood to start flowing properly in Arun's head. As his vision returned, Barney explained that he'd made an emergency course correction to avoid colliding with another cadet. The AI was now bringing him directly to the target.

The constant jinking grew even more frantic for a few moments before slamming to a halt. Barney had matched velocity with the target ship, positioning Arun at the far left of his fire team's patrol arc. The suit was now stealthed too.

Arun tensed. If all went well, the smokescreen would have hidden his entrance so that when the cloud of defensive munitions had degraded, Arun could rely on his suit to keep him invisible. If the smoke hadn't hidden him enough… he'd already be dead.

Arun relaxed and looked around.

Springer was in position to his right and Madge farther on. If Osman had made it through then he'd be farther still, hidden by the curvature of the ship's enormous hull. Arun gave Springer a thumbs up.

She ignored him.

He had a sudden urge to talk to her, but couldn't without breaking the training protocol. The only reason Arun could see his buddy was because the stealth function on these training suits was only a simulation. If this assault were real, Springer would be as invisible to him as to the enemy. That, and the point defense lasers would have opened up earlier and at lethal strength.

Arun looked over his section of hull. There were hatches aplenty and concealed areas under the forward shield projector where an enemy counter-strike force could assemble before attacking. There was nothing to report.

He glanced down and aft to where most of the cadets in the assault force were already swarming over the boarding points, simulating breaching by holding a boarding patch to the hull and pressing down until the patch turned green. Only then could they jump through the pre-drilled holes into whatever awaited them.

There was nothing he could do for the boarding teams now except guard them from surprise attack while they were busy. Arun turned his attention back to *Fort Douaumont's* bow.

From a distance, the training ship was a sleek wedge of metal, but up close the hull was much messier. The original hull design had been infected by a boxy, urban landscape that had risen, been cleared away, and then rebuilt countless times over the centuries to leave heat exchangers, gun emplacements, storage lockers, shuttle docks, maintenance bot housing, and retro-fitted defensive munition launchers.

If the blocky hull surface betrayed that *Fort Douaumont* had never needed to cut through the thickness of a planet's atmosphere, the forward shield projector was evidence that it had to press through a far more deadly medium: interstellar dust and debris. From a human perspective, the void was a vacuum. But the gulf between the stars was not quite devoid of matter, and even a tiny dust particle would hit with the force of a fusion grenade when the ship slammed into it at its top speed of 0.7 lightspeed. The apex of the filigree crown of shield rails extended nearly two klicks forward of the bow. In flight, the shield rails charged the interstellar medium, rolling it along the ship's beams in a magnetic slipstream.

Beneath Blue-5, the shield power array was laid out like a fan-shaped forest with its narrowest point aimed directly at the boarding point. If he were a defending officer, planning to sally forth against a Marine attack on the upper hull, Arun would deploy his counter-attack through this forest, which consisted of scores of the ten-foot high spiny boxes that powered the two upper shield projectors. Then he'd wipe out the boarding teams, taking them by surprise.

Arun hung above the power array, screwing up his eyes as he tried to penetrate the crimson-tinged black shadows cast by light reflected off Antilles, the nearest of Tranquility's moons. When the cadets had launched their attack on the orbiting ship, they had kept to the cover of Tranquility's shadow. For this simple exercise, *Fort Douaumont's* belly had been oriented toward the planet's surface, which shrouded the upper deck in that same shadow.

He switched to infra-red, but the power array was partially charged, meaning it glowed bright blue in his visor. Looking for the bots in infra-red was like looking for a flashlight on a star's surface.

It was no good. He switched back to the visual spectrum, but despite all the augmentations that uprated his sight, and Barney's best efforts to refine the image in his visor, all Arun could see were shades of black. He tried forcing his brain to concentrate harder. He was in so much drent already that he couldn't afford any mistakes. One more vulley-up and Staff Sergeant Bryant would kick him back down to the Aux levels. Alerting his section to an attack that wasn't there would be enough to earn that kicking. But the harder he made himself peer into the dark, the more it shimmered, his mind imagining fleeting patterns that weren't actually there.

What he needed were the sensors in his suit, but he was running his systems cold: active sensors could give away his position. So he left his eyes unfocused, relying on their natural motion-detection ability.

"Contact. Blue-4 going firm." The warning came from Mbizi Sesay. Arun had been good friends with Bizzy, close enough to hear the worry beneath his seemingly calm voice. "Eighteen hostiles bearing 350. Range 120 meters." Bizzy's voice cut off but that didn't mean he was dead. By broadcasting his warning, he'd also revealed his location underneath the ship. Bizzy could be moving to a new position, the g-forces unleashed squeezing off his ability to speak.

Alice's voice came over the command channel. "Gold-4 peel left. Gold-5 peel right. Enfilade hostiles in contact with Blue-4."

The temptation to turn and watch the action threatened to wrench Arun's head around, but he had his orders and they hadn't changed. Checking what was going on elsewhere in the battle was Madge's responsibility. Instead, he settled back into a watchful gaze. He'd spent countless hours in this state playing stealthsuit cat and mouse games set up between rival squads. That was good. That was routine, and routine was something he could sink into and ignore the fighting that raged behind and beneath him.

"Gold Command has boarded," said Alice. "Brandt has secured the upper two decks, and I'm forming up for attack on Target 1. Gold-3 follow.

Gold-6 remain stealthed as reserve. Blue-6 maintain position. Let's show those vets what we can do, Marines!"

Not only was Alice still alive but she sounded like she was having fun. That was a good sign. 'Target 1' was the bridge. Even though the Corps' alien enemies weren't expected to understand the human language, and even though battlesuit comms had encryption beyond the ability of human crypto-experts to explain, much less decrypt, the Jotuns insisted that Marines used code words for tactical objectives.

Arun's confidence lifted still further when Bizzy reported over the command channel that the enemy counter-attack had been repulsed with minimal casualties.

Arun sensed victory, but only for a few seconds. Down there… in the shield generator array… he thought he saw movement.

He strained his eyes trying to tell whether this was an attack, but he couldn't be sure. He had to get nearer.

To remain in stealth mode, albeit simulated, his suit could only move slowly. Arun approached the suspicious area as fast as he dared, snapping a flash-bomb off the equipment patch on his hip, and slotting it into the launcher beneath his carbine.

There was something there all right.

Directly below him, hatches had opened in the hull, spilling hostiles into the cover of the shield array generators. The enemy were scurrying spider-like training bots, the size of a human child but with lasers attached to two of their limbs. A fist-sized plate was grafted onto the central 'body' of the robots. If you hit that with your laser, the robot would deactivate — a combat casualty.

Already he could see dozens. More were spilling out by the second, forming up ready to rush the boarding party. The counter-attack on Bizzy had been a feint intended to commit the cadets' reserves.

Should he warn the others? He readied his carbine to fire the flash-bomb at the bots, but he daren't reveal his presence by broadcasting a warning as Bizzy had done. Instead he asked Barney to find a tight-beam comms route. Although he could turn around and see Springer, the stealth training protocol meant Barney pretended she was invisible. The AI simulated firing tight-beam pings at the probable location of his comrades, hoping to strike it lucky before being noticed by the enemy.

"Hold fire, McEwan. Activate LBNet." Madge had found him first, bouncing her order off Springer's suit.

The instant Arun switched to Local Battle Net, Barney changed Arun's visor to tactical-display mode, adding five blue dots to indicate the positions of his section comrades. Delta Section should have seven other cadets: Brandt had been promoted out, and it looked like Zug hadn't made it through point defense.

LBNet continuously connected everyone in the team using tight-beam links. It was risky, but more secure than broadcasting on Wide Battle Net. With the suit AIs now able to share what their wearers could see, and add what the AIs suspected, scores of enemy red dots erupted like an infestation over the terrain below.

"Hey, Springer," Arun called out. "Join me at the hatch? We can drop grenades in and then take the bots from the rear."

"Negative," Madge replied. "Assigning orders."

As Barney sketched an outline of Madge's intentions, Arun scooted off to comply, while Madge used words to duplicate her orders.

The shield generator array was a funnel aimed at the boarding point, but the funnel drained between a pair of shield array projectors. The shield rails that charged the interstellar medium fed out of these 30-meter diameter tubes, which were pointed forward, angled toward the starboard and port bows. Each of the two Delta Section fire teams would take a position on top of a shield projector. When the bots passed below, the Gold fire teams at the boarding point would pin them down, and then Delta Section would rake the bots with flanking fire.

It was obvious, though he hadn't seen it.

And that was why Madge was section leader.

By the time Arun was in position, lying prone atop the starboard shield projector, and using the ridge that ran along its crest as cover, Barney was telling him the bots were already beginning to swarm on the other side of the projector.

The temptation to stick his head over the ridge to see for himself was powerful, but the fear of screwing up the operation was greater. He glanced to either side. Osman and Springer had rolled onto their sides, checking their flanks for bots. They appeared calm, but of course it was impossible to be sure in their ACE-2/T training suits. He turned back to face the enemy. Blue dots showed Madge, Del-Marie and Cristina on the reverse slope of the other projector — the two fire teams keeping in touch by means of signal repeaters slapped over the ridges.

One of the blue dots moved up the slope. It was Madge.

"Ready on 3," she said. Simultaneously, the red dots rearranged and firmed as Barney received an update on their position: Madge had sneaked a visual of the enemy surging below them.

The bots fired first. Not at Delta Section but at one of the teams at the boarding point.

"Contact!" screamed Lance Corporal Yoshioka from Gold-3. "They're coming at us from behind." She sounded surprised. Why wasn't Yoshioka in on Madge's plan?

But there was no time to worry about Yoshioka. Madge counted down. "3… 2… 1… Now!"

Arun raised his carbine over his head and fired his flash-bomb. Without waiting for its effect, he scrambled over the ridge and opened fire with his laser, Barney applying a charge to the suit that glued it to the projector on a rough approximation of standard gravity.

Barney was ready for the explosion of light from the flash-bomb, limiting its effect to be merely dazzling. The bots, though… they acted stunned.

Perfect!

Arun raked them with laser fire. From the feet of his first target, he played his aim diagonally up to the right and then down again, stitching a repeating pattern of simulated death.

They might be bots but they still acted confused, staring up, seeking for the hidden threat that was scything them down.

Yeah!

This was the therapy he needed!

He tried to imagine he was shooting Tawfiq and her skangat monkey-bitches, Instructor Nhlappo for trying to get him executed to save her butt, the traitors who were drugging his section…

"Cease fire!"

So soon? The feeling was too good for Arun to release the pressure on the trigger, but the thermal cutout on Arun's carbine obeyed Madge's order for him anyway.

He knelt as he picked a new position to switch to while his carbine cooled.

There was movement. There… from the heap of robot bodies.

He froze.

No!

But they were dead… The bots… he'd seen them fall!

The combat bots rose from death, picking themselves up on spindly limbs. One rotated its bulbous sensor node and looked straight up at Arun. It didn't pick up its weapon, just *stared*.

Arun scrambled back behind the projector ridge. "Corp—"

Too late! His warning died with his comms connection. Stiffened cords erupted over his suit, immobilizing him. Barney wasn't there any longer, and the AI had taken his tactical-display and vision enhancements with him.

That look from the bot had killed him. Arun was certain. But… but that was impossible.

The charge on his suit that had stuck him to the ship went too. As the momentum from Arun's backward scramble carried him off the shield projector, his boot snagged briefly on a cooling fin, transforming his feet-first reverse into a head-over-heels tumble away from the warship. He bumped into a laser emplacement and off into space at the speed of an arthritic worm.

The veterans would be in no hurry to resurrect the dead cadets after the exercise, which left Arun with more time than he wanted to ponder how Delta Section had messed up so badly.

His answer wasn't long in coming. Delta Section hadn't screwed up at all: the exercise had been sabotaged.

Doubts gnawed at him, growing stronger as his distance from the ship stretched ever further. Until now he'd dodged the clutches of the conspiracies swirling through Detroit. He had begun to feel as if he were acting out a daring tale of adventure, something he would look back on one day and laugh.

No longer. Although his body was tumbling helplessly through the vacuum, he knew his fate was held fast by the traitors, gripped as surely as by a powered gauntlet.

There would be no Human Legion now.

Chapter 48

"You may turn around."

After the veterans unlocked the suit AIs of the dead cadets, they had then ordered Delta Section to stand facing the bulkhead in a passageway on Deck 14 of *Fort Douaumont* to contemplate their failure.

Now, after an hour with his visor up against a vertical sheet of metal, it was time for Arun to face the conspirators, for surely the veterans must be in on the set up.

In theory, Gold and Blue Squads had been victorious — after a fashion. Casualties had been high; tempers higher. The other cadets had taken the homeward shuttle long ago, but Arun suspected the rest of Gold and Blue had never been more than cover for what was really taking place here. Delta Section's day was far from over.

As he turned — an awkward movement without gravity but with his boots sticking to the deck like glue — all the overlays and vision enhancers in Arun's visor shut down, reducing it to a transparent bulge at the front of his helmet. Even his helmet lights failed. Gupta had taken control of his helmet.

To Arun's unaided eye, the only light in the utter black of the passageway came from the lamps mounted to either side of Gupta's helmet. They burned like fusion torches.

Arun shut his eyes. The lamps burning through his eyelids scarcely dimmed.

"McEwan!" bellowed the sergeant. "Stand at attention properly!"

Arun opened his eyes and squinted into the blazing light. Gupta held his gaze before walking down the line, halting again in front of his first victim.

"After you were in position above *Fort Douaumont*, did you hear Cadet Lance Sergeant Belville's instruction?"

In the airless passageway, there was no direction to Gupta's voice, the sound of his words coming only through Arun's helmet speaker.

"Yes, sergeant." There was a subtle note of desperation in Madge's voice. They all assumed the sergeant's words were meant to trap her with no possible means of escape.

"What were her orders?" asked Gupta.

"To guard the boarding teams against counter-attack, sergeant."

"And did you carry out that order?"

Madge hesitated.

"Answer me, Majanita! Or would you prefer me to first explain the concept of carrying out orders?"

"No, sergeant"

"Then answer, damn you. Did you carry out your orders?"

"Yes, sergeant."

"*Yes, sergeant?* Really? Then explain how your section failed to warn the boarding party of an attack coming from your sector? And why Delta's defense was such a steaming puddle of drent that you might as well have been back in Detroit, chowing down in the mess. Were there actually any cadets inside those ACE-2/T suits? Were you actually? Frakking? There?"

"Yes, sergeant."

"Then how do you explain your vulley-up?"

Arun glanced left to where Madge was pinned by Gupta's helmet lamps. Should he speak up? Shit happens, for sure, but Madge didn't deserve this. It wasn't fair.

Then he faced front, sharpish. He'd been warned before about not thinking things were fair. Besides, he bet Gupta knew what had really happened better than any of them.

"You!" bellowed the NCO.

Gupta took two bounds along the passageway to come to a position looming over Arun. He jabbed a gauntleted finger at Arun's chest.

"Do you think you're special, McEwan?"

"No, sergeant."

"Then why were your eyes on Cadet Corporal Majanita? Did you have something to say?"

"No, sergeant."

"Oh, really? Well, you do now. Tell us whether your section commander carried out her orders."

There was no hesitation. "Yes, sergeant."

"Interesting. Then explain how the enemy brushed aside your defense so easily that they wiped out Gold-3 unopposed."

"There was a fault with the bots, sergeant. We shot them but—" A red alarm sounded inside Arun's brain. A sensation he'd been trained to associate with going offline. Gupta had shut him out of the local comms net. Arun finished his explanation anyway. "We shot them, but they got back up and shot us. Frakk! They didn't shoot us. One just looked my way and I was dead. It wasn't our fault."

"Not your fault. Not *fair*? Not – *fucking* – fair? Your overactive sense of justice forced Staff Sergeant Bryant to send you down to join the Aux. Looks to me like he wasted his time. Are you hankering to reunite with your Hardit friends?"

"No, sergeant."

"Then let me remind you one final time. Life is not fair. This exercise was not fair. Wasting my breath talking to an idiot cadet is not fair. Do you still believe the bots malfunctioned?"

Did he? What was worse, lying or complaining? Lying to a superior was a capital offense, so it wasn't much of a choice. "Yes, sergeant. They malfunctioned."

"Oh, I'm sorry. Does that mean your section is off the hook? That your screw up wasn't your fault?"

"No, sergeant. Drent happens. We have to succeed despite that."

Arun pictured Gupta chewing over Arun's words behind his opaque visor. Gupta eventually responded: "I don't believe a word you've just said. But at least I detected a faint flicker of intelligence, which is as much as I can hope for. You've reported a suspected malfunction to your NCO. And now I'm telling you that I don't care. What should you do about the rogue bots now?"

"Nothing, sergeant."

"Good. You will not speak of bots that don't stay down. You will not speak of equipment malfunction. You will not talk about the events of this day at all, except to admit with the appropriate and deserved level of shame that you frakked up and let your comrades down. You will not speak of this to anyone at any time, ever. That is a direct order. Do you understand?"

"Yes, sergeant." Arun understood very clearly. If he ever talked, he would be disobeying a superior, and the penalty was death.

But there had been more meaning than that in the NCO's words. Equipment malfunction was an ever-present hazard. This was usually down to cyber-attack, not poor design or lack of maintenance. The Hardits had been mining this system for many thousands of years. Back when *Homo sapiens* and *Homo neanderthalis* were scrapping for domination of the Earth, the most valuable raw materials of Tranquility's system had already been extracted and hurled out into the interstellar trade routes by giant mass drivers.

That meant the system had long been a target for robot spies launched by rival empires. Counter-espionage bots scoured the asteroid, moons and comets forever discovering tiny automated factories pouring out nano-sized spybots to observe, challenge and test defenses.

Equipment malfunction should be investigated but Gupta was trying to snuff out any word of this. Which only confirmed what Arun already suspected: that Gupta was part of the conspiracy. And yet… Surely there were far simpler ways to silence a cadet who knew too much?

A green light clicked in Arun's head, and he knew he was back on the public comms net.

"This was your first zero-g exercise under my instruction," said Gupta. "You let me down. It is now my task to shake each of your scrawny hides until either a Marine tumbles out, or you die in the attempt. I don't much care either way. What I do care is that there should be no losers in my squad, because out there in the wider galaxy there are no losers in the Marine Corps. Why is that, Cadet Koraltan?"

"Sergeant," answered Osman briskly, "because only the best make it as Marines."

"You can cut the parade ground bullshit, Koraltan. That's for children. The reason why there are no losers in the Corps is because losers are a liability. No NCO would risk his or her entire unit in order to shield one unreliable Marine. Do you imagine the White Knight Empire provides a network of military hospitals to care for Marines who aren't fit for combat duty? Out at the front, liabilities are quietly abandoned to the void for the good of everyone else. No Marine left behind? That's a saying from long ago and far away. I don't care whether you call it murder or natural selection, but if you don't earn my trust by the time I lead your squad out to war, I'll kill you myself. Understood?"

"Yes, sergeant."

"I hope you do. And now for the good news. I've taken pity on you. Instead of going home to Tranquility, I'm going to give you a chance to start earning my trust without delay. I've booked you a place on my old boat, *Yorktown*. You're going to be doing EVA drill."

Arun kept his expression blank. Inwardly, his mind was spinning out of control. *Yorktown*? That was a Tactical Unit assault warboat, recently returned from the frontier wars for refit and upgrade. Just when he thought he was beginning to peer through the web of deceit to see what was going on here, Gupta had clouded the picture once again.

Perhaps he would find the answers on *Yorktown*.

Chapter 49

There was a helluva lot of black in space, Arun mused, not exactly for the first time. Facing out to space from his *Yorktown* EVA chute, he saw a field of black, peppered with infinitesimally small silver dots. Sergeant Gupta would appear somewhere in the void — when he was good and ready — darting in front of Delta Section on his one-man flitter. The exercise was simple. The disgraced cadets had to keep their eyes peeled until they spotted him, and then they had five minutes to catch him. Anyone who didn't manage that would not be going home. Ever. Or, at least, so the NCO had promised them. Gupta had seemed so pissed that Arun wasn't sure whether he was exaggerating.

Arun had been entombed in his EVA chute for three hours now. The sergeant might appear in the next second, the next hour, even the next day. They had no choice but to wait, their natural sleep patterns kept at bay by their augmented Marine bodies.

Whatever changes the alien scientists had wrought on his flesh, they did nothing to stop the hunger gnawing at Arun's belly (breakfast had been 14.3 hours ago) nor did they stop imaginary lights flickering across his field of vision as his mind got its revenge for staring so hard for so long by playing tricks on him.

He issued a mental command to his faceplate to overlay astro-navigation interpretive information. Moons were ringed and named. So too were distant mining craft, as were ore shipments in their transport capsules that would shepherd them along the light years to their destinations. If he stared long enough at the tiniest dots, they would reveal themselves as stars or comets, their names appearing on his faceplate. And if he stared longer still, he would see summaries of composition, and political and economic status.

What he really wanted was to access combat mode. But his suit was not set up to show his commanding NCO as an enemy threat, no matter how Arun felt about him. Astro-navigation mode should still show up the NCO, but Arun no longer trusted his suit, and so he switched off the interpretive mode and relied upon eyeballs alone.

The ghostly blue fringe of Tranquility's outer atmosphere entered Arun's field of vision, followed inevitably by the rest of his home planet as *Yorktown* continued her spin. He had no chance of spotting Gupta against the disk of purple-tinged clouds and azure seas, so he closed his eyelids. In the cocoon of an EVA bubble, that wasn't easy, but he decided it was better to rest his eyes for a few moments.

As his eyelids shut and the dark closed in, Arun felt fear. At first, it was a curious sensation. Fear was not an emotion that came easy to a Marine's altered mind. Even in dangerous situations, such a shooting away at an advancing horde of Troggie guardians, he was always so charged with a chemically-exaggerated combat high that he hadn't time to think. But now he did. He could do nothing *but* think.

He was plastered like a squashed bug to the outside of an orbiting Tactical Unit, a spherical warboat that usually served as the assault vehicle for a squad or two of tac-Marines. In his EVA chute, he could barely move, and certainly couldn't speak or even breathe. There was a reason the chutes were nicknamed *gibberballs*.

What if his NCO never did show? What if there was some elaborate scheme to cull the oversupply of Marines? Much of what the aliens did made little sense, but Arun was absolutely certain that the value their alien masters placed on each human life was precisely zero.

Fear, boredom, hunger, and betrayal. Arun was not having a good day. He would have loved to speak with Springer, or Osman, even Madge. But in an EVA chute, everything was stuffed with buffer gel, even his helmet and the inside of his mouth. Talking was impossible.

Tranquility slid away out of sight and Arun stared once more into the field of black.

Still nothing.

The Extra Vehicular Assault chutes were tubes set flush into the hull that terminated in an amniotic bubble filled with buffer gel. The Marine inside was supplied through nutrient and waste tubes that connected inside their bodies via their suits. The gel allowed oxygen to pass through the Marine's skin into the bloodstream, and to remove carbon dioxide through the reverse process.

In combat situations, deploying Marines to the position where they were most needed was a seriously dangerous business. The buffer gel that filled all empty spaces inside the amniotic bubble, and the suit itself, could protect a Marine against thirty second bursts of 16g acceleration while keeping at least 80% of the occupants conscious and no more than 5% fatal casualties.

Scuttlebutt had it that they were trialing a gibberball rated for 19g acceleration. The bubbles themselves were unaltered but the human occupants were upgraded by having their eyeballs replaced with artificial versions that would not pop under extreme acceleration. The brain fluid too was pumped out and replaced with buffer gel before each assault.

Arun's amniotic bubble could, in theory, keep him alive for years. Zug often insisted that this was the future intended for their distant descendants. Zug was strangely at ease with the distant prospect of cyborg Marines, but even he accepted that being encased in buffer gel – and so unable to move talk or breathe – for more than a few days would drive anyone insane.

The TU continued to spin about its center in a spiraling pattern that placed each EVA chute back to its starting position every 4.8 minutes. Thanks to the damned counters and timers he could never turn off, Arun knew for a fact that the TU was on its 38th cycle since the exercise had begun.

On cycle 39, the fear he'd experienced almost as a curiosity began to really bite. This could be the White Knights' new mode of murder: to entomb marines in their amniotic prisons until their minds were ruined. But why? It made no sense.

By cycle 41 he had it. Aliens were cruel for a reason and he knew that reason now. Disobedience was punishable by death, the sentence carried out by the assault carbines of an execution squad formed from the friends and squadmates of the guilty Marine. At least it was quick. As for death in combat, every Marine cadet accepted that was their most likely fate, one day out there in the stars, fighting for a contract signed on Earth centuries ago. Death in space combat was so quick you would never know you'd been hit. Anyone who couldn't cope with that prospect had been weeded out years ago.

But if a quick death was something they were prepared for, it would be something else entirely to be kept for a week or more in their gibberballs.

Once returned to the base on Tranquility and paraded as an example, their bodies would be physically healthy but once proud young men and women would be reduced to pitiful gibbering wrecks.

Pour encourager les autres, as Zug would say.

Arun fought against the sense of entrapment. He thought of Xin, imagined kissing those vital lips… but Xin was out of his league. His fancy battleplaner brain had caused only heartache. The idea of her falling in love with him was so improbable that he only felt even more of a loser.

Alone… Abandoned… Sacrificed…

And drugged! He should be able to handle the wait but whatever they were feeding the other cadets was driving his brain wild. He'd never make it.

Desperately, he replaced Xin in his mind with Springer. It was her lips he focused on, not to kiss but to hear her speak words of comfort and reason. It helped. A little. He reinforced Springer with Zug, the calmest person he knew.

But all imaginary Zug would do was shrug and say repeatedly: "You must die to encourage the others."

That was it.

Arun broke.

He screamed!

Inside his helmet, stuffed with buffer gel, his scream sounded like distant thunder. Then the gel was pushing itself down his throat, He was drowning. He swallowed a quantity of the tasteless gloop, but when his throat released, more gel had pushed into his mouth and stuffed itself down the back of his mouth, pushing, suffocating, drowning. He knew he should shut his mouth but the need to scream and gasp for air was stronger than his sense of reason. He gagged, but the link between gagging and vomiting had long been removed, so he kept on choking and gasping and drawing in yet more gel that pushed further down into his gullet.

Arun was drowning. Every instinct screamed that he was on the cusp of death, that he must *act* now! He was drowning! Yet he couldn't die. The gel was supplying him with oxygen. He knew that, but what help was knowing because he needed to breathe and could only drown and keep on drowning?

Enough reason returned to his mind for him to order the EVA chute to launch.

It refused. Barney knew that the cadet inside him was ordering a launch for the wrong reasons. Only when the launch criteria had been met would Barney relay a launch instruction, and Barney would know when Arun was lying.

And so Arun continued to scream, continued to drown…

And drown…

Drown…

———

Arun's mind became so lost in the hinterland of death that he had no idea how long he had been drowning before Barney snapped him out of his funk with the mental equivalent of pouring an ice-cold bucket of water over his head.

Around him, he saw a glittering halo of sparkles — gloops of buffer gel flash-frozen in the cold of space. The others had launched!

He braced himself and then willed his EVA chute to launch.

Nothing happened.

He tried again. *Come on, Barney. Damn you!*

Barney explained. <Launch initiation failed. Equipment failure. Shipboard AI notified and launch override requested. Standby.>

Arun braced for launch. He calmed and relaxed his throat until the gagging eased. The idea of being deliberately driven insane seemed ridiculous now, the result of spending time in this gibberball while doped. To experience yet another equipment failure… maybe this really was a cyber-assault? That was bad, but not as bad as being murdered by your superiors.

He watched as Osman, Springer, Madge and the others converged on a jittering dot that his faceplate overlay said was Sergeant Gupta. His squadmates closed in on their target and chased it around the back of the TU and out of sight.

"Why have we not launched?" he said. Or tried to. Even Arun couldn't hear more than an incoherent grunting, and Barney made no reply.

Seconds turned to minutes.

Minutes stretched into hours.

He fought a rearguard action against the approach of insanity. He imagined resting his head on Springer's chest, his head cradled in her arms. Even in his imagination, Springer was pissed at Arun for letting down his comrades again, blaming the sabotaged training bots on him. Too angry to speak any words of comfort, her embrace offered just enough comfort for Arun to keep a fingerhold on his sanity.

Chapter 50

His legs kicking over the pit of despair, Arun held on to his sanity by his fingertips, time stretching beyond any meaning.

And then, without warning, he was hurled back into the physical universe in a frantic blur of events.

Nutrient and waste tubes retracted. The buffer gel pulsed out of his suit, his helmet, but not his throat. He choked, panicked.

The skin of the EVA bubble blew out in a million tiny fragments and he was shot out into the vacuum, buffer gel freezing all around.

His lungs quivered, protested, screamed for the air flooding into his helmet but none could make it through the gel still clogging his gullet. Without the gel supplying air through his skin, he was choking to death.

He tried. He tried so hard, but he could not breathe.

A tear came to his eye. *It mustn't end like this!*

Then a deeply embedded instinct took over. He gulped and belched simultaneously. It was confused and painful but whatever he'd done worked.

He was breathing.

He was alone.

Arun tried radioing *Yorktown*, but Barney reported the warboat was refusing comms. He decided to scan the outside for a hatch, or better still a camera that he could wave into. Then he thought better of it. The *Yorktown* crew already knew he was here. His EVA port had just opened for frakk's sake.

His answer came when a bright speck detached from the starscape and came in on a looping trajectory around *Yorktown*, decelerating to halt side-on a hundred meters away from Arun.

The distant speck had grown into a TS-32(c), a utility shuttle configured in troop carrier mode. The side of the main section facing Arun folded up, ready for boarding.

He couldn't imagine a more obvious invitation.

A whoop came from Arun's mouth, a sound as weak as he was exhausted.

That won't do, he decided. So he flipped his suit over in a series of somersaults, the zero-g equivalent of jumping up and down while punching the air in triumph.

Someone was going to a great deal of trouble to lure Arun to a time and place of their choosing.

He laughed. This was more like it. He was living an adventure and loved it.

Too many people whose opinion he valued had called Arun an idiot recently. Well, they could go vulley themselves because he was unlucky, not stupid.

He realized that what had sapped his morale these past weeks was the fear that he would die pointlessly and unremarked, his life amounting only to a few lines in the regimental records that no one would ever read. That shuttle was as clear a sign as he'd ever get that someone powerful thought Arun was important.

Earning the contempt of his battalion had hollowed him out, leaving him a void inside a brittle shell. But if he didn't die now, he was confident he'd claw back the trust of his comrades one day, refilling that void inside with the sense of belonging that had once sustained him. He was already making good progress with Springer.

As for teetering on the brink of destruction so many times recently, that only energized him.

What was it Hortez had said on that first trip to Alabama? *Things happen around you, McEwan*. Dear Hortez. How had his friend's ending played out?

Arun instructed his suit AI to head for the shuttle.

C'mon, Barney, let's prove Hortez right.

Chapter 51

Arun watched the external video feed to the passenger cabin as the shuttle's AI touched the craft down gently. They landed on a mid-sized lump of rock that would once have been an asteroid much farther out from the sun, but had been captured and towed to a Lagrange point between Tranquility and one of its moons. The gravitational pull between planet and moon canceled out at these Lagrange points, making them an excellent place to dump things, such as old spacecraft and tamed asteroids, because they would stay where you left them rather than clutter up the already crowded orbital paths around moons and planets.

This rock had a simple landing pad of fused and flattened rock, set a short walk away from a cavernous hole that led down into darkness.

Arun checked his suit comms. Only the shuttle's AI was registering as a node on his local ad-hoc network, and it was refusing to answer any of Arun's questions. The shuttle's cabin was airless and unpressurized, designed to disgorge a squad of armored Marines within seconds. With no one talking to him, the journey and landing had been silent, other than the sound of his own breathing.

Arun expected to be contacted by the AI controlling operations on this asteroid. But if such an intelligence existed, it was hiding from Arun. There was no sign of technology at all, other than the artificial nature of the crude landing pad.

Without a doubt, this was the most remote place Arun had ever been.

Untraceable would be another word for it.

All these thoughts floated through Arun's mind but failed to catch there. While he'd been trapped in his EVA bubble, his Marine's enhanced physiology had suppressed sleep, kept him concentrating on tiny dots in space for hour after hour, and had filled him with such a sense of threat that his muscles had powered up ready to leap and bound, but had found themselves unable to push effectively against the entombing buffer gel that had drowned him relentlessly.

The elation he'd felt when he first saw the shuttle had consumed his final reserve of strength. Now he was exhausted almost beyond the capacity to care any longer. Whoever had set this up had gone to so much trouble that it was pointless to resist. Arun thumbed the door pad, and half jumped, half floated down onto the landing pad.

He took long, bounding jumps along the path to the cavern. After fifty paces stumbling through the winding cavern entrance, Barney switched his faceplate to infrared but there was no heat source to serve as illumination: the walls were as cold as space.

He stopped and laughed. Out of habit, he'd been trying to avoid drawing attention to himself, but the idea of remaining undetected was silly, so he activated his helmet lamps.

The twin patches of illumination revealed a crudely hewn tunnel with a floor that was flattened and textured for improved grip. Arun had expected the entrance tunnels to be just large enough for him to carry out a long micro-g bound without cracking his head on the roof. It was far larger than that.

He searched his memory for zero-g mining. He knew almost nothing, but after a few seconds, facts vomited themselves out of a deep store, unpleasant to access but ready for use all the same. Whether this new knowledge came from artificial memory stores or had been implanted during Second Sleep he had no idea. But he did know that asteroids were normally assessed for mining potential by lozenge-shaped robots that would drill holes just large enough for them to drag themselves through. Larger tunnels could wait for when full-scale mining began. He saw images of asteroids being actively mined, and those fully mined out. But there were no signs of the equipment, tailings or port facilities he should be seeing in either scenario. So this wasn't a mining asteroid at all. But what was it?

It took another half hour of following twisting tunnels, and worrying whether he was circling round on himself, before he heard the hum. The tunnels were airless, but there was a faint vibration running through the floor that Barney picked up and fed in a cleaned and amplified form through his helmet speakers.

At first, Arun thought this was the electrical hum from a power source. Then, after immersing himself in the sound for a while, he changed his mind. It reminded him of listening to radio wave emissions from the sun. No, that wasn't quite it either. There was an organic quality to the hum. It was alive.

Whatever the hum's source, it gave him a beacon to aim for. Time seemed to speed up once he had a clear objective. Soon he emerged into a cavern painted with abstract symbols on its walls. Tracks ran along a ceiling, and from one of those tracks hung heavy brown drapes that ran across the room, hiding whatever lay behind from his sight. Barney was convinced that the hum's source was just behind the curtain.

"Approach the hanging barrier!"

The voice in his helmet was mechanical. Could it be a Trog? The voice was identical.

Arun walked to the curtain and then halted.

"Turn off your light and remain stationary."

Arun turned off his helmet lamps but switched his faceplate to infrared. All he could see was a faint circular smudge right in front of him that shifted and swirled. It could easily be his mind playing tricks.

Whatever it was stayed motionless, throbbing gently in front of him. As the minutes dragged on, Arun became convinced he was making up the image, and yet something tangible was there: the hum. Under the fizz and swash, he heard — or thought he did — an echoing thump. A double pumping sound, as if twin hearts were beating.

A flash of heat came from overhead. Switching back from infra-red to visible spectrum, Arun saw that the ceiling was glowing with a diffuse blue-tinged light, and that the curtain was drawing back to reveal a… creature of some sort. But if this were a living thing, its evolutionary route was not one that had led to limbs, spine, torso, and head.

The thing was a blob, colored an impenetrable blue-black, about eight feet tall and three wide. The blob was surrounded in a rough sphere of orange liquid that fizzed and bubbled. It looked as if the orange liquid kept its shape through surface tension alone, because it wasn't inside a container. At the top of the central blob — what Arun thought of as its head — tubes connected with the orange surround, pumping out ribbons of silver fluid. A similar setup at its 'feet' sucked darkened streamers back inside its central core.

"Thank you," said the blob through Arun's helmet. At least, Arun assumed it was the blob that was speaking, but there was no sign of a translation box, no mouth parts, and no nodes registering on his suit comms.

Conversations were so much easier when you stuck to sound waves through air.

"Why am I here?" Arun asked.

"I — we — wish to see inside you."

"What? Dissection? Isn't that a bit old school?"

"It is not your body that interests us."

"You're going to read my mind?"

"We read your destiny."

"Oh."

"And your mind."

"You can…? Why?"

"Your future is — can be — important."

That's what Little Scar had told him. And the colonel had learned this from… "You're a Night Hummer!"

"You are correct."

"And all the weird stuff that's happened. Training bots that revive. Bad comms. Being left to drown for so long. That was all you?"

"I requested this event sequence. Disorientation and exhaustion is an aid to see inside your mind. To feel your path without the resistance natural to a sentient."

"Surely there must be an easier way to… to *read* me?"

"There is."

"Then why not use it?"

"You do not want the answer."

"Eh? What do you mean?"

"What I said."

Arun wanted to punch this annoying blob. Could he actually do any damage if he did? He shook his head. The Night Hummer was many levels of importance above a human Marine cadet. There would be reprisals.

"Feeding us combat meds. Running guns off planet. Was that your doing too?"

"No."

"Do you know anything about them?"

"No."

Liar. Arun was learning how deeply all the conspiracies were embedded into Detroit. Everyone knew more than they let on. And if this Hummer was in cahoots with Gupta – Arun was nearly convinced of that now – then it had to know something about the traitors on Tranquility.

The blob was probably laughing at him, those bubbles an expression of its contempt for the puny human. Nothing riled Arun more than aliens smug with the certainty of their superiority.

With difficulty, Arun sucked in his anger and snarled: "Do you realize how much trouble your little games have caused me and my squadmates?"

"No."

"Corporal Majanita will probably be demoted — that'll kill her. The battalion will be awarded demerits, which will make it even more impossible to climb out of the Cull Zone. I might be executed as a consequence of what you've done."

When the Night Hummer gave no reply, Arun prompted: "And?"

"And? Please elaborate."

"And don't you care that you've caused so much trouble?"

"I do not care."

"You're a skangat, then. You know that?"

There came a pause. Then the Hummer replied: "Yes."

"Yes? Yes, you're a skangat?"

"Correct. My translation device tells me that *skangat* is a term humans use on each other to communicate disappointment in the other's behavior, or to indicate aggression, possibly leading to physical combat. Is this correct?"

"Right on both counts, pal."

"Thank you. Then I am a skangat."

"Frakk! I can't even insult you."

"That assessment is probably accurate. Without long practice, interspecies communication is significantly less rich than between sentients of the same species. However, I estimate that if we communicate regularly over a period of no less than several weeks, and if you apply yourself to your task, then it might be possible for you to insult me."

"Is that's what's gonna happen? We're going to be stuck together for weeks?"

"No. I have completed my examination. You will leave shortly and only see me on one more occasion."

"Then why…? Oh, what's the use? Tell me this, then. What did you see inside my mind? What is my path?"

"It is best that members of your species are not given details of predestination. Your species is not evolved for that."

"And yours is?"

"Correct."

"Why?"

"Defense."

"So you — what? — see a threat coming and change the future so you avoid getting tropied?"

"The broad thrust of your speculation is correct. Our precognitive capability is an adaptation of our feeding process. It is why my kind has an understanding with the species you call White Knights. They feed and guard us. We tell them the future."

Arun thought back to the conversation with Little Scar. The Jotun had said Arun was important, another human too. Maybe two. "Luring me here," he said, "was that part of your defensive instincts?"

The Night Hummer made no reply. It rolled back a few paces before coming to a halt. Then it rolled forward again before repeating the pattern. Was it pacing?

It took three minutes before it answered: "yes."

"Then I do what? Do I shoot an invader who would otherwise have killed you?"

"Probably not."

"But I am important to your future?"

"Yes."

"Do I save you?"

"No. You are my killer."

Arun's vision reddened momentarily as combat rage took a hold of him. If the Hummer had brought his killer here, it could only be for one reason: the creature saw Arun as a threat, one to be eliminated.

Arun leaped at the blob. He had to kill the Hummer before it killed him. He sailed through the airless space aiming to bring his hands together in the place roughly corresponding to a human's neck. He penetrated the outer orange skin easily enough but then… he was gripped! The blob rolled back, absorbing his momentum, but his hands were held fast.

Arun pushed up until his feet were pointing at the ceiling. Then he swung himself back down in an arc pivoting on his hands. He never finished the maneuver. A cavity appeared in the center of the Hummer. A split second later, Arun was sailing through the vacuum to land on his back a dozen paces away. The thought just had time to run through his head that to throw him such a short distance showed restraint and skill before he hit the floor and was rolling back like a ball, and kept on rolling until he gently smacked into the wall.

The Night Hummer, meanwhile, had effortlessly kept pace with him, propelling itself by waving its surface in contact with the floor. He'd seen vids of Earth snakes move like that. It made sense if micro-g was your natural habitat.

"You misunderstand," said the Hummer when Arun had come to rest. "You are my killer, yes. But it is not your intention to kill me. You try to save me. You will fail. Probably. Hopefully."

"Hopefully? Why hopefully?"

"Because then your path is not what I foresee."

"And I'm important, right?" Arun scrambled to his feet. "Hold on! If I'm important, "

"Probably not. But the future is a forest of potential paths. You can change your future to make that more likely. This is why we stay aloof. Interference rarely works well. I have a personal interest in you because you kill me."

"What do I do that is so important?"

"You should not hear predestination."

"Who is the purple human?"

"You cannot make me tell you your destiny. Nor can you cast words and phrases in my direction, fishing for my reaction."

Okay, buddy, we'll see about that. But first, a change of tack. "Is this your natural habitat? Do you live here?"

"This facility is readied for occupation by a troop of my people. Sadly, my companions are not arriving. The White knights treat us like vegetables, to be planted in gardens such as this and tended, and weeded, left to grow information. But we are not vegetation, and I do miss company."

"So what are you telling me? That all the hell I've been through this past day… and more… it's so you have someone to talk to?"

"No!" A pressure wave coursed through the Hummer, striking the floor hard enough to lift Arun a few inches off the floor. "I am not so trivial. I must have you here to see deeper, to see the pattern of what you call past and future. Understand, human child. Your cultural history talks of the pattern of the future being a vast tapestry woven by the Fates. Each sentient life is a single thread."

"You're quoting the Loom of Thessaly, right? The Earth supremacists are always going on about the importance of Classical Greek culture."

"Perhaps they are correct to do so. The Loom of Thessaly remains the most accurate model your species has yet devised to explain the nature of reality. In this model, individual sentients are caught in the tyranny of the tapestry's pattern. They can struggle but never break free, and if you stand back a little, the struggles of individuals are invisible against the purity of the larger pattern. But sometimes special threads arise that… Your model suffers from a critical lack of dimensions at this point. Let us say that these special threads tie off the old pattern and influence the Fates to begin weaving a radically new design."

"And I'm a special thread, yeah?"

"You might be."

"Can be? What must I do to become this be this new-pattern guy?"

"You must make a choice. The pattern you make possibly saves your species from extinction and elevates the status of humans everywhere. Many other races too benefit in this future."

"Sounds nova. Where's the catch?"

"You must make an oath. It binds you to the future that saves your people. If you break your oath, the path diverges. The pattern corrupts, and you may accelerate your extinction."

"Go on."

"Do you promise to adopt my people as the client species of the humans? You must re-house, guard and cherish us. There are future times when you will choose between your friends and your promise and you must choose your promise, or the future will corrupt."

Arun laughed. After all he'd been through. Such madness! "Hummer, that's crazy talk. That's treason, for starters. The White Knights would sterilize the entire planet if they got wind of it."

"You are correct."

"I don't believe for a nanosecond that I could make this happen even if I was insane enough to try."

"I know. Yet you must promise sincerely. Saying meaningless words is not sufficient. The oath must be real."

"And in any case. The White Knights get you these hollowed-out rocks to live in. You have your understanding with them. Why change that?"

"Because the White Knights cherish randomness, mutation and the potential of creative destruction. We represent a predictable future. Our nature is utterly repugnant to them. They loath us more than any other species, and yet they cannot ignore our usefulness. Within a century from this time, we are labeled scapegoats for White Knight setbacks. They exterminate us."

"And you want me to protect you?"

"Yes."

"From the White Knights, the most powerful species I'm aware of?"

"Correct."

"You're mad."

"I can see into the future."

"You're also a liar. You refused to tell me the future because I'm not evolved enough, apparently. But you've just told me what will happen. "

"I have. I only reveal small details. They are obvious. You learn them yourself soon."

"Good for me." Arun's stomach rumbled in irritation. He hadn't eaten solid food for almost two days and his stomach wasn't one for philosophy and long-laid plans. Without food, Arun wasn't saving mad orange blobs or anyone else.

"If I refuse?"

"That is unwise. A tragedy. But you will eat and drink nonetheless, and the shuttle shall return you safely to your home."

"Food! Where?"

"Follow."

The Hummer shimmered over to the far end of the room, to the portion that had been hidden behind the curtain. If the blob had lips, Arun would have kissed them because there was a pressurized accommodation bubble. Through the clear plastic walls he could see a table and chair. There was a hotplate with steaming sauce and meat…"

"There is beer too," said the Hummer. "I am told humans enjoy beer — although you soldier-children are denied the experience. And roast meat and other palatable items. There is plenty of air, and an inflatable bedroll for you to sleep upon. When you are refreshed, tell the shuttle to return you home."

Arun knelt down to unseal the outer door of the airlock. As he started to crawl through to this one-man chow-hall, the alien spoke through Arun's helmet speaker.

"Human!"

"What?"

"Your oath. Will you swear to protect my species? To guard and cherish us?"

What was this, a marriage ceremony? He supposed it was. Perhaps this was the most important moment in human history since President Horden signed the Vancouver Accords that had bought Earth White Knight protection by selling human children into slavery. Maybe this was even more important than Vancouver.

Or maybe this was the rambling of an intelligent blob driven insane by loneliness.

He sighed. On the far side of the airlock was dinner. That was far more real than all this speculation.

"Well," said the Hummer. "Do you swear?"

"I do so swear. I shall cherish and nurture your people."

The airlock flashed a blue light and slid opened. Arun was inside, lifting off his helmet and smelling rich aromas of meat and vegetables and gravy. He shrugged. *Aliens!* If only they were all such dumbchucks.

Chapter 52

"Since your return from the auxiliary, you have not spoken of traitors and drugging."

Pedro was lounging in the lamp heat of his basking station, his face regarding Arun with expressionless eyes as always. While the insectoid's face was physically incapable of smiling, frowning, snarling and all those other human expressions, Arun was certain he was learning to pick up on the alien's other cues, from body posture, linguistic phrasing, those tireless antennae and who knew what else?

If he was reading the signs right, Pedro was saying that this was a topic they had buried for too long.

Arun shook his head. "Not going to happen, big guy. Too dangerous."

If only they had somewhere private to talk, then Arun would dearly love to ask his friend for advice. But that first trip to the orbit could be put down to meeting on neutral ground. Meeting there regularly would look to outside observers like plotting insurrection.

"And I'll tell you another thing that's dangerous," Arun said, "continuing these little chats without you opening up. You won't tell me anything about your military capability, your population numbers, or give me a detailed map of your nest. Hell, you refuse point blank to tell me what they did with Hortez when he hung up his microphone. Colonel Little Scar hasn't yet asked me to report back on my liaison mission. But he will. So far it's been all one-way: I give you info; you confuse the hell outta me. You've helped me, for sure, but you've given me nothing that I can give to the colonel. You call yourself my friend, but on this you've let me down. Badly. Possibly fatally."

Pedro's legs were folded underneath. Each pair in sequence now pushed him up a little before dropping back down. The result looked as if Pedro were bobbing atop ocean swell.

Arun knew this meant the insect was delighted at Arun's words. Dongwit aliens! He'd been trying to tell off the Trog.

"I am not permitted to reveal certain secrets," said Pedro when he'd finished bobbing, "but I have nearly finished the compilation of a dossier containing everything else we know about ourselves, from our earliest history, through our pheromone language, and on to the best examples of our love poetry. Expressing the essence of my people using your human language proved more difficult than I thought, which is why this took far longer than my initial estimate. The greatest challenge was to transform information into understanding. *Human* understanding. The dossier will be uploaded to the base network tomorrow, and access granted to your softscreen account."

Arun didn't know what to say. The more he replayed Pedro's words, the more stunned he became. "You did all this," he said when the faculty of speech returned, "for me?"

Pedro curled his antennae in amusement. The bulky alien was laughing at Arun's expense. "No," Pedro said. "I did not do all this. A team of over five thousand assembled this for me. The majority of the nest's research capability was diverted to serve your needs. Now do you believe I have let you down? Badly. Possibly fatally."

Arun grimaced. "Sorry, Pedro. Horden's Children, big guy. Look at you. You're an overgrown ant, and yet you've made me feel ashamed. How the hell have you managed that?"

Pedro tilted his head down and folded his antennae flat against his head. He was in deadly earnest now. "It is not my people of the nest who have made you feel guilt, it is your human sense of empathy. This is important, Arun McEwan. You are important. We have offered similar information to the Jotuns on many occasions, but they lack the mindset to *understand*. You humans are far more socially elastic, enough to accept and bond with us. Jotuns are admirable in many ways but they are culturally rigid, brittle even. They can only relate to you humans as dwarf Jotuns missing a pair of arms, and with limited intelligence. And it is because they relate to you as orphaned and mutilated children that they are so protective of you — more than you realize."

"And your lot? You're tunnel-dwelling colony beings. Jotuns can't relate to you at all."

"Precisely. Which is why they wish to use you as a conduit, an intermediary to interpret the information we give you because they cannot."

Arun was about to get up to convey his thanks by rubbing the insect's head. But he held himself back because Pedro's antennae were still tight against his head.

"I'm afraid I must raise again the subject of traitors and gunrunning," said the Trog.

"No. I thank you for your help, but you know as well as I do that tunnel walls hear everything."

"That is not accurate," said Pedro — still in super-serious mode. "I do not know this as well as you. I know this far *better* than you do."

Arun barely heard the words. Despite the heat from Pedro's basking lamps, the air had chilled.

"I have never spoken to you about gunrunning," he said.

"Correct. Listen, please, Human McEwan. This is important. It is not only tunnels that have ears. Did you believe the surface was unmonitored? And if your words have reached my ears, then any traitors who might exist will have heard them too."

Pedro sure had a knack for springing ugly surprises. The only way the alien could top this was if Xin came walking through the chamber entrance to see for herself how the color had drained from Arun's face. Arun trembled with fear. Any one of his comrades and NCOs could be a traitor. Give him someone to shoot at and he'd fire back, no problem. But he hadn't the courage to take this.

"I perceive you understand the danger," said Pedro.

"No kidding."

Pedro acted puzzled. "I agree. This is no time for humor. I believe that very soon, events will escalate into unconstrained violence. You need a refuge, and sending you pheromone passes in the mail is inadequate."

Pedro sprang from his basking shelf, kicking a cloud of dust from the dirt floor. He jumped on Arun who was sitting in his leather sofa chair.

Arun was suddenly aware of how big his friend was. What did he weigh? Three hundred pounds? More?

Pedro ripped Arun out of the chair and flung his bulk onto the human's shoulders. Arun's vision exploded into stars when the back of his head thumped into the ground.

When the fight came back to Arun, it was too late. Pedro had him pinned down good and proper. He threw everything he had into a wild roll to the left, but he didn't move an inch.

Frakk! This Trog was strong.

A sharp claw appeared at the end of one of Pedro's upper limbs. Arun heard the claw *snikk* through his shirt and then stared in disbelief as the claw peeled open his flesh. Then the pain hit him.

"Get off me! *Get off!*"

"Hold still!" Pedro ordered calmly. "This won't hurt a bit."

Arun relaxed a tiny degree. Then Pedro cut much deeper, flicking lines of agony into Arun's chest cavity.

"Agghh!" Arun screamed continuously until Pedro paused to reach for something in his thorax belt. "I thought…" hissed Arun through gritted teeth, "thought you said it wouldn't hurt."

"I said it won't hurt a bit. It will, in fact, hurt a lot. And if you struggle it will hurt a whole lot more."

Frakk! Arun must have been around aliens too long because he actually believed Pedro. Whatever crazy thing Pedro was doing, he wasn't trying to kill him. Didn't mean it wouldn't, but it wouldn't kill him on purpose.

Arun activated his emergency meditation triggers, which transported him to a safer place in his mind, leaving the pain in his body.

No sooner had he left his body — or so it seemed — then Pedro leaped off him and the sights and sounds of the chamber colored and flavored once more.

"All done," reported Pedro.

"All of *what* done?"

"I have implanted a pheromone amplifier-emitter under your sternum."

"What the…? I mean, what makes you…" Arun sighed. Every word he spoke cost its weight in agony. "Why?"

"For a start, you can throw this away." Pedro snapped off the pheromone identifier around Arun's neck. "Your new implant identifies you as a nest brother. Its scent charge should be good for about 160 years."

"For a start. You said, *for a start*." A wave of pain consumed Arun. They both waited until it ebbed sufficiently for Arun to speak. "What else have you done?"

"It is not only a dumb scent emitter. It is connected to your endocrine system."

"My what? My hormones? Are you telling me you've turned my hormones into scent signals?" The idea was hilarious. Arun vaguely noticed that the pain had gone, replaced with such giddy good cheer that the room was spinning,

"Essentially, yes. In theory you could learn to control this. You could learn the rudiments of my language."

"Look, pal. I'm seventeen. In a couple years, maybe five at most, I expect they'll ship me out on a troop ship. I don't expect to return. I'm not some kind of scribe. You're confusing me with another species. I'm a human. We shoot at people or we clean out the head. That's about the range of our career options."

"It seems that way now. Perhaps one day you could command whole legions of nest warriors with that device in your chest."

Arun stared. He waited for his friend's antennae to twist in amusement. When they didn't, he burst out in laughter that brought the pain crashing back over him.

Those visions everyone else kept having about him weren't right, after all. Arun wasn't going to become a great human freedom fighter, leader of the all-conquering Human Legion. Nope. Future annals of military history would record him as the great ant queen.

Arun the Ant Queen.

Frakk!

He was still laughing on his way back home when he was arrested on Level 7 on suspicion of taking narcotics.

He laughed all through the night in the detention cube. He laughed so much that each motion became agony, the muscles deep inside his chest bruised beyond purple and into ultra-violet.

He was still laughing as he cursed Pedro.

In the end the medics took him for an exploratory poke around in his chest to find out what the alien had done. He was still laughing as the anesthetic took him under.

He awoke with a head that felt like auto-cannons were laying down rapid fire inside. After a quick feel of his chest confirmed that Pedro's gift was still there, he groaned from something other than the pain. He was going to be a Troggie nest brother for the rest of his life.

What the hell would Xin make of that?

Chapter 53

Arun kept his buoyant mood all the way back from this evening's Scendence team training session, until the moment he turned off Corridor 622 and into the passageway to his hab-disk. Being this close to his home soured things. He tried to wrest back his cheerfulness, but it was like grappling a cloud of smoke.

An alert in his head warned him that inspection was in only ten minutes. He stepped up his pace. Every night he practiced with Xin's Scendence team, and every time he stayed away later. Guess he was cutting it a little too fine.

He started to run.

Physical exertion usually made him feel good. So did Team Ultimate Victory. As the 8th battalion's only remaining entry in the championship, Xin and Arun's team were beginning to attract a fringe of supporters, helpers and wannabe coaches. For the first time this week, final year cadets had joined in. The next night even a few veterans had turned up to lend their support.

Despite these newcomers' seniority, no one questioned Xin's place as unofficial team leader. Arun might be the expert planner and strategist, but that was not the same thing at all as leadership. Xin took charge as naturally as breathing, and she insisted that all team members trained together, despite their different game roles.

Now that he was back in the team — Pedro having declared his appearance was a one-off — Xin had relaxed around Arun, even giving a few rare words of praise.

Arun remembered every glowing word.

And when her tight lips softened into a dimpling smile, all the threat and hardship of his life sloughed away. To catch fleeting glimpses of happiness — was that what the free people of Earth felt?

On the threshold of his dorm, with 130 seconds before inspection, Arun came to a halt. He took a deep breath. Xin might have softened, but his squadmates' coldness had solidified into ice, blaming him for all their troubles.

Only Springer backed him, although sometimes with lukewarm support from Madge.

This was an asymmetric cold war. Arun couldn't fight back because they were right to blame him.

Reluctantly, he entered his home.

"Here he is, McEwan the Maverick. Tell me, pal, is Team Ultimate Victory going to live up to its name?"

What the…? Arun took a moment to work out why his brain was buzzing in confusion. The question had come from a figure lying in Brandt's rack. But this wasn't the cadet lance sergeant. The voice was too rough, his body too slender. A novice? And why was no one ready for inspection?

The impostor sat up. His head was shaved, revealing a lateral scar burning a zigzag path across the top of his skull. He was small, but that face was too weathered to be a novice's.

"Who the hell are you?" asked Arun.

Anger lit up the newcomer's eyes momentarily, rapidly fading into a look of resignation. "Man, I'm whacked. I've been asleep for ninety years, which works out well for you, pal, 'cos I'm too tired to beat the crap out of you."

Arun looked to his comrades who were watching in silence. *Hoping I'll trip up again.*

The newcomer continued. "Name's Umarov. I'm Blue-6's replacement for the guy who got himself promoted out into Command Section."

"Arun," said Springer, "Umarov is a veteran."

Umarov snorted. "Hardly. A few days after making Marine, they shoved me into the ice store. According to my body clock's reckoning, I was iced only yesterday. You could say I've been a Marine for five days, or ninety years, depending on how you count it. Either way, you lizards are still cadets, which means I outrank all of you. For now. That's why inspection is canceled permanently. Sergeant Gupta says it's a waste of his valuable time to schedule nursemaiding you like kids, now that I'm here. If you fall out of line, he'll kick my butt into the next star system. Simple. I like him."

None of the other cadets disputed this. Zug gave a tiny shrug. It was all true, then.

Arun saluted. "Congratulations, Marine. Days or decades makes no difference. Graduation is a proud achievement."

A frown came over Umarov. He hesitated, chewing over his next move. "You have no idea how much has changed. But this gung-ho attitude is worst of all. The others told me you don't fit in, McEwan, but you're just like the rest of them, acting as if you're proud to be in the Marines. Do you really believe it is an honor to serve in the Corps family?"

"Of course, Marine Umarov."

"No, don't call me that. And don't even think of calling me sir. That's for instructors and officers – collaborators and murderers, mostly. You call me by the rank I earned. *Carabinier*. It's the basic rank — *was* — and it's called that because our primary weapon is the SA-71 carbine. It's a title that makes sense, unlike your crap. I mean…" He glanced at Madge. "*Corporal*. And–" He gestured at Del-Marie. "*–Lance corporal*. Where the hell did those names come from? And *lance*! In the name of Horden's Hairy Hindquarters what is a fragging *lance*? Can any of you filthy skangats tell me that?"

No one answered.

"Didn't think so. Morons and lizards, the lot of you. Seems like while I was on ice they discovered the off switch for the human brain. So long as I'm still your superior, you will address me as carabinier. Understand?"

"Yes, carabinier," said Arun.

"As I was saying, we obeyed orders because my generation was too cowardly to face the consequences of disobedience. To be born in a Marine farm was to be sentenced to a hellish servitude. Are you not slaves?"

"Wait," said Madge. "You were raised on the farms? You grew wheat and barley and all that drent?"

Umarov's eyes narrowed. "It's been nine decades since I walked these passageways. I expected a few words to change. I didn't expect you to butcher the entire English language."

"With respect, carabinier," said Madge, "we speak Human, not English."

"Jeez." He grimaced. "This is a prime slice of awkwardness. You'll be my NCO sooner than you expect, but for a little while you're just a spotty little kid who doesn't know shit. Let me tell you for a fact, you're speaking English. Badly. If you don't know that, it's because of the Jotuns' eternal messing with our heads. They probably want to stamp out any sense of loyalty to the various groupings of old Earth. They didn't bother in my day. All we knew of Earth were fairy tales so corrupted in the retelling that they no longer made any sense. To us, *English* was just the name of a language. I'm guessing it means something more, now that you can read the history books."

"Carabinier," interrupted Del-Marie, but Umarov cut him dead with a cut of his hand.

"No, Sandure. Don't tell me your history lessons. I don't want to know. Not tonight."

"I wasn't. I was going to warn you. Your words could be considered… verging on disloyal."

"Good for you, kid. You might be a lizard, but at least lizards have backbone. The rest of you sorry lot are just worms."

Del-Marie brightened under the praise.

"But you score zero for intelligence." Arun nearly laughed at the look of disappointment on Del-Marie's face. "In my day the regime was so tough you had to think carefully before taking each breath. You could even be punished if you didn't go to sleep lying in your bed according to regulations; on your back, dead center, head pointing up with arms by your side palms down. For those of us who survived that crap, they loosened up a few months before graduation. They gave you back a little of your humanity to make you a better soldier, just in time for you to use it on the front line. It's obvious that hasn't changed."

"But, carabinier," said Madge. "*We* aren't nearing graduation. Your words could be dangerous for us to hear."

Umarov shrugged. "Another fair point, but still wrong. I'm not the only one to get thawed out. I just got the short straw and ended up with you freaks. There's whole companies of my class forming up. Don't you get it? They're calling up the reserves. I don't think you gotta worry about being years off graduation.

"Anyway. Crap! Give a guy a chance to think, why don't you? I only started thawing out this morning. Brain's still running on anti-freeze. Keeps getting distracted. *Farms*. Did I plow fields of dirt or something? No, I did not! I was raised on a *Marine farm*. They tell me this place is called Detroit now. Before that it was Alpha Base. Can't have been that very long 'cos in my day this stinking hole was called Marine Farm #3 and I was crop 167. If you come from the persuasion that the simplest explanation is the one that's most likely to let you survive one more day, then you'd interpret that as meaning we'd been farmed for 166 years before my crop. Me? I'm cursed by a sprinkling of intelligence. Enough to see this world of lies for what it is, but not clever enough to do squat about it." He looked across all the cadets in the room before sniffing with disdain. "So they've prettied the words and now you love the Marine Corps. I hope there's more to this change than bullshit, because from where I'm sitting, you look a right bunch of prize chumps."

Confused looks passed between the cadets.

"Chumps! Sheesh! I mean you're idiots. *Fools*. You've all got a vacancy between your ears. They've gilded your cage and suddenly the Human Marine Corps isn't your sentence, it's your proud family! Jeez!"

"I don't think so, carabinier," said Zug, trying to put deference into his voice.

Umarov nodded at him to go on.

"I am sure you are correct that our officers have realized that fear and brutality are neither the best ways to instill fighting spirit, nor to train Marines who act intelligently. But I believe there is more to it than that. Our veterans and instructors give us such different explanations about our place in the galaxy. I guess it depends on when they were raised and where they have been stationed. But I do see a pattern. The more recently they have fought, the more likely they are to believe that we are fighting for a worthwhile cause. We fight for Earth's dignity. For humanity's right to be taken seriously by a hostile galaxy that regards us as the ultimate underclass. And it isn't just the fighting. If I were called on to carry out the Cull on my comrades, I would do so without complaint because that is just as much a part of fighting for our dignity as rushing an enemy strong point."

Umarov shook his head. "Just nine decades ago, we were farmed. I like to think we were a more specialist crop than wheat, for instance, but still a crop to be grown, harvested and shipped out to meet demand. Does a blade of wheat have dignity? Eh? Even if it did, would it make a blind bit of difference to its fate?"

Del-Marie gave his most expressive Gallic shrug. "Perhaps, carabinier, the truth does not matter. If we *act* as if we have a purpose, if we pretend that we have dignity, then our lives as soldier-slaves are more bearable. Perhaps we are living a lie, perhaps we are… *chumps*, but surely that is better than the truth if that truth is unbearably hellish?"

Umarov closed his eyes. "You're no longer human, are you? I mean, you're probably right, Sandure, but God help me, you've moved on and left humanity behind. You're all built like the back end of a destroyer, and other than you, Sandure, with your silly shrug, there's barely a hint of expression on any of you except…"

Umarov pointed at Arun. Except that one. He thinks too deeply. And she…" He pointed at Springer. "She cares too much. Thinks she's the great Earth Mother. And the rest of you? It's like they cloned the most unimaginative drones of my generation, fed them super growth hormone, and have been interbreeding them ever since. What's wrong with you? We're in our dorm! Hello? It's where you let off steam? I expect a little stupid banter, the stronger reminding the weaker ones who's in charge, and I expect grumbling. A lot of grumbling. Soldiers should always grumble. It's one of the basic laws of the universe."

"*Les grognards*, carabinier," said Zug.

"Laygronyards? That's the modern word for grumbling is it? What kind of dumbass word is that? One you never use, I'll bet, because you're all like machines on standby mode, waiting to be fully activated in the morning." He shook his head. "*Laygronyards*? Shit! You fragging scare me more than the Jotuns."

What was Zug playing at? He'd talked of these *grognards* before. It was a French word — meaning *grumblers* — that had been the nickname for a corps of elite French soldiers. Arun liked the name, though. It sounded very human.

Umarov grabbed a softscreen and started to figure out the controls. The rest of the room remained silent and motionless.

"What? Oh, for crying out loud," groaned Umarov. "You're dismissed. Go do whatever robots do in their free time. Just leave me the hell alone."

Arun considered helping the carabinier struggling with his softscreen but decided to wait a while. He grinned. Like him, Umarov was an outsider, and one who saw immediately that there was something screwy about the attitude of the cadets.

Arun thanked Fate for bringing him a natural ally. Change was in the air, and that meant the next time he left his Scendence training, he might have something worth coming home to.

Chapter 54

Striding along the curved corridor of sector F7 on his way to the shower tunnel, Arun grinned when he thought back to how Umarov's arrival last night had shaken up the frigid atmosphere in his dorm.

Ever since that stupid tunnel exercise, his life had gone from drent to drenter. Zug and the guys could go vulley themselves for thinking Arun had brought it all on himself. So what if all their cold-shoulder drent was due to them being drugged? That wasn't a good enough excuse.

Arun had made his choices but he stood up for them. Why shouldn't he? He wasn't a loser. It was just the universe trying to make him look bad by conspiring to trip him up all the time.

Well, nuts to the universe too, because he was feeling good right now. It was 06:42 and he'd just finished his solo morning workout: three circuits of Ring 7 – the second-longest ring in the hab-disk – followed by a half hour pushing and pulling against resistance channels in the gym.

Even being an engineered freak, courtesy of centuries of White Knight tinkering, had its plus points. Did the humans on Earth feel such a flare of unquenchable energy first thing in the morning? From what he'd heard, they mostly fell reluctantly out of bed in a semi-torpor that would hold them for hours. Whereas, thanks to his augmented body, Arun felt not just that he could climb a mountain before breakfast, but that he needed to, or else his body would explode from all the pent-up energy inside his muscles.

He walked into the F7 shower room, giving a vague wave of greeting to the other cadets stripping off on their way in, or on their way out, putting on fresh underwear and fatigues from the bins provided by the Aux.

Arun had his shirt off and was about to tug down his gym pants when he saw Zug and Osman up ahead, naked and about to enter the shower tunnel. When they spotted Arun, they glanced at each other and then grabbed gym pants from the bin and put them on.

"What's up?" asked Arun. He spoke carefully, not wishing to antagonize them.

Zug and Osman faced off against him.

Osman folded his arms. "You'll have to wait," he said. "Springer's in there."

Arun shrugged. "So?"

"So you wait till she's dressed. The tactical order chart says you're a member of our squad, but you aren't part of our team. You'll need to give our women their privacy."

"*Your* women? You're crazy, Osman. What, you think you own Springer? That she's stripping off for your pleasure? She's just getting clean, man. Stop being such a… *chump*."

"Yeah, I'm with Bryant's blue-eyed boy," said a voice from behind: Lance Corporal Yoshioka from Gold Squad. She threw her gym clothes in the bin. "I don't care about your lovers' tiff. Stupid Blue Squad guffoons. I do care about whether I stink. Get out the frakking way!"

Osman stepped aside.

Yoshioka strode into the shower tunnel, giving Osman a shove for good measure on her way in. She still blamed Blue Squad for letting the combat bots shoot her from behind in that frakked-up boarding exercise on *Fort Douaumont*.

Arun dove for the gap she had opened between Zug and Osman, but they were waiting for him. Osman pushed him back so sharply that Arun slipped on the wet floor and fell onto his backside.

"It would be best for you," said Zug, "that you make an effort to be polite, whether or not you believe our request for privacy is justified."

Arun felt the anger boil over inside him. Anger directed at Zug. It was Osman who'd pushed him, but Osman had always lived life to binary extremes. You were his mortal enemy or greatest friend, sometimes both on the same day. Back before he became a cadet, any unresolved disagreements would torment Osman such that he couldn't sleep, but the next day, Osman would shrug and forget whatever had troubled him so badly the day before.

That was what made Osman such fun to be around, or used to. It also made him the exact opposite of Zug. Calm, considered, consistent, it was Zug's disapproval that had really turned the squad against Arun.

He couldn't get his revenge on Zug here. But he would. Oh, yes. Zug — *Zhoog* as he insisted it was pronounced — would get his just deserts soon enough. But for now…

"Fine," said Arun, still sitting on his butt. "I'll wait."

"Make sure you do," said Osman, his anger burning so hot that he could barely speak.

Osman and Zug threw their clothes in the bin and followed Yoshioka into the shower tunnel. Arun hovered just outside, feeling increasingly uncomfortable as a steady stream of cadets entered the shower room, or emerged naked at the other end.

The F7 shower room wasn't reserved for Blue and Gold Squads, but it was nearest to their dorm rooms, and so Arun knew most of the cadets coming into the room and giving him some hard stares.

No one said anything. They didn't have to. He was acting like some kind of deviant, lurking in the shower to steal glimpses of nude flesh.

Arun shut his eyes and clenched his fists. How had it come to this? Only moments ago he'd been buzzing.

Now Zug and Osman had ruined his morning.

Skangat lizards!

Arun stripped off and walked into the shower tunnel.

As he lifted his arms to accept the spray of foaming detergent, Arun felt eyes watching him warily. One of the girls from Gold Squad turned her back on him.

This was getting ridiculous.

Arun yelled through the spattering noise of the shower jets. "Hey! Hey, Zug!"

The big guy turned around.

"This is all your fault, man."

"No, my friend," said Zug. "It is your own doing."

"I'm not your friend."

"Yes, you are."

"You're wrong. And I'll tell you one thing, Zug the Perfect – Zug the Frakking Aloof. You'll know what it feels like one day. Maybe right now the universe is stacking the deck to deal you a frakked-up hand. Sooner or later you'll have a run of bad luck"

"I am certain you are right. One day."

"One day? Nuts to that. I don't want bad luck to happen to you one day. I want it *now*. Do you hear, Zug? I hope today is the worst frakking day of your life."

But the cadet who still called himself Arun's friend had already turned away and was lost behind the steam and spray of water.

Arun was on his own.

———

On his way back to the dorm room, someone leaped out of a side passageway and grabbed him by the shoulders.

Arun was about to deck his assailant when he recognized something in that touch. That scent.

He turned and stared wide-eyed into Springer's face.

Her eyes glowed violet with emotion.

Well, Arun was emotional too. He was furious at Zug and disappointed at Osman. But his anger was all jumbled up with regret and loneliness, and he'd never been angry with Springer. Everything inside churned into such a confused mess that his jaw moved up and down, but he didn't know what to say.

He didn't think he needed to. Springer looked into his face and seemed to understand what he was feeling better than Arun did himself.

"Help me?" he whispered.

"I heard what happened in the shower," she said. "You need to sort this."

Arun bellowed in rage. His pulse raced, his limbs shook. "How the frakk can I do that?" Arun couldn't keep the anger out of his voice. His shoulders slumped. He hadn't wanted to bark at Springer.

Springer didn't scream back; she laughed as if this were all a game. "You're not alone, Arun." She shook her head in mock pity. Which was weird. Arun had never seen her act like that before. "It's you boys. It's your testosterone making you into idiots. I was talking this over with Majanita last night. She said she thought they give you Marine boys added testosterone to bulk you up, make you fight better. But they give you too high a dose. If not testosterone, *then they must be giving you something similar.*"

Arun nearly missed Springer's emphasis. She wasn't talking about testosterone. "I'm surprised Madge finally bought into your theory," he said, a flash of understanding connecting them as he looked into her eyes.

"I've been working on her for a while," Springer replied.

"You're amazing. I ever tell you that?"

"Not nearly enough, Arun."

"Guilty as charged." He just about managed a grin. "But I still don't see how that helps me."

Springer shook her head. "That's because you're a guy. You're no different from Zug, Osman and the others. You boys are acting as if all you understand is confrontation. Instead of a frontal assault, switch the direction of your attack. Try empathy instead."

"You mean, see it from a girl's perspective?"

"Frakk it, Arun! You've got a lot to learn. No, not at all, but if it helps you to think of it that way then, yes, try thinking like a girl."

Arun started by taking in deep breaths through his nose, holding and then blowing out a smooth stream of spent air through his mouth.

"Not now, sweetie," Springer teased. "Have you forgotten? Gupta switched schedule to put us up in orbit. *Again!* We move out in fifteen."

"I know. It's like he's deliberately keeping us off planet."

"That's not important now. Just think on something Madge said to me. It might help with Zug and the rest. She said we're all gene-modified, brainwashed, drugged up combat kids. But deep down we're still the same species as our Earth ancestors. They evolved a set of social behaviors to cope with the challenges of life on Earth. Sometimes our minds decide they recognize the problems we face on Tranquility and reach for the bag of coping behaviors our ancestors brought with them from Earth. We act a certain way even though we don't always know why."

"So you're saying that Zug is acting like a pre-tech savage and doesn't even know it?"

Springer frowned. "Majanita sees it like this. The boys in the squad are treating me like I'm their little sister. They're closing ranks to protect me, a female, against the unwanted attention of the outsider male who wronged me, who dishonored the clan. That's you, in case your brain hasn't woken up yet. If you reason or fight them you will only make it worse. The one way to resolve this is to earn the right to rejoin the clan. Do something dramatic that proves your loyalty to our *testosterone*-addled boys. Does that make sense?"

Arun nodded. "Is that all?"

Springer rolled her eyes. "Actually, there is one more thing to think on."

"What's that?"

"This…" Springer raised herself on tiptoes, leaned in, and kissed Arun on the lips.

It was no more than a chaste peck, but Arun couldn't help but touch the spot where Springer's lips had brushed against his.

That was the most beautiful thing anyone had ever done for him.

Arun hurried after Springer and into a dorm filling with unhurried activity as the section prepared to spend for a stint of unknown duration practicing void combat.

Suit AIs were checked, the head visited, silent words spoken by the more spiritual. Umarov was helped through the modern drills, grumbling at all the stupid changes and venting his frustration at everyone around him in a stream of unfamiliar curses.

All that ceased dead on 07:00 when, unexpectedly, a tone sounded through the speakers recessed into the walls, followed a moment later by a woman's voice. It was not a voice Arun recognized, but it was one that was clearly used to being obeyed.

"Attention! All cadet units report to the main parade ground immediately. I say again. All cadet units report to the main parade ground immediately. That is all."

The entire force of Detroit cadets was only assembled for graduation day, the Cull, or executions too serious to be handled at battalion level. But none of those were due.

Arun's fellow cadets weren't unresponsive robots now: they looked stunned, turning to each other for explanations.

But there was one person who didn't look surprised.

"Sorry, kids," said Umarov. He was sincere too, his grouchiness replaced by hollowed-out sadness. "I guess you're gonna grow up even quicker than I feared."

Chapter 55

Detroit nestled in a valley floor beneath the dusty red peaks of the Gjende Mountains. So deep were the shadows, it was said, that a natural-born Earth human would need a torch to pick their way around the valley floor. Arun was not a normal human. The wide avenue meandering toward the parade ground was clear for his eyes to see, as were the obelisks at either side that displayed bas-relief carvings of fantastic martial creatures. Or possibly they were portraits in sculpture of the previous residents of the base. It was not a species that Arun recognized. Although his eyes could see the path, the colors of the valley floor had been leeched out. Arun saw everything in monochrome shades of malevolent red.

If it weren't for the ominous circumstances it would be a pleasant walk. The air was thin up on the surface, but the winds were light for a change and the temperature comfortable.

At one point the avenue had been crushed under a fallen mountain top. A fresh and unadorned path detoured around the obstruction.

"What caused that?" he asked Majanita, pointing to the rock fall that blocked the path.

She shrugged. "I don't know. But it's no landslide or natural erosion."

"A meteor strike perhaps," suggested Arun.

"More likely a kinetic torpedo."

Suddenly Arun felt exposed out here on the planet's surface. That made him the opposite of the Jotuns who could not bear to be underground. At least Arun's fear was rational. A ship in orbit above the valley floor could do some serious damage. Being underground with a few hundred meters of dirt above your head was much safer.

At 07:36 they reached the parade ground, an oval cut into the side of the mountain. The gouge went back 800 meters and was 100 meters high, the roof being the smooth, flat underside of the mountain above. It was as if an impossibly large stonemason's chisel had cut a groove into the side of the mountain.

"Look!" said Brandt. He pointed to the densest concentration of cadets at the center of the oval. "Look for our battalion flag."

He must have good eyesight, thought Arun, because he couldn't see any flags himself. But as they made their way toward the center and saw that at regular intervals there were indeed square banners mounted on five-meter poles.

There it was! The gold circle on a black background of the 412th Marines with a silver number 8 in the lower left corner. It was a simple design but enough to swell Arun's heart with pride.

Sergeant Gupta was waiting for them. He marshalled them into ranks and files to his satisfaction, repositioning cadets until he was happy.

Then he marched in and out of the lines saying: "Keep your dignity at all times. Never forget. Keep your dignity!"

The cadets came to attention in perfect parade ground posture and waited. They had been bred and trained for waiting, which was just as well. The parade deck was huge, but there were around 130,000 cadets across all four regiments. Assembling them took a while.

"Welcome, cadets," came a woman's voice once all the cadets were assembled. "My name is Sergeant Bissinger."

Arun recognized Bissinger's voice as the woman who had ordered all cadets to parade. There were no obvious speakers to carry her voice, but her words reached Arun's ears with crystal clarity.

"I shall not say good morning," she added. Arun knew Sergeant Bissinger was as senior a veteran as they came. Although it was always tricky to determine the rank seniority of the human commanders due to the rule that no human could take a rank above senior squad NCO. Seniority was pretty much a word of mouth thing, but Arun's guess was that Bissinger was the de facto human base commander.

"Today," said Bissinger, "is a tragedy and a necessity."

Arun heard himself groan.

"Today you cadets face the reality of your lives. That we all of us have won freedom for our home world but that it is we who must pay the price."

If only he were in his suit. Barney would fire him the drugs to make this much easier.

"We are all of us soldiers of the White Knights, our ultimate leaders who glory in change, mutation and experimentation. They believe the elimination of failed experiments is indivisible from growth and renewal. Creative destruction is not merely an ideal that they cherish, but has been incorporated deep within their biology and planetary engineering. We humans do not mutate with the rapidity that our masters are blessed with, but the White Knights demand that all servant species perform their own emulation of our masters' ideal of creative destruction."

Arun found his eyes blinking uncontrollably. Was he crying?

"Our human way of handling this tradition – one sanctified by our masters – is called the Cull."

Frakk! He *was* crying. For years he'd dreaded this moment. It shouldn't be happening now. It was too early in the year. But off schedule or not there was a deathly inevitability about the events that would roll out over the coming minutes. All that talk of winning more points to escape the danger zone was too late now for graduation year cadets in the bottom-ranked battalions. One tenth of them were about to die, and there was nothing anyone could do to change their fate.

Eyes front, watching the officer who wasn't an officer address them from a platform almost directly in front of him, Arun was nearly surprised by Sergeant Gupta when he walked behind his rank of cadets.

"Keep your dignity. Do not disobey."

Sergeant Gupta kept repeating his litany. But what was dignified about people murdering each other? And all this pain only to ape the freakish beliefs of a bunch of faraway alien vecks?

Once Gupta had passed him, Arun's eyes drilled holes in the sergeant's back as he marched away.

Easy for you, thought Arun. *You're not up for execution duty.*

Then Arun turned his head and looked around him. Only then did he understand the layout of this grotesque exercise. The three battalions in the Cull Zone were lined up in front of Bissinger's platform. The other 29 battalions were arranged in a semicircle around their doomed comrades. *Observers to what was about to unfold.*

There was a blur of movement and then Gupta was in Arun's face, glowering. The sergeant's breath came in short, rasping gasps. It sounded as if he was a raging bull, raring to tear Arun apart, but restraining himself from violence only by a titanic battle of will.

Snapped back to attention, Arun kept his eyes forward, which was filled by a view of his NCO's forehead. Sweat was beginning to bead in the craggy furrows of Gupta's frown.

The NCO's battle for control went on. His breath quickened even faster. Arun tensed, ready for Gupta's attack. To fight with a superior would mean immediate execution. So he readied himself to leap for the ground, where he would curl up and hope his injuries would not kill him or, worse, render him unfit for service, which would mean being dumped back into the Aux.

"You dishonor them, boy." It had taken nearly two minutes before Gupta had gained enough control to spit those words. "We are fighting a war here. A war for survival. Today is one battle. There will be casualties."

Gupta stepped back half a pace, close enough to still intimidate Arun, but far enough away that he could fix him with his glare. "Are you a coward, Cadet McEwan?"

"No, sergeant."

"Really? Only a coward would be so frightened by the thought of battle casualties that they hate their commander."

Arun's heart lurched. Had Gupta read his thoughts?

"It's good to be scared in battle," Gupta growled. "It gives you an edge. But real Marines don't stare at their commander's back, blaming them for the war. I ask you again. Are you a coward?"

"No, sergeant."

"Then what are you?"

Gupta stepped back another half pace and waited for an answer. Arun couldn't work out whether this was a drill sergeant's parade ground psycho-trick, or whether his life depended on his next sentence. Perhaps both were true.

But Arun had played this game before at school, even before then at crèche. His entire life since waking from the freezer had been lived under the hawk-like gaze of the instructors.

"I'm stupid, sergeant. Too dumb to realize I was in a battle."

Gupta rocked back on his heels, as satisfied as he was likely to get any time soon. "That's the correct answer. And stupid Marines are only one iota better than cowardly ones. Idiots get their squad killed. Today is your first real battle, McEwan. I will be watching you. If you show cowardice or stupidity, I *will* know. Understood?"

"Yes, sergeant."

Gupta considered Arun for a few moments. "Eyes front," he snapped. Then in a quieter voice he added: "Remember that no matter what you are called to do, whatever horrors you witness, you do it for the Marines. Most of all, we're fighting for Earth. Got it?"

"Yes, sergeant."

In perfect step, Gupta marched off to the front of Blue Squad, turned on his heels and faced his cadets. And waited with the rest of them.

Over the coming minutes, Arun could sense small groups of people from the condemned battalions march to the front and return a little later. He daren't get a good look after Gupta's grilling. How had Gupta seen what he was up to? Was it a veteran's sixth sense? Was he under invisible surveillance? Maybe it was just bad luck and his guilty face had given him away. Until he found out, he decided to act as if Gupta really did have eyes in the back of his head.

Then it was Blue Squad's turn. At a command barked by Gupta, they filed out in a neat column and followed him up to the platform. He thought back to that bawling out in Little Scar's office and realized he was being filmed too. He pushed back his shoulders, squared his jaw, and marched with as much dignity as he could muster.

Sergeant Bissinger stood alone on a stone platform raised about fifteen meters above the parade ground floor. It was a hexagon twenty meters across that had been carved out of the rock; or rather, left behind when the parade ground had been carved. In front of the hexagon was a polished metal drum, and alongside, what appeared to be the same kind of armory cabinet that was scattered around the hab-disks.

Sergeant Gupta ordered the squad to halt. Then he separated off ten cadets and told them what to do. Arun wasn't in that first group. He got to watch first.

The picked cadets each put their hands into a hole cut into one end of the drum. They lined up, gripping something in their palms, but Arun couldn't see what until Gupta ordered them to open up their hands.

They were pebbles. Smooth round pebbles. Half were colored black and half white. The cadets replaced the pebbles in the drum. Those who'd picked white marched back to their place in the crowd. Those with black lined up in front of the armory cupboard.

Sergeant Gupta opened the cupboard door. Inside was a firearm rack holding five SA-71s. It was similar to what Arun was used to, except this cupboard had a feed from underneath. If these were the weapons of execution, they would need more than five. There must be scores waiting out of sight to replace those taken from the cupboard.

At Gupta's signal, the five cadets each took a carbine in turn. At his next command, they armed them ready to fire. Four of them immediately returned their carbines to the cupboard, lined up again, and then marched back to the battalion's place in the crowd.

That left one cadet holding a carbine. Laban Caccamo, his name was, from Hecht's Alpha Section. Dark hair, thick eyebrows, muscular, popular with the girls. He was an ace at flying radio-controlled drones. In happier days as a novice, Caccamo had joined in with any fun and games going around, especially if it involved playing pranks on his friends. He did what his training instructors told, and he did it well but not exceptionally.

At that moment, Caccamo couldn't help being exceptional. Every cadet in Detroit was watching him and what he would do.

Caccamo snapped to attention, saluted, and then marched around to the back of the hexagon. He was lost to sight.

Then it was Arun's turn. His group of ten included all eight cadets from Delta Section plus Lewark and Bizzy from Beta Section.

Gupta gave them instructions, but Arun wasn't listening. He was hardly going to forget what he had just seen.

By the time his turn came around to put his hand into the drum, he was convinced that it would be him joining Caccamo in the execution squad. He had to reach in deep to find it. The pebble he drew out was warm to the touch. Arun gripped it so tightly that he felt his hand bruise.

He stood in a line facing the crowd. Cristina was to his left. Zug joined him on his right, the final cadet in that group of ten.

The cadets in even the most distant battalions could clearly see Arun's plight, due to their uprated vision. If they chose to. How many of them opted to see a defocused blur instead?

"Show your hands!" ordered Sergeant Gupta.

The cadets each raised a hand in front of them, palm up, and opened their fingers.

Arun didn't feel fear as his hand opened to reveal the color of his stone; he just felt numb. Sure enough, his stone was black. He quickly glanced around him. Zug had a black pebble too. Cristina's was white.

The five cadets with white stones wheeled right in readiness to march away. Cristina whispered hurriedly to him. "If you do it now, you'll not spend the next two years fearing what it might be like."

Because I will already be dammed? He did not dare to speak the words in his mind. Cristina's words were no comfort but the warmth of her sentiment was. He couldn't imagine the males in his squad offering any words of comfort.

The line-up in front of the armory cabinet consisted of Arun, Zug, Springer, Lewark from Blue-4, and Del-Marie.

Sergeant Gupta opened the armory cabinet and Arun picked out a carbine. He was so used to the heft of the SA-71 that it normally felt like an extension of his body, but this railgun felt awkward. If the weapon was a part of his body, then this was a part that had turned cancerous. It was sickening, alien. He wanted to throw it far away from him, but he steeled himself instead to hold it as if this were an everyday gunnery drill.

And as with a gunnery drill, Arun flicked the switch to arm the carbine and read the ammo supply from the stock display. His weapon was charged, and an ammo bulb was in place, but the stock display was faulty.

To his astonishment, only Del-Marie replaced his carbine in the cabinet and went back to his place in the crowd, presumably because it had no charge or no ammo. Arun and the other cadets picked for execution detail glanced at each other nervously. Then they gave smart salutes to Sergeant Gupta and marched around the back of the hexagon where the executioners were lined up, marshaled by a veteran Arun didn't recognize.

Every few minutes they were reinforced by blank-faced cadets, arriving in ones and twos, and occasionally in larger groups.

As the selection played out over the next hour, it became clear that there was a strong random element to the selection. Sometimes all the carbines in the cabinet were armed and sometimes none. But over time the numbers began to average out and Arun saw the pattern that was emerging.

There were around 175 cadets in a company, and the battalion had eight depot companies in the graduation year. That made 1,400 due to be Culled.

The G-1 and G-2 years for 8-412 had another eight companies each, which made a pool of 2,800 executioners. The G-year cadets were to be decimated: one in ten would be executed. Arun had assumed that meant there would be 140 executioners picked, but instead there was to be one executioner for every member of the G-year. Did that mean they were all to be killed?

They heard a hiss. From around the sides and top of the hexagon came clouds of lurid orange. The smell hit them. Arun swallowed hard, fought to keep control. Once he'd gotten over the shock of being gassed, it didn't smell or taste so bad. And if it was toxic, it wasn't so toxic that he could see anyone keel over. In fact, it tasted of burned biscuits and almond flavoring.

Human veterans advanced toward them from out of the billowing orange. For a moment, Arun thought it was his detail behind the hexagon that were to be killed, and the veterans their executioners. But the vets led them back around the hexagon and into the heart of the unfolding spectacle.

Sergeant Bissinger cleared her throat and addressed the parade. "Every world inhabited by our masters, the White Knights, is blessed by the Sacred Mists of Renewal, more commonly called the Flek. We cannot release the Flek here on Tranquility because it would kill us all. This orange vapor we release in emulation of the Flek as we…" She paused, just briefly but Arun caught it "…reach the climax of today's ritual."

The release of the pseudo-Flek gas had been timed so that as Arun and the other executioners came around the hexagon they appeared to the waiting crowd to emerge from the mist at the moment Sergeant Bissinger finished her speech. The veterans led the execution detail to their places. They lined up facing the hexagon in 47 rows of 29 cadets. Each rank had a veteran to either side, a veteran from another battalion.

The mist cleared to reveal pale faces staring back at them. Twenty-nine cadets from the year of graduation stood with their backs to the hexagon, each a couple of paces apart. The other cadets due to be Culled awaited their fate a short distance to the left, already organized into ranks of 29.

Twenty-nine executioners would fire their carbines at twenty-nine battalion comrades. Arun understood now why his stock readout wasn't working. It was a cruel trick. All of the executioners would fire on a comrade, but only one in ten of the weapons had live rounds. Arun had never fired at another human being. That was just about to change. Whether he would kill his target was something no one would know until a split second after he fired.

Arun was in the third row. At least he wouldn't have to wait long to find out.

The first rank of executioners moved forward a pace and spread out a little so that each faced their victim head on.

Arun stared into the faces of the condemned, who awaited their fate with quiet dignity. In a few seconds, perhaps two or three would die. Maybe more or maybe less if this part of the Cull were as random as everything else. Most, though, would live.

That still didn't make this all right,

Gupta had called this a battle. Arun wouldn't flinch at going into battle with the possibility of ten percent casualties. But this wasn't combat whatever Gupta might say. This was humans copying their betters, a foul mockery of an utterly alien ritual. Surely it was going along with killing your comrades that was stupid and cowardly, not questioning the murder?

The front rank raised their weapons.

Was Arun prepared to defy orders? Was anyone here?

The front-rank veterans faced in at their cadets, raised their arms… and then threw them downward.

A ragged volley of shots rang out. Three of the condemned slumped to the bare rock of the parade ground, bloody chunks blasted out of their bodies.

Dead before they hit the ground, thought Arun. Flenser rounds aimed at the heart. A quick death, but a messy one.

He wondered why he was analyzing the execution in such cold detail, and then realized he was distracting himself from looking into the faces of the front rank of executioners as they filed back to the rear of the execution detail.

He couldn't look upon them because in a few moments he would have become one of them. He knew he wasn't going to rebel. He didn't have the will to disobey orders.

When in doubt, obey orders. It was all he'd ever known. And if that meant he was a coward or stupid then so be it. What he did know for certain in that moment was that he was a slave.

The 26 survivors of the Cull picked up the corpses of their fallen comrades and carried them round to the rear of the hexagon. Without delay they were replaced by the next group of 29 condemned cadets, stepping carefully so as not to slip on the gore-splatter rock.

It felt dreamlike as Arun watched the front rank of executioners spread out to match their victims, raise their carbines and fire!

This time, one cadet from 8-412 fell down dead.

This time Arun did look at the executioners because something was wrong. The whole ritual was wrong, he thought, but now something had disrupted the smooth workings of the execution process.

The veteran on the right of the front rank marched in front of her detail. She halted before one particular cadet. It was Olmer, one of the original members of Xin's Scendence team.

Olmer dropped her carbine. The sound of the ceramalloy-plastic blend striking the rock floor made Arun cringe. He'd never heard the sound of a dropped railgun before.

"I can't do it!" Olmer screamed. "I can't fire. You can't make me."

If Olmer was panicking, the effect of this disruption on the cadet she had failed to shoot was even more dramatic. The condemned started to cry.

The reason soon became clear.

The veteran drew her sidearm from its holster and shot Olmer in the head. Then she turned to the condemned cadet who by now had slumped down onto her haunches, her head in her hands.

The veteran shot her through the heart.

Of everything he'd seen so far that day, the sight of the cadet slumped against the hexagon waiting her fate was the cruelest by far. If Olmer had obeyed orders, then the older cadet would probably still be alive. Everyone saw that drama unfold. Everyone got the message. Arun had never attended the Cull before, but he'd attended executions. It was always the same.

Disobey orders and you will be killed.

Breathe so much as a word of dissent against the White Knights, and it won't be just you who is killed.

Arun did what he always did. Suck up the anger and humiliation and stored it for the future. Everything on this planet was designed to control the slaves who lived here. But if he survived to graduate as a Marine, one day he would get away from Detroit.

He made a vow. He swore it on the blood of his murdered cadet comrades, and on the hellish memories that their murderers would carry for the rest of their lives. Unlike Olmer, he would *wait*. Over time he would stack the chances in his favor. One day he would revenge all of humanity against the White Knights.

And then he found himself lined up opposite a tall boy with hooded eyes staring back at him with quiet dignity. Arun recognized the face but didn't know the name. Good, that made this a little easier.

Arun raised his carbine and trained his sights on the cadet, aiming for his heart. Usually when he fired, he was wearing armor and had Barney to direct his aim. Manual aim was so much more personal and if he had to go through with this then Arun preferred to do it himself. To hide behind Barney would be disrespectful to the cadet, who was calmly looking at the business end of Arun's carbine.

I will revenge you, Arun promised the condemned cadet. He took off the safety and heard the whine as the barrel charged in preparation to fling a shell at four times the speed of sound. The railgun had already been set for the required distance of an execution shot.

The Human Legion.

Desperate to think of anything other than the horror all around him, Arun clutched at a speck of hope for the future. Gupta had talked of a Czech Legion that had survived impossible odds behind enemy lines, and Springer's vision had hinted that it might be Arun's fate to lead a modern-day equivalent. He'd been too busy trying to survive to think these treasonous thoughts. Now he could think of nothing else.

One day, I swear, there will be a Human Legion. Arun made his vow in the privacy of his head and kept his mouth rigid. Even to mouth the words would be disastrous. *The Human Legion will be a beacon of hope to all humankind,* he continued silently, *and I will play my part in that story. I promise you.*

Then the veteran gave the command and Arun squeezed his trigger.

Flenser rounds consisted of an aerodynamic shell that broke apart about two meters before the target to release pairs of tiny blade-encrusted balls connected to each other by monofilament wire.

They were designed to tear great holes through unarmored targets.

Arun saw the results on human flesh. A micro-instant after he began to take in the sight, he heard the crack of the flenser casing open and the wet ripping sound as the casing's contents struck home.

The cadet's left chest disintegrated, leaving behind scored bone, gristle, and tatters of bloodied cloth from the clean fatigues she had picked up from the laundry shelf a few hours earlier.

Arun hadn't shot her. This was the cadet alongside.

An irritated whine and click came from Arun's carbine as it tried repeatedly to select a round from the ammo carousel, but he knew it was empty. He'd been spared.

He glanced up at the cadet that he had aimed at. He was looking back, not at Arun but at the person to Arun's right.

Arun followed his gaze and looked into Zug's face. Zug who had just shot dead a cadet from his own battalion.

Zug the Aloof, Arun had called him earlier.

He wasn't so calm now. He looked deathly pale. Then he started retching.

Arun willed his old friend to keep it in.

On the march to the rear of the execution detail Zug held it in about half way. Then he vomited, all over Arun's back.

Arun thought back to the boneheaded curse he had thrown at Zug in the shower earlier that morning.

Sergeant Gupta had been right all along. Arun's words in the shower had been those of a coward.

And a stupid one too.
Arun's shame was complete.

PART IV

You're all Marines Now

Human Legion INFOPEDIA

Terminology
MARINE

The term, MARINE refers to both the soldiers and military organizations whose primary function is one or more of the following:
* Close assault and boarding of space-faring vessels.
* Defense of space-faring vessels against close assault and boarding.
* Assault from space against the defended surface of a planet.

The term is widely used to describe the relevant military forces of most political entities within the Trans-Species Union.

The original Earthly military meaning of marine (water-borne rather than space-borne military forces) is now referred to as 'littoral marine' or 'seaborne marine'. Referring to a member of such a unit as a 'wet marine' is a sure way to start a fight.

The military term 'marine' is not capitalized in general use, although marine organizations will frequently capitalize when referring to themselves. Since the accounts you are now reading are about the Human Legion, and its predecessor/ rival, the Human Marine Corps, we capitalize as 'Marine' when referring to those organizations. We, the authors, are ourselves mostly Marines. Whatever the grammatical niceties that proper nouns might demand, it is impossible for us to think of ourselves as anything other than *Marines* with an upper case 'M'. To call us mere *marines* would be an insult.

And, we would argue, an insult to our ancestors, for we were not the first Marines by a long way.

Seaborne marines were critical in ancient Earth history. In the Battle of Salamis (-480CE) Greek Marines played a crucial role in defeating the much larger Persian forces, helping to set the cultural underpinning of what would later be called Western Civilization.

A ship-boarding technology called the *corvus* enabled Roman Marines to win naval supremacy in the Mediterranean Sea (around -250CE), ultimately meaning the Romans defeated their arch rivals the Carthaginians to become the dominant regional superpower for many centuries.

The next major innovation in seaborne Marine forces came two thousand years later with the development of a much larger self-contained, combined-arms Marine army that could fight wars almost unaided. This was the United States Marine Corps.

It is widely speculated by modern-era Marines that the military units formed from human slaves following the Vancouver Accord were inspired by the US Marine Corps. Others regard this as wishful thinking, pointing out that while the Human Marine Corps might draw inspiration from the fighting spirit of their US ancestors, the segregation and racism inherent to their command structure more closely follows the army of the British East India Company in the early 1800s CE.

Whatever the truth of that argument, we the Marines of the Human Legion acknowledge the rich heritage of our Earthly military ancestors, and indeed those from other planets. We recognize their example and transcend them, because the Human Legion is not based in the past. We have a single mission: to fight for a better *future*. A future for us all.

Freedom *can* be won.

Chapter 56

Scorched, perforated and abused for decades — despite all that, *Fort Douaumont*'s long, lazy tumbling caught the sunlight and gleamed, an incomparable jewel for an instant… and then the moment was gone, and the training hulk was space dross once more.

Fort Douaumont teased Arun. He couldn't take his eyes off her in case he missed another glint of hidden beauty.

Frakk, I must be bored!

It had been less than a day since the Cull — since Zug had shot dead an innocent cadet. After drent like that went down, the powers that be liked to split up the cadets and keep them busy.

So they'd shipped Blue and Gold squads up to Gupta's old TU, *Yorktown*, where they'd stuck the cadets into EVA gibberballs.

An orange and red flashing blob marred the serenity of the silent scene of beauty laid out before him: Sergeant Gupta with his battlesuit set for high visibility. The NCO was sitting on a flitter waiting for the exercise to begin. Hell, he must be just as bored as Arun, wishing he were wherever Gold Squad's Sergeant Searl had ended up.

They might have rushed them up here, but now the cadets were trapped in the amniotic gel bubbles, those in charge were in no hurry to launch them.

Instead of the robot defenders they normally faced, the old hulk would be defended by veteran marines, one of whom was Arun's brother, or so Gupta had said.

The exercise should be a blast. Why didn't they get it started already?

Arun had now spent hours in this gibberball trying and eventually failing to be interested in his brother. Hell, he didn't even know the guy's name. It wasn't as if he'd ever talked with his family. Instantaneous communication was possible to each Marine ship but was far too expensive to waste on human chit-chat. Why would you care about anyone out-system anyway? You had your family right here on Tranquility.

The Corps is your family. You need no other.

It dawned on Arun why he kept thinking about family. He wasn't just bored; he was lonely too.

But talking wasn't easy when you were stuffed inside a bubble of buffer gel. After his last experience of endless drowning, he wasn't going to open his mouth no matter how much he needed to talk.

But maybe there was another way.

The TU was essentially spherical with the EVA chutes recessed into the hull. The outer surface of the amniotic bubbles pushed out from the warboat's hull like festering pustules on a victim of the red pox. But there were also vanes sticking out from the hull. He'd always assumed they were radiator fins. He should be able to bounce a tight comm beam off them. See if he could raise Springer.

Arun had plenty of experience of talking with aliens who used thought-to-speech to communicate in the human language. In theory you could do the same with a suit if its AI knew you well, and so did the AI of the person you wanted to talk with.

He tried to form the idea in his mind, to explain to Barney what he wanted. He pictured Springer. Cute freckles, a cautious smile and violet eyes.

Then he spoke the words slowly in his head.

<Springer. Can you hear me? Springer!>
<Arun. You?>
<You — what? Sorry, Springer. I can't understand you.>
<Idiot. Keep word simple.>
<OK. Understand.>
<You OK. Arun?>
<I bored.>
<Me too.>
<Zug?>
<Zug? Query?>
<Zug speak you, Springer?>
<A little.>
<Zug not speak me.>
<I know.>
<But I worry about Zug.>

<I know you do.>
<Do you?>
<Of course, Arun. Whatever explanation, we're not the same as them. You know that.>
<I suppose.> Arun had an urge to change the subject. <Your words coming through clearer, Springer.>
<Guess AIs are good at learning. Can't believe never talked like this before.>
<Usually focused on watching for an enemy. This time they've just stuck us here out the way.>
<Be loyal, Arun.>
<I am. Why do you say…? Oh, you mean loyal to Zug. I don't know what more to do.>
<Don't wimp out, McEwan. Give them time. Give them reasons to accept you again.>
<That could take years.>
<Is that a reason not to try?>
<No.>
<Don't give up, Arun.>
<I won't—>
<Good.>
<—ever give up—>
<I know.>
<—on you.>

Arun choked on a swell of adoration for Springer. Buffer gel pushed down into his mouth. Not again! He froze — not breathing — not even daring to think. When eventually he relaxed again, the gel hadn't pushed in far. He wasn't drowning. But the link to Springer was broken.

Maybe that wasn't such a bad thing. They had strayed onto the most dangerous topic, and who knew might be able to listen in? Especially with Arun unreliable due to his oversupply of emotions that ambushed him constantly. What had he meant just then with Springer? Was he in love with her? Was he reaching out for any human contact? Or was he just scared?

Arun pushed against the gel to shake his head. Man, he was such a vulleyed-up wreck, and he had no idea how much he could blame that on the mind-altering drugs he was being given. He'd sidestepped execution somehow, but it could only be a question of time before he was kicked out of the Marines… probably through an airlock without a suit.

Damn these long stretches encased in the gibberball. He'd rather face an enemy battle fleet than the thoughts in his own head.

Something flew past, too quick to see properly.

Was the gibberball finally making him see things?

But when he asked Barney to replay and slow down the image — he learned it was real all right. Something was moving very fast toward Tranquility.

Barney interrupted the playback to show a real-time view of a second object flashing past. The interval between the two: 11.4 seconds.

Arun had only a limited view from inside the gibberball. Whatever had whizzed past had disappeared out of his left field of vision. He couldn't see Tranquility either, except in the planetshine brightening the side of *Fort Douaumont* that faced his home world.

What he *could* see on the extreme left of his viewpoint was a dot Barney identified as Orbital Defense Platform 74. Twelve streaks of white curled and twisted away from the platform, gyrating wildly but with only one possible target.

Horden's bones! If the defense platform had launched missiles then this was for real. Tranquility was under bombardment.

And Arun was at war!

Chapter 57

Four objects had been launched against Tranquility, at 11.4 second intervals, followed by… nothing.

Was the attack over?

Arun tried to form another link to Springer. Perhaps she had a better view of what was going on.

Barney wasn't playing ball, though, refusing to make the comm link.

After 41 seconds, he learned that the bombardment hadn't ceased. A streak of light on a new trajectory etched a line across Arun's vision pursued by a spread of missiles from Orbital Defense Platform 74.

This time he saw the explosion as two of the defensive missiles blew up the projectile.

Yes!

His elation froze a moment later. The missiles hadn't contacted the projectile far enough away… some fragments from the explosion must have carried on. Platform 74 flared into a brilliant blue-white bloom that forced Barney to dim Arun's visor. Platform 74 was gone.

If a brace of missiles couldn't stop those projectiles, they must be moving with a staggering amount of momentum. Was this the nightmare scenario they used to scare each other with as kids? A bombardment by the mass drivers that were designed to send ore shipments across the stars? But there were failsafes. The system defense fleet could shut down mass drivers remotely. Had they turned traitor too?

Finally someone spoke. "We're all seeing this. Standby." It was Gupta, still out there somewhere on his flitter. He'd stealthed his suit but was connecting to Wide Battle Net, which enabled Barney to mark the sergeant's position with a blue dot even though he remained unseen.

The next shot slammed into *Fort Douaumont*.

The projectile passed straight through the old hulk. Arun imagined the disappointment of whoever was firing at them when the old ship didn't explode. It had no main armament, fuel or air to blow up, but the old ship was crippled all the same, just not in such a showy way. The hull twisted, sheared, broke asunder. Then another projectile hit the stricken ship, sending fragments of metal weighing thousands of tons shooting in all directions, leaving a glittering halo of shimmering shards.

The power of the projectiles was almost beyond human comprehension, but whoever was launching them didn't have much military sense. Why waste time taking out a useless abandoned hulk? Then a shock hit him when he remembered *Fort Douaumont* hadn't quite been abandoned. His brother had been on board.

Arun's concern for a brother he'd never met didn't have time to take root, because if the enemy were trying to take out the threat from nearby ships, that meant the next target was the TU!

There were mass drivers scattered on moons throughout the system, essentially the same as the railgun inside his SA-71 carbine except scaled up to the enormous degree necessary to fling packages of refined ore across the gulf of interstellar space to be received by resource-hungry star systems. Transit times between star systems were measured in centuries. But if the mass driver was on one of Tranquility's moons, its projectiles would be only seconds away from the planet.

Arun knew he was ceasing to be a bystander when, even through the buffer gel, he could feel the TU throb with a massive power build up.

Sergeant Gupta's voice came into his helmet. "Listen up, cadets. You haven't impressed me so far."

Arun's view blurred. And then settled. The TU had spun around. He was facing the dusty red ball of Antilles, the largest of Tranquility's moons.

"My advice to *Yorktown*'s captain is to leave you where you are," said Gupta, "that you're a liability. She says that if we've spent all that training budget on you over the past 17 years…"

Then *Yorktown* was moving. Man, was she *moving!* Even stuffed with buffer gel, the breath was being crushed from Arun's body. Lump hammers pounded his skull tirelessly. He closed his eyes. He'd never experienced such acceleration before. It felt like he was being squeezed into a sticky dot on *Yorktown's* outer hull.

Then the lump hammers softened into wooden mallets; the vise crushing his chest mellowed into the fists of a Jotun warrior pummeling his ribs, and Gupta continued his words. "After 17 years of training you should damned well be a useful asset. *Yorktown* is moving to assault the traitors who took out *Fort Douaumont* and are bombarding our homes on the surface. We compromised and decided to offer you a choice. Are you going to take this opportunity to prove to me you're Marines? Or are you going to be spectators? Which is it to be?"

"We're Marines, sergeant."

As far as Arun could tell, every cadet in the Blue and Gold squads had answered in the same way at the same time. Himself included.

Maybe he wasn't so different from the others.

A bubble of pride put a little grin onto his face.

The TU corkscrewed sickeningly as it approached Antilles.

"Very well," Gupta growled after a few seconds. "It makes my guts crawl to call you sorry lot Marines, but here's the plan. Rebels have taken over a mass driver on Antilles. We think their main target is Detroit. Defense Command estimate a 90% chance that their defense shield can keep out a direct hit for the next hour. After that our shield effectiveness degrades rapidly, and everything that breaches the outer atmosphere is going to hit *something*. If we're lucky we might have as much as two hours to shut them down before the upper levels of Detroit are turned to slag, or buried under shattered mountain fragments."

Yorktown lurched sideways so unexpectedly that Arun's heart and lungs were left miles behind. Another bombardment shot past.

"Here's our problem," continued Gupta. "The rebels have thrown a thick cloud of rock fragments — pebbles really — above and around their base. We don't know how they've done it, but it makes for an effective barrier. *Yorktown*'s weapons can't penetrate that rock cloud, but the enemy can shoot out. They've created a force tunnel through their shield that provides a launch window for their mass driver, but we can't get a firing solution through it. Friendly system defense boats are hours away. There are no other combat vessels nearby. We need boots on the ground. You!"

"But, sergeant," said Brandt, "our weapons–"

"Are training poppers only?" finished Gupta. "Did you really think they'd design and build you separate carbines just to be toy guns in training exercises? They're fully functional except we haven't given you any ammo bulbs. You've got two default modes we never told you about because you're not meant to know this yet. There's a pulse laser capability and an emergency railgun mode. Standby..."

Arun held his breath for 8.5 seconds until Gupta spoke again. "Your deployment starts in 72 seconds. Your suit AIs know how to unlock your carbines and have updated maps of the moon surface. Cadet Lance Sergeant Belville, you have command. Brandt is your deputy. Form up in the depression 4 klicks northwest of the mining base. I've marked it on your maps. We'll land a second scratch team of veterans, Force Alpha. Wait for them to attack. Then move in and—"

A familiar jolt hit Arun like a hundred Marines in full armor jumping on his spine. Then he was tossed into space with the familiar sensation of gasping for air.

By the time he was alert and had stabilized his spin, Sergeant Gupta had finished his talk and the surface of Antilles, dusty gray rocks streaked with rust, was fast rising up to claim him.

He asked Barney to fill him in on his carbine's capability. Quick as you like.

―――――

Arun had thought he knew all about the SA-71 carbine. Turned out he didn't. The weapon was designed to be the ultimate in robustness and flexibility with a power pack that was so long lasting that it might as well be magical. What had been hidden from them was that there were two default modes for when the standard-fit ammo carousels were exhausted. He'd always dismissed the rumors that there was secret information they only trusted Marines with once they were already on a troop ship headed out-system.

Said a lot about how humans were viewed by their betters.

One of these hidden options was a pulsed laser beam that would rapidly eat away at even the SA-71's battery charge. The strength of the laser pulses quickly degraded in an atmosphere, but in vacuum this was a credible weapon.

The second option was referred to as *shardshot*. The Marine grabbed whatever material was to hand and packed it into a tube concealed within the weapon's stock. A combination of grinders and laser drills would chop the toughest materials into dust, which would then be compressed into ballistic pellets and shot out of the barrel in railgun mode. Barney warned him that neither the carbine nor the suit could counter the recoil from shardshot rounds.

The recoil would kick like an angry Hardit.

And selecting the right material was critical to achieve a decent muzzle velocity. Something with metal content would be good.

Arun grinned when Barney told him this. The mining bases were situated on Antilles because the moon's rocky surface was rich in zinc, copper, iron, and manganese.

That should do it!

Chapter 58

As he plummeted feet-first toward the moon, Arun could see other white smears falling like hail against the black of space. *And if he could see them…*

Gold and Blue squads looked like gunnery training targets as they descended in their gleaming white suits.

Arun couldn't help but imagine bright lines extend from the surface of Antilles, connecting a laser battery to each white blur in an obscene diagram of death.

Then Barney braked — hard enough to take Arun's breath away and make his vision blur. When his senses returned he was ten meters above the moon's cratered surface. Barney had braked early enough that he came down with only as much force as if he were stepping off a bottom stair back home.

Barney used a virtual arrow to indicate the rendezvous point. Arun was running there from his very first step on the moon.

Turned out running wasn't easy. He kept jumping high above the ground and had to tell Barney to push him back down to the surface. It was frustratingly slow.

He was at home in zero-g where Barney could zip him around effortlessly. But in the moon's low gravity, the suit's motive power was much reduced. Barney could lob him over an obstacle but couldn't run for him.

Arun briefly considered scampering on all fours before finding a steady loping gait that would look ridiculous if anyone were there to see it. But Arun was on his own. Alice Belville had told them to stick to Local Battle Net, which meant tight line-of-sight comms only.

A few hundred meters from the rendezvous, Arun finally encountered another cadet: Tanweer Aburto from Gold Squad. Seconds later, Barney added more dots to Arun's tac-display as the suit AIs began to ping signals off each other.

Ahead Arun saw that what the sergeant had called a depression looked like a shallow quarry pit covered by a few centuries of dust.

He couldn't see more than a few hundred meters into the depression due to the swirl of pebbles thrown up by the rebels as a defensive shield. From a distance the shield fragments looked like static. Barney speculated the pebbles were actually tailings from the ore crushers. Arun didn't care. He could already see what he wanted to know: the pebble shield didn't extend as far as the ground. There was a narrow gap underneath.

Up close, the pebble shield looked more like a miniature asteroid belt bent to the rebels' will and sped up to lethal velocities.

Arun halted. If he kept to even this low gait, he would bounce high enough to be pulped.

Aburto had the solution. The Gold Squad cadet hit the deck and rolled. Laughing, Arun copied him. It was like being a four-year-old again. Arun clung to those memories as he rolled under the rock-storm, the silent blur of death.

The ground underneath was littered with rock fragments that had fallen out of the shield. Would his training armor stand up to any rocks falling out onto him? As he spun forward, Arun grabbed some of the fallen rocks in his free hand, keeping his carbine low to the ground in the other. Maybe they would make good shardshot? He'd only collected a few small rocks before he was spinning too fast. He brought his arms beneath him as he accelerated. He was inside the depression now; rolling down the edge and picking up speed.

Then he hit the bottom and bounced — tumbling and dazed out of control and heading for the blur of swirling rocks.

Barney stabilized Arun's suit. Just at the moment that the sense of up and down began to reassert itself, the first rock hit Arun, spinning him helplessly. Then another strike.

But Barney had control now, enough to push Arun down out of the rock cloud. And once he'd touched down, Arun could run to safety because the depression was deep enough to give him plenty more headroom.

Seven other cadets were there already. He kept away from the others, keeping alert for anyone else in Delta Section to appear. Extended order drill demanded a minimum of five meters between each cadet and ten meters between sections, but that was difficult to make sense of when hardly anyone was here yet.

Some of the others appeared to be praying. Had their morale crumbled so easily?

Then he remembered about the shardshot ammo and realized they were filling their weapon stocks with dirt. He joined in, using the rocks he'd grabbed out of the shield. Barney gave Arun a virtual thumbs up. Just as he'd hoped, the shield pebbles were mineral-rich tailings, not moon dust. They would make excellent shard bullets.

Arun looked up and noticed Stok Laskosk from Blue Squad's command section was nearby. He looked lost.

Arun walked over and patted Laskosk on the shoulder.

"Hey, Stopcock. Nervous?"

Heavy weapons specialist Laskosk, or Stopcock as he was universally known, looked at Arun as if trying to decide whether this was an insult. He shook his head. "It feels wrong. I always imagined I would have my missile launcher over my shoulder. Instead…" He held up his carbine. "We're firing chewed up wads of moondust. Not what I expected."

"Look on the bright side," offered Arun. "Without your launcher you're no longer a prime target for snipers."

"What's your problem, McEwan?" It was Lance Corporal Narcisco, also from the command section.

"Nothing, lance corporal."

"Good. Then piss off like a good little boy. You're bad luck, McEwan. Keep away from me."

Arun retreated, almost stumbling into Springer.

"Don't mind them, Arun," she said. "Stopcock is scared, that's all."

"Are you?"

"No."

Arun laughed. "Me neither. Well, scared of letting down my buddies. Not scared of getting killed."

"Seventeen years of brainwashing and drugs and re-engineering didn't go to waste after all. Guess we're not so different from everyone else." She paused. "I'm glad you've got my back, Arun. I think that fights off the fear."

"I'm glad you're here too, Springer."

"Me too," said Osman who'd just arrived. "I mean… now the shooting's about to start. I guess I can't stay angry at you, McEwan."

"Keep minimum five meters separation," snapped Majanita to everyone in Delta Section, once they had all assembled in the depression. Privately she added for Arun's benefit: "I know it's not your fault that bad luck's followed you around, McEwan. Right now, I don't care. I think you're a liability. Since I'm stuck with you, I want you to do everything you can to prove me wrong. Can you do that?

"Yes, corporal."

"Good. The first thing I want you to do is shut the frakk up. I don't want a peep until we contact the enemy."

Arun shut up.

Above him, the black sky was dominated by Tranquility's huge disk, its planetshine bright enough to cast shadows even though it was day on Antilles. An angry ripple spread out from a hole in the froth of cloud cover as the first enemy projectile broke through the planet's defensive shield. The fireball on the planet's surface briefly lit up the clouds in shades of orange and red.

As ordered, Belville made them wait until Force Alpha had launched its attack.

It wasn't difficult to see when that was.

Over the mass driver's expected location, two balls of hot violet light exploded: a pair of plasma grenades. The explosions spread fingers of jagged light in an arc over the driver but never reaching closer than about fifteen meters from the target.

"Frakk! That's some force field. Didn't even scratch it."

The words came from Force Alpha, the handful of veteran Marines deployed separately by *Yorktown*. Until this point they'd been undetectably silent, but now they were noisy. In fact, they were making as much of a clamor as possible, keeping the enemy's attention away from the hidden cadets.

"Power drain must be staggering," said another Marine. "If only we could get to the power source and shut it down."

Arun winced because that was such a clumsy hint to the cadets. But then, as he reminded himself, his time as a Hardit slave had taught him most aliens weren't interested in human languages. He had to hope there were no traitor humans listening in.

"Keep silent," Madge reminded her squad. Then: "Advance to assault positions."

The cadets scrambled up to the lip of the depression, ready to move out.

Sticking your head over a parapet was a surefire way to get your brains blown out. The designers of the ACE-2 battlesuit had solved this by providing periscope worms: an optical cable that extended out the top of the helmet. The cable was so thin that if an enemy could detect your periscope, you were as good as dead anyway.

Arun extended his periscope worm, and he saw for himself what the cadet scouts had already reported.

Gold and Blue Squads were deployed in an old quarry pit several hundred meters to the north-west of the rebel mining facility. The nearby pits had long been mined out, but the buildings remained to service the mass driver. The driver was situated in a natural crater on the far side of the complex. A simple platform rested on the shallow slope of the crater. Superconducting hoops were mounted along the platform's length.

Arun watched those hoops accelerate another ore package to such speed that even if the rock shield hadn't hidden its progress from view, the projectile would have disappeared over the horizon within a handful of seconds. After a sub-orbital arc around Antilles, it would escape the moon's gravity on its brief journey toward Tranquility.

Between their position and the mine base, they could see trenches zigzagging in a ring around the buildings and extending out toward the mass driver.

Keeping to LBNet denied the cadets eyes in the sky. All they could tell was that some kind of defensive positions had been prepared for them. They might be facing an unoccupied trench, or a defensive hive protected by AI controlled GX-cannons and combat drones.

They hadn't a lot of choice either way.

From the enemy positions concentrated around the driver, dozens of streaks suddenly shot toward the Force Alpha Marines.

The missiles hit, lighting up the horizon with a series of explosions.

Force Alpha had launched two grenades. The rebels had replied with at least thirty missiles.

Arun jumped inside his suit when Barney unexpectedly lifted the worm's eye to look up into space. The silver bullet of the mass driver's previous launch had reappeared overhead. It had traveled in a slingshot around the back of Antilles and was now on its way to his home planet.

From where he waited, sinking in to the dust of Antilles surface, the projectile's silent journey looked serene. It was difficult to believe that if this glowing spark reached Tranquility's surface the impact would flatten a city.

"Look!"

It was Springer on a private channel.

Arun cut the feed from the worm and followed her finger pointing at the mass driver. He didn't understand. Not daring to break Madge's order to be silent, Arun raised a hand palm-up in a gesture of confusion.

"Look at their counter-fire."

He watched as the rebels dug in around the mass driver fired another volley of missiles at Force Alpha. This time he saw what Springer meant. The missiles didn't jink in the way that Stopcock's would if he had his shoulder-mounted launcher with him. Instead the rebels' missiles were traveling in straight lines, which meant they were crude rockets, not intelligent missiles. And rather than spread them out in a barrage pattern, the rockets were being fired straight at the firing positions the Marines had used to launch their grenades.

Didn't they realize that the Marines would have hopped and rolled away to new positions the instant they'd fired?

"The rebels don't stand a chance," said Springer. "They're strictly amateur."

Arun was beginning to agree, but then they saw movement from the enemy positions facing them. Rebels moving through the trench system to reinforce the defenses around the mass driver.

Arun laughed at his enemy. They looked so ludicrous. They'd dug these trenches but the idiots were in such a hurry that they were bouncing in the low-g, making their torsos pop into sight and then disappear as if they were on trampolines. It looked like some kind of virtual game for kids. Arun wanted to play. Doubly so because he could see the aliens were Hardits, and he had a score to settle. He itched to bring his carbine to bear and try out this new pulse laser setting on the bouncing monkeys.

But the order never came.

Arun estimated 40 rebels had moved off to tackle Force Alpha. How many remained to face the 50-odd cadets of Blue and Gold Squads?

"Go!" ordered Madge.

Time to find out.

Arun scrambled over the lip of crumbling moondust and charged the enemy trenches.

Miniature explosions of dust erupted all along the enemy trenches. This was the suppressive fire from the even-numbered cadet fire teams, and it was doing its job of keeping the enemy's head down because Arun didn't see any return fire.

Arun's team had to charge forward as fast as he could for two hundred meters before taking cover and providing rapid suppressive fire to shield the even-numbered fire teams as they caught up.

He wasn't scared. He hadn't time to be because all his concentration was spent on making progress without bouncing high into the sky.

One thing he did notice, though, was a missile corkscrewing from Force Alpha's position toward the mining complex.

It didn't get far.

Anti-missile defenses sprang into action from three points around the mass driver. Scores of ultra-fast missiles lifted from the ground to take out the invader. The Marine missile was nimble but not enough to evade this level of defense. It was blasted from the sky.

Arun hadn't time to regret its loss. He'd reached his first objective. He spotted a small crater and dived into it. At half a meter deep, it wasn't much, but it was better than nothing.

As he readied to fire, Arun checked his tac-display. Madge, Osman, and Springer had all taken up positions a short distance away. Barney wasn't reporting any other casualties, but he hadn't time to check beyond his comrades in Blue-5. He was zooming his visor display onto the enemy trench, about two hundred and fifty meters away, when Madge gave the order: "Shardshot. Rapid fire!"

He couldn't see any rebels, so Arun picked a segment of trench opposite him and opened up.

Frakk! The weapon had given him a slap of recoil like a nuclear explosion.

He'd intended to rake the enemy position, with fire but had squeezed off one aimed shot and a handful so high they were probably heading up into orbit.

If he hadn't been in armor, the damned thing would have broken his collar bone.

He braced himself more firmly and set to work. He couldn't call it rapid fire, but it was as fast as the recoil would allow without sacrificing accuracy entirely.

"Overwatch," ordered Madge. Arun ceased firing and kept a close watch on the enemy trench, ready to shoot at any rebel brave enough to present themselves as a target.

But Madge's order confirmed what he'd already guessed. The enemy had either abandoned their trench, or were luring them into a trap.

If this were a trap, they were headed right into its jaws because the cadet fire teams made their leapfrogging advance until they reached a stopline fifteen meters from the enemy trench.

The enemy had not returned fire.

From the far side of the mining complex, Force Alpha's battle against the rebels continued its noisy progress.

The veteran Marines yelled into Wide Battle Net for backup. They fired more missiles at the mining buildings, only to see them shot down, and they gave orders to imaginary units to make flanking maneuvers. For all their efforts to pretend they were more of a threat than they actually were, Barney estimated there were only five Marines in Force Alpha. Six tops.

Then Madge gave the order to close the distance to the enemy trench and Arun forgot Force Alpha. All he could think of was what he would find waiting for him.

Blue Squad would use a boost from their suits to leap over the trench, while Gold Squad would assault inside the trench.

He sailed over, covering the trench line with his SA-71, but it really had been abandoned.

Trench warfare was the opposite of the flexibility of zero-g space combat that was the focus of Tactical Marine training. Even with his limited training on the matter, the trench looked to Arun like a hastily constructed channel. Crude cover and recently built. A far cry from the defensive warren an attacker would be faced with if they tried to assault the Detroit base from the ground.

Arun advanced, making for his next target: a cuboid segment of the mining complex that looked grafted on to the main building. This was to be their route inside.

Behind him, Gold Squad reported that they had secured the trench. There weren't any booby traps — at least no explosions — but perhaps there had been motion sensors or watching cameras because moments later a volley of rockets streaked into the trench.

"Remain on LBNet," ordered Belville. "They know we're here now, but not how many of us are here. And once we're inside they will lose us. Blue Squad, hurry up and get me a breach."

Arun didn't hear Belville's orders for Gold Squad, but his tac-display showed them abandoning the trench, crawling a short distance toward the building to take up a defensive line near Blue Squad. Marines instinctively distrusted static defenses. Hiding behind a trench or rampart wall robbed you of maneuver options and surrendered initiative to the enemy. Marines won their battles by attacking, and no one launched an attack while cowering in the bottom of a ditch.

With rocket explosions raining down rock fragments behind them, Blue Squad got to work.

Brandt marked out a flat section away from any bulges or exterior features, and ordered Corporal Hecht's Alpha Section to break through. Alpha tried using assault teeth, but the monofilament spikes extending from their carbine muzzles were optimized to cut through flesh and bone, the modern equivalent of the ancient bayonet. The rotating spikes skidded against the wall, scarring it, but snapping and blunting the assault teeth.

Next they tried melting their way through using their carbines on the new pulse laser setting. New to them, anyway.

Brandt assigned each section in his squad a portion of a diamond shape large enough for an armored cadet to pass through.

If Arun were in charge he would have concentrated the lasers on a single spot. Not a hole large enough to pass through but maybe after a breach the pressure escape would rip away a large chunk of wall. At least they would know how much laser power was needed to push through.

But Brandt wanted an entry point from the get go. They burned deep scores into the fabric of the building but they were burning deeper into their carbine power packs. Barney reported power had depleted by 80% already and falling rapidly.

Belville brought over a section from Gold Squad.

The mining building had shielded them somewhat from the enemy rocket volleys. But the rebels must have moved to a better position, because a fresh volley of explosions rocked the ground behind him. Their fire was increasingly accurate.

Barney marked two red crosses to show Gold Squad casualties.

It got worse. The dust thrown up was already causing laser bloom — scattering the beams aimed at the outer wall, robbing them of power.

"Move closer," ordered Brandt. "Get those lasers within ten paces of the wall."

Arun moved to obey, very conscious of what would happen if he were standing too close to the section of wall when it blew out.

"I know it's dangerous," said Brandt, "but every second we are delayed out here imperils our mission."

But they were spared that horror. Without any warning, the diamond they'd already cut through the wall flew out, landing on the moon's surface and skidding for twenty meters. Luckily no one was in its path.

Blue Squad blasted the far side of the breach with a volley of shardshot.

Arun couldn't see what was inside, because first the air, and then anything in the room that wasn't tied down, exploded out through the breach. Blue Squad was engulfed in a rain of softscreens, hats, empty plastic bottles and other detritus of what Arun guessed was a store room. The water vapor in the air flash-froze and began to fall as snow.

To anyone inside this bridgehead room, the vacuum sucking remorselessly at the air would sound like a howling gale. Outside in his suit, the violent depressurization was eerily silent.

Cutting holes into enemy warboats was fundamental to tactical Marine doctrine, so the cadets knew plenty about depressurization. Through a Marine-sized breach the air would be escaping at about 200 mph. That was plenty to incapacitate any opponents not strapped down and braced for a breach. After about 25 seconds, the wind would have died down to around 80 mph. That was when Brandt gave the order to go in.

The cadets lowered their heads and pushed against the wind. Getting through the hole was the worst part. As the cadets partially plugged the breach, the air pushed at them even harder as it tried to escape. Once they'd popped through the hole there was still enough air to hear alarm sirens above the banshee screech of the wind.

Cadet Caccamo from Alpha Section was first in. At the far side of the bridgehead room the door to an internal corridor was still open. He raced for the door but it shut before he could reach it. The wind dropped abruptly, making the cadets who'd struggled in topple flat on their faces.

Under the illumination of flashing blue lights mounted in the ceiling, Blue Squad began to form up inside the bridgehead. Even before the rest of the squad had made it inside, Hecht was by the door control with Alpha Section, ready to advance up the corridor on the far side.

"Brace for depressurization," he warned. "Opening door in 3 - 2 - 1 - now!"

Nothing happened. The door ignored him.

"Could be security lockdown," Del said, "but probably refusing to open into vacuum. Let me see if I can hack it."

"Very good, Lance Corporal Sandure," replied Brandt. Hearing his comrades refer to each other by their rank still felt freaky to Arun.

Del hadn't even reached the control panel when the door suddenly opened, and another blast of air rushed out to flash freeze as it entered the depressurized room.

Arun covered the doorway with his carbine, but no one emerged. With the swirling mist it was difficult to see, difficult to even stand up against the wind. Then he saw two dark cylinders rolling his way along the floor.

"Grenades!"

Arun dove for the floor. In the low gravity, the maneuver was agonizingly slow. In fact, the wind trying to blow him out of the crude hole in the wall was stronger than gravity. He didn't even make it to the ground before the grenades exploded. The blast smacked him down and skidded him along the floor before slamming him into an equipment cupboard. Gleaming pairs of boots fell off the shelves, showering down upon him in slow motion.

The wind, he realized, had stopped.

As Arun got to his feet, Barney reported that his armor had not been compromised. Idiot monkeys! They'd used high explosive grenades — mining charges, probably. In the near-vacuum, there was hardly any medium for their shockwave to travel through. Someone standing a meter behind Arun wouldn't have felt a thing. He laughed as he got to his feet and immediately found himself in a raging firefight.

He took a moment to read his tac-display. Beta and Delta Sections had rolled, knelt or gone prone to take up firing positions that maximized fire on the door without shooting comrades in the back.

Hardit miners — about a half dozen so far — were racing into the room, spraying fire wildly. They were shooting slug-throwers: kinetic weapons that shot metal bullets powered by a chemical explosive.

A hammer blow hit Arun on his chest, which was already bruised from his drop to the moon's surface. He'd been shot by a bullet, but Barney reported his suit's integrity had been degraded but not compromised. A suit unable to cope with a few high energy impacts from small objects was little use in a real space battlefield.

Arun wanted height. Barney read his intentions, lifting his master gently off the ground and then, with a kick of brutal power, threw him to the ceiling, coming to a shuddering halt, but not so rapid that Arun blacked out. Barney had been Arun's most intimate companion for so many years that the AI knew how far he could fling Arun without breaking him. In a crowded room in the midst of a firefight, speed was vital. Gaining height was a big risk, but so too was staying in the same place when he'd already been hit once.

Arun willed Barney to reorient his visor display so that the ceiling was 'down' and the floor 'up'. Gravity might insist that it knew the correct direction of down, but it was weak enough on the moon that the motive system on Arun's suit could compensate, if it operated at maximum power. He shut his eyes, reframed in his mind, and opened them at the same time as bringing his carbine to bear on… Osman. His firing solution was blocked by his friend who was attempting the same maneuver. Arun crab-walked out of Osman's way. Osman was cartwheeling through the air, firing as he went. Osman was always flashy like that. Then Osman's aerial dance missed a beat. He was jerked backward, making him fling out his hands in a primitive instinct that made no sense here, upside down on a low-g moon.

Arun watched helplessly as Osman's helmet shattered. In the low-pressure environment of the nearly airless room, the higher pressure in Osman's suit forced out a plume of blood, flesh, and faceplate splinters.

Osman was dead!

Arun braced and fired. Brandt had ordered them to conserve ammo. The pellet supply was limited without reloading, but Arun didn't give a damn as he sprayed the rebel miners. If he needed to reload, there were plenty of spare SA-71s that no one was in a state to use any longer.

Hellfire! He'd forgotten the recoil again, thumping away at his shoulder with such violence that he sprayed his fire high, which from his position on the ceiling meant firing down at his fellow cadets.

Arun lifted his finger off the trigger before he accidentally shot his friends. Shifting firing position by rolling once to the right — mentally oriented upside-down all the while — he fired again on the Hardits as rapidly as he could.

He got one, he was sure. Shot the little veck until he'd nearly decapitated it, enjoying seeing the Hardit twitch under the flail of the shardshot. Maybe it was the miner who'd killed Osman. He hoped so but in the confusion of a firefight that was more a hope than certainty.

"Cease fire!" ordered Brandt. The firing stopped. The cloud of dust and other debris began the slow process of settling to the floor, unhurried in the lazy gravity.

Madge issued an additional order. "McEwan, stay at top. Springer, stay low. Secure the corridor."

Arun acknowledged and moved off for the corridor that led beyond the shattered door. His mind was still reframed so that everyone else appeared to him to be walking upside down. Everyone but Osman. He had to push past Osman's corpse.

Still obeying its last command, Osman's suit AI kept its master's battlesuit positioned with its boots on the ceiling, making Osman's arterial flow spray onto the floor below like a red sprinkler.

Arun snatched a glance at their dead opponents. They were in simple vacsuits — not combat hardened. He hoped to recognize Tawfiq or one of the other Hardit tormentors of the Detroit Aux, but the suit visors obscured the faces of their wearers. He imagined the faces inside stretched into shapes of agony.

Arun pushed past Springer who was hugging the door frame, using it as cover, and advanced 20 paces along the ceiling before taking a prone position behind what looked like an atmosphere scrubber mounted in the ceiling. Blue warning lights were mounted every three meters along the ceiling before it turned right after twenty meters. They flashed a decompression alert. Arun willed Barney to remove the lights from his visor display so they didn't obscure his line of sight.

There was no sign of movement ahead.

Even without air, the corridor wasn't completely silent. A hum of power transmitted itself through the material of the ceiling. Without needing to be told, Barney would be listening tirelessly for the sound of enemy footsteps.

As he waited, Arun's thoughts turned to the weapons he'd smuggled to Alabama. Had he supplied the rebels? He wanted to assume 'yes', but… Tawfiq had been smuggling SA-71s and combat armor, not these rifles with the simple kinetic rounds.

Thinking of weapons made him realize that a pressure seal somewhere ahead had closed, leaving the corridor in vacuum. *There was very little to diffuse a laser beam.*

"Setting carbine to pulse laser," Arun said to Springer.

She hesitated — probably considering the power already drained from cutting the hole through the outer wall. "Good thinking, Arun."

In his tac-display, Springer was a strong blue dot, a short distance behind him, and with a slight tail on her dot's head, meaning she was a little below him. She'd taken cover behind a trolley, her carbine barrel resting on a pile of water bottles.

"Springer…" Arun said uncertainly.

"What? Osman? Yes… I… I saw."

Never letting his attention slip from the corridor ahead, Arun spent several seconds trying to work out what he wanted to say. He couldn't talk about Osman. Not yet. But there was something else…

Eventually he said, "I'm sorry, Springer."

"Why? You couldn't have saved Osman."

"No, not that. For letting you down about Xin and Scendence. I'm sorry."

"For frakk's sake, we've been over this already. Don't get all weepy on me, McEwan. Keep focus."

"But Osman. Do you think he really forgave me?"

"I don't know, McEwan. But I do know that if you get me killed because you're too busy being sorry to keep alert, I'll never forgive you."

Barney had no difficulty keeping alert. He smeared garish orange over Arun's view of the corridor turning, meaning he'd detected something but was unsure what.

"Contact threat," said Arun.

"Confirmed," added Springer. Her suit AI would probably be giving her the same warning as Barney, but Arun had been drilled to always seek confirmation. Suits could be damaged or make mistakes. Worse, they could be compromised through electronic warfare attack.

Maybe Barney had detected the vibrations of running feet, of heat radiating from a sweating body, of unnatural light fluctuations. Whatever bothered the AI was getting stronger because the orange flash he'd superimposed had turned an angry red. Barney was sometimes wrong in his suspicions, but Arun trusted them enough to place his full concentration on the manual sights of his carbine, braced as he was, upside down behind a ceiling unit.

A Hardit head appeared around the bend, searching the corridor for threats.

Had the rebel seen them? Arun didn't think so because the monkey slunk toward them on three limbs, the fourth holding its rifle stock. The Hardit's tail grasped the weapon's pistol grip.

Barney overlaid the Hardit with a short-tailed red targeting dot, and added two more dots for the two other rebels Barney was now confident were hiding just out of sight.

"Contact three rebels," said Springer.

"Confirmed," said Arun.

"Support required?" queried Brandt. Barney zoomed the tac-display out and up from the advancing Hardits, tilting it so that Arun could see what was happening behind him. One of the Gold Squad cadets had taken up position in the doorway that fed into his corridor, his suit acting as a relay for LBNet.

"Negative," Springer answered. "We can take them out."

The lead Hardit beckoned its two hidden comrades with a wave of its rifle. If the flashing decompression lights were blinding it, then its targeting capability must be limited to three eyes staring over an ugly snout and out through a dumb transparent visor.

This would be easy!

"I'll take the leader," said Springer.

"Roger." It didn't make sense for them to both hit the same target.

As soon as Barney said he had a good firing solution, Arun opened up. The lead Hardit was just bringing its rifle to bear, its two followers not even as ready as that.

Too late, monkeys!

Using short, cutting motions, Arun fired his pulse laser at the second Hardit.

He knew he'd scored a hit. So had Springer, but then they had to face the difference between a low-power pulse laser and a full laser connected to the additional power packs they usually carried in space.

Their pulse lasers turned themselves off for a second to recharge.

They were effectively unarmed for what felt like an age. The remaining Hardit failed to make use of its advantage. All it could do was stare in horror at its fallen comrades.

Arun almost sympathized.

Their lasers had gashed open the Hardit suits but left little or no exit wounds. The pinkish spray fountaining out of their compromised suits did more than prove the Hardits had been injured, they were high pressure jets spinning the Hardits off balance. One injured Hardit got off a wild shot before both were on the floor, their weapons dropped.

Arun's carbine had recharged. He killed the remaining Hardit with a headshot, firing simultaneously with Springer.

The other Hardits were still alive, but not worth wasting battery power on.

By the time the jets out of their depressurizing suits had calmed, the Hardits would be too oxygen starved to be any threat.

"Three miners tropied," reported Springer, but no acknowledgment came from the bridgehead. They'd lost LBNet.

What were they playing at back there?

LBNet didn't reconnect for nearly two minutes. When it did, Arun's irritation vanished, because Barney updated his tac-display by planting red crosses over the blue cadet dots. Casualties. Lots of them, and they'd only captured one room so far.

Barney had added a double yellow halo to Brandt's dot, meaning he was now tactical commander.

Alice Belville was one of the red crosses.

Oh, hell!

"Listen up!" announced Brandt. His speech-making was cringeworthy at the best of times. His voice sounded doubly uncertain now. "We've suffered eight killed, two wounded. We've lost Lance Sergeant Belville, so I have command. Blue-6, reinforce Blue-5 guarding the corridor approach. Gold Alpha and Beta Sections will stay behind to guard the bridgehead and the wounded. The rest, grab ammo for yourselves and Blue Delta Section and…"

Brandt's voice faded. Arun groaned. Alice never hesitated like that. If she'd survived, they would be halfway to the base command center by now.

"Medics?" asked Brandt on the open channel. "How long to stabilize the wounded?"

"Three minutes, lance sergeant."

"The rest of us have three minutes to tear this room apart searching for anything useful. Questions?"

No one spoke.

A few seconds later, Madge took a position next to Springer, the rest of Delta Section spreading out around her.

"Good to see you, corporal," said Springer.

Arun winced. He didn't know what to say to Madge even in a simple greeting. How could he greet the remaining member of his fire team without mentioning Blue-5's missing member: Osman?

When Barney signaled another alert, Arun almost groaned with relief. He was overlaying the view of the corridor turn with a flashing orange warning.

Seconds later a Hardit head peered around the corner. Arun waited for it to move closer, to get a clearer shot. But this time the rebels weren't playing ball. The head disappeared out of sight. Barney, meanwhile, was firming his estimate. There were more rebels massing this time. Many more.

"Contact approx 20 rebels," Arun reported.

"We'll vape 'em easy," said Madge. "Two of you took out three of them with ease. Now there's six of us and they will be choked by the corridor's narrowness."

Arun thought she was talking away her fears. He didn't like the sound of that.

He readied to fire.

Any second now.

But the Hardits stayed around the corner as if waiting for something. Were they inviting the cadets to attack?

Why was no one giving orders? This wasn't a waiting game. It was a race to save his home from obliteration.

"Contact, 90 hostiles," he heard over LBNet.

Confirmation soon came from his tac-display. Out on the moon's surface, the rebels had retaken their trenches and were shooting through the breach and into the bridgehead.

The cadets were pinned down and outnumbered. Surely they had to take the fight to the enemy without delay. And who was nearest to the enemy?

Arun was.

Cold fear struck through Arun's heart. He wanted his combat meds.

Brandt's voice entered Arun's helmet. "Gold Squad will defend the bridgehead. Blue will push through the enemy in the corridor. Blue Delta Section. You're point."

Arun took a deep breath. The moment he reached the turn in the corridor a dozen rifles would fire at him.

"Blue-5, advance along the ceiling," ordered Madge. "Take the corner. Blue-6, give pulse laser covering fire. Aim low. Ready on my mark."

Arun wanted to say something — anything — to Springer. But everything he could think of sounded demoralizing. So he kept his mouth shut and tensed his legs in readiness.

"Wait!" Madge ordered.

Arun didn't understand until he glanced at his tac-display. The Hardits were advancing.

"Fire on my command!"

The last Hardit attack had been hesitant. This time the Hardits came at the cadets in a rush.

Three of them had come round the corner. Five of them. Seven. And they weren't carrying rifles. They had SA-71 carbines. Oh, frakk!

The leading rank of rebels launched grenades.

"Fire!"

As he pressed the trigger to release the laser bolt, the enemy grenades exploded, filling the corridor incredibly quickly with thick smoke. Had the laser shots got off in time before the smoke grenades scattered them to harmlessness?

All he knew was that he couldn't see the end of his barrel, but Barney insisted the Hardits were still coming.

Switching to shardshot, he raked the corridor. He extended his assault teeth too.

The Hardits were firing back. Fragments of the scrubber unit he was sheltering behind flew past his face. He felt a kick in his left chest, just below the collar bone.

Then the firing stopped, all sides unwilling to fire into the fog, fearful of hitting their own side.

Barney used the brief respite to inform Arun that he had been shot. That kick he'd felt was a kinetic dart passing through Arun's body. Barney insisted he'd fixed the suit breach and anesthetized the wound. Nothing to worry about.

Good enough, thought Arun. Out of the choking mist a looming blur rapidly solidified into a Hardit rebel, carbine at the ready.

He — or she — might be better armed than the first line of Hardit defense, but not better trained. The rebel scanned ahead for targets but wasn't looking up at the ceiling.

Arun spun his assault teeth and thrust down in to the rebel's shoulder. *Let's see how you like that!*

The needle-like teeth sank in through the vacsuit, embedding into the soft tissue beyond. Then Arun set the teeth spinning at 1000 rpm, ripping a jagged hole through the suit that released a geyser of pulpy, red spray.

Before the dying Hardit had finished slumping to the floor, another attacker pushed forward through the mist and stumbled over its comrade. Arun jabbed at it with his assault teeth, but the rebel tripped before he could connect, falling headlong. The unexpected motion confused Arun. He missed. More rebels were passing beneath all the time.

The atmosphere scrubbers must be pretty powerful because the smoke was starting to clear.

When they did, they would reveal Arun to be alone in a sea of rebels.

He glanced behind him, convinced he was about to be stabbed in the back.

With a last blind jab from his carbine, he snapped his attention back to his front. No one there either, just the thinning smoke.

Stay still and die. That what the Corps had taught him.

So he moved. Forward.

The closer he got to the end of the corridor, the thinner the smoke got. LBNet was still unavailable. He should probably try WBNet but he'd been ordered not to.

He could see a heap of Hardit dead below him. Around the turn in the corridor, Barney estimated a half dozen rebels — the enemy's final attack wave.

Was he really going to take them on alone?

Arun paused, then dropped down to the floor to plug in an ammo bulb from one of the fallen Hardits. If he going to die doing something stupid, he wasn't going to do so firing pellets of chewed up ore tailings.

"You are another hero, yes?" said a scratchy voice.

Arun looked up to see a Marine on the ceiling: the replacement, Umarov. "More like another idiot, carabinier. Yes."

"Good lad."

Hearing another human voice was all he needed to restore his morale, despite the enemy waiting around the corner. And the army behind them.

Umarov shifted around so he was standing on the right-hand wall of the corridor. "Stand on the wall opposite me," he ordered.

While Arun moved to comply, Umarov dropped his carbine and drew a combat blade in each hand. They were like nothing he'd ever seen: crescent moons attached to either end of a hand grip, the blades glistening with drips of what looked like fluorescent puss.

"Let's see what they make of old-fashioned poisoned carbon. Suppress them until I engage. Go!"

This was it.

Arun ran along the corridor wall, to meet his fate. At the last moment, he told Barney to select rocket rounds. He hadn't many, but they would make more of a show for the untrained rebels.

Then he was rounding the corridor and firing. His finger didn't release from the trigger until the rocket rounds were spent and he was firing kinetic darts so fast that his recoil limiter tripped out.

And still he was running at the Hardits.

Umarov was on them now, limbs extended in a whirlwind dance of cuts and kicks. Killing elegance.

Umarov had their full attention, which meant somehow Arun had survived against all odds.

He extended his assault teeth to join Umarov in the melee.

But the Hardits seemed to be getting farther away, not closer.

And gravity felt as if it were strengthening.

His legs were weakening.

What's happening Barney?

His suit AI brought up a damage summary. Arun had been shot five times. Barney had sealed his suit, but fixing the holes in his master's body was another matter entirely.

But what about the Night Hummer prophecy? I thought the future needed me?

Arun clung to that protest as everything slowed.

And went black.

Chapter 59

A bell rang for Arun, beckoning him to his place in the afterlife.

He hadn't expected this.

To be dead: yes. But afterlife? He'd assumed that was Jotun propaganda.

"Yes, that's it. Welcome back."

The voice came through his helmet speaker. It didn't have the gravitas of a supernatural being. It sounded familiar.

He opened his eyes onto the medic tapping Arun's helmet with her gauntlet. It was Puja, or Lance Corporal Puja Narciso as she'd become. She was Command Section's medic.

He'd had a thing for her in novice school. She'd felt the same way too. Briefly.

She smiled. "I've still got it, ain't I, Arun?"

"I guess so, l… lance—"

"No!" She put a finger to his lips, or as close as his helmet would allow. "Don't 'lance' me. Not yet. You shut up and rest for a minute."

"Am I dying?" Arun croaked. He couldn't feel pain. But his body felt as if all its life-force had leeched away, leaving nothing more than dust held together by a memory of once-strong flesh and bone.

Puja paused, working out her story. She sighed. "You've taken multiple hits. A lot of trauma and blood loss. But I've patched you up and given you a transfusion. Bottom line: Stay in bed. Light duties for minimum three weeks. I'll check up on you in the morning."

"Seriously?"

"Of course not, you donker. We're heavily outnumbered and most of us are already dead. You're good to carry a carbine and that's all you need to know right now. Corporal Majanita can fill you in on the rest in a minute. Just as well you aren't human."

"What do you mean, I'm not human?"

"Well, have you ever studied a pre-Contact medical textbook?"

"No, of course not."

Puja grinned, making her visor transparent so Arun could see. "Good. Don't bother, 'cos you'd be wasting your time. Whatever the hell we are, we aren't *Homo sapiens*, that's for sure. You'd be dead if you were."

Puja's grin, flashing that cute gap between her incisors. Yes, he remembered her smile.

"McEwan?"

He tried to work out where he was, but he couldn't see properly. Hey, did someone say most of them were dead?

"Frakk! Spoke too soon."

He didn't want to think of dead friends.

"Arun. Come back to me, Arun!" begged a memory of a girl who'd for an intense few weeks had meant the universe to him. Puja had been his first kiss. It seemed a lifetime ago. He closed his eyes and dreamed memories of better days, of a teenage girl back in the days when she wore too-tight fatigues, not a poly-ceramalloy battlesuit.

Chapter 60

"You're alive then."

Arun opened his eyes. He was in a room he didn't recognize, his back propped up against something. A lot of people were rushing around. People in battlesuits. And they were glowing vision-enhancement blue because there was very little light. One battlesuit was standing over him. Inside was a woman.

"Puja?"

"Dream time's over, lover boy. I'm not Lance Corporal Narciso." She studied him for a moment. "Do you recognize me?"

The woman made her visor go clear. He squinted at her face. It seemed familiar. "Corporal… You're Corporal Majanita."

"Damn right I am."

"You don't want me."

She laughed. "What I want isn't worth squit. You're in my section and I'm giving you 60 seconds recuperation time before I need you ready to use this." She thrust something into his hands. It was an SA-71 carbine. His carbine.

"Here's the sitrep. We beat off the rebel counterattacks, but it wasn't easy. We've lost half the cadets who dropped from *Yorktown*. Cristina and Osman are both dead but, frankly, we've gotten off lightly. Gold Squad's down to about section strength."

A chill, prickling sensation marched up Arun's spine. *So many dead?*

"Where are we now?" he asked.

"Don't interrupt. We think this is the main control room. We made a mess of the doors coming in, helped by some drills the monkeys were kind enough to leave for us in the bridgehead. Del tried hacking the computer systems but doesn't think that worked. Zug had a brainwave and found power cables running through a conduit in the roof. We cut them. The main lights went out. The power hum in all the machines running here died too."

"But how do we know for certain that we've turned off power to the mass driver? Or the force shield protecting it?"

Madge hesitated. "We don't. We can't raise Force Alpha on WBNet — the monkeys are jamming us. So Brandt's ordered us to stay here. Make sure the monkeys don't sneak in and turn the power back on."

"Shouldn't we try to link up with Force Alpha? At least recon the mass driver?"

"Did God visit you in your dream and promote you to sergeant?"

"No, corporal."

"Then the lance sergeant still outranks you — thank the Fates… I think. And there's this tradition that means you kinda got to do what your superior says. Humor me. It's a Marine thing."

Madge turned away, adding: "One last thing. The base has set up pressure plugs, meaning any pressure loss is sealed automatically by a kind of gradual force field. So we can't repeat the trick of cutting a hole in a door and watch the poor vecks inside tripping over as their air rushes out. And now that we're back in an atmosphere, grenades and blast weapons — they're gonna hurt a whole lot more."

"Those pressure plugs," cut in Zug. "I've studied the theory. Playing with the laws of nature like that doesn't come cheap. Which means there must still be a lot of power running through this base. Power they could re-route to the mass driver."

"Thank you for the interruption," snapped Madge. "Makes me feel a whole lot better. I'll pass it on to the lance sergeant. You worry about keeping your eyes on the northern approach." She kicked Arun's feet. "You too. Recuperation time's over."

Arun tried standing up. There was a slight wobble, no more. There wasn't even any pain. In fact, he felt completely numb except for the tingling sensation of his gauntleted hands gripping his carbine.

Barney's medical summary explained that Arun had been stabilized just this side of death, patched up, and set running again. The reason Arun wasn't collapsing in a swoon was because, instead of using the battlesuit motors to amplify Arun's muscle movements, Barney was pretty much running the suit himself by guessing Arun's intentions. If he were outside of his battlesuit, Arun would probably be in a coma.

But at least he wasn't getting any worse. A near-coma would just have to do.

Arun was behind a huge equipment bank. He imagined it would normally be winking lights, heat and a power hum. Currently it was a cooling metal box. Even in the emergency lighting — putrid green bioluminescence seeping out of the walls — the box looked pretty shot up by the cadet attack. With Barney's guesses helping to make up for the lack of illumination, Arun saw that he was in a 12 by 10 meter rectangular room filled with dead computers, power equipment, and consoles.

There was a door to the north which had been fused shut and then cut through and peeled back from the outside. Must be where the cadets had drilled through. A mound of spent SA-71 sabot casings on the far side of the door told the story of what had transpired.

Corpses were piled up against one wall — human and the more numerous Hardits mixed together.

To the south, a second door was propped open, leading out onto an approach corridor. The Gold Squad survivors were guarding that approach.

Arun's eyes dimmed, his breath quickened. He closed his eyes, felt like he was swaying but he knew Barney wouldn't let him fall. He didn't want to open them. Didn't want to see. Not yet; he was still too weak.

Hiding didn't help, though. He could remember what he'd seen in the tac-display clearly enough to count the Gold Squad dots. There were 8 survivors of the 31 who'd dropped from *Yorktown* just 83 minutes ago. From Blue Squad, 21 had made it this far.

He wanted his heart to feel as numb as the rest of his body, but he felt only aching loss. And Cristina… she was gone too.

A jumble of memories jostled to overwhelm him: happy times with Cristina, of arguments and impossible boasts he'd traded with Osman. He opened his eyes to escape, and tried again to take in his surroundings.

He was crouched alongside Madge and Springer behind the metal-skinned box. The alien writing and dead display screen set into the box told him nothing about its function or inner contents.

Behind a similar box next to them crouched Del, Zug and Umarov.

They were facing the northern corridor approach. They couldn't see it in visual because the boxes were in the way. They didn't need to. If anything came at them from north or south, every cadet would see it on their tac-display. Delta Section would simply leap up, fire, and then drop back down behind cover.

Arun unsnagged his mind from speculating what might be transpiring around the mass driver, and his memories of fallen comrades. He settled his concentration instead onto the dots and wire-frame schematics of Barney's tac-display.

Seconds turned to minutes.

Nothing happened.

Like the training missions where he remained floating in space, keeping watch on the void, once Arun had settled into the rhythm of observation, he could keep his concentration fixed for hours. He'd been bred for this, *engineered*.

So it came as something of a shock when his concentration was broken by someone rapping on his helmet with the barrel of an SA-71 carbine. It was Springer. Her faceplate blanked to transparency, an internal light in her helmet illuminating her features. She smiled. It was forced, but the affection warmed him.

He blanked his own visor, automatically lighting the inside of his helmet. A little glare reflected off the inside of the visor.

Arun was struck by the look of concern that shone out of her eyes like violet jewels.

Springer pursed her lips and blew him a kiss from the inside of her helmet. With faceplates touching so that the sound wave could travel directly into his helmet, he could hear the sound as if from a great depth underwater.

"That was a vac-kiss," she breathed in a voice that Arun found teasingly steamy, but he recognized was the sound of Springer speaking from her heart despite the distortion of speaking faceplate-to-faceplate. "When we get back home," she continued, "I'll give you a real one."

"Then I'd better make sure I stay alive," said Arun, grinning.

"Be sure of it. *No Marine left behind.* They used to take that seriously, you know, those old Marines on Earth. Bryant might laugh at that, but I don't. I can't leave you behind, Arun."

A burst of warmth flooded through Arun, spreading out from his heart and into an uncontrollable grin that filled his face. He fantasized entwining his suit with Springer's. There was an annoyingly rational part of his brain that Arun wished he could turn off, but maybe one day would save his life. Right now it was reminding him that human hormonal responses were dangerously amplified by combat stress, a dangerous side-effect of their re-engineered physiology that would normally be overcome by the use of combat-stim drugs.

A harsh aural assault of white noise made Arun flinch. He brought his free hand to cover his ear. Of course, that made not the slightest difference to the noise attacking him through the speakers inside his helmet.

Arun gritted his teeth and hung on tightly to his sanity until the noise ceased as suddenly as it had hit him. It had lasted six seconds.

"Cut it out, you two," bellowed Majanita inside his helmet. "You're both on a charge. Brandt's seen you. If you two loved-up shunters let yourself be distracted a moment longer, I'll be on a charge too and you will be reported for dereliction of duty. What's wrong with you, Springer? I thought you were too smart to get yourself executed."

Arun and Springer both answered at the same time. "Sorry, corporal."

Even with his attention back on the corridor approach, Arun couldn't eject from his mind the fact that Springer was standing next to him. He imagined he could feel the warmth from her body. A body that if freed from their suits would fit perfectly pressed against his own. His arms would wrap around her, gently squashing her warm flesh against his. Arun's hand would stroke through her mess of auburn curls, moving slowly so as not to pull painfully at her hair, gently untangling. Then his hand would slide down to cup the underswell of her buttock and press his fingertips into her yielding flesh…

He pushed those thoughts far enough away to realize that Majanita was right. His faulty body chemistry was going to get them both shot if he wasn't careful.

Arun let out a long breath and then ordered Barney to administer combat drugs.

He wasn't sure what they were doping the cadets with, but he couldn't shake off memories of the last time he'd been on stims. He'd ended up naked, his image plastered all over Detroit.

What would it do to him this time?

He didn't feel a thing as the meds went in, but then he felt a crust form over his heart. Fantasies of what might be were replaced with obsessively detailed observation of the here and now. Lusty romance evaporated away to leave indifference, which soured into hatred, and finally the need to kill.

"Here we go again," he mumbled.

Combat drugs were unique to each individual. Really they were a cocktail of psychostimulants and endocrine effectors blended to an individual's requirements, and adjusted and tuned after each use. The exercise was made more difficult when administered into a young body still changing through the natural hormones of adolescence.

He tried to hold onto the memory of Springer's kiss, the lilac glow from her beautiful mutant eyes. He could recall the images of Springer with full fidelity, but although he could remember the fact of her love and concern for him, the emotion behind those facts had now drifted far out of reach.

Human emotion had become alien to him.

He wanted to hate that loss but couldn't. All his hatred was aimed at the enemy.

Springer had always looked out for him, ever since that time when he'd stood up for her when they were both ten years old. When the leader of the most vicious girl gang of their year had asked Springer to join, her reply had been to fill the gang leader's bed with steaming porridge, just before bedtime. Springer's other friends had thought that hilarious when the news reached them, but not Arun. He tracked down his missing friend to a disused corridor where he found her surrounded by jeering gang members. Arun stepped in to protect Springer.

His presence made no difference. Both of them were beaten senseless.

When they'd awoken in neighboring infirmary beds, she smiled as best she could through cut and swollen lips and called Arun her hero. It was the first time he'd seen her violet eyes glow, a warmth that stirred his heart. But then she said something that still chilled him: "You cared. You came because you cared. No one else did. No one else could. Thank you for caring."

Even back then, loyalty to the Corps was firmly instilled in all novices. But caring for others was a weakness, and good Marines had no weaknesses. Emotions were being eroded from the human genestock of the Corps. As a little boy, his mother had warned him never to reveal that he cared. But Springer knew his secret.

Arun shut out the memories of Springer and locked them away next to times remembered with Cristina and Osman. He had no need for such weakness.

The drugs had released him from that burden.

Now all that mattered was killing the enemy.

And killing was good.

Without warning, Arun's tac-display vanished, leaving him staring out of a dumb visor of transparent polycarbide at the big block of cold metal in front of him. In the near-dark he could barely make out the edges of the equipment block.

He jumped up, carbine ready, but before he cleared the top of the equipment box, his visor display went completely white. Words appeared on top of the white.

++ TRAINING OVERRIDE ++

++ DO NOT SHOOT! INCOMING MARINES ARE FRIENDLY ++

Was this a trick?

If the rebels could subvert the cadets' suits, then sending messages would be simple. Speaking like a human would be tricky, but any AI could write a simple sentence in any language it knew.

"Hold your fire!" The command came from Brandt, or at least that's what Barney was telling him. Brandt added: "But keep your weapons trained in case this is a deception."

That's all very well for you to say, thought Arun, *but how am I to train my weapon when I can't see out?* Barney anticipated his next thought and informed him that the air was mildly poisonous and would not be easy to breathe, but if Arun wished, the helmet lock could be released so he could take it off and see who was approaching with his naked eyes.

As he was considering whether that was wise, Brandt announced: "I have visual. It's the *Yorktown* Marines. It's Force Alpha."

Arun's faceplate lost its whiteness and his pulse calmed down. On tac-display he saw four new marines had joined LBNet. The double-halo of command had switched from Brandt to Ensign Thunderclaws, a Jotun name if ever he'd heard one. Thunderclaws was bounding toward them from the north like a swift six-legged dog, a creature Arun had seen many times in Earth recordings, though he'd never seen a dog in combat armor.

"I repeat, this is no trick," said Brandt. Frankly, thought Arun, if the rebels could fake a Jotun in a suit then they deserved to win.

"Sir, why did we lose Wide Battle Net?" asked Brandt.

The officer replied: "Our WBNet transmissions had to be bounced off *Yorktown* and boosted in tight beams to punch through Hardit jamming."

Oh, shit, thought Arun. *That meant...*

Brandt asked the question in Arun's head. "Is she lost, sir?"

"Negative," replied the Jotun. "*Yorktown* is evacuating key personnel from orbital platforms. She is merely out of range." The Jotun was speaking through a voicebox machine, sounding identical to Pedro. Arun wondered whether his friendly Trog was going to survive this rebellion, whether he would debate Arun's part in the operation with his usual alien weirdness. He was surprised to find that he looked forward to that talk.

Of course, there was the little matter of Arun surviving the day too.

Arun stood up and took a good look at the Marines coming his way.

There were three of them, in gray battlesuits, though their coloration could change in an instant. Unit insignia marked them as 9th field battalion, 412th Marines — Arun's regiment.

Two of them carried SA-71s, the third an HG-11c machine gun, which was essentially a heavy version of the SA-71 in railgun mode. Kinetic darts fired from the HG-11c reached greater muzzle velocity due to a stronger electrical charge and a much longer barrel, which was braced by a small flip-out bipod rest.

Arun counted four ammo belts slung over the machine gunner's shoulder, each holding scores of magazines, which were blocks of charged metal, pre-stressed to split along ballistic shapes, a little like perforated paper. The ammo alone must weigh well over a hundred pounds. Sometimes Marine armor was used to turn humans into beasts of burden. Unglamorous yet effective.

The machine gunner was coming directly toward Arun. Or, more likely, to take over his position.

Arun stepped back a few paces to allow the machine gunner to select his or her position, but the gunner immediately switched direction to come straight for him.

Arun froze.

"Are you Arun McEwan?" asked the Marine – a corporal according to suit markings – when they were standing toe-to-toe.

"Yes, corporal."

"Blank your visor and let me see your face."

Arun complied, standing at attention while this guy just stared at him.

Arun desperately wanted to query Barney's tac-display to ping this Marine's ID, but he couldn't do that with a blank display.

Then the Marine blanked his own faceplate. That was even worse. The Marine peered at him through bulging eyes tinted an artificial blue. The Marine's face was young — thirty perhaps? — and might have been considered handsome if not for the scar tissue that covered one cheek and cut across his nose and brow. Here was a Marine who had taken a plasma blast to the face and survived.

You didn't get to be a G-2 Marine cadet without knowing how to deal with older kids throwing their weight around. The first rule was to avoid being seen as weak. Then, if you get picked upon anyway, you took it on the chin and waited for payback until you were older.

This guy had probably picked on Arun at random. Singling him out to make an example to the other cadets to remind them who was in charge. But then, why bother? The Marine's eyes stared into space for a moment, as if recalling a precious memory. His face crumpled a little and his lips moved, preparing to say something laden with emotion.

Just before the man could speak, Springer beat him to it. She had checked her tac-display on Arun's behalf.

"Arun, he's your brother. Corporal Fraser McEwan."

But… he thought his brother had died on *Fort Douaumont*. They must have been on *Yorktown* all this time, never having set out. If Arun survived long enough for his combat meds to work their way out of his system, he expected he would feel pleased about that later on.

Fraser looked about to speak but he was interrupted by the Jotun officer. "I salute you human Marine children," said Thunderclaws speaking the human language with his own voice. He switched back to the artificial voice of the translator unit. "You have shut off power to the mass driver. The bombardment has been halted. The force shield protecting it still functions. Half of Force Alpha — three Marines — occupies the attention of the rebel positions near the driver. We have traveled here undetected, entering through the bridgehead you established."

Arun half-expected cheers to ring out. But the other cadets were, like Arun, so drugged up with the need to kill that victory didn't interest them.

"However, the engagement is not over. The rebels are sending an assault force to deal with us. Until this point, you have only encountered annoying little monkeys — not an equal foe. Now you will face their elite. They are still hardly a martial race but you should regard them with a little less than utter contempt."

Had Arun just heard a little light racial abuse directed by one alien species at another in human speech? There was a time, not long ago, when Zug would have been fascinated by that.

Ensign Thunderclaws broke off conversation, gestured at one of the Marines, and turned his attention to some other task. What that task might be, Arun was not privy to.

"I'm Sergeant Rathanjani," said the Marine the ensign had gestured to. "You've done okay for a bunch of kids but you've a shitload to learn. For starters, don't look at me! We're in a battle for frakk's sake. Keep watching the approaches to this room. That's better. Now, here's the sitrep. We estimate 10 to 20 hostiles heading our way. They will be heavily armed and armored, and their objective will be to kill us if they can, but more importantly to pin us while their engineers boot up the secondary power and control systems, and then recommence the bombardment of Tranquility."

"Sergeant," asked Brandt, "what about reinforcements?"

"Don't interrupt, cadet. Anyone else got a stupid question or maybe want a comfort break before I carry on? No? Good. System defense boats ETA two hours. Navy ships in about five. Last I heard, both were still on our side but we've traitors somewhere in the system. Tranquility orbital defense is not set up to bombard our own moon. Anything else that could help was taken out in the initial salvos. It's down to us. If these monkeys keep us pinned down here, then by the time the warboats arrive, you won't have homes to go back to."

"You're still kids," said Arun's brother. "Still believe the crap they teach you in novice school. So let me educate you. We're human Marines. We fight two wars. One is the war that the White Knights give us through their Jotun officers. The other is a longer war, a hard-fought war of attrition and tiny incremental gains that will last centuries. None of us will survive to see this other war end. This is the war for respectability. Whatever bullshit you might hear in Detroit these days, the White Knights only took on we humans as a client race to piss off the Cienju. They're lizard aliens who had taken control of the Earth, and would have enslaved us all to ship them ore from the Solar System. The White Knights don't think of us as being fit enough to clean their sewers. We're only here out in the stars playing Marines as a face-saving measure, to make it look as if the Knights wanted us all along. It's down to all of us at all times to prove to our alien masters bit by tiny bit that we are worthwhile, that we are a surprisingly valuable asset. Because if we don't, then one day they will decide that the Earth and the rest of their empire will be simpler if they were no longer infested with humans. If we are to die today, make sure we die well."

His brother wasn't great with the old motivational, thought Arun. If he weren't in the grip of his combat drugs, his brother's speech would make him want to crawl into a corner, curl up, and await his doom.

The Force Alpha Marines suddenly disappeared. They must have stealthed their suits. The SA-71s attached to their invisible suits disappeared too. But Fraser's machine gun wasn't stealth-capable, hovering in mid-air as if suspended on wires.

"Cadets, keep to Cadet Lance Sergeant Brandt's deployment," said Sergeant Rathanjani. Barney used the sergeant's broadcast to place a fuzzy outline around where he thought the NCO might be. "Force Alpha will operate as mobile reserve," continued the sergeant. "Keep alert. Attack is imminent. And heed Corporal McEwan's words. I know some of you might be a little young to hear the truth, but that's hard shit. Today is the day you grow up. You're all Marines now. If you do die, then die well. That is an order. Good luck."

Chapter 61

The door to the northern approach was still fused shut, but while the humans waited for the attack, Beta Section had used the drills to widen the opening in the door, and then post a picket guard on the far side.

"Incoming! North corridor defenses, prepare to fire."

The warning came from Sergeant Rathanjani. *He must have a better AI than me,* considered Arun because it took another few seconds before Barney picked up the threat on LBNet and threw it up onto Arun's tac-display.

Four rebels were advancing along the northern corridor, still hidden for now beyond the right turn. It almost felt like a re-run of the attacks along the corridor out of the bridgehead room, though with one difference. The rebels were plodding nearer at an astonishingly leisurely pace. Barney was getting firmer data now and was confident enough to show tight red circles to indicate the estimated position of the leading two rebels. Arun didn't get the impression they were moving slowly because they were hesitating.

They simply weren't in any hurry.

Arun decided he was frightened.

It was a weird feeling. He didn't *feel* frightened — all he felt was calm anticipation of killing the enemy – but he knew with conviction that he was scared. It was like watching someone else shaking with fear.

He glanced at Fraser's position. His brother was invisible, but his long-barreled gun was wedged securely in a slot set into an equipment console, and aimed through the opening in the north door. When his brother got to open fire on the rebels, they wouldn't stand a chance.

Then a combat fugue descended on Arun like a cool mist. His universe shrunk to his gun, his tac-display, and the enemy. An enemy he would kill.

The first rebel edged around the turn. LBNet activity flared as the suit AIs of the Marine cadets in the corridor assessed the attacker, firing packets of updated information and assessment at neighboring suits.

The AIs were MPQX-8 units: built on massive parallel quantum architecture and rated a minimum 8 peta decisions per second. That made them decidedly second rate, but plenty fast enough for Barney to start suggesting firing solutions within a tiny fraction of a second. What he wasn't offering were killshots, and that wasn't good enough. Only killing would slake Arun's bloodlust.

Arun sprung into the air, getting above the cover of the equipment bank so he could see the rebels in realsight.

As soon as Arun crested his cover, Barney zoomed his visor viewpoint onto the leading rebel, who had now advanced far enough to face Arun head on.

The rebel wore some seriously heavy armor. He looked like a column of vehicle tires stacked one upon the other, and then partially melted so the bottom was wider than the top.

Arun remembered seeing sections of this armor before — in a broken wooden cargo box on the way to Alabama.

There were no feet and no head in this armored cone, but there were two bulges at the shoulders. Two stubby little tubes ending in gauntlets showed where the hands went. One of those gauntlets held the barrel of a plasma blaster. The stock and trigger were held by a black snake that Barney whispered was the rebel's prehensile tail.

Arun aimed for the tail.

With Barney anticipating his intentions, all Arun needed to do was point his carbine roughly where it was needed and let Barney steady his suit and adjust the position of his hands and arms. As a safety precaution, Arun still had to pull the trigger.

As he did so, he felt a gentle nudge of recoil, and watched Barney register a hit.

The rebel's blaster jerked and then accelerated a ball of plasma out of its barrel — aimed at Arun. But the shot went wide, melting a section of door instead of Arun's head. Before he fell back behind cover, Arun saw the rebel's weapon and tail dance under a hail of fire. The blaster was dropping to the ground now, the enemy's tail whipping back behind its body. A cloud was blooming around the rebel, debris from his disintegrating armor.

An aperture opened in one of the rebel's shoulder bulges and a stream of fire streaked down the corridor, exploding in a ball of energy.

Rocket attack!

The shockwave took hold of Arun while he was still falling back behind cover. It tossed him onto the floor.

He heard a human cry of pain and suddenly remembered that it wasn't just him and the enemy. There were other people here too.

Barney understood his new concern and showed him the cadet casualties out in the corridor. No one in the central control room had been wounded so far. The rockets must be set to low yield, the enemy unwilling as yet to obliterate the equipment in the control room.

Another rocket strike rocked the corridor.

"Aim for the skirt."

A third rocket hit.

"Aim for the skirt!"

By the time Arun had scrambled back onto his feet, Barney had marked the Marines stationed out in the corridor with a red cross. *All dead.*

"We're hurting him!"

It occurred to Arun that he was hearing Corporal Majanita's words. She was important, and he was supposed to pay attention. Battle was so much easier when it was just him, Barney, and the enemy. But Barney had betrayed him, raising the volume of Majanita's words until his helmet rang like a bell.

Damn those combat drugs.

Damn reality without the drugs even more.

Arun gasped, stumbling backward. It felt like waking up suddenly from a nightmare. He shook his head. He felt normal again.

"Aim for the skirt on the lead rebel," Majanita shouted.

Standard doctrine said he should shift to a new firing position after each burst of fire to frustrate enemy counter fire. But the room was too full of Marines to offer opportunities for new cover, and the enemy fire was wild anyway.

More importantly, his urge to kill would not wait.

Arun jumped up again from behind cover and ordered Barney to hold his position, hovering a meter above the ground. He aimed through the thickening cloud of smoke, dust, and armor fragments, at the feet of the rebel, who had now advanced about another four paces toward their room.

Majanita must be right. Behind the blob of armor was a monkey with two legs on the ground and slowly walking the bulky armor their way. There must be at least some space cut away from the armor in front of the monkey's legs, or else the Hardit would trip over. Which meant the armor was thinner there. Probably.

It was the best plan Arun could think of.

Just before he put his first shot into the skirt, he heard a screaming hum of power rise to a crescendo, and unleash in a deafening whine. Barney selectively dampened the noise, which Arun recognized as a heavy-duty linear accelerator powering up and then spitting out a hellfire of spinning rounds. It was his brother opening up.

Arun fired too. Rapid blasts at the enemy's skirt. He left Barney to continue firing while he looked at the other rebels. There were five in total. Two had advanced several more paces toward the room, weathering the hail of fire, uninjured so far. The three at the back were not carrying blasters. They didn't seem to be carrying anything. Other than the low-yield rockets — which he suspected were being used as a distraction — none of the rebels were firing.

"What are they up to?" he asked.

"Don't know. Don't care," replied Majanita. "Just kill them."

And they were. The skirt armor of the first rebel gave way, splitting into a dozen fragments that spun away under the firestorm coming from the humans.

The veterans put grenades into the gap that had opened in the armor. Arun figured that was one enemy down and shifted aim to the next rebel. His brother beat him to it, hammering the rebel with a stream of bullets aimed at his head. The rebel had no faceplate or helmet. Or if he did, it was hidden inside the mound of protective armor that offered no obvious weak spot.

No weakness, except perhaps simple physics and the concept of levers. The rebel either tripped, or the kinetic push from Fraser's fire toppled him over backward.

Arun heard a roar of shared hatred go around LBNet. He didn't join in. He was readying to aim at the three rebels who stood in a line at the rear.

But they had readied their own attack. As one, the rebels were using their dexterous tails sheltered behind their backs to throw metal objects.

Was this a grenade attack? Nerve gas?

Neither held any fear for Arun but the three round disks of metal they'd thrown hadn't been aimed at the Marines. Instead, one flew at the ceiling and two on the wall to either side.

Fraser fired on one of the rebels at the rear. Most of the humans were shooting at the rebel who had just fallen onto his back. Arun aimed at the thing on the ceiling.

An instant before his finger squeezed the trigger, a curtain of shimmering purple fell across the corridor, a force shield emitted from the devices on the walls.

Anything touching the energy barrier flashed instantly into plasma. Arun's round gave a flicker when the energy barrier disintegrated it. Fraser's machine gun rounds gave a ferocious light display but could not punch through.

The fragments of blasted armor flared. So too did the body of the second rebel who had fallen across the path of the energy field. A fist-sized swathe of the Hardit's body, running from shoulder to shoulder, had simply ceased to exist.

Arun was about to shoot through the force shield at the rebels behind, but stopped himself. He'd put such a hail of railgun darts into the armored rebels that his ammo was running low.

"Switch to laser," Brandt ordered. "Concentrate fire on the upper shield generator."

"Negative," countered Sergeant Rathanjani. "That's a 37-P tactical force shield. Save your power, we've nothing that can punch through that."

"At least there is one advantage," added Fraser. "The barrier is unidirectional. We can't fire at them. But they can't fire at us either."

"Unless they switch it off," added the sergeant cheerfully.

This was turning into a disaster.

Arun perched atop the equipment bank he had used for cover. His armored body sank into the deep pile of spent sabots. He watched the surviving rebels shuffle slowly backward and out of sight. With no shots firing into it, the energy curtain calmed. Coils of gold and crimson snaked along its surface until settling into a standing wave. Arun stared entranced at the shimmering energy field, which was framed by a corridor blackened with scorch marks and littered with the ruined corpses of his comrades. The way the rebel bodies lay amid heaps of armor dust on the ground, pointing toward the force shield, looked as if they were abasing themselves in worship of the shield's majesty. It was a horrifically beautiful sight. Arun recorded a high fidelity static image of this view, to appreciate later if he should survive this day.

What is this? he thought. *Are the drugs exciting my sense of artistic appreciation now?*

"Get a squad south," said Thunderclaws through his voicebox. "Their armor is the BA-2-G ground assault model. I know it well. Good frontal armor. Much weaker at the back. Get behind them and take them out."

"Fraser, Beder, with me," ordered Rathanjani. "Brandt, give me your best fire team."

Before Brandt could reply, Barney flashed a new threat alert. This time from the southern approach to the control room.

It was too much for Arun. Something inside him broke.

What are those disgusting three-eyed monkeys up to now? If I could just pry those frakking cowards out of their frakking armor, I'd rip their stinking fur off. And they do stink, I know them. I hate them. I wanna kill them all. Medical alert. Come here! Let me kill the frakking… frakking… Emergency cognitive sequester… Pound them! Pound 'em! How do you like that, eh? Smash the monkey bitch vecks. Every… single… last… frakking… Sequestering NOW!

Arun was alone.

He was nowhere.

He'd been angry. Yes, that was it. Run straight into the Hardit troops and beat the life-force out of them with his bare hands.

Or had he imagined that?

If he'd been running then he should have remembered seeing the room speed by. He remembered nothing like that. Couldn't remember his fists pounding alien flesh. Couldn't recall anything except anger… and argument. With Barney?

Barney, are you there?

He was a Marine — at home in the vacuum. But this was true void.

He had no existence.

Only a memory.

He clung to that memory and held on tight. He didn't want to die.

He was Arun McEwan. If he forgot that, there was no one else to remember he had ever been. There would be nothing left to rescue.

Minutes turned to months. Years stretched and thinned to become pale decades of oblivion.

Once there had been a universe and he had lived within. Time had passed there in a way he could comprehend. Night had followed day. Cause led to effect.

Now he was cast adrift in a timelike infinity. He told stories of himself, desperate to keep his memory alive because memory was all he was. For a long time he told stories about others too, but then he realized the cold truth. Those others… he'd only dreamed them.

Relentless eons of time eroded his stories, leaving weathered husks, mere rumors of a physical existence: color, heat, life. Love.

Finally, even those last nubs of memory wore away and he drifted in the nothingness. He just *was*.

Then… a change.

Still there was nothing here. No sounds. No sights. The utter void. And yet the void was bounded in a way he could not fully describe, except that boundary was *shrinking*.

Time had no measure here. A second. A century. They were the same. But time had gained one property. Time had a direction now, and it was running backward. Effect led to cause. Day preceded night.

Time was accelerating in its backward surge.

Light returned. He was moving from darkness to light. He remembered color and searched for it, but there was none.

Then taste returned.

Oblivion was hurtling at breakneck speed and tasted of bitterness and spit.

He sped through the barrier of light and out into the physical universe.

He sucked in stale air and felt it chill his teeth as he drew it in and *breathed!*

"Corporal! It's McEwan."

"What the hell's up with him now?"

"Dunno. He just, *shuddered*."

There was movement nearby.

"Arun! Arun, can you hear me?"

Arun opened his eyes and looked through Springer's blanked visor and onto her face. Her eyes gleamed with concern. He had seen this sight before. Did that mean he was still dreaming? It had been such a *long* dream.

"Arun, it's me."

"Springer?"

"Yes. Oh, yes. You've been acting weird for about ten minutes. I thought I'd lost you for good."

"I'm sorry."

"Shhh!" Springer nudged her faceplate against Arun's to speak in private. "Del thinks your suit AI shut down your consciousness and took control. We didn't want to ask the veterans if that was possible because…" She whispered. "It wouldn't look good on your record."

Arun backed away from his comrade. "I'm sorry. I'm so sorry."

"Shut up, McEwan," snapped Madge.

"Don't be sorry," added Springer, irritated but not without sympathy. "I've forgiven you."

"I know," said Arun. "I'm not saying sorry to you, violet eyes, but to all of you. To my family, the Corps. I worry too much. You know I do. I feel too much. I can't shut out my humanity and become a combat machine. Hortez should've had my place in the Corps. LaSalle. Even Adrienne Miller or the lowest Aux. I don't deserve to carry this SA-71. I'm not a Marine."

It was only when Brandt and the veterans turned to stare at him that Arun realized he'd spoken out loud. His secrets spilling out from his gut because something had torn, and he couldn't hold them in. He was overwhelmed by the emotions of love and loyalty and the sense that he had betrayed himself and everyone around him. If only he'd not given into his obsession with Xin. If only he'd loved Springer back as she deserved.

Arun sobbed. Thoughts of what should and could have been grew heavier until the burden was too great for his shoulders. He shrank into a clumsy fetal ball, cowering on the floor.

People were trying to talk to him, but he couldn't understand. Someone peered into his face, but he shut his eyes.

A little lucidity returned. Enough to hear what Sergeant Rathanjani was saying. "I don't care whether his mind's been sequestered. I've heard enough," said the sergeant. "Shoot this cadet. I'm sorry, Fraser. I don't know whether its cowardice in the face of the enemy or combat shock. Either way, he's a liability."

"Understood."

"I don't want that cadet dead," said Thunderclaws.

Even Arun could feel the charge of surprise explode through the room. Why would a Jotun waste time with a single, unimportant cadet?

"It's his combat meds," said Fraser, "They used to do the same to me before my implants took. I know what to do. I'll make sure he's never a problem again. Come here, brother. This won't hurt."

"Quickly!" snapped Thunderclaws. "We're wasting time."

Arun stood before his brother.

"Take off your helmet," said Fraser.

Arun did as he was told. Frakk! It was cold. He took a breath. The air tasted tainted with poisons and burned his lungs with its chill.

Meanwhile Fraser had removed his gauntlet and was sneaking his hand inside Arun's clothing until he could press his palm against Arun's bare neck.

"They told you I was your brother, didn't they?" asked Fraser, using a speaker mounted in his helmet to communicate.

Arun nodded.

"Knowing the Jotuns, they never told you I am your *twin* brother."

Did that matter at this point? wondered Arun. The question seemed to consume Arun in a recursive spiral until, when his legs buckled and he slipped out of consciousness, he barely noticed.

Chapter 62

Arun had no clear idea of what the afterlife would be like. Some Marines claimed to have preserved religious teachings from Old Earth, but he was suspicious of anything claimed to be from the home planet. The Jotuns freely provided what they said were copies of religious texts from Earth. He was doubly suspicious of that.

Soon after he'd first witnessed an execution, Arun found himself drawn to the array of temples to be found in Detroit, curious about religion for the first time.

Now he found himself floating in a sky of gold and crimson swirls. Was this purgatory? He tried to remember his religious teachings.

The memories of those visits to the temples came easily to him. He was *thinking*… his mind spinning furiously like a freewheeling supercomputer searching for a problem to solve.

That didn't sound like purgatory. Maybe this was *bardo* — the in-between state.

Then a bright light came into being in front of his eyes. It seemed to beckon him. A destiny awaited Arun, some problem that he knew only he could solve.

He opened his eyes but immediately squeezed them shut. The light was blinding.

"And he's back."

The words used his brother's voice. The light dimmed and Arun opened his eyes cautiously.

He was still in the control room of the mining base, his feet dangling helplessly in the air and held in his brother's arms. His brother was hovering near the ceiling.

Alongside, Stopcock was cradling a captured drilling machine in his arms as if he were hugging a pet quadruped. The device looked like a miniature tank with four stubby legs and a conical drill for a head.

Arun's helmet was back on, pressure seals locked.

"Welcome back, Cadet Prong," laughed Madge.

"I think he had to come back to us because he was missing his Troggie boyfriend," suggested Del-Marie. "In any case, Corporal McEwan assures me you won't keep winking out on us. No more swooning for you, boy. You're fixed"

"Not quite," said Fraser. "You may need to ask your suit AI to remind you of orders because your short-term memory is going to be shot to crap while my nanites fix you. Other than that, you'll function fine but you won't remember a thing."

"But don't expect us to forget what you said while you were delirious," added Del-Marie.

"Or what you do next," said Madge.

Springer, Arun noticed, said nothing.

"If you've quite finished…" growled Sergeant Rathanjani, though Arun sensed amusement in his voice. "All teams ready to execute on my mark… Go!"

At ground level, the sergeant led his team in a decoy attack to the south.

Fraser counted to five and then pointed to Stopcock, who activated his drill. The cutting teeth on its nose cone whirled into a blur and a pale blue lance of light erupted from its tip, the distinctive color of a Fermi beam operating in atmosphere. At the focus point of the beam, the laws of sub-atomic physics were thrown out of the airlock. The matter in the ceiling was reduced to a squirming mess, easily gouged away by the drill teeth in a shower of trailings.

Four seconds later, the roof was breached and all the air in the room was racing to escape out into vacuum outside, trying to suck Arun out with it.

That was all Arun could remember.

Fraser McEwan, it transpired, had experimental augmentations. Hormonal factories had been implanted subcutaneously, intended to solve the problems with combat drugs by making them self-administered and tuned by bio-feedback.

There was a secondary purpose too. Human Marines and crewmembers could go for tours of decades or even centuries without leaving their ships.

Troopships were not spacious. Depression, violence and other psychoses grew commonplace as lengthy tours outstripped anything evolution had prepared humans for in terms of living together in cramped conditions. The implants aimed to upgrade the very nature of human society by allowing a direct communication of moods and simple information between individuals by touching implants to the skin of another human, and using the hormonal nano-transporters to travel into the other person's system.

This *gifting*, as the Marines called it, was new and it was experimental but it worked. Fraser's biology was close enough to his twin's that he could purge the combat drugs that were messing with his head, and replace with something far better tuned to Arun's physiology than anything that Detroit's medical staff could supply.

Fraser had been right about the side effect on his memory as Fraser's nanites battled Detroit's combat drugs.

Arun remembered nothing. He had to rely on his surviving comrades to explain the events afterward. Given the number of wounds he'd taken, Arun felt lucky to be alive, his periods of unconsciousness no cause for shame. Not his surviving comrades, though, who found Arun's progress through the battle to be a constant source of amusement. They even named the engagement after him.

To the survivors, it would forever be known as the Battle of the Swoons.

About the time Fraser's nanites were temporarily destroying Arun's short-term memory, the assault force that contained both McEwans was scurrying away across the roof of the base. Wide Battle Net was being jammed by the rebels, but the loss of comms affected the enemy too. The thirteen heavily armored rebels were vulnerable to being cut off from each other. Fraser exploited this, making hit and run raids, drilling through walls, and surprising the enemy detachments from behind before the slow-moving rebels could turn in their bulky armor and fight back.

Arun had a brainwave. When Force McEwan sneaked back into the building via the breach they had first cut into the wall from the outside, they had found Osman still hanging upside down. Arun removed his comrade from his suit, laying him to rest in gravity's embrace, but dragging Osman's suit with him. Corporal McEwan had a more advanced form of battlesuit, one able to switch his visor to share the view anyone in his command was seeing at the time. Even dead members of his command. They'd left Osman's body behind, but his suit AI was still on active duty, buried in an armored band across the chest of his suit.

Osman's helmet and suit AI made a perfect scout, peering around corners as they played cat and mouse games with the rebels through the maze of corridors, always trying to hit the armored rebels from their lightly armored rear.

Arun remembered none of this. His first dim recollection was of their attack on the secondary control room.

The main objective of the Hardits in their heavy armor was to keep the humans pinned down while their engineers could boot up the secondary control room and re-route power to the mass driver, recommencing the bombardment before the system defense boats blew them off the face of Antilles.

The Hardits had been only a whisker away from completion when Stopcock cut through the wall, allowing Arun, Majanita and Springer to rush through while the rest of Force McEwan was pinning down the enemy fighters tasked with defending the room.

The engineers surrendered immediately, complying without hesitation when Majanita ordered them to kneel with hands on heads.

When Corporal McEwan joined them, he began shooting the prisoners and ordered the others to do the same.

Majanita complained that this was murder, and Arun could remember Fraser's reply clearly. "Murder suggests the rule of law, but in war there are no rules, there is no law. There are only winners and losers. Murder? What authority declares one action to be acceptable in wartime and another to be murder? Such a body doesn't exist."

Majanita told Arun later that Fraser had been calm throughout the rest of the battle. But when he shot the prisoners, he was impatient, as if he didn't want to give them a chance to talk. But what could the Hardits say that Arun's brother didn't want to be heard? It made no sense.

Had Arun obeyed and shot the unarmed Hardit technicians? He didn't ask, and no one offered to tell him.

Perhaps the events with the prisoners troubled him so much that his brain commandeered all of its limited capability to record them. He had no memory of the skirmishes and raids that followed; of the victories and casualties, he knew nothing.

It wasn't until the final firefight that an image seared across his mind so vividly that it overcame all forgetfulness.

He was running, his breath hot in his helmet, his vision fogging with the exertion. Stabbing pains jolted up his legs and into his ribs, his head. Everything hurt because Arun's body was screaming its need to shut down and die, but Arun was forcing himself beyond the limit of endurance. And all because there ahead of him, on the edge of a heap of bodies blocking the blood-slicked corridor, lay Springer.

She'd been caught in a lethal rocket blast and now she was down with her lower leg blown off. Below the knee, her suit was growing an emergency seal, simultaneously fusing shut the spray of Springer's arterial blood.

"Get back, Cadet McEwan!"

The order came from Ensign Thunderclaws.

For the first time in his life, Arun disobeyed a Jotun.

Springer was down. There wasn't time to explain to the officer why that mattered so much.

Arun blacked out.

When he came to, he found he'd only been out for three seconds. Loyal, clever Barney had kept him moving forward. Arun was now coming down into a crouch over his wounded comrade. His wheezing gasps were bubbling, leaving the taste of blood on his lips.

He checked Springer's suit integrity and requested a medical update from her suit AI. She was stable, it told him, but she couldn't take any more damage. Arun had to get her away.

That was when his fogged-up brain remembered he was in a firefight.

He glanced up at the Hardit defender who'd unleashed the volley of rocket fire. He was still standing there in his huge battle armor, being blasted at by the Marines, like a titan wreathed in fire. His rocket launchers were ruined and his armor near blasted away. But behind him two more titans were turning around, ready to launch everything they had at the humans.

Where once they had set their rockets to low yield to avoid damaging their vital equipment, now they were cornered and desperate to take as much human life as they could.

Where was his carbine?

Arun tried to remember what had happened to it, but the corridor was a mess of debris and blinding flashes.

The Hardit titans had nearly turned around.

Arun picked up Springer to carry her to safety.

But after he'd lifted her only a few inches, his vision swam so furiously that he had to set her back down.

How did she get to be so heavy?

The officer's voice came loud into his helmet. "Curse you, human."

Arun looked behind at the Jotun. Thunderclaws was ten meters away, in a small group of Marines in open order. He watched as the seven-foot tall hexaped dropped his weapon and closed the gap between them in an astonishing burst of speed.

A quick bunching of six limbs and Thunderclaws was tumbling up through the air, but he'd overshot - - aiming for a bruising impact against the ceiling. When the officer slammed into the roof, Arun saw that this was all part of his maneuver, two limbs pushing gracefully against the ceiling and sending the bulky armored alien down to land… directly on top of Arun!

In the moment before the Jotun thumped down on top of him, Arun got on all fours over Springer, trying to shield her with his body.

A crushing weight fell over Arun, leaving him spread-eagled over his wounded buddy.

He found he was still alive, though, still breathing because the officer had extended all six limbs, using them like pillars to support the shield that was the Jotun's body.

Hardit explosions engulfed them.

Arun felt them as a white flare that seared every molecule in his body.

He should have died. He would have, a dozen times over today, if he had been a mere human. The White Knights, or their bio-engineers, had made him something far stronger than human, but Arun could push his battered body no further.

Barney could, though.

Now that the corrupting combat drugs had largely been scoured from Arun's body, Barney could implement the standing order to keep badly wounded Marines conscious. The suit AI refused to allow Arun the easy escape of slipping into blackness.

This wasn't kindness. A conscious Marine had a higher chance of staying alive long enough for a medic to reach him.

Around him, the battle raged on.

Arun's body persisted. His visor was smeared in blood. He was crushed under the bulk of Ensign Thunderclaws, unable to move his suit. The only movement from Thunderclaws was his alien blood flowing over Arun like a crimson waterfall.

Barney tried to show him a zoomed-out tactical display, but Arun's mind had been beaten up even more than his body and his thoughts shied away from the fighting.

Arun was alive and conscious, but his battle was finally over.

His comrades would have to handle the rest without him.

PART V
A Promise Made Good

Human Legion INFOPEDIA

Key concepts
—The regimental system

The earliest regimental system originated in the Earth continent of Europe a development of that continent's first nation states: France and England. An English regiment of the 18th century British Army, for example, would typically have three battalions. A 1st battalion of the best men and equipment would fight overseas in the continental European wars. The 2nd battalion remained in England to defend the home country. A further depot battalion billeted at the home base would train and equip new recruits, sending a stream of replacements out to the main two battalions and possibly perform garrison duties. The depot battalion would often be little more than an administrative concept, manned by a scattering of accountants, invalided veterans, and the idle rich masquerading as officers.

When the army needed to be expanded rapidly to meet the demands of a new war, all the government needed to do was raise additional battalions for the existing regiments.

The regimental system set up for the Human Marine Corps had to cope with completely different needs.

The Human Marine Corps was mostly employed in the Eighth Frontier War, a series of fluid probes and parries by the Muryani and Amilx around lightly held, minor systems situated 10-40 light years from Tranquility.

When the depot battalion in France or England sent out replacements, they would reach the front line battalion within a few weeks. But if the two depots on the planet of Tranquility sent out similar streams of replacements to frontline battalions, the journey would be not weeks but decades. European replacements could sometimes take months chasing down their battalions in a fast-moving campaign. At modern distances of light-years, and transportation cruising speed typically half the speed of light, the problem of straggling replacements looking for their unit would make the whole depot system a joke.

So instead of sending small streams of replacements to the front, fully formed companies or battalions were sent instead. As the strength of frontline units depleted due to losses, they merged and merged again. Veterans with leadership capability were sent back to leaven the green cadet battalions with a few experienced Marines.

As for the problem of how to expand the army in the face of a crisis, the Human Marine Corps solved this by constructing reservoirs of cryogenically frozen Marines to be thawed out when needed. Indeed, it has often been speculated that the only purpose of sending the Tranquility battalions to the frontier was to experiment with human military units under battlefield conditions. Any military contribution to the Eighth Frontier War was coincidental. The main purpose of Tranquility was really to breed and freeze huge armies of loyal Marines who would be thawed and retrained to the latest standards when a major war sprang up.

Detroit alone was thought by some authorities to store over four million frozen Marines, each in a cryo box designed to be shielded from cosmic rays and micrometeorites and magnetized so the boxes would clamp together.

Transport ships would have towed these boxes in their millions between the stars.

It would have been an astonishing sight, like city-sized reefs of frogspawn glittering occasionally in the dark of space.

This topic entry has mentioned the Human Marine Corps, but what about the Human Legion? At this stage in the Human Legion's development, the administrative policies for battlefield replacements are something for the future, but for our human warriors, at least, no one has suggested a better approach than that used at Tranquility.

Until someone devises a better system, it looks as if the regimental system, originating from Earth's ancient history, will spread through the galaxy for millennia to come.

Chapter 63

As soon as Staff Sergeant Bryant strapped himself into his harness he gave a thumbs up to the camera. The shuttle eased away from the orbital elevator dock without delay. Destination: the as-yet unnamed human-Trog base under construction on Antilles.

Arun and two former Gold Squad cadets were sitting on the bench set against the opposite bulkhead. The cadets had all been wounded in the attack on Antilles, and were hitching a ride back there, back to their new posting on the moon.

Bryant took his time to size up the cadets.

"You did well, Cascella," said the NCO. "You too, Abramovski. I read how you were quite the marksman, picking off enemy leaders rallying their troops to counter-attack through the bridgehead. I expect every Marine to be an expert with the SA-71, but it takes special aptitude to be a sniper. If we weren't dumping you on this frakking moon, I'd put you in for sniper assessment. I haven't the authority to get you back to Detroit, but I've made a note on your record recommending you for assessment if you do return."

"Thank you, Staff," said Abramovski coldly. Arun had liked the pale-haired girl back in novice school. She had a big heart and warm eyes, but the instant she was in the presence of a superior, her face became as unyielding as ceramalloy.

"You keep your thanks in reserve, cadet. A sniper's role is not easy." Bryant paused. "I'll say it once more. I'm proud of you two." He didn't just say the words, he glowed with so much pleasure that enemy targeting systems would mark the shuttle out as having a hot payload.

To their credit, Arun's two new cadet squadmates – even Abramovski – glanced at him with embarrassment on their faces when Bryant proceeded to ask them about their injuries and treatment. Arun didn't exist for Bryant. The senior NCO utterly blanked him, which wounded Arun deeply. After risking his life to save Springer, having put himself in the line of fire alongside his comrades, hadn't he earned enough respect to be acknowledged as existing?

Clearly not to Bryant.

Waiting for Arun on Antilles was a place in the new Indigo Squad, formed from the survivors of Blue and Gold. Would they treat him any better?

Arun turned his head away from Bryant and set his mind back to earlier that day when the medics had let him look in on Springer. She was still in an induced coma, looking scarred but peaceful, wrapped in clear sheeting like a logistics package. He'd found it difficult to believe but they'd told him she would follow in a few weeks.

Springer would never blank him. He'd done right by his buddy.

That was good enough for him.

Frakk the rest of them.

An hour later, Arun was on the parade deck, looking for his place in Indigo Squad's lineup. Not an easy task, because other than electric lamps directed at the front of the deck, where the officers would stand, the only illumination was a dim bio-lume red oozing up from the floor. The *parade deck* was actually a cavern literally chewed out from under Antilles' rocky crust.

How had the Trogs managed to construct all this? Just three weeks earlier, Arun had been fighting a battle about a klick from here. The dead moon of Antilles had no plant roots, water, rotting vegetation or even weather — none of the things that would produce soil on a living planet. Under a layer of powdery dust, the moon was made of cold, hard rock. But the floors and walls looked the same as the packed soil tunnels of the Troggie nest where Arun's adventures had begun. He looked again. Perhaps the walls were a slightly grayer color, and the caverns in Tranquility hadn't had those stone columns supporting the vaulted roof. It was difficult to say in the ruddy gloom that rose from the floor, transforming a parade of human cadets into something that looked more like a demonic horde assembling in the fiery depths of hell.

But his eyes soon recalibrated for the light conditions, and he found his place in the line. Madge was now leading a new Delta Section. Zug, Del and Umarov were in that section, along with two survivors from Gold Squad: a stocky girl called Azinza Sadri, and Kolenja Abramovski whom Bryant had recommended for sniper training.

There was a space left for Springer.

He thought of Cristina and Osman. There were no spaces left for them.

"Welcome back, friend," whispered Zug as Arun pushed past.

Madge ignored Zug's infraction of speaking while on parade. "Park yourself at the end of the line, McEwan," she ordered. "And for frakk's sake, try to keep out of trouble."

By the time Arun had taken his place, the two senior figures inspecting the parade were taking theirs.

Bryant was there wearing an expression like a plasma bomb two seconds from going off. He trailed half a pace behind the commanding officer. Arun didn't blame Bryant because the new ruler of all personnel on Antilles — including Hardits and humans — was a Trog!

For a moment, his heart leaped when the insect-like creature curled his antennae in faint amusement, just like Pedro used to. It couldn't be Pedro, though. Surely not. Because this was a Trog at a different stage of their weird lifecycle.

He missed Pedro's excitable nature, his playfulness. This Trog commander was very different. For a start it was much larger, almost struggling with the weight of its body. Unlike Pedro's gleaming carapace the commander's abdomen was a barrel of blisters. Dead skin — or chitin, or whatever the big aliens were made from — sloughed off as the commander walked, leaving a scabrous trail on the floor.

The alien reared up on its hind legs and surveyed the paraded humans through eyes that were milky and red-lined where Pedro's had been gleaming black jewels.

It spoke through a voicebox device that hung loosely from its neck. "Humans need ritual," it said in that familiar approximation of human speech. "I give you a ritual of welcome. And a token of our thanks."

Something made Arun snap a glance at the ceiling, noticing that half of Indigo Squad was doing the same. He started, the roof was about to collapse, crushing the life from them. But instead of death from above came… scents! Pleasant odors. Evocative ones all mixed together in a way that made no sense at all, but were astonishingly beautiful. Taking a deep breath, and closing his eyes, the smells transported Arun to ripe topside fields bathed in golden sunshine. At the same time he imagined the rich security and comfort of warm blanket on a cold night. His blanket was shared with the spicy scent of a lover impatient for his touch.

He knew the Trogs experienced the universe through smell, but Pedro had never hinted that they could do this. Arun didn't have the words to describe what the aliens were doing, and frankly he didn't want them. The experience was magic. And magic was a treasure better experienced than explained.

All too quickly, the smells dissipated. Arun opened his eyes, and once more they were an underground assembly of 34 cadets, with Sergeant Gupta lined up beside the front rank.

"I see from your facial expressions that our gift was well received," said the Trog commander. "We are pleased. In time we will grow nest warriors of our own, but that is many years away. Until then, this moon will be garrisoned by humans. You are the first human warriors to take on that responsibility. As of this moment you are re-designated soldiers of the 1st Antilles Brigade."

Bryant's face was so pinched that it looked about to turn itself inside out.

"I am not a warrior," continued the alien, ignoring the staff sergeant's disgust. "I am not a general. I was a scribe until very recently, a role that you do not have in your Marine Corps, but means I was a seeker of understanding. I understand that human warriors need the comfort of a chain of command. Whom must they obey and who must obey them? Your colonel has agreed that I shall take the rank of captain. You humans also want everyone you meet to have sex. Therefore, I designate myself male, and take the human rank-role-identification as Captain Pedro, Governor of Antilles and Great Parent of the Antilles Nest."

Arun peered intently at this Captain Pedro. *Could this really be Arun's friend reborn?*

"Colonel Little Scar has also agreed to reinforce you with another squad of cadets from your battalion. They shall be a little more experienced, being one training year ahead of you."

Arun's heart skipped a beat. Pedro loved to interfere and knew all too well of Arun's interest in one particular cadet in the year above. It *had* to be his Pedro.

But to share a distant posting on a silvered moon… It sounded like some romantic drent out of old Earth, but if that was what Pedro was angling for, Arun wasn't convinced it would end well.

"As some may know, I learned much about humans from my friend Cadet McEwan. Now that I am a great parent, I have no time for luxury. No time for friends. Soon I shall select scribes to continue my work in exploring what it is to be human, so that we may aid each other in the future. McEwan's special role is at an end, but as token of appreciation, I have decided to let him choose which squad will join you."

You conniving little veck. Pedro had set him up. *Do I choose Xin or not? She'll hate me if I do, but… but Pedro's brought her within my reach!* The lingering effect of the Troggie scent magic teased Arun's mind with the illusion that Xin was waiting for him, just out of sight… underneath that illusory blanket.

"What is your answer?" Pedro prompted, pointing a limb at Arun.

"Thank you, sir. However, I regret to say that we have a chain of command for making decisions. I defer my choice. It is Sergeant Gupta's to make."

Pedro flicked his antennae back. His body might look different, but his gesture of anger was unchanged. "With my people, to refuse a gift dishonors the one who bestows the gift. Is this so with humans too?"

"Yes, sir."

"Then do not dishonor me! The decision is yours to make alone. If you refuse then I shall decide for you. You have 20 seconds."

Skangat! Arun guessed whom Pedro would pick. Well, he wasn't going to get his way this time. "Sir. I select Baker Company, Bolt Squad."

Pedro froze. Arun felt the insect regarded him out of those watery eyes as the silence stretched on. Why had he picked the Bolters? He knew a few cadets in the squad but none of them well. He'd always liked the unusual name, and the lightning bolt emblem. The most important thing about Bolt Squad was that Xin wasn't in it.

"Very well," said Pedro eventually. "I have noted your choice. Bolt Squad it shall be." He jigged his antennae in agitation. "To my brave human warriors of the 1st Antilles Brigade, I say again: welcome, and serve well."

The humans saluted as their new commander limped out of the parade deck.

Once Captain Pedro was out of sight, Arun thought Bryant would say his piece, but all he could manage was to glower at the cadets. He appeared at a loss for words, not exactly a state Arun associated with veteran NCOs. In the end all he could say was, "What a steaming pile of crap," before shaking his head in disbelief.

"There should be an officer handling this kind of ceremonial drent," said Bryant. "The Jotuns love parades but... Well, you can tell by their absence what they think of this Antilles garrison. This 1st Brigade nonsense. We'll continue your training as best we can. I've managed to rustle you up an orbital training environment for 48 hours, but training facilities from now on are ad hoc, make do, and only if you're lucky. Sergeant Gupta has very capable hands, but they can't practice magic. Isn't that right, Sergeant?"

"No such word as *can't*, Staff Sergeant," replied Gupta, who was standing to the left of the front line.

That won a half-smile from Bryant. "Even so, I want you back in Detroit where you belong. We have plenty of trained Marines to thaw out if we need a garrison, and a regiment of engineers to build the facilities. However, Sergeant Bissinger says we should play nice with the Trogs for now. Apparently the Trog *officer*"—the way Bryant screwed his face made it plain what he thought of Pedro's place in the chain of command— "has specifically requested that the garrison should comprise cadets because *their minds are more flexible.*" He sniffed as if assaulted by a particularly offensive odor. "Needless to say, those are not my choice of words. Nonetheless, you are here. I do not know whether you will ever graduate as Marines or re-integrate with the rest of Charlie Company. However, I am certain of two things.

"One. You are Marine cadets and represent the Corps on this moon. You will uphold the honor of your regiment and fulfill your mission to the best of your abilities. That mission is to prevent another insurrection. There are over seventeen thousand Hardit miners on this moon. The ore shipments launched from Antilles and elsewhere in this star system are the vital pulse of the regional economy. You will ensure those deliveries continue."

The staff sergeant peered at the cadets as if searching. Then Bryant's gaze found its target: Arun!

Bryant continued. "Two. Your brothers and sisters who fell here did so with honor. With one exception, you are not to blame for being posted here. I do, however, know the one individual who deserves blame. Cadet Arun McEwan, come forward!"

Arun marched with leaden legs to stand before Bryant. He felt the pressure of all those eyes staring at his back as he snapped a salute.

"Sergeant Bissinger has forbidden me to throw you out of the Corps. You can thank your alien supporters for that." He started circling around Arun, a predator seeking a weak spot. "You could, however, quit voluntarily. Will you quit, cadet?"

"No, staff sergeant."

"Due to your overactive sense of justice, I had to send two good cadets to join the Aux for a week. They were lucky to make it back. It was you, McEwan, who put your sisters in harm's way. I ask again, will you quit?"

"No, staff sergeant."

Bryant halted, and leaned in. Arun could feel the sergeant's breath on the back of his left ear.

"Hortez!" Bryant bellowed loud enough to make Arun flinch. "LaSalle! Two good young men dead. Cause of death? The colonel's punishment after you lost your mind during a training exercise, because you weren't Marine enough to handle combat stims. Will you leave the Corps and allow someone better than you to take your place?"

Arun paused. It was getting harder to say no. He hadn't thought about Hortez for days now. That was shameful. "No, staff sergeant," he said, but he knew his voice lacked conviction.

"About face!"

Arun turned around to face his comrades. Now he could see the 34 pairs of eyes all focused on him, malevolent beams of contempt in the hellish parade deck.

"No one escapes the Cull," Bryant told the assembly. "Not even on this godforsaken moon. If the battalion is in the Cull Zone in your graduation year, then you will be considered for decimation no matter where you are stationed. Some of you in Indigo Squad were forced to fire upon your battalion brothers and sisters in the recent Cull. It was you, McEwan, who ensured our battalion was chosen to endure that grief. Their blood on your hands. You brought the shame on our regiment that pushed those cadets into the Cull Zone. Do you still believe you deserve a place amongst your brothers and sisters you see before you?"

Bryant spoke cleanly and calmly, without rancor. His words, though, were barbed and tipped with the most agonizing poison of all: the truth.

The past few months had been a hellish sequence of vulley-ups and bad luck. Arun hadn't deserved much of it, but he'd been the cause all the same. Back when all this crap had kicked off, the freshly minted Cadet Arun McEwan would have looked into the faces of his brothers and sisters and caved.

The staff sergeant was waiting for Arun's reply. So too were his Indigo Squad comrades.

Now that Arun's eyes were adjusting to the hell-light, he saw the Indigo Squad faces looked supportive, not contemptuous. And he'd grown up these past weeks. No longer was he just some kid trying to fit in, he had a destiny. If there was the slightest chance that his future lay with a Human Legion fighting for freedom, then that was worth the price others had paid. And more. Far more.

"Well, McEwan? What is it to be? Do you deserve your place in their ranks?"

He'd made solemn oaths. To the Night Hummer to protect its species, and to the Culled cadets to avenge their deaths. Was his word good?

Yes, it was!

"Yes, staff sergeant. My place is with them. One day I will make you proud."

"Very well, you may return to your place."

As Arun marched back to his place, Bryant addressed the squad. "The training shuttle departs Docking Bay 2 at 16:20. McEwan?"

"Yes, staff sergeant."

"Be at Docking Bay 1 at 16:10. For this exercise, you're coming with me."

Chapter 64

With a protesting screech of its hull, the shuttle braked suddenly. The deceleration tested the harnesses of the two armored occupants of the passenger compartment, yanking them up off the bench, trying to dash their brains against the overhead.

But the shuttle was configured as a troop carrier. The harnesses were good for far more extreme stresses, and the bulkheads had already folded out of sight before Staff Sergeant Bryant had finished shouting: "Out!"

Arun slammed the harness release and pushed away. Less than two seconds later, Arun and Bryant had deployed, SA-71 carbines at the ready, and the shuttle was already blasting away.

The shuttle had braked but not to a stop. Arun had been taught long ago that there was no such thing as being at rest in space. Everything moved in relation to something else; you had to frame an inertial reference based on what was important.

Of maximum importance right now was the target of this void deployment exercise: a signal buoy orbiting Antilles. A quick check with Barney showed the shuttle had bequeathed them a textbook 3 klicks per second velocity directed at the buoy.

So far, so good. Except the point of close void assault was to concentrate your forces to overwhelm the enemy defenses. The only way to prevail was to have enough Marines to soak up the inevitable heavy casualties as you closed.

But there was no sign of the other shuttle, which carried the remainder of Indigo Squad.

It was just Bryant and Arun.

They were alone.

Just the way Bryant must have planned it.

Arun had a split second to react. Had Bryant brought him here to murder him?

There was no other possibility.

It was him or Bryant. The first to shoot would live.

Arun told Barney to initiate emergency evasive maneuvers for five seconds that would end with his carbine with safety off and aimed at the NCO.

Nothing happened!

Bryant had locked up Arun's training suit. He couldn't move.

But Bryant could. Already, the NCO was out of sight, behind Arun.

By switching to external camera, Arun got a visual on Bryant. He expected to be staring down a barrel, but Bryant had clamped his carbine to his thigh and was pressing his thumb down on a control box in his hand.

Arun flinched. But all he felt was a popping in his ears.

"EMP bomb," explained Bryant. "Nanoscale spybots are clever little skangats, but the one downside of being so small and so simple is that they aren't strongly EMP hardened. I've blasted a 50-klick privacy sphere. God help us all if I'm wrong."

Arun had learned his lesson about speaking out to his superiors. He said nothing.

"I'm proud of you, cadet. You've repeatedly shown backbone and initiative."

"But Staff—"

Bryant cut Arun's query off with a cutting gesture. "I know. I handed your ass to you in public. Now that we're in private — hopefully — consider your ass handed back, with my compliments. Best guess is that your fun and games in Alabama spooked the Hardits so bad that they thought we'd rumbled them. They launched their rebellion before they were ready. Thousands died. If it weren't for you, that figure could have been millions. The rebels could have won — at least in the short term. In the long term, even if they'd won this system, their insurrection has probably earned extinction for their entire race. Why here and now? We still don't know."

"Which makes me think the rebellion was part of a wider operation still ongoing," said Arun.

"I agree. And that kind of instant analysis combined with the initiative and planning abilities you've demonstrated leads me to think you're a natural leader. What do you say to that?"

"Thank you, staff sergeant. But I don't think I'm cut out to be an NCO. I'm not a natural leader of people."

Bryant maneuvered to take a position facing Arun. With glare reflecting off the NCO's faceplate, Arun couldn't see his face. From the jerking of Bryant's suit, Arun had the impression he was nodding in agreement.

"Right answer," said Bryant. "Good. That's what I wanted to hear you say. You're right. Maybe with a few more years on your clock you'd make a passable lance corporal. Maybe not. I'm not talking about you being a leader of men and women, I mean a commander of combat units. Armies perhaps. Commanding a unit and leading the Marines in that unit are very different things."

"You mean… like an officer, staff sergeant?"

"I do, McEwan. Last I heard there weren't any officer vacancies for our race in the Human Marine Corps."

Bryant closed the gap between them so their helmets kissed. He spoke faceplate to faceplate. "But there *will* be in the Human Legion."

Panic flared through Arun. How the frakk did he know about the Human Legion?

"NCO privilege," explained Bryant. "You're still in a training suit and I have the override. I can do more than lock your suit's motors, I can also listen in to your words. I can only hope the Hardits' human allies didn't know how to do the same."

"You think there are human traitors too?"

"How else could they have drugged you cadets? They still are, by the way. I daren't let on that I know that. They're doing it to turn you into unquestioning robots. If Charlie Company were ordered to fire on friendly units, I don't think many could shake off the drugs enough to question that order."

"But surely they can't keep this secret indefinitely," said Arun. The conspiracies were starting to make sense. "Which means… which means they will make their move soon."

"Agreed."

"But… the Human Legion? Where do you get that name? I have never uttered those words."

"Stow the chatter, McEwan. We haven't much time. You might not have said them, but you did hear them spoken once by…" He broke off to check records. "By Cadet Phaedra Tremayne."

"Springer?"

Bryant laughed. "*Springer.* Is that what you call her? I like that. Very human." He paused, keeping the faceplates in contact. "Damn. The rest of the squad is coming. Listen, trust the colonel, your Trog friend, myself, and Sergeant Gupta. And Cadet Lee. There are a few others but best you don't know who. Hopefully the traitors aren't after us specifically, but they can kill us just as surely if we get in their way. Stay alive and keep your profile low. You have a responsibility to the future. I hope one day to serve under you in the Human Legion. *Sir.*"

Arun was too stunned to reply, but amidst that explosion of surprise, he logged the mention of Cadet Lee. Did Bryant mean Xin Lee?

Bryant moved away releasing the system lock on Arun's suit, which meant Barney suddenly carried out the emergency evasive maneuver Arun had demanded when he'd tried to shoot Bryant.

Arun wasn't ready for the sudden 5g zigzags. The universe became a fuzzy blur of violent motion. When his senses came back fully, he was half a klick away at the edge of a squad of cadets deploying in open order, and his neck was screaming in protest at the whiplash. To add to his woes, Sergeant Gupta's voice screamed at him through his helmet speaker.

"McEwan. *McEwan!* Get your sorry ass into position. Did you just black out on me? Don't tell me you blacked out."

"No, sergeant. I did not black out, sergeant." Which was close enough to the truth. Arun's world had grayed, not blacked.

"Then what the hell are you doing out of position, you useless veck?"

"Sorry, sergeant."

"Umarov is worth ten of you, McEwan. Next time you screw up, you're back with the Aux permanently and I'll thaw out another Marine from Umarov's vintage. This is your last chance."

"Thank you, sergeant."

"Don't waste my time thanking me, McEwan. Just get your ass in position and we can finally get started."

Arun grinned as he maneuvered into place. It felt good to have allies.

Chapter 65

The next two weeks were exhausting but were the most glorious Arun had ever enjoyed. Their Detroit hab-disks had housed the ultimate luxury: Aux who would cook, clean and wash. On Antilles there was no one else to plumb in the head or clean any blockage. Sergeant Gupta demanded there should be no slippage in hygiene standards, which meant the cadets not only had to cook but clean the galley afterward. Fatigues also had to be not only clean each morning but crease free.

None of this would be possible if not for the Trogs, whose tunneling and construction ability was miraculous. They built rectangular rooms with level floors for human usage, constructed drainage and ventilation channels and hardened conduits for power and data feeds. Their arterial corridors were broad: wide enough to take ten humans abreast, plus at least one line of the monorail system which the Trogs used to transport mounds of heavy equipment, spoil, and Trog workers.

The tunnel system already stretched for several klicks around the Hardit base Arun had fought over in the Battle of the Swoons. Given a generation or two, the entire moon would be honeycombed with their tunneling.

Best of all was the pleasure of sharing honest toil with the brothers and sisters of his unit. He wasn't sure why, but he was accepted once more as part of the unit. Perhaps it was trying to save Springer's life? He also suspected that they weren't being constantly fed combat drugs any more, though he had no way to be certain of that. Sergeant Gupta had taken Arun to one side and explained that sometimes when a group of untested Marines first comes under fire, invisible bonds are forged between the survivors that are stronger than animosities built up over the preceding years.

Springer would be back soon. She'd be able to explain what had changed.

The Trogs were everywhere but it was impossible to guess their number when all scribes and all workers looked identical. The one Trog Arun considered to be an individual was nowhere to be seen… until the day before the reinforcements from Bolt Squad were due to arrive. Arun was given an order to report to a deep level where he had never been. He guessed the summons had not come from a human.

"Didn't think you were going to see me again," Arun told his old friend who had been waiting for him. Pedro seemed to be growing into his new body. The dead 'skin' had flaked away to leave a rough carapace of mottled gray, with ridges running around his body like hoops around an ancient wooden barrel. His legs had atrophied. Arun wondered whether they would eventually drop off, a body part not required in great parents.

"This is the last time I plan for us to have a conversation," Pedro replied.

"So this is for old times' sake, eh?"

"Arun McEwan, do you recall why our first planned encounter was on that orbital platform?"

"So we couldn't be overheard."

"Correct. Orbital platforms have heavy defense against infiltration by nano spies. And now too, finally, is this area of our new moonbase. We may speak freely."

"Let me guess. You're going to tell me that the Night Hummers have spoken of Xin too. That's she's part of their prophecy."

Pedro whirled his antennae in consternation. In his old body, Arun reckoned, he'd be scampering around too.

"But you are accurate," said Pedro when he'd recovered. "How can this be so?"

"I have my sources."

"This is excellent news, if surprising. Our hopes for freedom and expansion rest on both your pairs of narrow human shoulders. If you knew this already, perhaps your shoulders are a little broader than I thought."

"Nice human metaphor, pal."

"I thank you."

"What I don't know," said Arun, "is how the purple girl fits in. Little Scar talked of a purple girl."

"I know nothing of this. I do not think Lee Xin will change her color. My guess is that this purple human is an adaptation of your species bred for camouflage on worlds rich with vegetation. Foliage on most planets is purple. I enjoy speculating with you, but this is only a guess."

Arun thought that over. Little Scar had talked of someone arriving at Tranquility soon. No point guessing, though. He'd just have to keep an eye open. "You've been a great help, Pedro," he said, knowing the old Pedro would glow with pleasure at the praise. "Really. But now you're cutting me loose. I understand that, but since I'm on my own, do you have any last advice for me?"

"Only what Sergeant Gupta tells me he has been trying to tell you all along: to keep your head down and wait for your chance."

"Is that it?"

"No."

When Pedro didn't elaborate, Arun grinned and placed a hand on Pedro's rough carapace. "I know you too well for you to confuse me, my friend. Pedro, please tell me what else you have to tell me."

"You are mistaken. Anything I have not told you is self-evident."

Arun laughed. "Have you forgotten that you regard the male human brain to be blinkered and sex-obsessed? What is self-evident that we have not yet discussed?"

"That I will aid you if I can, but I have no influence outsystem. That if you need refuge in the Tranquility system I will try to provide it here on Antilles."

"Is that truly it? Nothing more to tell me?"

"There is plenty more. However, there are things it is best you do not know. Otherwise if you were interrogated…"

"Yeah. I get it." He gently caressed Pedro's feathery antennae. Under a covering of downy hairs, they were surprisingly stiff; cracked too, like perished black plastic. He'd never ditch his Cadet Prong rep if any human saw him, but Pedro was his good friend, and communicating through touch was a human thing.

"I never did get around to touching you there," Arun said. "Does it feel nice?"

"Oh, yes. Y - e - sss." The artificial voice distorted, growing fuzzier until becoming a low rumble. It had never done that before. Then Pedro's legs buckled, giving way under him,

Arun snatched his hands away, screwing face up in disgust. "You're kidding me. That's not… I mean I didn't just…?"

When Pedro recovered, he curled his antennae and answered: "Your sex obsession continues to amuse. When I was altered to morph into a new great parent, I passed by the reproductive stages, never to reclaim them. I am incapable of what you would call sexual arousal. Your touch was merely very relaxing."

"Thank frakk for that. Well, I guess if that's all you have to say, then it's farewell, you big lunk. It was good having you as a friend."

"I have not ceased being a friend, Arun, but now I must be a secret one. The action of Ensign Thunderclaws drew a great deal of attention to you. It has been noted and questioned. I gave you the choice of your reinforcements so that you could demonstrate loyalty to your nest brothers and sisters. I do not wish to further the sense that you are special. That is why this is our last meeting. Farewell, human McEwan."

With that, Pedro turned and swam through the wall.

Arun blinked, barely believing his eyes. In his morphing body, Pedro was struggling to walk, but he swam through the chewed rock as if it were his natural element.

How the frakk did he do that?

Arun inspected the wall, remembering back to that first training exercise when the Troggie guardians had emerged through the tunnel walls. Yet they had struggled to dig him out of the hole his grenades had scooped out for him. The packed earth or rock dust Pedro had disappeared into felt powdery and glistened with slime. He thrust his hands into the wall which parted until he'd nearly pushed in up to his elbows. Then the earth hardened.

Idiot! Arun yanked his arms back, but it was too late! The soil had hardened around him. He screamed for help.

He was lucky some passing Trog workers were nearby. They came racing through the passageway, milling around in confusion when they got to Arun. He waggled his upper arms, trying to communicate that he was stuck.

They looked at the wall. They looked at the human who had summoned them. They looked at each other.

Then one rubbed its antennae over Arun's shirt, over the spot where Pedro had implanted his scent communicator.

Now the big aliens understood, flinging themselves at the wall in their eagerness to free Arun.

Arun understood too. It wasn't his human screams that had summoned the Troggie workers, it was his distress interpreted by the device, and translated into pheromones, just as Pedro's box translated the scents he communicated into human speech.

When his limbs came free, the cramps he felt in his arms were excruciating, but Arun ignored that and filled his mind with a sense of gratitude.

By the way the workers scampered around, rubbing themselves against him, the Trogs were basking in his praise.

Arun grinned. Being queen of the ants could prove pretty useful. Though he started to have doubts as he dusted himself off and went to rejoin the rest of his section, who were readying to patrol the mining area where the insurrection had started, an exercise in being seen. Five Troggie workers followed in a neat column behind Arun.

He began to wonder what Madge would say if he didn't find the pheromone that told them to clear off.

Chapter 66

On the day Bolt Squad was due to join them in the growing Antilles tunnel complex, excitement spread through Indigo Squad like a fever. By way of welcome, the cadets constructed an item that could loosely be described as a cake.

Umarov said this was madness. Having a party with Indigo would be the last thing on the newcomers' minds. If he were in their place he'd want to rip the heads off everyone in Indigo and spit down their necks.

Umarov always complained. It was just his way. But he meant what he said because he stuck close to Arun all day, explaining that the cadet needed protection more than anyone. He even guarded Arun when they showered after the two had spent a day showing a Marine presence at a cluster of heavy element mines, about 150 klicks east of their main base.

Although they called them *showers*, water was far too scarce to be blasted at dirty cadets. Instead they stripped off and rubbed into their bodies a warmed-up ocher goop, which looked like fine moon dust mixed in with the kind of degreasing agent used to clean machine parts. Then they used plastic scrapers to lift off the cleaner. It sounded primitive but was surprisingly effective, leaving their skin cleaner and more refreshed than the Detroit showers.

"I still don't get why you're so worried about Bolt Squad," said Arun as he scooped the cleaning slime from his calves. "You've graduated, which makes you senior to them. I know Gupta asked Madge to run the section, and we could all see a few days ago that you and Madge have finally sorted between you how that works."

"You noticed our bruises, eh?"

"The limps were kinda obvious too."

"Get to the point, McEwan. Technically I outrank all the cadets in Bolt Squad. You want to know why I don't just order them to play nice."

"Well?"

Umarov shrugged. "Enlarging the group means we need to re-establish the new pecking order, same as I did with Majanita. Can't be avoided.

Fighting human nature never works. I'm just here to keep you alive, pal. The rest is up to you."

Arun walked naked through the slime-coated floor and out into the passageway followed by Umarov. Clean fatigues were waiting in the dorm chamber. Back in Detroit he would've picked fresh fatigues from the bins in the shower block. Laundry was one of life's practical details they hadn't yet perfected.

"Now you've settled in, do you ever feel like taking Madge's place?" Arun asked. "Or Brandt's? *Lance sergeant Umarov.* How does that sound to you?"

"Worse than a death sentence," growled Umarov. They entered the dorm warren, making for their section's chamber. "The First Law of Soldiering still applies today. *Never volunteer for anything.* You'll learn one day."

"But Brandt, Del and Madge — none of them volunteered," protested Arun. "They were picked as NCO tryouts."

"Maybe," Umarov admitted as they entered their chamber. They waved a greeting at Brandt, Del-Marie and Sadri, who was one of the new members of the section. "But you're forgetting the Second Law of Soldiering — never stand out. Your cadet NCOs broke the Second Law and paid the price. No offense, Lancer Del."

Del-Marie looked up from the softscreen he was studying with Brandt. "None take, Grognard."

Arun laughed. Del and Umarov had understood each other from the start. The one time Arun had tried calling Umarov *Grognard*, the carabinier had given him an icy stare of warning.

Simultaneously they all fell silent when they sensed a disturbance following Arun and Umarov through the dorm chambers.

It might be Bolt Squad.

Arun climbed into his pants and hunted for his shirt. Then he caught sight of Del and Brandt getting to their feet and face the entrance. They looked seriously pissed.

Abandoning the search for his clothes, Arun turned around, just in time to duck under a flying fist. The shoulder barge that followed knocked him to the ground.

"This is your fault, McEwan."

He looked up at Xin Lee's face.

What the hell was she doing here?

"No," he said. "No, it's nothing to do with me."

"Get to your feet," she hissed, "so I can knock you down again."

Two more cadets burst in, both female.

"You kids listen up," shouted one of the invaders. "We don't want to be here." She pointed at Arun. "He is the worst of you, but I blame you all. If you know what's best for you, keep out of our way. We run this moon now. When you're off duty, you stay in your dorm. The rest of Antilles is off limits. Understand?"

Arun and the other members of the team all looked to Brandt for leadership.

"Save your threats for someone who will listen to them," said Brandt, sounding even more pissed than Xin. "You've no right to order us around. Besides, when Cadet McEwan was ordered to select a squad to join us, he didn't pick you. He picked Bolt Squad."

"But we *are* Bolt Squad." The speaker emerged from the adjoining chamber and pushed in front of the newcomers. "Cadet Lance Corporal Lee was transferred to our squad two days ago. So was I. Care to explain why?"

Xin's arrival had been a shock, but the identity of the newcomer made Arun's eyes pop so wide they threatened to explode. Standing in front of him was Chief Instructor Nhlappo. Except she was clearly in charge of the Bolt Squad expedition. Given the stripe on her shoulder, she was now Lance Corporal Nhlappo. Here, no doubt, to give him hell.

"Answer me!" she bellowed.

"Ma'am, sorry ma'am."

"Don't give me *ma'am*, McEwan!"

"Sorry, Lance Corporal."

"So now even you understand, McEwan. You *are* to blame because you are an alien-faggot. If the colonel had punished you rather than myself, Hortez and LaSalle, then you would never have been able to stick your tongue up whatever passes for Troggie butt." She frowned at Umarov, as if trying to figure out his role. Then she shrugged. "Carry on, Bolt Squad."

"Yes, lance corporal," answered Xin and the two other Bolt Squad cadets. They were panting, eyes wild and teeth bared. Eager for a fight.

"Oh, frakk!" said Del-Marie. "They're on combat stims."

Nhlappo withdrew out of sight behind a phalanx of more Bolt Squad cadets who advanced into the chamber and spread out, hugging the room's edge.

Xin nodded. It was a signal to attack. All three of the cadets who'd first arrived leaped on Brandt, pummeling him on the ground. The others in Bolt Squad — another dozen cadets — stood at the ready, daring anyone in Indigo Squad to intervene.

Arun dared. He dodged out of the clutches of a lunging Bolt Squad sentinel, and jumped onto the bundle of bodies that had formed over Brandt. He grappled, trying to reach into the writhing mass and pull attackers off his lance sergeant. Umarov was running interference behind him.

A kick to his nose threw Arun off the writhing bodies but only for a moment. He dove back in, riding the punches and kicks to get purchase. Del-Marie and Sadri were somewhere in this confusing melee too, but the mass of limbs was too confusing to make out. Finally, Arun got a good hold of a leg and levered himself backward. The legs kicked and thrashed but he pulled the attacker off Brandt.

The attacker rolled to one side before springing to her feet. She glared at Arun. It was Xin. *Figures.*

Her beautiful dark eyes flashed danger, immobilizing Arun with horror even when those eyes were coming straight at him. He snapped out of his stupor just in time, slipping under her headbutt and throwing her over his shoulder.

She grunted when her head sent a chair spinning and she landed with a thud onto her back.

Arun took in a rapid glance of the combat. Umarov and Del-Marie were on the deck, held down under a crush of attackers. It was Brandt, Arun and Sadri against Xin and the other two. Three on three. And if combat stims really were in play, this was a fight to the death!

Xin was scrambling to get up, but Arun was already over her, pinning her down with his weight through his knees. He lifted his weight momentarily, but only to get a twisting action from his hips to maximize the power behind his fist that he launched at her pretty button nose, aiming to shatter it and drive the bone fragments into her brain.

With his fist just two inches from her nose, Arun realized what he was doing and snapped out of his combat rage. He gasped, pulling his punch. It still struck home, but was a stinging slap rather than a lethal strike from a trained 17-year-old killer.

Xin seemed to snap out of her combat state too. Her eyes snapped open, staring wide-eyed at Arun. Was she shocked at her violence? Impressed with Arun?

No, neither! Xin shook spasmodically. Her stare tracked him as he twisted off her, leaving her to her fit. Something clattered to the floor beside him. It was an electro-stunner that had fallen out of Xin's fingers. She'd been about to ram it into his gut when someone had sent a shock bolt into her. Horden's frakking children! What now?

Arun got to his feet, assuming a cautious crouch as he checked for this new threat.

Trogs were swimming through the walls, bowling over the Bolt Squad perimeter from behind. Each Trog was holding two weapons that looked like modified SA-71 carbines.

There were about a score of Trogs. The cadets of both squads were still or writhing on the ground, shocked by stun rounds.

Blowing up the enemy was simplicity itself. But to blow someone up *slightly*, without permanent damage, was anything but. Which meant these Trogs had been armed with specifically anti-human stun rounds.

Everyone in the chamber had been shot except Arun.

He put his finger to the faint bulge in his sternum. Had his pheromone implant saved him? The Trogs waved their weapons at him but seemed uncertain whether to shoot.

When the shocked humans began to recover enough to sit upright, one of the big insects brought out a voicebox and brandished the speaker about its abdomen like a trophy.

"Attention, human younglings. This is a message from your great captain commander, whom we call the great parent. Your presence here is to assist in the defense of a key imperial asset. Your selection as warriors is an honor. It is mandated that you do not render each other inoperable. The great parent's authority over all sentients on this moon is paramount. Anyone guilty of… *acting naughty*… will be… *tropied*."

Arun struggled to keep a straight face as the bewildered cadets rubbed at their heads, wondering whether they had really just heard those words. Of course, this was Pedro having fun again, inserting recordings of Arun's voice toward the end of his speech. Arun's smile vaporized. Pedro had played him for a fool, giving him the choice of reinforcements and then bringing Xin anyway. Nhlappo too. Was she in the plot with the good guys?

The artificial voice came louder now. "You will all now separate and return to your respective habitation chambers to await punishment from human commander-adults."

The groggy Bolt Squad cadets picked themselves up and shuffled away, the fight shocked out of them.

As Xin passed through the door, she stopped and glanced back at Arun.

He grinned and blew her a kiss. With his chances with her well and truly blown, he might as well act as if it were all a joke.

Arun expected her to respond with the twisting hand gesture that meant she wanted to rip his heart out and devour it.

She didn't. Instead, she winked.

She *winked!*

Chapter 67

Del-Marie set his spoon down beside his bowl of chow-hall gruel and glared at Arun across the table. "If you don't shut your mouth, McEwan, I'm going to rip out your hamstrings and use them to sew your lips shut. Permanently."

"Just making conversation, lance corporal."

"No, McEwan. You prattling on about your illusory love affair is not conversation. It's a monologue and I'm sick of it."

But she winked! Arun kept that memory to himself as he began to puff with indignation. An age ago, when Delta Section, Blue Squad were brand new cadets, Springer and Arun's prattling had lightened the section's mood. Osman's antics had also helped to entertain the unit as they made their first step along the journey toward being Marines. Osman was dead and Springer still absent. Arun was trying to keep up the morale of his exhausted comrades. Trying to turn back the clock…

A red mist enveloped Arun. He answered with venom: "Does it offend you because it is a woman that I want for a prong-buddy? Would it be better if I talked of sharing my rack with one of the men? How about Stoney from the Bolters. He's—"

"Oh, please. You're just embarrassing yourself. You never were very good at doing anger. Love is love, Arun, in all its forms. It excites us. Thrills and teases us with the promises of paradise, but we know we risk being tumbled into the lowest form of misery when love fails. Life without love would be as cold and lifeless as the void. I like to hear other people talk of love, however they experience it. Just not you."

Arun frowned. "What's the matter, Del?" When Del-Marie started up with his poetic phrases, it meant something was seriously troubling him.

Del-Marie shook his head, disappointed. "Your prattling about Xin fills the room like a gaseous emission from your backside. It's crude and stale. We all want to ignore it but it just keeps coming until we're all choking on your emanations." The chow hall — a crude cavern with a scattering of tables — was bubbling with laughter by this point. "And yet your words are ultimately nothing more than warm gas that dissipates to leave nothing behind of any consequence."

"And the rest of you?" shouted Arun at the others as he got to his feet. "Is that what you all think? That I'm a joke?"

He searched the faces for support. Madge was laughing at him, as were the cadets from Hecht's Alpha Section. Zug looked thoughtful.

"Yes, Arun," said Del-Marie. "I speak for everyone in the section. It's been nearly four weeks since this Xin creature arrived, and you still haven't stopped talking of your undying love. On the rare occasions when you do see her, you're too tongue-tied to do more than nod and grunt, and try ineffectually to reduce your drooling. She tried to gut you with an electro-stunner, for frakk's sake!"

"That's because Nhlappo gave them all stims."

Del sighed. "The girl who loves you is due back tomorrow minus her leg. You love her too, you're just too dumb to realize because you've bewitched yourself over this Xin. Snap out of it, Arun. You're not thirteen years old anymore. Act like a man. In a little over two years, you and I could be boarding a troopship to go to war. Sooner, if you believe Umarov. I don't want to fight alongside a little boy who's too scared to talk to girls. The Bolters have their own chow hall. If you're so interested in Xin, why aren't you there?"

Ungrateful shunters, the lot of them. Arun blanked Del-Marie and sat back down, contemplating his gruel.

Zug wouldn't let Arun go. "Our real problem is that we've lost Springer, just when we need her most. She isn't just the funny one with the silly ideas and spooky violet eyes. She's the one who keeps us together. Call her our emotional hub, if you like, our squad's heart. We need our heart because so many things have happened at once. First you embarrassed the colonel and then you let us down by abandoning your Scendence team mates."

"Hey, that's not fair. I thought you'd gotten over that."

"Stow it, McEwan," said Majanita. "Zug's doing the best he can to sugar coat. Would you prefer it if I told you how it really is?"

Arun kept his mouth closed.

"Rightly or not," continued Zug, "we all felt at the time that you had let us down. I've heard rumors that we have been fed low-level combat drugs for weeks or more. Maybe that's true and influenced our reaction. Then there was the Cull."

"I know," said Arun. "Sorry, man."

"I executed a fellow human being. A nineteen-year-old girl from our own battalion. Our scores were added to hers and we didn't earn enough to keep her alive. In a very small part, we are all responsible for her death, but it was me alone who killed her. It has changed me, Arun. I can't yet explain how, but I am not the same person I was when we started this training year."

"Then the frakk-up when someone rigged the training session on *Fort Douaumont* against us," said Madge. "We still don't know why. And the rebellion. The Aux. Osman and Cristina dying. Our posting here at some whimsy of your alien friend, which has cut us off from the training system. A lot has happened in a short space of time."

"What we're saying," added Zug, "is that we've gone through a period of transition. We can no longer pretend to live in a world where innocence is permitted."

"So, what you're saying is that… what? We've all gone through drent and I should shut the frakk up because I'm too childish?"

Zug held Arun's furious gaze for a few moments before replying. "Yes, that is what I'm saying."

"Fine! You can all go vulley yourselves. Maybe Xin is a pathetic fantasy. Yes, she's out of my league. And I do see that Springer is beautiful and loving and better than I could ever deserve or hope to find in another woman, but at least I still think of love. My body is still capable of feeling passion. Is yours, Zug? Who do you dream about at night? I hear nothing from you. I don't even know whether you prefer women or men."

"Then your powers of observation are limited," said Zug.

Arun ground his jaw. "What about you, Del-Marie? There was a time when you would be forever sneaking off to spend time with Barnard. Now that he's stuck back in Detroit, you never mention his name. Weren't you in love?"

"I loved him very much." There was a catch to Del-Marie's voice. "But he loved me a little less it seems. I do not blame you for our exile to this exhausting little moon, but like it or not, it is a fact that we have been banished. It would take great sacrifice for Barnard to wait for me. Barnard is of the opinion that one must take one's pleasures where one can, while you still can, for we could all die tomorrow."

"I thought it was only Umarov who thought like that," said Arun.

Zug tapped Arun on shoulder. "Barnard was a member of the execution squad too."

"I'm sorry, I didn't know."

"Yes, well I'm not surprised," said Del-Marie. "That's kind of my point. Anyway, as Barnard says, we have to take one's pleasures where we can. I have an attachment with Jimmy Hellenstein now."

Arun knew Big Jim from Bolt Squad. Was scared of him, to be honest. "I'm glad to hear that you're happy," said Arun. "Happ-*ier*," he corrected himself when he saw misery cloud Del-Marie's face.

That was *it!* Arun was furious with his squadmates and disgusted with himself. He abandoned his chow and stormed off.

Del called it exile, but one good thing about the Antilles posting was being at liberty to wander the fast-expanding base, and having gaps in the daily schedule to take advantage of that freedom. Arun intended to check out the new lower level but only made a few hundred meters through the winding tunnels when he came across Jimmy Hellenstein coming the other way.

"Hey," said Arun in greeting. Since the violence of their arrival, the two squads had developed a rough accommodation with each other. It wasn't friendship. Not yet.

Jimmy nodded back.

"Errm." Arun felt he needed to say something but had no idea what. He wished Springer were here. "Look, ah, Hellenstein…"

Jimmy halted in front of Arun, looming over like an instructor about to chew out a novice, studying him. Judging. Jimmy was a good six inches taller than Arun and probably about the same wider at the shoulders. Arun felt like a child in comparison.

"It's Del-Marie," said Arun. "I've just left him at our chow hall. He's had a hard time and he's feeling it today. You will look after him, won't you?"

Jimmy gave a slight nod. He looked away for a moment. He seemed to be thinking over something, was about to say something to Arun but then thought better of it. Instead he rested a hand on Arun's shoulder.

"I have a message for you from Xin," he said. "She wants you to meet her in our dorm chamber."

Jimmy leaned in slightly and spoke with menace into Arun's ear. "Xin is in my section." He tightened his grip on Arun's shoulder. "I expect *you* to look after *her*."

Arun swallowed hard. Did Jimmy's message mean what he hoped it did? Jimmy was still leering down him, his expression hardening.

"Yes," said Arun hurriedly. "Xin means a lot to me. I would never do anything to hurt her." Then he remembered that he was the reason Xin was on the moon. He added quickly: "Not on purpose."

Jimmy, gave a hard stare back. After a few seconds, he relaxed a little and nodded. "Make sure you don't." Then he sighed and seemed to loosen. "Go to her now," he added, with something approaching warmth in his voice.

Then he walked off. Arun detected no joy in his gait. He hoped Del-Marie would be okay.

As soon as Jimmy had turned the corner and was out of sight, Arun forgot about Del's troubles.

He ran to Xin.

Chapter 68

Xin was waiting on her rack, hugging her knees and deep in contemplation.

The adjoining dorm chambers were surprisingly full of Bolters, either pumped with excitement or as lost in thought as Xin. Something was up, but all Arun cared was that the rest of Xin's section had made themselves scarce. They were close enough to privacy for Arun to screw up his courage and sit beside her, stretching an arm around her shoulder.

She looked up at him with mournful eyes. He expected her to shrug him off, but she dipped her head and leaned into his embrace, shifting until her head nestled comfortably against his shoulder.

Through the thin material of her shirt, Arun's touch electrified to the feel of her muscle and bone as her shoulder gently rose and fell with her breathing.

And so they sat in silence, huddled together on a rack in a Trog-chewed underground hole under an airless moon.

This wasn't how Arun had imagined this moment at all.

Take your pleasures where you can. Umarov would laugh at him forever if he hesitated now.

Taking a deep breath, Arun slid his hand under Xin's chin and gently lifted her, gazing into those dark eyes that had been the focus of so many dreams.

He meant to kiss her but… those eyes… they were deep wells of sadness.

Suddenly he understood. *Taking your pleasures where you could* – it had never occurred to him that *he* would be the pleasure being taken, the reason why Xin had summoned him.

He drew back. "What's wrong?"

She rubbed at his lips with her thumb, as if wiping them clean of words she did not want to hear.

"Not now," she said. "Not yet."

Then the fire of her spirit ignited. The old Xin was back, pushing him back onto the rack, kissing him all the way down.

They rolled and squeezed, pressing up against each other in a frantic melee of hair, and lips, and limbs.

But as quickly as her passion had flared, it now guttered and went out, stranding Arun in Xin's stiff embrace.

He laughed. Whenever he dreamed of making love with Xin, clothing never seemed to exist. Now that he was lying on her rack in real life, not only were they both dressed, but his feet were still encased in dusty boots.

"Sorry," he said when he noticed her following his gaze down to his footwear.

"So you should be," she replied in mock anger. She scooted down the bed and removed his boots. After a salacious glance that Arun took care to commit to long-term memory, she loosened his pants and proceeded to strip him naked.

As soon as she was done, Xin darted under the covers. Arun dove in after her and started yanking off her clothes too.

She squirmed and gasped in playful protest, any resistance only part of her fun.

When they were naked together, his fingertips traced lazy circles up the softness of her inner thigh.

That didn't get the reaction Arun was after. She went rigid.

He'd pushed too far!

But then she leaned back on folded arms and released a long, long sigh — one of tension released rather than erotic passion.

"That's it, twinkle eyes," she whispered. "Keep doing that, and never stop…"

―――――

"I have to go," said Arun about an hour later, with as much relish as the condemned walking to their place of execution.

Xin leaned over and looked him in the eye. "Stay."

"I can't be AWOL. Not even for you."

"Stay till the end, Arun. Hellenstein was on his way to see Del-Marie Sandure. So your unit will know. They'll understand that you should be here."

"It's not my crew who bother me. Sergeant Gupta and Corporal Majanita—"

"Will understand."

Arun sighed. "It's time. You need to explain."

Xin spent several seconds searching for the right words. She looked up at the roof, ignoring Arun. "Bolt Squad will embark on the transport shuttle leaving Docking Bay 2 at 05:30. Destination: fleet transport *Themistocles*."

"What is your role on *Themistocles*?" he said carefully, dreading the answer.

"The G-year and G-1 year companies of 8th depot battalion have been detached to form the 87th field battalion. My cadet years are already over, Arun. We've all graduated. All my life I've wanted to earn my place out in the stars as a Marine. I want to go but… only when I was ready. I was having a blast back in Detroit."

He kissed her sad eyes. "Scared?" he asked.

"A little. It's whatever threat is making them rush us out when we're not ready. No one is saying what that is, but it can't be good."

Arun gave her a nod, as if he understood what she was going through. He embraced her against his chest and held her there.

Jimmy Hellenstein and the rest of Xin's section returned soon after. They made a show of ignoring Arun and Xin.

Xin tapped Arun on the head. "Don't mind them," she said. "Will you stay with me until I embark?"

Arun nearly said she ought to be spending the time with her comrades. Then he remembered she'd been transferred because of Pedro's interference. Her friends were still back on Detroit. She knew Arun better than anyone else on this little world.

From along the dorm warren, a boisterous group of newly minted Marines launched into song.

"Of course," he said. "Let's join in the fun."

Chapter 69

Early the next morning, Arun accompanied Xin as far as the broad transit corridor that zigzagged its way to the embarkation point for Xin and the other Bolter Marines. Waving her off at the shuttle airlock, like a distraught parent, would hardly help her settle into her new role. So he hung back at the junction, applying a gentle pressure to her shoulder.

She came to a halt, turning around but not able to meet his eyes.

Xin needed him. Arun knew that. But however hard he tried to find words that would boost her morale, everything that reached the threshold of his lips sounded too trite to speak.

Eventually it fell to Xin to squeeze his hand and break the silence. "Things happen around you, McEwan. I like that about you. And you *are* kind of cute. But there's another reason why I want to stay close to you."

"Shush!" He pressed a finger hard against her full lips. "You and I are special. You know that, right? Well, so do I."

Xin's eyes went wide. He had to stifle laughter because she looked farcical with wide eyes and his finger still on her lips.

Then she gave a curt nod of understanding. How much did she really understand? Had she too talked with the Night Hummer?

"No need for us to brag about it," he said, withdrawing his finger.

"We'll be each other's little secret," she breathed, acting the part of an impassioned secret lover. "Fate is about to separate us. But we must do everything we can to let each other know where we are. One day, I believe, we *will* be reunited. Our destinies are entwined."

Then something happened that Arun would never forget but neither could he ever explain how it came about. Maybe Xin's words were too close to revealing the truth and he needed to shut her up. Perhaps he wanted to test how much of her lover's act was rooted in truth. Whatever the reason, he found he had swept his lips against hers and she was responding and kissing him greedily. She slid one hand around his neck, resting the other on the small of his back. Arun was barely conscious of his hands, and cared less about the Marines flowing around them on their way to the shuttle; his attention was limited to the brush of her lips, the warmth of her mouth.

When, eventually, they broke, it was only to take a quarter step back so that Xin could rest her gaze in Arun's.

Arun chose to believe Xin's feelings were genuine.

They stood there in silence — for how long, even Arun's time counters couldn't tell — until they were disturbed by the rattle of an ore-laden truck coming along the hover-rail out in the main corridor. With blinking eyes (was that a tear?) Xin mournfully cast down her gaze and walked away with head high, and kitbag over her shoulder.

She didn't look back.

Arun didn't look away. Not until Xin had disappeared around a turn in the tunnel.

Sighing, he made his way back to his comrades. Keeping Xin as an impossible fantasy lover would have been so much simpler.

He shrugged, managing a grin.

Simplicity was overrated.

Chapter 70

With over an hour to go before reveille, Arun's section should have been asleep, but when Arun slunk back into his dorm chamber, he was surprised to be greeted by a ragged cheer.

Umarov had activated his nuclear-powered snore, oblivious to the universe, but the others were drifting in a place between light slumber and quiet contemplation. Not Del-Marie, though. He looked drained of blood.

Of course. Jim had been here, to say his farewells to Del.

"How was it?" Madge asked Arun.

Arun frowned unsure of the answer himself. "Not at all what I expected," he replied. "Intense. Painful."

Madge nodded back. "Tough luck, brother. I envy you. Can you believe that?"

"I'm not sure I can, corporal."

"You only had a brief time with her, Arun, but… You've come away with a powerful memory you can treasure forever. Of all of us here, only Del can claim to have experienced anything like that."

"I hope you aren't including me in your assessment!"

Arun span around. "Springer!"

There she was, framed in the doorway. Other than a walking stick, her outline looked the same as ever. A grin split her face from ear to ear. Those wild brown curls and violet eyes gleaming from her playful face were still there, despite the burns. But the dimples when she smiled had gone.

"Hello, Arun." She swung her kit bag onto the nearest rack. "Anyone miss me?"

Arun hung back while the others mobbed Springer with high-fives. Even Del planted a lingering kiss on her head.

The others gave them space, Arun and Springer facing each other an arm's length apart.

"I crept back in so as not to wake you all," Springer said. "I should have guessed you'd still be up, discussing Xin. Nothing changes, eh?"

"Just passing the time till you came back," Arun said, feeling more awkward than he believed was possible.

She gave him a look that said she didn't believe that.

Arun tried again. "She was lonely. She just wanted someone to hold her on her last night."

"Dear Arun, there's more to it than that. They brought me in early on the same shuttle that's transferring Xin's squad to the troopship. By the look on her face, when I passed by, I could tell she was leaving something precious behind. Surprise, surprise! That turns out to be you."

There was an acidic edge to her words, but the teasing glint in her eye was vintage Springer.

It was enough.

He closed the gap, trying not to look at her burn-damaged face, and kissed her.

Her lips felt as cold as stone, and her flesh didn't move quite as it should.

He hated himself for noticing these details when all that mattered was that she was alive and back with him.

He embraced her. She should fit perfectly into the snug of his shoulder as if they were built for each other, but her stance was wooden, her weight in the wrong place.

No matter. He would hold her in his arms for as long as it took until she could feel the love that permeated his embrace reach through her injuries and touch her heart.

He wanted to let her know how sexy she was too, but… but Springer could see through any lie. She was damaged, and he hadn't gotten used to that yet. But he would. They had plenty of time.

Del-Marie rescued him. "Still getting used to your new leg, Springer? I noticed you limping."

Springer drew back, winking at Arun as she did.

"I'm getting there, lance corporal," she said. She walked over to the rack she'd claimed. Del was right: she limped, the soft plastic tip of her stick going *tap… tap… tap…*

"Is that permanent?" Arun asked. "I mean the new leg."

"Yeah."

"But you can't walk properly."

"So?" She shrugged. "It's powered. My new leg works well inside armor. Better than your flesh one."

Springer sounded genuine. But that was horrendous.

She must have caught Arun's look because she asked him: "Do you remember when we were novices running through the fields near Alabama? The instructors were in our face all the frakking time, telling us what pathetic weaklings we were every step of the way?"

Arun laughed. "It was easy to believe we were hopeless. We'd be gasping but they never seemed to even break sweat. The countryside was beautiful, but I used to hate those runs."

"Good, because none of that matters now. None of us will ever run through those fields again, nor anywhere else. Not in the flesh. The next time we run will be in armor."

"No," said Arun. "The Trogs can build tunnels so quickly it scares me. Even stuck here on this moon, we'll get things settled down and have miles of tunnels to run through before breakfast. Just like the old days."

Springer swung her legs over so she could lie back on her rack. "Today was Xin's turn to go to war. I expect tomorrow it will be ours. The rest of our lives will be spent either in cryo, zero-g or combat armor. No, I don't miss my leg. Now someone turn the volume down on Umarov, 'cause I want to grab some kip while I can."

Arun moved to Umarov's rack to roll him over, but stopped when he saw Springer was already asleep.

"Do you think she's right, corporal," he asked Madge. "Will we be called up tomorrow?"

Zug laughed, a sound Arun hadn't heard for a long while. "She was speaking figuratively," he said.

"True," Madge agreed with a fleeting smile, "but to answer your question, McEwan. When was the last time Springer was wrong about anything? Now, everyone, get some sleep!"

Arun tried, but he wasn't like Umarov or Springer. The room could be shaking with the retort of field artillery, the levels above collapsing under an orbital bombardment of kinetic torpedoes, but those two would sleep right through.

But when Arun closed his eyes, his mind only filled with the rhythmic *tap… tap… tap…* of Springer's walking stick.

It sounded like a countdown.

Chapter 71

Clang… clang… clang…

A metallic beat advanced on Arun, wrenching him out of his sleepy fog.

He'd been dreaming of Springer's walking stick again — as he had done every time he'd slept in the two weeks since she'd returned — but his brain composed itself enough to insist that this noise was real. And could be a threat. He opened his eyes – muscles firing up ready for action – but the sound was only one of the ship-rats up on the walkway, here to make final sleep checks on her crop of cryo pods.

It was a surreal sight. With the pods recessed into the floor at shoulder height, the chamber did look like a field of decapitated heads, with the ship-rats their farmers.

The cryo-drugs were adding drag to every thought, making the rats walking above Arun's head look even more otherworldly than when he had boarded *Beowulf*.

It was difficult to believe the runty ship-rats had come from the same stock of Horden's children as the Marines. With their long, slender necks — and limbs to match — they could be elves of human myth, if not for the spiky hair dyed in bright primary colors. Their childlike stature brought out a protective urge in Arun, but unlike the children on Tranquility, who were bred to be Marines, the ship-rats possessed an ethereal, exotic beauty.

Arun grinned. Ship girls were hot!

He made himself think of Xin, about two light days away on *Themistocles*. Did he still feel she was a slender bundle of cuteness? Oh, yes… but compared to the graceful ship girl — who was now close enough for him to smell her perfume of machine lubricants and cryo chemicals — Xin was as bulky as… as an elephant.

He laughed, remembering his first conversation with Pedro, when the big insect had agreed that only an idiot would compare anything to an elephant.

No, this was no good. The girl had distracted him. He should be drifting away by now.

Once again he activated the calming process embedded in his mind, and felt the endorphins surge and mix with the cryo drugs in a cascade of blissful fuzziness.

A positive mental state increased the chance of surviving the revival process. The trick was to concentrate on the good things in life, to go into cryo-sleep with your head filled with all the reasons why you wanted to wake up.

He let his mind touch on memories of his unlikely friendship with Pedro, of other friends: Zug, Springer… and Fraser, who had been promoted to lead *Beowulf*'s small Marine detachment, and had been so pleasantly surprised to meet his brother on board that his handshake had carried on for ages. Then there was Xin… Umarov too… And Osman… Hortez…

Hortez.

He felt a pang of regret — he would never know how Hortez had met his end.

A new shame scoured him, guilt at how easily he'd shrugged off Cristina's death.

No! These negative thoughts were getting dangerous. If you went into cryo with worries on your mind, you'd come out a paranoid wreck.

He directed his thoughts to once again play over Xin. When he'd gone into those Troggie tunnels, she'd been nothing more than a dream. He wasn't sure what they were to each other now, but whatever it was, it was real.

As his thoughts slowed, merging into an ocean of tranquility, he felt his jaw unclench. Xin and Hortez were the kind of loose end left after every campaign. What mattered was that as a cadet he'd had just one primary objective: to become a Marine.

Arun had done that. His first campaign had ended in victory.

Now he was going to war. Two weeks after an executive order had redesignated Xin's year as Marines, the same had happened to Arun's. Calling him a Marine was an even bigger stretch of the truth than it had been for Xin, but what mattered right now was that somewhere on this ship was a full ACE-2 battlesuit allotted specifically to him — Arun McEwan — and he couldn't wait to try it on. Of course he couldn't: he'd been bred for this.

The ship-rat had reappeared over his head, checking his details on her softscreen. Her face was creamy soft, and when she glanced at him, gifting him a flirtatious smile, her brown eyes lit with character.

His drooping eyelids narrowed on the sight of her moving on to the neighboring cryo pod, fixing an image of her beautiful hair: shades of indigo and violet that ran to bright lilac at its tips.

No! He mustn't sleep. Not yet!

Suddenly Arun was fighting the drugs that were trying to still his heart before freezing him. He was swimming up from the depths of an icy sea, desperate to break the surface before everything went black.

Who are you? he asked the girl, not sure whether he'd actually spoken the words aloud. If he made any sound at all, the girl with the purple hair showed no sign of hearing him.

He closed his eyes. The icy depths claimed him, and he was sinking into darkness.

Her voice penetrated his dark tomb. "Problem?"

"Your hair," he whispered.

"My what? My hair? What about it?"

He wrenched open one eye. She was crouching down over him, her face shimmering.

He frowned. Trying to force his fading brain processes to explain why her hair was so vital.

Ship-rat fashion was to dye hair, the more vibrant and unnatural the shade the better. This girl's hair was more natural — subtle, blended shades of… Almost like…

"Your hair… it's like Springer's eyes."

She smiled but looked confused.

"I mean," he added, every word now a life-or-death struggle. "I like the way you. Color. It."

She laughed. "Thank you," she said. "Although, actually I don't color it. It's a mutation. Listen—" she paused a moment — "you really need to stop talking, Marine… Arun McEwan. But I *will* remember you. I promise. We can chat about how you like my hair when you wake. See you in six months, Arun."

The ship-rat closed the lid, sealing him inside. With his last flickers of consciousness, he finally remembered what was important about her hair. This had to be the purple girl Little Scar had spoken of. The transparent lid was frosting over, but he could still see her walking to the neighboring pod, where Umarov awaited his turn. Arun wanted to shout out but the power of speech had left him.

A yearning for the purple girl was the thought that froze in his mind as his body locked solid in stasis.

———

Elsewhere on the ship, Arun's slide into unconsciousness had not gone unnoticed.

"Is he under?"

"Sleeping like a baby, ready for freezing."

"And you're set up to give him our little present before he's frozen?"

"No need. I've already delivered my package."

"Good. I don't know what makes you so special, Arun McEwan. But I *will* find out. And once I have, I'll kill you myself."

Join the Legion!

Read de-classified Infopedia entries!

Be the first to hear mobilization news!

Get involved with the telling of the Human Legion story!

Read short tales from the worlds of the Human Legion.

Read the next chapters in the Human Legion story before they are published!

HumanLegion.com

Human Legion INFOPEDIA

Category: Equipment - personal weapons
Text copied from predecessor Organizations
— Human Marine Corps:- Detroit Base
— Category: equipment - personal weapons
— SA-71(h) carbine
— Firing options

The SA-71(h) assault carbine is designed to be the main assault weapon for space-borne humanoid troops. The (h) sub-variant has been adapted slightly to suit human physiology and responsibility level, but the ammunition and control systems are compatible with other weapons throughout the SA-70 range.

Humanoid planetary defense forces are generally equipped with the SA-72 rifle, which has a longer barrel, higher muzzle velocity, larger caliber rounds without sabots, and no energy beam or stealth capability.

The requirement to be suitable for use by space Marines gave the weapon designers a priority for robustness, endurance, and to reduce recoil, because in zero-g combat an uncanceled recoil kick will send a firer into an uncontrollable spin.

On any given day, an SA-71(h) might be shooting back at ambushers high in the jungle canopy of a hothouse world. The very next day, the same weapon might be in the vacuum of deep space, bathed in cosmic radiation and wielded by a marine encased in a battlesuit that would be his or her sole source of air, power, and ammunition for several days. The carbine has been designed to be reliable enough to cope with any environment without question.

As a result, the SA-71(h) has enormous power endurance, ammunition flexibility, and recoil absorption.

There are three main firing modes:

1. RAILGUN.

An electrical charge is applied to superconductor rails running along the weapon barrel. The rails are arranged in a helical pattern to impart spin to the round as it leaves the muzzle, thus improving accuracy. The ammunition management system supplies a round of the type selected by the firer and fits it to a sabot created on the fly from the sabot resin reservoir. The sabot ensures optimum superconductance and mechanical fit to the rails. Sabots also permit the standard kinetic round to be much smaller than the railgun caliber thus allowing ammunition cartridges to hold many more rounds.

On full power, the railgun generates enormous heat and imparts a heavy recoil force at the breech of the weapon. Providing the recoil dampening system is not overcome by sustained fully automatic fire, this energy is automatically absorbed at up to 80% efficiency, being used both to heat the reservoir of sabot resin and to recharge the weapon's power pack. In limited-gravity environments the motors in an ACE-series battlesuit can cancel most of the remaining recoil automatically. [See 'Effect of combat environment on SA-71(h) carbine performance'.]

2. BEAM WEAPON.

A phased array in the gun stock can emit lasered energy beams in the x-ray and visible bands.

The x-Ray beam drains such a huge amount of energy that the maximum firing rate possible is approximately one shot per hour. The advantage and disadvantage of the x-ray beam is that it has limited interaction with physical matter. It is best employed in massed volleys against very large targets such as capital ships, space stations, and city-sized ground targets — although the usefulness is reduced for ground-based targets protected by planetary atmosphere. An x-ray beam volley can have a devastating impact, or none at all. It is the most unpredictable of all weapons available to the Human Marine Corps.

The visible laser beam is the most common firing option for use in vacuum. Beam diffraction limits effective range to around 20 klicks, though unhardened sensors can be dazzled at much greater ranges. To maximize power effectiveness, the laser beam will operate in low-power targeting mode until the battlesuit AI detects a hit, at which point it will automatically up the power rate to maximum. In the timeframe of the human operator's worldview, this shift from targeting to lethal power is instantaneous and requires no human intervention.

3. GRENADE LAUNCHER.

Specialist munitions may be slotted into the launch tube situated underneath the main barrel. Grenades are low accuracy and limited range specialist munitions powered by chemical explosive. Many Marine units are now discontinuing the grenade launcher, replacing the capability by an improved supply of specialist munitions fired through the railgun.

4. ASSAULT CUTTERS.

For close combat situations monofilament teeth can be extended from the end of the barrel. They can be rotated at 1000 rpm for maximum penetration. Care should be taken if the cutters are employed in a lateral, raking motion as the blades may snap off. As well as a melee weapon, the cutters have some limited capability to act as a general-purpose drill or cutting tool, although the blades will blunt rapidly. Assault cutters are optimized for cutting through flesh; they are not suitable as an entrenching tool.

— **Some information on this topic has been excluded as you have insufficient access privileges** —

This infopedia section was extracted from humanlegion.com

Human Legion
INFOPEDIA

Category: Strategic context:
— FTL communications

The principle behind faster-than-light (FTL) communication is *quantum entanglement* allied with bit hybridization. Channel-linked paired particles (known as *chbits*) are split into two, but retain a ghostly connection between them that is unaffected by distance (but only when measured in the three main spatial dimensions). Although 'FTL comms' is the standard term, a better practical description would be *instantaneous* communication.

Tech specialists would decry both terms because the information transferred across the channel link is neither truly faster than lightspeed, and using the term *instantaneous* obscures the potential for this method to transmit information across entangled chbits that are separated not by distance but by time.

Whatever you call it, the key is that a tiny item of information can be passed from one particle to its entangled twin, and by using many particles, data can be transmitted along the channel in the same way as, for example, electrical pulses along a copper wire. The drawback is that in passing this information to its twin, both particles lose their entanglement.

For each particle, transmission and reception is strictly single-use only, but of course the solution is to have large blocks of entangled chbits that wear away gradually with each transmission.

However, producing entangled pairs of communication blocks is a very expensive process, and transporting one half of a block of entangled material to another star system is only possible at sub-light speeds, which can take decades. As a result, although there is no theoretical limitation, these practical considerations mean that FTL bandwidth is extremely restricted. An admiral could use FTL comms to issue orders and receive reports from a fleet 60 light years away, for example, but would not expect to receive detailed telemetry, nor remotely control combat drones.

Even the local fleet commander faces the problems of sub-light communications when maneuvering the forces at her disposal. A space battle is typically fought over an area up to a light minute across. If a targeting laser reports to its weapon system that it has a firing solution for an enemy cruiser one light minute away, what it is actually reporting is that it knows where the enemy used to be located one minute earlier. If the weapon responds by sending a lethal energy pulse at the target (taking another minute), then an enemy vessel at 0.2 lightspeed would have traveled over two million miles during the intervening two minutes.

One critical difference between FTL and conventional communications is that the equipment required by the former is so compact. There is no need for the kind of concave dishes, aerials, or power sources that might reveal the location of a transmitter to an enemy. Nor is it possible to intercept or jam the signal. A node in the quantum telegraph network could be small enough to embed inside a battlesuit, or bury deep within an unremarkable asteroid. Nonetheless, even passive FTL capable comms are detectable by patient and numerous observers. And such observers exist because at a microscopic scale, war is underway in all star systems in which minuscule spy robots from enemy powers try to evade detection and report back on the location of FTL communication nodes, amongst other intelligence.

If the FTL nodes are uncovered, an enemy might launch a raid, such as in the following scenario.

A fleet of raiders descends upon a lightly defended star system, overwhelming local military forces. This could be tens of light years behind a contested 'frontier' (there are no 'front lines' in space).

One of the first acts of the attackers is to destroy FTL communications facilities, because that immediately cuts the system off from the rest of the defending empire. Almost certainly the defenders will retain hidden assets within the defeated star system, reporting back on what the attackers are doing. These may be sentient observers but will also include nano spies dispersed throughout the star system. But if the invaders are successful in eliminating the FTL comms, any further reports will be limited to the speed of light. Given the typical distance separating inhabited systems, that means a gap of 10-20 Earth standard years during which the defending empire is completely blind.

Raiders will usually take a few months or years to plunder and refit before heading off for their next target, confident in the knowledge that any relief force from the defending empire would be decades away. History also records more imaginative uses of this blind period, such as using a raid to screen the arrival of a full invasion fleet that will use this blind period to construct battle cruisers deep inside enemy territory.

***A note on the use of gender.** The Trans-Species Union recognizes four principal genders as well as a neuter state. Gender neutral literature will use all possible pronouns in such phrases as: "An admiral will use FTL comms to issue orders to his, her, sie, ser or its fleet."

Within military organizations, language needs to be fast, concise and clear. Using all five gender pronouns every time is unthinkable. The convention developed within the Human Marine Corps, and inherited by the Human Legion, is to use the female pronouns – 'her' and 'she' — to represent gender neutrality. Most senior officers of the Jotun race are female, and this convention was adopted from them.

This infopedia section was extracted from humanlegion.com

INDIGO SQUAD

Start reading the second book in the annals of the Human Legion now…

INDIGO SQUAD
Chapter 01

Arun McEwan's heart swelled with pride when he accessed the internal camera feeds, and saw himself lined up with the rest of Charlie Company in *Beowulf's* dorsal hangar. The Marines twitched with eagerness to emerge and take the fight to the enemy.

Whoever the frakk they might be.

But it was fear, not pride, that made Arun so impatient to launch. He was scared that in the action to come he would reveal himself. Fed a constant dose of combat drugs, even while in cryo sleep, all his other comrades were doped-out mental wrecks, left with as much initiative as the dumbest robot. Well, maybe not the slightly smaller armored figure to his left: Springer. Marine Phaedra Tremayne, known to Springer to anyone without a deathwish, was his best friend and fire team buddy. The drugs had less effect on her, as with their comrade, Umarov, but they all acted as if they were as doped as the others. Hidden conspiracies swirled around Arun like a persistent stink. He'd hoped all that had gone away when he left Tranquility System on *Beowulf*, but here it was even worse and felt more urgent. Playing dumb now might just give Arun the edge he needed when the traitors made their move.

"Ready to launch on my mark," ordered Staff Sergeant Bryant, on behalf of their silent alien officer, Captain Mhabali. Bryant had become an unexpected ally back on their depot planet of Tranquility, but now he had succumbed to the drugs along with almost all the other humans.

"Ten… nine… eight…"

From his camera feed, Arun watched the ACE-2 combat suits flick from field gray to matt black, shimmer and then disappear. Charlie Company had activated stealth mode.

"Seven… six…"

With the waiting over, Arun's worries were draining away.

"Five… four…"

Arun McEwan had an advantage over everyone else in the company: his future had been foretold by the strange alien creatures known as Night Hummers. Unlike the others he had a destiny. The cause of human freedom would not let him die today.

"Three… two…"

Arun knew he would be coming back.

"One… go!"

Arun placed his life in the virtual hands of his battlesuit AI, Barney, who hurled him into space a split second after the hangar doors snapped open. The Marines emerged into a bloom of light across the electromagnetic spectrum as *Beowulf* simultaneously launched a barrage of kinetic torpedoes and blew smoke, both intended to cover the real attack, a close assault by the stealthed Marines.

The 'smoke', which consisted of sensor-reflective streamers, semi-intelligent decoy drones, and a dozen types of EMP flash-bombs, obscured *Beowulf* as the warship pivoted through 180 degrees and used her main engine to brake, applying enough power to keep out of effective firing range, but not so much that she fried Charlie Company in the quantum-effect cone extending hundreds of meters out of her zero-point engine.

Within minutes, Arun had left *Beowulf* far behind and drifted slightly to one side. The smoke had dissipated, and the kinetic torpedoes — which were on a parallel vector to the Marines — were dark in the visible spectrum, though still launch-hot in infra-red.

None of that mattered. What counted was whether the enemy warship had seen the Marines. That would determine whether most of them lived or died over the coming hours.

Beowulf's attack plan was simple. The enemy ship was 20,000 klicks ahead and Charlie Company was on an almost identical vector to the enemy ship, except *Beowulf* had been moving slightly faster. That extra velocity was enough for the barrage of torpedoes to hit in about an hour, and the Marines to arrive, ready to board, about ten minutes later.

Missiles and x-ray bombs from their sister ship, *Themistocles*, had crippled the enemy's main propulsion in a brief firefight as she'd flashed past 26 days earlier. The hostile ship's maneuvering thrusters could spin it in any direction and nudge to either side, but that made negligible difference to its velocity of nearly 15% lightspeed. Unless the enemy repaired her main engine, the target ship was essentially headed in a straight line that would not stop until the end of time.

Barney estimated they would reach long range for beam weapons in approximately ten minutes. Until then, Arun was alone with only the sound of his breathing, and the fears in his mind for company.

He tried to get a visual on the target, but at this range it was no more than a faint dot. So he stared instead at home. Tranquility, or rather its sun, was still less than a light year away, making it the brightest object in the blackness of interstellar space. He thought back to happier times, messing around with his mate, Osman, in novice school, and chatting late into the night with Springer. Then there had been that night on the moon when he held in his arms the most beautiful woman he'd even known.

But his maybe lover, Xin Lee, was on *Themistocles*, only about two light days distant, but the difficulty in matching vectors meant she might as well be a galaxy away. As for Osman, he had been killed in the rebellion Arun had helped to put down. Springer lost her leg in the same fight, and was out there now, practically within touching distance, but as invisible to Arun in her stealthed battlesuit as, hopefully, they all were to the enemy.

He smiled. Thinking of Springer always did. Arun's life had mysteries and threats by the bucketload — not least the mysterious purple girl that the pre-cog Night Hummers had talked of — but thinking about them wouldn't help him now.

Springer would be by his side in the fight.

As she would be afterward, when they celebrated victory.

That was more than enough.

―――

After closing for fifteen minutes, when the target vessel had grown enough for Arun to see it was a rough cuboid shape, the enemy opened up with lasers.

The kinetic torpedoes were dumb bullets, without maneuver capability of their own, which made targeting them child's play.

Unlike in an atmosphere, there was nothing in space to scatter a beam weapon, robbing it of power. What limited a laser's effective range was diffraction, the inevitable spreading out of beam diameter. What started as a tight beam at the laser's focal point, had spread to a five-meter diameter disk by the time it played over the torpedoes.

Diluting the laser's energy over a wider area turned it from a death beam to a pleasant heat lamp.

Nonetheless, in the near-absolute cold of space, that relentless heat lamp was deadly, warming the torpedoes in an uneven way.

After another ten minutes secondary lasers opened up, pulsing their energy, so that the torpedoes rapidly heated then cooled.

It didn't take much longer before the outer surface of a few torpedoes cracked. The material pitted, ejecting little plumes of debris.

To Arun, the effect looked so gentle, but it was enough. The torpedoes slowly tumbled and drifted.

There! The first collision. One torpedo had knocked into another, causing both to fly off on a new vector, narrowly missing others on their way out of the barrage spread.

And with every meter they grew closer to the enemy ship, the business ends of the laser beams narrowed, increasing the effect.

Arun grinned. The torpedoes were only a distraction, cover for the most deadly weapon in *Beowulf*'s armory: its complement of human Marines.

The fact that the enemy hadn't fired on the Marines meant they hadn't seen them.

Yet.

Oh, but they would do soon.

By the time they were ten minutes away, Arun was counting down the seconds before boarding, impatience adding a rasp to his breath.

He'd been bred and engineered to fight.

3,000 klicks and closing.

He couldn't wait.

The story continues in INDIGO SQUAD…

HUMANLEGION.COM

Join the Legion!

Receive a free eBook starter library!
(Summer 2018: The Sleeping Legion prequel novella: 'The Demons of Kor-Lir', Revenge Squad novelette: 'Damage Unlimited', Human Legion short story: 'Hill 435', Human Legion novelette: 'The Battle of Cairo', and Four Horsemen Universe novelette: 'Thrill Addict')

Read de-classified Infopedia entries!

Be the first to hear mobilization news!

Get involved with the telling of the Human Legion, Sleeping Legion and Revenge Squad stories!

Read short tales from the worlds of the Human Legion.

Experience a gruesome end as a redshirt.

HumanLegion.com

Printed in Great Britain
by Amazon